Advance Praise for
Tearza

"Every reader can relate to the world Peter Carlson creates. The daughters of two single parents become best friends. While the kids delight in getting together, their parents focus on managing the many demands of their lives. Carlson does a masterful job of exploring the conflicts that arise from the past. Themes of loss and the fear of risk play against the promise of friendship and the possibility of something more. This story made me think in new ways."

Barb Lundy, author of The Fiction of Stone

"In *Tearza*, Pete Carlson delivers a heartwarming story of Ryan and Tearza, two survivors of loss and heartbreak, navigating their way through child-raising and careers. With four young girls in the middle nothing is simple. It's a second chance to get love right, though Carlson skillfully reminds the reader that failure and resilience must play their roles first, and only with time and determination will the two discover what's meant to be."

Harper McDavid, Author of Zapata, Winner of the 2020
Colorado Book Award for Romance

D1028441

Tearza

Pete Carlson

CALUMET EDITIONS

Minneapolis

**CALUMET
EDITIONS**

Minneapolis

First Edition December 2020
Tearza. Copyright © 2020 by Pete Carlson. All rights reserved.

This is a work of fiction. All of the characters, names, incidents, organizations, and dialogue are either the products of the author's imagination or are used fictitiously.

Printed in the United States of America.
10 9 8 7 6 5 4 3 2 1

ISBN: 978-1-950743-40-7

Cover and book design by Gary Lindberg

Tearza

Pete Carlson

Memories are gifts we can open and reopen throughout our lifetimes

To my family and friends

Also by Pete Carlson

Ukrainian Nights

Winter

Prologue

Slivers of sunlight broke through the thinning storm clouds leaving snow drifted high against the windows of my small studio. During the night, a thick blanket of new snow like a fresh coat of white paint had covered our backyard hiding any trace of yesterday. I wished it would be that easy to wake up and find my regrets buried for good.

Earlier this morning, Jim had stormed out of the house with his gym bag and briefcase. Stupid, but like most arguments between married couples ours was over nothing and ended badly. A tiny issue had set off Jim's temper, and I had no idea why. After he left, I dropped the girls at school, looking forward to having some free time to paint. Back home, I had just set up the easel when my cell phone rang. My heart jumped and I glanced at the caller ID, but it wasn't Jim, so I didn't answer. He hadn't texted or emailed since he'd left—not usual for him. Confused and hurt, I pondered whether to call him at the office and apologize but decided to wait until he was at lunch.

On the small table next to my elbow, several brushes and blades formed a semi-circle along with a dozen twisted, half-used tubes of oil paints. Like old friends, they waited patiently for me to do something with them. For several minutes, I sat on a tall stool in front of the easel, but the canvas remained blank. Frustrated, I shut my eyes and wondered, *how do you paint a regret*?

I thought of my mother, remembering how she had first taught me to paint. We were close together in the summer kitchen back on the farm, and she smelled faintly sweet from the barn after morning chores.

"What should I paint?" I asked her.

"That's up to you."

"But I can't see anything," I said, pointing to the empty canvas.

"You're trying too hard," she whispered. "Let it come to you."

"I don't understand. How can I do that?"

"Close your eyes, my dear, and think of something that makes you happy."

At first, everything was black, and then after several seconds a stroke of green appeared across the canvas of my mind—the color of summer grass. Suddenly, I saw dew sparkling in the first morning light. When I opened my eyes, Mother smiled.

"Do you see it?" she asked.

"Yes," I said, amazed. "But how does that work?"

"It comes from where you dream, but you have to let go first."

Still mad at myself over the earlier argument with Jim, I closed my eyes and tried to think of my blessings, not my regrets. Once I let go of the anger and the harsh words I couldn't take back, I saw what was hiding behind my guilt. Before the image disappeared, I mixed three colors together with my brush and then moved it to the canvas; I hesitated for a moment; the first stroke was always the hardest. Like the first word in a book, the first note of a song or your first kiss, I told myself, you have to take a risk, and so I did. After the second stroke, my hand didn't control the brush anymore. My eyes didn't select the colors. The painting emerged by itself. I was an observer, not the painter. Suspended in time, I worked feverishly, but I hadn't made much progress before the phone rang again.

It was the hospital. I never finished the painting.

Chapter 1

Tearza

My lawyer, Jon Hogan, frowned as he joined my accountant and me in the large conference room. I was surprised he had returned without the buyer or his lawyer. Jon's black dress shoes squeaked as he walked across the polished hardwood floor. He slumped into the leather chair next to me and tossed the purchase agreement onto the table. He reminded me of my dad, maybe because he was about the same age. Deep creases etched his forehead giving him a serious look. His steely blue eyes were as strong as his handshake. After exchanging a tense look with my accountant, he grumbled, "Commitments don't mean a damn thing to people anymore."

The sale of Jim's business was the last unsettled issue since his death eighteen months ago. My thoughts drifted to the faces of my two young daughters, because if this sale didn't go through, I didn't know what I would do.

A dozen manila folders littered the long conference table, along with cell phones, calculators and unfinished drafts of the closing documents. The room smelled of stale coffee and soured tuna salad from the half-eaten box lunches. The confidence I had arrived with had gradually waned as a stream of lawyers shuttled back and forth between the conference room and the buyer in an adjacent room. Occasionally, the lawyers asked me a question or handed me something to sign, but mostly I sat alone and waited.

Jon was Jim's business lawyer. We had met on a couple occasions, but I didn't know him well. For several minutes, Jon hunched over the purchase agreement crossing out sections and scribbling notes in the margins. Sometimes he paused, leaning back in his chair and looking up as if counting the textured ceiling tiles. Finally, he set his pen down and slid the purchase agreement over to Greg, my accountant.

"See what you think," he said.

I couldn't stand it anymore. "Will somebody please talk to me?"

"Wait a second," Jon said. "I want him to look at this first."

Greg's finger moved slowly down the page, carefully reading each change and occasionally comparing things to his financial statements. After a few minutes, he shrugged and nodded. "I agree."

"What does that mean?" I asked.

Jon's Christmas tie hung loosely around his neck and dark circles ringed his eyes. Slowly, he removed his reading glasses.

"Tearza, here's the—"

I interrupted him. "Do we have a deal?"

Jon sighed. "I know this is difficult, but here's where we stand." He handed me a copy of the latest term sheet.

None of it made any sense. I stared at the analysis until I finally admitted, "I'm not good with numbers."

"Skip down to the bottom of the last page."

My heart stopped when I saw the final price. "Is this a joke? This can't be right. The price is way lower than the original offer."

Jon doodled on his notebook. I reached into my purse for some Advil because my head throbbed. I prayed another migraine wasn't starting.

"They can't change this, can they?" I looked back and forth between Jon and Greg. "We have a signed purchase agreement."

His jaw tightened. "They're back-trading on us."

I slammed my hand on the table. "Tell them no. I won't sign this."

"I already did."

"I hate lawyers."

Jon glanced sideways at me.

"I mean them, not you. Do you think this ploy is because I'm a single woman and Korean?"

"I'm not sure. Jamison is without a doubt a chauvinist and he has a sketchy reputation as a racist. He believes that he has leverage and is attempting to use it."

I rubbed my forehead in frustration. "What options do we have?"

"We can sue for performance, but that will involve an expensive, protracted fight that could take at least a year or more to resolve if we have to go to court."

"Screw 'em. Jim worked so hard to build this business. I won't let them do this." I pushed the agreement away and the pages scattered.

"It's not that simple," Jon explained. "Some things came up in their due diligence, things we didn't disclose because we didn't know about them. They're accusing us of withholding information."

"What?" I said.

He took a swallow of coffee, stood up, and walked to the window. The room was on the forty-eighth floor, high above a river that ran through downtown Chicago. "They're playing hardball. Their lead attorney, Jamison, loves to do this. I've sat across the table from him in the past." Jon turned to my accountant. "Maybe you should explain."

Greg slid his chair closer to me, flipped through several pages, and then pointed to the liabilities listed at the bottom of Jim's financial statements.

"What we didn't know until recently was that Jim had refinanced the business before he died. Unfortunately, he didn't get a chance to finish some major contracts he expected would pay off the loan. Bad timing. It's hard to sell a service business at the highest price when the key revenue generator isn't there to complete the contracts." He shuffled the papers together, then mumbled, "I'm sorry."

Jon turned back from the window, chewing on a stir stick. "Here's my suggestion," he announced. "Let's bring them in and see how bad they want a fight. We might be able to negotiate a better price without a trial." He walked over to the table and tapped their latest offer. "We have nothing to lose at this point."

"Should we warn Tearza?" Greg asked Jon as if I weren't in the room.

Jon looked at his wristwatch, glanced down the hall through the glass wall of the conference room, and nodded to Greg.

"Tearza, listen carefully," Jon said, those steely eyes burning into me. "When they come back, do not speak. Do not react or show any emotion to anything they propose. The buyer will bring in two or three lawyers to intimidate you. They'll watch your reaction for any clue as to how you feel. It can get very uncomfortable, but that's part of the negotiation. No matter what happens, don't say anything. Let me handle it."

"Okay," I said as my heart started to race. "But what if I make a mistake?"

Jon patted my arm. "You'll be fine if you just don't show any reaction at all."

"If you say so."

I braced myself as the buyer and his team of lawyers entered and took a seat across from us. They all stared at me expressionless. The buyer's senior attorney offered his hand. Cold and almost wet, it made me want to wipe my hand on my skirt.

"I'm Bob Jamison," he said without a smile. His eyes darted around the table and then he introduced his associates. "To my right is Travis May and to my left," he paused for effect, "is Ryan Olson. He's in charge of litigation."

Ryan was around my age with an athletic build, sandy hair, sun freckles, and black glasses he kept pushing back to the bridge of his nose. He wore the same black power suit as his associates, but it didn't seem to fit him. A spot of food from lunch stained his slightly askew light blue tie, which reminded me of Jim.

While Mr. Jamison was making introductions, another lawyer quietly slipped into the far end of the conference room. Older and distinguished looking, he leaned casually against the wall and listened as Jamison cleared his throat to begin the next round of negotiations.

Jamison placed both hands flat on the table and announced, "Okay, let's get down to business. We're walking away from this deal if you don't accept our price."

Jon quickly responded, "You do what you want, but we're prepared to go to court and sue for performance. We didn't hide anything because my client wasn't involved in her husband's business. Your team did a lousy job of diligence and now you're using that as an excuse to lower the price. I'm telling you right now, your strategy doesn't work."

The room became icy silent, each side waiting to see who would speak first. Jamison rocked back and forth in his chair, twirling a fancy gold pen in his fingers. He lurched forward. "You have no case and you know it." He glanced down the table and pointed out Ryan. "He's your worst nightmare. He hasn't lost a lawsuit in five years. You do not want to see him in a courtroom."

Jon was slow to anger, but as the conversation deteriorated, he stiffened in his chair. Finally, he'd had enough and growled back in a voice that made the hair on my arm stand up. Jamison's eyes flared, but as he started to respond, the mysterious lawyer at the end of the conference room interrupted him.

"Pardon me, but can you excuse us for a moment?" he asked politely.

Surprised, everyone turned in his direction as he motioned for the buyer and Jamison to follow him out of the conference room.

"Who's that?" I asked Jon after they left.

"That's Andy Peterson, the managing partner of the firm."

"What are they doing?"

"I'm not sure," he said. "Andy's a good guy. However, Jamison's a piece of work."

Several minutes later, Jamison and the buyer returned without Mr. Petersen and sat down. Jamison's eyes narrowed as he wrote a number on a sheet of paper from his notebook, tore the page out, and pushed it across the table.

Arrogantly, he crossed his arms and threatened, "This is our last offer. You have fifteen minutes to decide or we'll see you in court." At his lead, he and the other lawyers abruptly stood up and silently filed out.

Jon glanced down at the number on the sheet, scowled, and slid the paper over to me.

I looked at the number and then back to Jon. "What should I do?"

"Take it," he answered wearily from across the table. "It's better than I thought they'd offer us. I know Andy. He did us a favor out in the hall because Jamison was dying for a fight."

"Do you know what this does to me?" I said.

"It isn't what we expected either."

"But you don't understand."

Jon glanced nervously at Greg. "How bad is it?"

Greg played the calculator like a pianist as he went over the numbers. Finally, he looked up and adjusted his oval, wire-rimmed glasses.

"By the time we take into account the various fees, debt payoff and taxes, we're left with this." He pointed to the last number written on the ledger sheet.

I gasped.

"Are you sure?" Jon asked.

"I could be off a little, but not much."

I threw my hands in the air. "We didn't have much in savings because Jim put most of the income back into the company. We were using my salary as a scientist at Northwestern University to pay our monthly expenses."

Jon grimaced and walked over to the credenza. He pulled out a roll of Tums from his pocket, peeled off two, and washed them down with a Coke. Slowly, he turned around and crossed his arms.

"What about Jim's key employee life insurance?"

"Can somebody explain what kind of insurance you're talking about? I don't know of Jim having any other than his life insurance.—which was worthless because he committed suicide."

"Most companies carry insurance on their key employees to cover disruption to the company caused by the loss of a critical executive until they can hire a replacement," Jim explained.

"Remember," Greg said. "I checked into that right after he died. Apparently, Jim let the policy lapse because he was short on cash. He was under a lot of stress and told his insurance agent that once the economy turned around, he'd replace the life policy."

A hot flash made me dizzy. Suddenly everything made sense—all the dumb arguments over nothing and the wasted hours of marriage counseling. No wonder Jim was so depressed and moody before he died. Why didn't he tell me? I thought the sale of the business would make up for the lack of insurance. Now, with that gone—

I took off my sweater and looked for a window to open. The last time I'd felt this nauseated was when I was pregnant with Ella.

Greg glanced at his notes. "You shouldn't have to sell your house or do anything drastic based on the sale proceeds as long as you manage the income you have from your job at the university."

"I forgot to tell you," I frowned. "The university experienced a severe reduction in federal funding and my program was cut last month. They gave me four weeks of severance pay and a box to carry out my personal things."

Jon winced, walked over to my chair and put his hand on my shoulder. "I'm so sorry. I did the best I could."

"I know. It's not your fault."

An hour later, I walked out of the law office in a daze and starving for some fresh air. Squinting in the strong sunlight, I fished for my sunglasses and car keys. I couldn't believe it. First, Jim's suicide—and now a group of shitty lawyers had stolen what was left of his business. How could this happen? I had no job, a small check from the sale of Jim's business, and two young girls to raise. My marriage wasn't perfect, but eighteen months ago I had everything…

Now I had nothing.

Chapter 2

Ryan

Hundreds of passengers slowly inched forward in lines that snaked through JFK airport in New York. Some swore constantly at the airline agents, TSA personnel, or anyone within earshot while the rest of us shuffled along mute, resigned to the fact there was nothing we could do about the snowstorm. It took my boss and me over an hour to clear security. Once inside, the concourse looked like a temporary refugee camp. People lined the hallways talking on cell phones or working on laptops; families huddled together sharing food and trying to keep track of the little ones; college students on Christmas break listened to music and surfed the internet. Many had that dazed look you acquire when stranded in an airport for too long. With only seven days before Christmas, it seemed like half the country had booked last minute business or shopping trips before the holidays.

As we reached our gate, I searched the monitor for our flight number, hoping that our plane from New York to Chicago hadn't been cancelled. Multiple delays and cancellations had already stranded hundreds of people. I tried to ignore the odors of fast food and stuffy air. As I waited for our flight status to scroll onto monitor, I cursed quietly when the agent announced that our flight was delayed again. *Damn,* I thought, *if our plane doesn't leave in the next thirty minutes, I'll miss the girls' Christmas concert.* I reached into my pocket, peeled off three Rolaids, and returned to my seat in the waiting area.

I opened my laptop and started a list of Christmas presents for the girls. I couldn't believe how fast this month had gone by, especially after starting work on cases in New York City six months ago. I loved the Big Apple with the energy of its nine million people crammed on an island only two miles wide and thirteen miles long. There's no place like the Greenwich Village on a warm summer night. I always felt so alive surrounded by people from every corner of the world and the cacophony of Latin, country, and rock and roll music. My mouth watered whenever thinking about the aromas from street vendors and outdoor cafes—hot pizza, tacos, and Italian sweet sausages sizzling with onions and peppers. Manhattan was a far cry from my youth in northern Wisconsin where the sidewalks rolled up at ten o'clock at night.

This was my third trip to the city in a month and I didn't know how long I could keep it up with two young daughters in Chicago. I was naïve when I joined the law firm of Steele & Peterson and hadn't fully comprehended the toll of constant travel and long hours. I should've listened to my wife Clair and ignored my dad. He was convinced that litigation was the fastest way to make law partner. I didn't conduct any research and blindly trained to become a trial lawyer because on TV, courtroom law was so dramatic. As a junior lawyer, I quickly realized that attorneys in family law make good money and also have a life beyond work.

Shortly after we married, Clair begged me to follow my other passion and become an author, educator, columnist—anything but a lawyer. I ignored her pleas because there was no money in journalism and I was sick of being poor. Now, seven years after law school, I'm a thirty-two-year-old divorced father working ridiculous hours. I should've been promoted to partner by now, but everything changed when Clair became sick.

We had just completed two long days of trial in New York and I was exhausted. Jamison, a senior partner in our law firm, came back from the check-in counter and scowled.

"Did you hear the announcement?" Jamison asked. "Our flight's delayed for at least another hour. Apparently, planes are backed up all the way to Brooklyn."

I groaned and said, "I promised Sara and Gracie that I'd be home for their Christmas concert tonight."

"Remind me. How old are your girls?"

I pulled a photo from my briefcase and handed it to Jamison. "See what you think. I was planning on using this for our Christmas card this year. Sara's on the left. She's eleven turning sixteen. Gracie's eight, but don't let her angelic smile fool you. She's my wild child."

Jamison smiled and tapped the picture. "I love it. The girls are beautiful."

"Lucky for them, they inherited everything from Clair."

Jamison handed the photo back. "We still have a little time. Maybe we can get off sooner than they predict."

"Fat chance," I said, and then tucked the picture back into my briefcase.

"Hey, you were a real tiger in court today," Jamison said.

I shrugged. "Not really. The other side made some dumb mistakes. I just took advantage."

"How about their CEO?" Jamison chuckled. "You pinned him into a corner, and then he broke down when he realized all his lies had caught up to him." Jamison whistled and slapped me on the shoulder. "You went for the throat. That was a thing of beauty. You reminded me of myself when I was your age."

"Thanks," I said.

His sudden friendliness surprised me. Jamison rarely gave out compliments unless it was about himself.—such an odd, eccentric fellow with a really mean temper. He had seemed unusually quiet all day. I always wondered how Jamison would've fared if not for Andy, our managing partner. They'd grown up in the same town and gone to law school together. Andy told me Jamison's life story over a couple off scotches one night, said he was a thin, pale child with thick glasses who was kicked around at school for being a smart nerd. Jamison once admitted to me that he didn't have a single date until his third year when he met Helen, a server at a café near the law school. They dated for six months and married a week after he graduated.

The practice of law was transformational for Jamison who gained from it an empowerment that mainly he used in a dark way. For the first time in his life he was in control. He experienced sadistic pleasure in making witnesses squirm or cry in the same way others had tormented him when he was young.

In truth, he was a caricature of an arrogant lawyer. Everything about him was exaggerated, from his manicured nails to his fake Rolex watch. He traded his glasses for contacts and styled his grey hair side-to-side with thick gel to cover a receding hairline. At five-foot-four in shoes with generous heels, he only purchased dark pinstriped suits because he read somewhere that they make you look taller.

As we sat in the gate area, I watched him pick at some white fuzz on his black overcoat and felt sorry for him. Nothing was worse than an insecure lawyer with a grudge and a razor-sharp tongue. He approached everything—a conversation, a case, or where to have lunch—as an argument he had to win.

I glanced at my watch again. Frustrated, I reached for the cell phone in my jacket.

Jamison nodded toward the television screen hanging from the ceiling. "Listen to those morons," he said. A panel of experts were debating the president's latest proposal to stimulate the economy. An economics professor from Columbia was explaining the need for the emergency stimulus when Jamison grumbled and pointed. "It's a joke. I know we have to do something because the market's in a free-fall, but what idiot came up with this bailout? This idea is dead in the water before it even has a chance."

I didn't respond—too exhausted to talk about the market and politics. I didn't have any money in the stock market anyway. I just wanted to get home.

Jamison turned his head toward me. "Remind me—where did you go to law school? Columbia, wasn't it?"

"No, I was accepted there but ended up at the University of Wisconsin."

"Why Wisconsin instead of Columbia?"

"Simple—I didn't have any money and they offered a full scholarship." I fidgeted with my cell phone. "It was always my dream to attend Columbia and live in New York City, but some things weren't meant to be. Anyway, I would've never met Clair and had the girls if I'd gone to Columbia."

I wondered why he asked me where I went to law school. He enjoyed reminding the office that he attended Harvard Law, so what did he care where I went?

"Ironic, isn't it?" he said.

"What?"

"Here you are, travelling to New York City for our firm all the time."

"Yeah, funny how life works. I just wish I had time to enjoy it."

"In spite of the economy, over the last two years our business has tripled in New York. If this keeps up, we'll need to increase our staff or open an office here." He scratched his chin and wrote something in his Day-Timer. "Are you and Tiffany coming back here next week?"

"Yeah, we start depositions on the North Dakota oil case next Tuesday."

"How often have you worked with her?"

"Only two cases so far."

He smirked. "She's effective, isn't she?"

I returned the look. "Interesting choice of words."

Jamison laughed. "When I first interviewed her at the firm, I asked how someone so pretty could be successful in the rough and tumble world of high stakes lawsuits and large corporations." He grinned. "You know what she said?"

"I have no idea."

"She batted her long eyelashes and said in a sweet southern drawl, 'It takes a little honey to catch a bee.' I hired her on the spot. I knew she was good."

"I agree. She may be easy to underestimate—at first because of her looks, but from what I've seen she's one of the smartest young lawyers in the firm."

"See me on Monday. I have a lead I want you to run down in the Quantum case before you leave next week."

A phone rang and it took Jamison a few seconds to realize it was his. "Jamison here." He walked a few yards away. "What? … When? Fuck…" He walked quickly in a circle. "Who else knows?" He glanced at me. "I'll call you when I land."

Jamison walked down the concourse so I couldn't overhear him. A few minutes he returned and sat down. His finger trembled as he scrolled through a list of emails on his phone.

"Bad news?" I asked.

Jamison smiled thinly and shrugged.

I couldn't put off calling Sara and Gracie any longer, so I moved away from the crowded gate area. My stomach churned as my call rolled into voicemail for the second time. I shifted the cell phone to my better ear and strained to hear above the crying babies, intermittent announcements, and CNN droning from flat screens around the room. I tried calling one more time and while the phone continued to ring, I looked at a monitor to check for updates on my flight. Finally, my nanny answered.

"Hi, Betty. Sorry but our plane has been delayed for at least another hour because of bad weather."

"Not again."

"I know. I can't help it."

"What about the Christmas concert tonight?"

"Can you take them?"

Sara, my oldest daughter, jumped on the other line. "Hi, Dad. What time are you getting home? They want us early to put on our costumes."

"Honey, I'm sorry but my plane's been delayed. I can't get home in time for the concert."

Sara's voice rose sharply. "But you promised."

"I know. I'll make it up to you."

"You've said that before."

She sounded so much like Clair, I thought. "Trust me, things will change soon," I said, hoping it wasn't a lie.

She didn't reply—already jaded by too many broken promises.

"Are you still there?" I asked, worried that she had hung up.

"Yes," she said, her voice barely audible.

Her voice faded in an out on the call so I moved closer to the window for better reception. "Sarah, can you put Betty back on the line?"

After several seconds, Betty said, "Hello."

"Betty, will this work for you?"

There was a long pause before she snapped, "Do I have a choice?"

"I'm really sorry. I can't tell you how much I appreciate it."

"Sure," she said sarcastically.

"But Betty—"

The phone went dead as she hung up before I could finish my sentence. Betty was our regular nanny but lately had acted more like my ex-wife. She constantly nagged me about working late and not spending enough time with the girls. She didn't understand, as Clair never did, how I was sacrificing all of this for them. I wanted the girls to live in a great house, go to the best schools, wear nice clothes, enjoy all the advantages that I didn't have growing up. *The girls will understand when they get older*, I kept telling myself.

Through an enormous window, I watched the planes fade in and out like ghosts in the falling snow and thought about seven years ago when my flight was delayed because of a similar snowstorm. That was the first time I realized Clair and I were in trouble. It was late and I had returned from another long business trip. I just wanted to get home to the girls, although I knew they would be asleep. Gracie was almost a year old and Sara was just a toddler.

Clair had hated my increasing travel, but each new case brought me one step closer to making partner. Even though she didn't work, staying at home with two young girls had been very stressful for her. At the time, I couldn't understand why she struggled so much, but whenever I tried to discuss it she became angry. Way too late, I realized that my stupid insistence that she quit her job as a realtor to be a stay-at-home mom was a major cause of Clair's depression. I wanted the girls to have a mom to greet them when they got home from school, bring treats to school on their birthdays, read stories in their classroom—all the things I had never experienced in my childhood. I had greatly underestimated how much Clair had loved her job, which she excelled at.

Add that colossal mistake to a big stack of other bad decisions I've made.

When I finally reached home late that night years ago, everything seemed wrong, as if I were the first person to arrive at an untouched crime scene. Two old newspapers lay scattered on the floor in the hallway along with several pieces of unopened mail. The kitchen and dining table were covered with dirty dishes and discarded food packages.

With each step I took, my apprehension grew. The living room air was thick with stale smoke and a cigarette butt smoldered in a full ashtray on the coffee table. The television was turned on to a home shopping channel with the sound muted. An empty wine bottle on the end table had tipped over and a second one was lying on the floor.

Not again, I thought. Clair was curled up in a tight ball on the couch with her back to me. Leaning over her shoulder, I carefully lifted the tangled dark hair covering her face and tried to wake her but she moaned and tried to push me away. Finally, I picked her up and carried her like a child into the bedroom, pulled back the sheets and tucked her in fully clothed. In the darkness, my anger dissolved into fear as I listened to her erratic breathing. The longer I stood there the more I wondered if our past was the only thing left of our future.

The boarding agent made another garbled announcement asking passengers to stay in the immediate area so we could board quickly when clearance was granted. Several confused passengers turned to each other to see if they heard the message correctly. I looked up at the monitor and prayed they wouldn't cancel the flight. I didn't want to spend another night in New York City.

Jamison came back with two cups of coffee and sat down. I put my cell phone away.

"Is everything all right at home?" Jamison asked.

"Fine, no problem," I lied. I was getting so close to making partner that I didn't want anything to screw it up now.

"Are you sure? You look like hell."

I felt like hell. Lack of sleep. Stress. No exercise. I had gained ten pounds in the last few months and my stomach was killing me. I took a sip of coffee and stomach acid started coming up.

"What's wrong? Is the coffee too hot?" Jamison asked.

"No, it must be something I ate." I gritted my teeth as I swallowed the acid reflux.

He frowned. "Cut the coffee and Coke. You live on that crap. And I watch you chewing on Rolaids all day. I know what I'm talking about because I gave myself an ulcer when I was your age."

I pointed to his cup. "Sure seems to have worked for you."

"Very funny, wise guy." Then he ignored me for the next twenty minutes as he scrolled through his emails. Finally, he put his phone away and watched a young couple giggling and sneaking kisses as they waited in a corner of the gate area. He smiled for a second and then frowned. Without taking his eyes off those kids, he asked, "How long has it been since your divorce?"

I almost choked on my coffee. Jamison was an arrogant man, not one for idle chit-chat, especially about anything personal. This was the longest conversation we'd had in the past year.

"Two years." I said slowly.

"Do you ever hear from her?"

"Rarely."

"Me neither." he said.

"Where's Helen living now?"

He ignored my question. Then, like an addict, he pulled out his phone and checked his email again. The cell phone was his security blanket, his way to ignore someone or change the subject. I remembered the ugly rumors about his marriage. The divorce had happened so fast I always wondered what was behind it.

A young mother seated across from Jamison was reading a story to her two daughters. Jamison put his phone back into his pocket and watched the girls sit quietly on her lap.

"How did your girls react to the divorce?" he asked me without turning his head.

"Gracie was too young to remember much when it happened. But Sara—well, that's been an on-going problem."

Jamison looked down and his finger made a circle around the rim of his cup. "I understand. My parents divorced when I was twelve. It's a tough age to lose parents."

"Actually, the divorce was a relief," I said. "A chance to resume some sense of a normal life for the first time since Gracie was born. If you recall, Clair developed postpartum depression shortly after Gracie was born, which led to alcoholism and drug abuse. The five years leading up to the divorce were a nightmare."

"That must've been rough," Jamison said. "I remember you missed a lot of work during that time."

I studied Jamison's face for a few seconds. He almost sounded as if he cared. Funny, how you think you know someone and yet you really don't.

"I've tried everything," I confessed. "But frankly, it's been hell on my daughters not to have a mother. Since the divorce, Clair only calls when she needs money. Every time she pops back into our lives it's like ripping a scab off an old wound."

Jamison didn't respond, but slowly nodded.

An older woman, who was playing cards with her husband across from us, suddenly slapped a card on the small carry-on they were using as a table. "Gin!" she howled with glee.

Her husband shook his head and started to shuffle the cards again. "You cheat," he teased.

"Sore loser." She rubbed her hands together. "Deal them."

I stared at the couple. Once upon a time, that was Clair and me. The way we used to be before she became sick. I was so close to getting everything—the partnership, money, house—if only.

"I know it's none of my business, but what happened to your parents?" I asked Jamison. "Why did they divorce when you were so young?"

Unconsciously, Jamison jutted out his chin and stretched his neck in a rapid motion like a gull trying to swallow a fish. It was a tick he was not aware of most of the time. This was a way of ignoring my question. "It's difficult, isn't it?" he finally asked.

"What do you mean?" I said warily.

"You know, living alone." He leaned forward and blew on his hot coffee. "At least you have the girls. I don't have anyone at home since my divorce."

Finally, the boarding agent announced, "This is flight 896 to Chicago." A cheer from a hundred passengers drowned her out. "We'll board in thirty minutes."

I glanced at my watch. The concert had started. Sara's words, "*You promised*," reminded me of the first time I had left home for college. My step-mother had cried and to my surprise Dad had hugged me so tight I could hardly breathe.

Before he let go, he whispered, "Keep your promises and you'll have no regrets in life."

Chapter 3

Tearza

It had been six months since we closed on the sale of Jim's business and yet the invoices kept coming. A pile of unpaid bills lay scattered on the kitchen table. A letter from our bank threatened foreclosure unless I caught up on my mortgage payment. I tried to figure out how long I could last with the small proceeds of the business sale, but no matter how I crunched the numbers I got the same result—seven months, give or take a month.

Frustrated, I pushed aside all the bills and wondered what the girls were doing with my parents on the farm. I studied the scratches and dents on the heavy oak table where the girls usually sat, each of them reminding me of a funny story, spilled milk and laughter. Then I looked at Jim's empty chair and fought back tears. *It isn't fair,* I thought. *Why didn't he talk to me?* Strange to sit in my kitchen without any place to be, lunches to pack, phone calls to make. I felt unhinged and alone for the first time since Jim's death more than two years ago. At first I resisted my parents' offer to take the girls for the weekend, but they eventually convinced me it would be good for them and for me. I could tell from the daily calls from Mom that they were worried about me.

After Jim died, I had briefly considered personally running our company, but I quickly realized I knew nothing about the printing business. And the girls were struggling —they needed me more than ever. The concept of suicide was impossible for the girls to understand,

and they missed their dad so much I put them into grief therapy. Endless questions haunted me every night. To make things worse, a few months after Jim's death I lost my job as a scientist conducting research on the effects of climate change to farmland across the country. Growing up on a farm, I realized how important good research could help guide farmers in the future. With my nose barely above water, I struggled to find a new path to pursue my passion for the land. The land was part of my DNA. I needed to keep my hands in the dirt and nurture my passion for flowers.

After finishing my morning coffee, I walked to the sink to wash some fresh berries. Glancing out the bay window, I noticed the deck thermometer was showing ten degrees. I shivered and wrapped my fuzzy, pink bathrobe tighter around my waist. Ever since Jim died, I felt constantly cold.

A knock on the kitchen door startled me. I panicked because I didn't want anyone to see me without make-up, glasses, and with my hair sticking out in ten directions. I froze, hoping whoever it was would go away, but then I heard three raps on the kitchen window. It was Ali, my best friend, smiling through the frosted glass and madly waving. Her wiry red hair almost matched the color of her ski jacket. Wearing her signature cowboy hat and Maui Jim sunglasses, she looked as if she had just stepped off a private jet from Aspen.

I had no idea why we were such dear friends. She was everything that I'm not. She was gregarious, crazy, a daredevil, never thought before she leaped, quick to laugh and cry, had no idea what would happen next, and could care less. I loved her, I suppose, because she was the only friend who always thought the best of me no matter what dumb things I said or did. She always made me feel as though I mattered to her.

Trapped, I waved back and pointed to the kitchen door. I wiped my face, quickly tied my hair back with a band and adjusted my robe before opening the door.

"This is a surprise," I said with a forced smile. "What're you doing here?"

"I'm on a mission."

"Oh really," I said, holding the door partially open.

"May I come in?" Ali peered around me as she pulled her mittens off with her teeth.

"That depends."

"On what?" Ali didn't wait for my answer, just stepped past me into the kitchen. She set her purse on the table and took off her coat before I could stop her. "How are you?" she said, out of breath. She always talked in rapid spurts, rarely finishing one sentence before beginning another.

"I'm—"

"Is it hot in here or just me?" Ali fanned her face.

"I don't feel hot but I could turn—"

"I heard about what happened with the sale of the business."

"From my mother?"

"No, Dylan told me."

"Dylan?" I stiffened. "He may have been Jim's best friend, but he has a big…"

"Tearza!" Ali said, quickly raising her hand in the air, "He's concerned."

I sighed. Dylan was Jim's college roommate and best man at our wedding. I never told Ali, but Dylan had called several times over the last few months. I know he meant well, but I was leery. In college, he had a crush on me while I was dating Jim. It was never an issue, but I didn't think his recent calls were just out of concern and I wasn't ready for anything like that.

"Good God, girl. Everyone's tried to contact you and no one has seen you for months," Ali seemed exasperated as she sat down in my chair. I watched her eyes roam over my checkbook and the bills scattered on the table.

I averted my eyes. "I know, Ali. I haven't been good about returning calls. It's hard to explain."

"We're worried about you," she said, and I believed her.

"Don't."

Ali frowned and picked up the letter from the bank. "Is there anything we can do?"

"I'm not helpless," I blurted out more loudly than I intended, grabbing the letter from her hand. "And I don't need charity."

Ali flinched. I knew that I had hurt her feelings, but I couldn't help myself.

"I didn't mean it that way," Ali said. "Actually, I'm here to recruit you."

"For what?" I asked sarcastically. "My expertise in laundry and housework, or for nursing skinned knees and broken hearts? That's about all I'm good for these days."

Ali lowered her voice. "You have to commit once you agree."

"My girls threaten to commit me every other week, is that good enough?"

Ali grinned, showing a mouthful of white teeth that would make a movie star jealous. "It may require a leap of faith."

"That might be a problem. I ran out of that long ago." I turned away, afraid to look at her. I was a puddle these days. It was embarrassing— breaking down in tears for no reason over stupid things that didn't matter. I stood up to start a pot of coffee and brought out some fresh sugar donuts to fill the awkward silence.

Ali pointed and wagged her finger. "That's definitely not on my diet!"

"You may want to reconsider. I made them this morning. They're still warm."

Ali hesitated and then picked one off the plate. "Are these from your mom's recipe?"

"Of course! She won a blue ribbon at the state fair three times." I licked the sugar off my fingers. "I always make them when—"

"You think of Jim?" she answered for me.

"They were his favorite." I wiped my nose with a balled-up lump of tissue from the pocket of my bathrobe.

Ali reached over, grasped both my hands, and leaned close to my face. Her breath smelled sweet-donutty. "Look at my eyes. You're my best friend. Please— talk to me."

How do I explain that sometimes I would find myself driving in the car and suddenly realize I'd missed a turn miles past where I should've been? How do I tell her about not being able to breathe when I have panic attacks for no reason in the middle of the day?

How do I admit that I'm thirty-four years old but couldn't go to sleep without a night light?

"If I tell you something," I said, still debating whether this was a mistake, "will you promise not to make fun of me?"

"I'd never do that."

We stared at each other. Finally, I said, "I dream about Jim."

"That's normal."

"This is different. Sometimes he comes to me during the night."

Ali shifted in her chair and began tapping her fingers on the table. "What do you mean?"

"Last week I was asleep in bed when I heard the door click. I felt a warm breath on my face. I assumed it was one of the girls trying to climb in bed with me, but when I opened my eyes, there he was."

"Who?"

"Jim," I said carefully, watching for her reaction. "He was sitting on the edge of my bed."

Ali's red eyebrows arched up as her eyes grew wider. She stopped tapping her fingers and stiffened in her chair. "What did he say?"

"He didn't speak but smiled as if he were making sure I was okay. We had drifted apart during the last year of our marriage. This was his way of letting me know he still loved me."

"What happened next?"

"When I tried to reach out and kiss him, he disappeared like a mirage. Then I found myself awake in the dark, afraid and doubting whether I could still tell a dream from reality."

"Oh, Tearza," Ali leaned over and gave me a hug.

"This wasn't the first time," I said. "Do you think I'm crazy?"

"You're not crazy," she said, wiping tears from my cheek. "My grandmother used to come to me in my dreams after she died. I was in high school at the time and really struggling. The visits stopped after I straightened myself out. I loved that woman."

"Ali, I swear it was as real as you and I are sitting here. But that can't be possible, can it?"

"That dreams are real?" she asked.

"Yes."

"I believe we learn as much from our dream self as when we're awake. I used to tell my grandmother about my wild dreams when I was a child. She always listened intently while I explained as much as I could remember. Once, I asked her if it was bad to dream so much. She smiled and whispered, 'Child, there is an old saying—dream your life, then live your dreams.'"

"Maybe I should try to dream my life differently," I said.

"Maybe you already are."

"Some dream," I said.

"Tearza, you always said your life was perfect—a dream-come-true."

"It wasn't perfect," I said quietly as I dunked a chunk of doughnut in my coffee.

Ali looked up. "What do you mean?"

"Things weren't as they seemed. We had been in marriage counseling for months."

"You're kidding!" Ali said. "I always thought you two were the perfect couple. None of your friends can understand why Jim committed suicide."

"Join the club." My lips trembled. "I would give anything to know why he became so depressed. He never revealed his pain to me. Maybe I could've prevented his…"

Ali interrupted. "Don't go there. You can't blame yourself."

I stood up and set my dish in the sink. "It doesn't matter now."

"But did he ever—?"

"He wasn't cheating on me if that's what you're asking."

"I don't know what to think."

"It's complicated," I said defensively. "Let's leave it at that."

Ali started to say something but stopped. She slowly surveyed the kitchen cluttered with two shriveled plants in the bay window, dirty dishes stacked in the sink, an empty carton of Chinese take-out, and a half-eaten bag of miniature Snicker's bars on the counter.

"What have you been doing lately?" she asked in a worried voice.

"Not much. What did you expect." I quickly gathered up the half dozen tissue balls off the table, stuffed them into my pocket, and then picked up her plate.

Ali stared at me for second and started to get up. She put one arm into her coat.

"Maybe I should come back another time."

"Please, I'm sorry—don't go." I grabbed the arm of her jacket and began to cry.

"Tearza, what's wrong?"

"Everything." I blew my nose into a wadded up tissue. "Do you want more coffee?"

"Where are the girls?"

"On the farm with my parents."

"How have they adjusted?"

"Marci stuffed her feelings inside. She's so much like her dad. Jim didn't like conflict so he just hid his feelings. That was part of the problem in our marriage. My mother always encouraged me to ask for what I needed. Jim couldn't do that. Marci reacts the same way when she's stressed or afraid. She refuses to talk about his death, and she's withdrawn into her own little world. Ella's too young to wrap her head around suicide. All she understands is that her dad's gone and never coming back. Both are working with a grief counselor. But I'm not sure it's helping. At least I'm doing something. It breaks my heart to watch them look at pictures of their father next to their bed before they go to sleep."

I stared into the distance and Ali played with her coffee cup.

Her face lit up. "Honey, what we need is one of Jim's famous Bloody Marys, not more coffee." She steered me back to my chair. "You sit here and point me to the liquor cabinet."

"But it's only ten in the morning."

Ali tilted her head back and let out a sound that was more like a howl than a laugh.

"Perfect time to have a drink!"

As she made the drinks on the counter, I casually said, "It was our anniversary this weekend."

"I know," she said without turning around.

"You remembered?"

Ali looked over her shoulder and smiled. "Of course, how could I forget? I was your maid-of-honor." She carried over the two drinks and sat down next to me. We clinked glasses and she said, "To us!"

I took a sip and almost choked. "How much vodka did you put in here?"

"Enough," she smirked as she licked some salt off the rim of her glass.

Ali made me laugh. I was such a lightweight but she could out-drink a sailor on leave. There was more than one occasion in college when she carried me home after a night-on-the-town.

"There you go," she said pointing at my face. "That's more like it. This is the first time you've smiled since I got here."

I took a few more sips of my drink and began to feel a warm spot in my stomach. "You know what the hardest part about losing Jim is?"

"I can't imagine." Ali pulled out the pickle slice and sucked on it like a Popsicle.

"Not talking about him."

"What do you mean?" she asked.

"No one will talk about Jim. Everyone seems afraid to talk about his death. Especially because it was a suicide. I believe they're afraid of hurting my feelings, afraid to make me feel bad—afraid to say the wrong thing."

Ali squirmed in her chair. "Grief is a hard subject."

I pointed at her. "See, look at you. That's exactly what I mean. I want to talk about Jim. I want people to tell funny stories about him." I put my head in my hands. "Even the girls won't talk about Jim."

"What about your friends? You and Jim have a great group of friends."

I teared up again.

"What's wrong?"

"I've learned a lot..."

"Go on."

I hesitated for second, before saying, "Especially about those who are my true friends."

"What do you mean?"

"We loved our friends. They invited us to everything—but only as a couple. There are a few women you know who have avoided my attempts to become better friends. I understand one can't be more than acquaintances with everyone, but it bothers me." I took a deep breath. "Thank God for you. I can count on one hand the women in my life who genuinely care about me. Since Jim died, I've never felt so lonely. No one calls or invites me to anything. I sit alone at home every night. I understand it's awkward for couples to include a single person, but I never imagined my friends would drift away so quickly.

"Oh, Tearza."

"I learned another thing I never expected—something that hurts just as much. I could be mistaken, but I believe certain people are avoiding me for other reasons."

"You're kidding. You're the sweetest person I've ever met. Who's avoiding you—and why?"

"I'm not telling, but you can probably guess." I bit my lip. "A few women have been avoiding me because I was adopted as a baby from Korea. I have an Asian face, and they don't seem to care that I lived in Wisconsin since I was six months old. I'm not white. That's all that matters to some people."

Ali frowned and reached for my hand. "I know. Some people are pigs."

"Remember when we were at a luncheon at Cindy's club and then Sheila, who I thought was a friend, introduced me to the table by saying, 'This is Tearza, she's from China?'"

"We were all embarrassed by that."

I shook my head and looked away. "I wanted to slap her! I've endured many other examples like that. There's a small number of woman who've dropped me out of their groups since Jim died."

"They're idiots. Small, shallow people you don't need. Remember, you are well loved. Screw the others."

"Yeah, well, you don't know the extent. Growing up on the rural farm in Wisconsin, we lived a quiet life. Small schools and churches, simple lives—everyone knew each other. I never felt discrimination at home. I never felt different than anyone else in my childhood. Not until I reached college did I experience discrimination because of my Korean heritage.

"The first time I realized some people viewed me as anything but an American occurred on move-in day at college when I met my freshman roommate and her family. They smiled and said the usual nice things like 'So nice to meet you, blah, blah, blah.' But the next day, when I returned from orientation, I saw that my roommate had moved out. At first, I felt ashamed. But later, I was angry. I realized that for some people, thankfully not all, 'Midwest Nice' was nothing more than a curtain that concealed racism."

Now that I had started to vent, I couldn't stop, so I went on. "After college, I moved to Chicago and frequently experienced racism in everyday life. Little things like when I had to submit numerous applications before I got approval to rent an apartment. On occasion, I was ignored while on the wait list at popular restaurants. Watching other people get seated before me when I was ahead of them on the list made me furious. Tiny slights felt like slivers—small, but irritating.

"And then, later, big things occurred, such as learning that other candidates received job offers for positions I was clearly better qualified. I could give you hundreds of examples." I took a deep breath. "It sounds silly when I verbalize these specific things now. Individually, I try to brush them off—but over time it swells into extreme frustration."

"I'm sorry. I didn't know." Ali said.

I shrugged. "For many reasons, and now in a new way, I treasure what it means to have friends of the heart—true friends." I reached over and grabbed Ali's hand. "True friends like you."

Ali stroked my hair for a second and then lifted my chin until I could see her emerald green eyes. "Tell me," she asked gently. "What can I do?"

"Promise you won't forget Jim."

"I promise."

"Or me?"

She didn't have to answer. The teardrop hanging from her eyelash was enough.

"Thank you." I wiped my eyes with the sleeve of my bathrobe.

We sat quietly for a moment when Ali reached up and touched my necklace. "I remember how beautiful you looked on your wedding day as you walked down the aisle. Your guardian angel pendant sparkled against your white wedding dress."

"Grandmother gave me her necklace the morning of our wedding," I said. "My grandfather had given it to her the night before they got married. He always said she was his guardian angel. Grandma always thought it was the other way around."

"That's beautiful."

"I was so nervous on our wedding day."

"Not as much as your dad." Ali laughed. "I remember how he smelled like Tabu."

"That's my dad. As a dairy farmer, he was paranoid that he smelled like his barn, so he'd always steal a dab of Mom's perfume before he went out in public."

Ali laughed even harder. "And the way your dad was hanging onto you in the back of the church... I didn't think he would make it down the aisle."

"When we were ready to walk toward Jim at the altar, Dad squeezed my hand and said, 'You are truly a gift from God. Mom and I have been so blessed to have you in our lives. You're my girl for the next sixty steps and then I have to give you up.' I tried to reassure him that he wasn't losing me, but he didn't believe it for a second. Then he said a funny thing. 'Remember when you were young and we used to polka in the barn on the runway between the cows?'"

"I can't picture your dad dancing in the barn," Ali confessed.

"He actually thinks he's a great dancer!"

We both laughed. And for the first time in a long time, I felt warm and happy.

"Tearza, have you made any decisions about your future?"

"No. After devoting so much of my life to my work, the girls, and Jim, I feel paralyzed. I don't know who I am anymore. Sure, I was a good mother and wife, but I lost myself somewhere along the way. It's ironic that we're talking about this because I read an article just yesterday about widows. The Hebrew translation of the word widow is, 'One who does not have a voice.'" I looked down at my left hand and rubbed my wedding ring. "That's exactly how I feel, as if I lost my voice when I lost Jim."

Ali sat back in her chair with her left knee bouncing up and down. I couldn't tell if she was thinking about herself or me.

Finally I said, "I'm sorry. I didn't mean to dump my problems on you. I have enough money to get by for a few months, but I have to sell the house and get a job and find an apartment to rent or—"

"Or what?" Ali asked.

"Or move home with Mom and Dad until I figure things out."

She searched my eyes for an explanation. "Move home?"

I changed the subject. "Ali, why did you come here today?"

"To convince you to come skiing with us this year."

We had gone skiing as couples every year since college. Was I ready for that? "I don't know," I told her.

"Please, it'll be good for you."

"I can't."

"We'll pay for it. It won't cost you a thing."

"What did I say about charity?" I repeated myself but not as sharply.

"Okay, but it would be fun."

"We'll see."

"At least think about it?" Ali reached over and grabbed my hand. "Please."

I nodded.

"Good. I have to leave, but I'll call you next week."

I stood in the doorway and waved as she pulled out of the driveway and then looked up to watch a jet passing high overhead. Its silver wings glistened, and a long vapor trail lingered behind it. The sky had the same lifeless, gray color as the day we buried Jim.

I closed the door and thought about my conversation with Ali as I cleaned up the kitchen. Since the girls were gone, I decided to go to the cemetery. I put on heavy boots and a ski jacket and took one last swallow of coffee. It tasted bitter, like my heart felt.

The cemetery was deserted. The snow swirled around hundreds of lonely tombstones that dotted the graveyard. As if it were happening now, I knelt down by Jim's grave and braced myself against the biting wind. The world suddenly went black and white, as if time had stopped, and I was back at Jim's funeral. I held Ella and Marci's icy hands while staring down at my husband's casket in disbelief. *This is not really happening*, I thought. Standing next to Jim, death seemed to seep from the grave. My nostrils burned from the stench and my eyes watered as I gagged on the taste of it. Struggling to control myself, I didn't remember anything else of the service until I felt water hitting my face. The priest had sprinkled holy water on Jim's casket, and those of us standing nearby got a few drops.

Suddenly, the service was over and everyone drifted away. I lingered next to the casket, while Dad took the girls to the car. Alone with Jim for the last time, I couldn't bring myself to leave until I felt Mother's hand on my shoulder.

"Tearza, look at my face," she said softly.

I stared into her deep, green eyes and my knees buckled as I clutched her winter coat. Mom quickly reached around my waist to keep me from falling. She didn't say anything for a minute, then she whispered, "Dear, we have to go now."

"But I never got to tell him…"

"What?"

"You wouldn't understand." And then I wept. "My God, Mom, how can I say goodbye now?"

"He knows you loved him," she said gently. "That's enough."

"Is it?"

Mom nodded and stroked my hair the same way she always did when I was hurting. Arm-in-arm, we walked slowly through the snow back to our car.

The memory of that day lingered as I brushed the snow away from Jim's tombstone and unearthed Marci's Mason jar. It was filled with special memories of her dad—two smooth, white skipping stones from the shores of Lake Michigan; a picture of the two of them fishing; a letter she wrote to him the day after he died, sealed shut until they met again; the king of hearts card from our Rummy Royal game; a plastic ring he won for her at the state fair; and two lightning bugs from the farm. I see Jim every time I look at Marci. She has the same physical features—tall, lanky, and athletic. And she has a similar demeanor—generous, sweet with a kind heart, yet at times reserved, moody, and judgmental. Ella, on the other hand, is the yin to Marci's yang. She's my spitfire, gregarious, emotions-on-her-sleeve comic who always makes us laugh.

I set the jar on top of the snow under his picture encased in the tombstone. Even though we had our share of problems, I took for granted that we would always share our life together. Now, all of that was gone. Jim would never get to celebrate Marci and Ella's sweet-sixteen birthdays, take photos of their first proms, or walk them down the aisles on their wedding days.

And I'm alone.

Kneeling, I clasped my hands together and spoke to my husband. "Jim, you have to help me. I can't do this alone. I'm losing the house. I lost my job. Marci's so angry that you are gone, and Ella's simply lost. What should I do?" I touched his photo and ran my finger over his eyes, down his cheek and then across his lips.

A large pine tree stood guard over Jim's grave. Suddenly, the sun peeked out from the clouds as silver wind chimes, a gift from our ski group, began tinkling on a branch above me. I trudged back to my car through knee-deep snow and drove home. When I pulled into the driveway, I noticed something sticking out of the kitchen door. It was a letter with a yellow sticky note in Ali's handwriting stuck to it. The note said, "I forgot to give this to you from Dylan. You were gone when I came back, so I stuck it in the door. Love you, Ali."

I began to read the letter from Jim's college friend.

Dear Tearza,

I miss you. I miss Jim. I know we haven't seen each other since Jim died. I wish we could get together more often, but I understand.

I never got a chance to thank you for asking me to give his eulogy. You understand more than anyone why it was too painful for me to say how I felt about Jim in church. After I wrote the eulogy, I knew that I couldn't do it. I found the speech in my drawer the other day and thought you might want to read it.

Tearza, we all miss you. I'll call you in the next couple of weeks.

Fondly,

Dylan

Behind Dylan's letter was his handwritten speech:

How do you describe the perfect friend? Unconditional, funny, big heart, father, best friend—I could go on for an hour. We never fully appreciate what we have until we lose it.

I want to share one story. After college, we spent one month in Nepal. At the end of the trip on a glorious day in the shadow of Mount Everest, Jim gave me a book, *The Bhagavad Gita*, to remind us of our time together. He had placed a bookmark on his favorite passage.

"The truly wise mourn neither for the living or the dead, because there never was a time when I did not exist, nor you, nor any of us. Nor is there any future in which we shall cease to be."

To this day, whenever the sky is blue, I hear a child laugh, ski in fresh powder, or take a walk in the woods, I can feel him. He's there, all around me, and I can hear him whisper through the soft wind in the trees, "No worries my friend."

Ignoring the cold, I leaned against the kitchen door and read the letter again. My breath came out in rapid bursts. Nauseated, my eyes filled with tiny flashing lights and I lost my sense of balance as if falling into a black hole. *My God*, I thought, *I'm losing it.*

Chapter 4

Ryan

The flight from New York didn't arrive until after midnight. I found the girls spooned together in Sara's bed. Their concert costumes laid in a pile on the floor. I sat on Gracie's bed, watched them snuggle and imagined their futures. They're so beautiful. After a few minutes, the pride gave way to doubts and fears. Instead of joy in my heart, I felt nothing but shame and frustration. For the first time in my adult life I knelt on the floor and prayed. My daughters deserve more from me, yet I'm in a box without a door out.

My alarm woke me at six-thirty the next morning. I rose and walked down the hall to the girls' bedroom. From the doorway I saw that Cooper, our golden retriever, had curled up on the end of Sara's bed while Gracie lay sprawled on hers with legs and arms stretched out in different directions. After Clair had left, Sara insisted we repaint their room pink with stars on the ceiling. Matching unicorn bedspreads and stuffed animals covered their twin beds and a dozen crayon and watercolor paintings decorated the walls.

Thirty minutes later, Sara woke with a fever and a bad sore throat. I rummaged through the medicine cabinet until I found the thermometer behind a box of Band-Aids. With a flashlight, I peered into her throat. Gracie imitated Sara by sticking out her tongue and saying, "Aaahh." Sisters—they have no mercy on each other. As I predicted, Sara's tonsils were red, swollen, and covered with white gunk. Probably strep again.

I switched off the flashlight. "We have to go to the doctor."

Sara frowned. "No way."

"Your mother never liked doctors either, but I have to know if you have strep."

"I'm not going."

"Come on, Sara."

She stubbornly crossed her arms. "You can't make me."

She was equally as obstinate as her mother. I looked at Gracie and said, "You talk to her. I have to call the office."

I checked my morning schedule. Damn—I had a deposition at nine and then two back-to-back meetings. Jamison would have no mercy. This would be the second time this month I missed work because of a sick child. I left a message with Susan, my assistant, to cancel all my meetings. Then I scrambled to get Gracie off to school and called the doctor's office to schedule an appointment for Sara.

Sneezing and coughing children, accompanied by anxious mothers, packed the doctor's office lobby when we arrived. Illinois was a Petri dish for flu and viruses from December to March. The only other man in the lobby was dressed in a suit and holding a young boy about the same age as Sara on his lap. His cell phone vibrated periodically and he kept looking at his watch.

A nurse appeared in the doorway with a medical file and read off the man's name. Our eyes met as he stood up, shook his head slightly and then carried his son down the hall.

I picked up a magazine. The cover story featured a young mother and her saga of battling postpartum depression. It seems a growing number of women are diagnosed each year with this serious syndrome that occasionally occurs after childbirth. I'd never heard of it until Clair and I had met with her internist to discuss her depression and drinking problems.

It was hard to pinpoint an exact cause. Clair said she had struggled even before Gracie was born. Although she loved her time with Sarah, Clair also loved her work. She missed the camaraderie of the other realtors and the excitement of getting a new client. After Gracie was born, Clair often woke with nausea combined with headaches. The days were long and tiring because Sara demanded a lot of attention as a toddler. In addition to lack of sleep and morning sickness, Clair felt isolated and alone because of my long hours at work and frequent travel.

The pregnancy with Gracie was much worse than with Sara. Clair spent the last ten weeks of her pregnancy on complete bedrest terrified she would lose the baby. Throughout the last trimester, every twitch or false contraction brought instant panic that Gracie was coming too early. The stress was unbearable, and each passing week was a gift, bringing us one day closer to when Clair could deliver safely. After she was born, Gracie cried for the first three months until we discovered she was lactose intolerant. Once Clair changed her diet, we had a quiet and happy infant, and I was positive everything would change for the better.

But it didn't. Clair never rebounded from the long ordeal. Even months later, she couldn't sleep and wept periodically for no apparent reason. I didn't know what to do, and neither did Clair.

After a series of medical and psychological evaluations, the doctors confirmed their suspicion that Clair suffered from postpartum depression syndrome. In addition to treating her medical condition, we added marriage counseling and enrolled Clair in a local Alcoholics Anonymous program.

We experienced a brief period of improvement, but then everything spiraled out of control. A tsunami of anger and blame engulfed our lives. Clair retreated into her own world and there didn't seem anything the doctors or I could do to stop it. Our relationship deteriorated until we couldn't have a normal conversation without arguing. She gradually lost interest in her health, me, and finally even the girls.

In the waiting room, Sara groaned, so I rubbed her ear and stroked her hair while we waited for our turn. After another half hour, the same nurse appeared in the doorway and called our name. She weighed Sara and then led us into an empty patient room. Sara lay quietly on the examination table. Her eyes drooped with a dull glaze and her ears were red. On the wall was a growth chart where kids could stand and measure their height. I did the same thing at home, periodically marking off the height of Gracie and Sara on a kitchen doorframe.

I remembered the joy of the first measurement entry when Gracie was two weeks old. Clair had carefully held her sister upright against the wall while I scratched a line at twenty-one inches. Sara was next. She was three years old and compared to Gracie was a towering giant at thirty-seven inches. Sadly, the higher I marked the lines, the more the girls and I grew apart. Instead of happiness and joy, the growth lines reminded me of too many tears and broken promises. Each one marked off my frequent failures.

The doctor confirmed that Sara had strep. He wrote a prescription and I drove home and put Sara to bed. The next morning, I woke early to finish work on a new case. Sara was too sick to go back to school, so I had to work from home again. Alone in the kitchen, I stared out the window. The slowly brightening dawn light revealed that it had snowed two feet overnight. The streets were deserted. Even the newspaper boys would have to wait for the plows.

I turned on a small lamp next to the pantry. Toys, dog bones, and various boots and shoes lay scattered across the floor like land mines. Barefoot, I moved around the kitchen trying to avoid making any noise that might wake the girls. I loved this time of the morning because I didn't have to think or make decisions. I could ignore the responsibilities of the coming day for at least one more cup of coffee while I played with Cooper. I sat down at the table, trying to concentrate on a contract, but instead I replayed the last argument I'd had with Clair in this kitchen before the divorce. I shivered thinking about what Clair had said to me two years ago.

◆ ◆ ◆

I hadn't heard Clair come in from the bedroom that early morning. I picked up my briefcase and zigzagged my way across the kitchen toward the door to the garage when a cold hand grabbed my wrist. Startled, I couldn't see her face, but her voice quivered in the shadows.

"I don't know who I am anymore," she said.

"Sometimes I don't either."

"I want us back the way we were—the way we used to be."

When Clair stepped into the kitchen light, I was surprised at how much she had changed. I should've noticed earlier, but I felt as if I were seeing her for the first time in months. Even though she had lost too much weight and her shoulder-length hair hung limply around her face, her vacant eyes made me afraid.

"Ryan, you have to make a choice," she said.

"A choice?"

We had been down this road many times before. For once, I wanted to leave the house without getting into another argument. Nevertheless, like a bull that couldn't resist the cape, all I saw was red.

"I can't go on like this," Clair said.

"Come on," I exploded. "I'm not the one who's drinking during the day. I'm not the one taking sleeping pills at night. Look, I can't help it if I have to travel for work and I can't be there to cater to your every need. Don't you understand? Making partner requires sacrifice." My fingers started to cramp from holding my heavy briefcase, so I set it down and put my hands on her shoulders.

"Don't touch me!" She shouted, pushing me away. "What you really mean is that I have to sacrifice!"

"What I really mean is, we *both* do."

"You sound like your father. He wants the damn partnership more than you do." She looked like she wanted to spit.

"Don't bring Dad into this again."

"Why not? He never liked me and you know why."

"Oh, please."

"He's a racist."

"We knew he would reject us when we decided to marry."

"You mean reject *me* because I'm not white. Your dad never respected me enough to care or even just ask me about my background. Even though my family immigrated to the United States from the Caribbean, he assumed I was from Africa because of my dark skin."

"I love you and that's all that matters. Mom blamed Dad's bigotry on his service in Vietnam."

Clair gritted her teeth. "Remember when he found out that I was pregnant with Sara?"

"You and I both know Sara wasn't an accident."

"Remember how he ranted and raved that I ruined everything—how you'd never go to law school now and it was all my fault?"

"I know. I'm ashamed of how Dad treated you then. And now."

"Well, at least your step-mother loved me," Clair sighed.

We stared at each other until she took a deep breath and announced, "I can't take this anymore. All you do is work. We communicate more by texting then we do in person. We live in a shoebox, you're gone all the time, and I'm sorry, but I can't raise the two girls alone."

"Once I make partner, everything will be better."

The room became very small, almost suffocating.

Clair shook her head. "You don't get it, do you?"

"Other people have problems and they work them out."

"That's not what I'm talking about. It wasn't like this when we first got married. You were fun and easygoing. You made me laugh all the time."

I just shrugged because there was nothing I could say to change her mind.

"Since you joined the law firm, all you talk about is money, making partner, your big idea to move us to New York City."

"What's wrong with living in New York City?"

"New York will not change who you are. You're still the son of a hard-working guy from northern Wisconsin."

Cooper jumped up from his corner and stood between us. The dog's sleepy eyes moved back and forth, silently refereeing the tension in our voices. He nudged Clair's hand with his wet nose. He was afraid, probably with the same fear I felt.

"You've changed," she said.

"Maybe we've both changed."

To my surprise, she reached out to brush a tuft of hair away from my glasses, but stopped, as if there was an invisible barrier between us. Now unsure, her hand closed and slowly dropped to her side.

"All I ever wanted was you—only you," Clair said softly as she searched my eyes. "Don't you remember?"

"Which part?" I asked. "You tell me, what part should we remember? And what part should we forget?"

I pushed the memory of that morning away and resumed revisions on the contracts. It was still dark when I finished. Cooper was whining by the backdoor, so I let him out. The wind was picking up again. I looked at the lonely streetlight illuminating the swirling snow and thought about how Clair and I had worn each other down during that terrible last year—battle by battle, bit by bit, broken promise after broken promise—each time cutting a small piece of love out of our hearts.

◆ ◆ ◆

After three days, Sara recovered well enough from strep to return to school. The girls settled into a normal schedule, but I kept falling further and further behind at work. Every night I lay on my pillow, my head buzzing with the long list of things to complete the next day. Every part of my life was stretched to the limit. The girls struggled, Betty threatened to quit, and Jamison constantly criticized my work.

Alone with only the moonlight to share my bed, I stared at the ceiling thinking about how close I had been to achieving everything I had wanted—if only Clair hadn't gotten sick. As much as I hated the fights, I still missed her.

Toward the end of our marriage, pain and anger filled our remaining time. Night after night, we'd lie in bed with our backs to each other. Only six inches separated us, but our hearts felt a thousand miles apart. Inevitably, during one of those long, cold nights, Clair woke me up and asked for a divorce. In the darkness, her words hung in the air like a death sentence. Neither of us spoke for a long time after that. I shouldn't have been surprised, but I remembered how my ears burned white hot as if I had a fever.

Next to my bed, a small alarm clock cast a faint blue light on the wall. I rolled over to look at the time—only four o'clock. Sleep always deserted me when I needed it the most. I got up and finished working on two depositions before I prepared breakfast for the girls.

While the two sleepy-heads sat quietly in the backseat, I drove them to school in silence. Cold air blasted out of the vents and my breath formed a hard frost inside the window as fast as I scraped it off. Shivering over the steering wheel, I struggled to see through the small frozen hole in the windshield and cursed winter, cursed my past, and cursed my life.

As usual, I was the first to arrive at the office. I glanced at the calendar on my desk: February 14. Ironically, Valentine's Day marked the second anniversary of our divorce. For years, Valentine's Day was one of our favorite holidays, but now I dreaded it.

A loud buzz startled me and I knocked over the calendar reaching for the phone. Susan said, "Ryan, did you forget your eight o'clock appointment? He called asking where you were."

I checked my watch. "Shit."

"Don't worry. I covered for you," she said.

"Thanks, you always save me."

"Does that mean I get a raise?"

"Sorry, the phone went dead." I pounded the receiver on my desk. "What did you say?"

"More money," she said louder.

"Okay, but you'll have to wait until I make partner."

"Deal. By the way, happy Valentine's Day—and don't forget to pick up flowers and a present for the girls." She hung up.

A few moments later, Susan walked into my office with files I needed for the meeting then picked up a letter from the top of the stack and handed it to me.

"This came in yesterday's mail while you were at home with Sara. I didn't open it."

"Why not? You know you have permission to open and sort my mail."

"I wasn't sure—it's from Florida," she mumbled.

"Oh." I stuffed the unopened letter in my briefcase. We both knew the letter was from Clair.

My next client meeting was the beginning of another crazy day of sprinting from one thing to the next. It was late by the time I finally got home. The girls met me at the door and told me to close my eyes. They giggled as they ushered me to the kitchen table.

"Surprise!" they yelled and I opened my eyes to candlelight, red hand-cut paper hearts, a plate filled with a large pile of candy hearts, and two hand-made cards. We toasted each other with sparkling apple cider, then Sara handed me two more Valentine's cards.

"These are for Mom. Can you mail them to her for us?"

"Of course," I said. "Did you know that Valentine's Day was your mother's favorite holiday?"

"Really?" Gracie said.

"Remember the snow globe you have in your room? That was my first Valentine's gift to her."

"I always wondered how Mom got that," Sara said.

"I found the globe in a strange shop that reminded me of my grandpa's old attic, which was filled with dust-covered things that hadn't moved for decades. I noticed the snow globe hidden behind a lamp in the corner of the store. I fell in love with the tiny Christmas tree inside the snowy landscape. When I asked the owner about the globe, he spoke in a funny voice that sounded like Truman Capote."

"Who?" Gracie asked.

"A famous writer. Anyway, this little man talked like this—'It's for dreams. If you're the rightful owner, you get to make a wish.'"

The girls laughed at my goofy nasal voice.

"Was Mom surprised when you gave her the snow globe?" Sara asked.

"I think so. But before I gave her my present, we shared beer cheese soup and a glass of white wine. While we ate, your mother drew a heart with our initials in the frost of the windowpane next to our table at the restaurant. In the candlelight, her deep, dark eyes drove me crazy."

"Dad, you're sooo romantic," Sara swooned.

"Your mother was—*is* beautiful," I said. "I fell in love with her the moment we met. She worked in a coffee shop near the law library. I was sure she must be one of those models you see in fashion magazines. Tall, smooth, cocoa-complexion with shoulder-length black, wavy hair—she was a stunning combination of European, African, and Caribbean features. I was so flustered that I ordered a scone and forgot the coffee.

The girls stopped talking at my description of Clair. Gracie twisted her hair, while Sara chewed on her lip.

I pointed my finger at each of the girls. "You know, you look so much like her."

They both blushed.

"Sara, you have the same eyes and long legs." I turned to Gracie, "And you have her smile and the same beautiful laugh."

"Did you give Mom the snow globe at the restaurant?" Gracie asked.

"I made your mother close her eyes, pulled the snow globe out of my backpack, and set it in front of her on the table. She was so surprised she clapped her hands. She said, 'Let's make a wish. Did you know that snow globes are magic?' I told her the shop owner had explained that to me.. Then she said, 'I'll tip it upside down, but before the last snowflake floats to the bottom we both have to make our wish.' "

As the snowflakes swirled and danced on their lazy journey to the bottom, she whispered, 'Isn't it beautiful?' I told her yes, but I wasn't watching the snowflakes."

"What were you looking at?" Gracie asked.

Sara rolled her eyes. "Mom, who else?" she said. "You're such a dope."

Gracie swatted at Sara. "I am not!"

"Come on girls, don't fight," I begged them. "Let's eat first, then you can open your presents."

After dinner, Sara helped me rinse the dishes. She'd been unusually quiet since I had told the story about Clair and the snow globe.

"Sara, are you okay?"

She didn't answer, so I decided not to pursue it. We continued to clean-up while Gracie drew pictures with crayons on the end of the kitchen table. Sara passed by the kitchen doorway as I put the last of the dishes away.

"Sara," I said, "stand next to the door. I think you've grown again."

She stopped and pressed her back against the wall.

"You're cheating!" Gracie pointed. "Dad, she's standing on her toes."

Sara made a face and stuck out her tongue at Gracie.

"Wow! You've grown another inch since last fall." I drew another pencil line. It felt strange to write the date, February 14, on the wall. That had always been Clair's job.

Gracie sat at the table pouting until I asked her to stand against the wall too. She jumped off her chair and stood as tall as she could, waiting for me to measure her. She hadn't grown at all, but I winked at Sara and drew a line about a quarter of an inch higher anyway.

Gracie went back to coloring while Sara walked to the refrigerator and looked at various pictures of our family taped to the door.

"Are you still thinking about the snow globe?"

"No."

"Then what?"

"Our last dinner with Mom." She rubbed her forehead. "You made everyone's favorite—grilled cheese with tomato basil soup for me, chicken fingers for Gracie, and for Mom I think you made shrimp alfredo."

"Good memory."

Clair had packed the night before to begin a new treatment program in Miami. She left early the next morning before the girls woke up.

Sara continued to look at the pictures on the refrigerator. Without turning around, she whispered, "You know, she never said goodbye."

"I'm sorry," I said, searching for words to console her.

"It's not fair," Sara said.

"I know."

I tried to give her a hug, but she pushed away and shrugged her shoulders.

"I've never asked you this before, but what was the worst part of the divorce for you?"

"Lying in bed with her the night she told us she was leaving."

"Anything else?" I asked.

"Her promises," she whispered and then walked away.

Spring

Chapter 1

Ryan

The snow had melted under a lukewarm sun. The girls burst out of the house with Cooper bounding behind, and Gracie leading the pack in bare feet despite the fifty-degree weather. Gracie squinted in the sunlight, her eyes nearly hidden beneath a mop of curly brown hair. Clair's features were obvious when you looked at Sarah, but Gracie was a mix of my family's genes and Clair's exotic Caribbean DNA. Gracie had her mother's mischievous smile and laugh, but my family's sturdy, Scandinavian characteristics.

"Dad, what're you doing?" Gracie asked.

I stopped raking. "Where are your shoes?"

"I hate shoes," she said while chasing Cooper around the yard.

"I know, but you'll catch a cold."

She ignored me.

"What in the world are you wearing?" I prodded.

She twirled around showing off three layers. The bottom one started with a swimsuit, followed by a layer of black leotards, running shorts, and Sara's blue soccer T-shirt, finishing at last with a pink tutu and florescent green cape.

I shook my head. "Whose wild child is this?"

"Come on, let's do something," Gracie begged. "You promised you wouldn't work today."

I bagged some dead leaves into a plastic bag and said, "I'm almost done."

The mail carrier had stopped by, so I walked down to the mailbox, flipped through the bills and junk mail, and then spotted a postcard from Sedona, Arizona. The front contained a picture of a mountain field of desert flowers surrounded by red rock canyons. I turned the postcard over and froze when I recognized Clair's shaky handwriting: "Spring's here. I feel better. I'll see you sometime soon. Give the girls a hug."

Above Clair's signature three words—"love," "always" and "fondly"—were scribbled and then scratched out, one on top of the other. I envisioned her chewing a nail as she decided which one looked best. I understood because I wasn't sure how I'd sign my name either. She had settled on "fondly."

I stared at the postcard wondering what she meant by "soon." Her last visit had started fine but soon degenerated into arguments over small things, which grew into big things, such as her custody rights and money. The girls were upset and I vowed not to let that happen again.

Sara and Gracie were now kicking the soccer ball around. Over the winter, Sara had lost her little girl look. Her long, gangly legs and arms didn't match her body anymore and her wavy black hair and violet eyes made everyone do a double-take. Clair once told Sarah that the Chinese prized the color violet because it represents unity transcending the duality of Yin and Yang. As Clair said this, Sarah looked like her mom had lost her mind. By contrast, at eight Gracie was still in that cute butterball stage with chubby cheeks and tiny round tummy.

I resumed raking, and after about twenty minutes the girls tired of soccer and begged me to stop. It was Saturday, my only day to catch up on my spring chores, but Sara, like Clair, knew my weak spots. As soon as she suggested ice cream, I abandoned my good intentions.

On the drive to the ice cream shop, we had a fierce debate about which flavors were the best. We continued to argue as we entered the shop and the girls bumped into two girlfriends. I didn't recognize them, but they seemed to be good friends by the way they talked and giggled for a few minutes. Finally, they ambled along the cooler pointing at all the flavors.

A high school boy with bad acne and a silver scooper waited impatiently for the decision of an attractive woman, probably the mother of my daughters' friends, who was licking small wooden tasting spoons. She was a peanut, at least six inches shorter than me. I vaguely recognized her, but from where I couldn't say. Regardless, without make-up or jewelry, her delicate features radiated natural beauty.

Gracie waved at me and pointed. "Hey Dad, look! They have your favorite—chocolate chip cookie dough."

The pretty woman looked up from the cooler when she heard Gracie yell. At first she smiled, but then squinted at me and said, "You were one of them, weren't you?"

"Have we met before?" I asked.

"In the conference room of your law firm."

"When was that?"

She frowned, placed her hands on her hips, and then I remembered. This was Tearza Regan, the woman in the blue polka-dot dress. The widow trying to sell her husband's printing business.

"I hope you're satisfied," she said through her teeth.

"Why?" I asked.

"Do they only bring you in for tough cases?" She cocked her right eyebrow. "Or only when they need someone to crush widows out of their life savings?"

"I don't remember the details, but didn't the sale end up at a fair price?"

She moved a half-step closer to me and growled, "You have no idea..." Suddenly, she realized the girls were all staring us. She continued to glare until Gracie pulled on my hand.

I looked down. "Wait a second, Gracie, I'll be right with you." I turned back to Tearza. "We were doing our job. Just like your attorney did for you."

Tearza was going to say something, but she stopped when Gracie tugged my hand again. Her eyes were ablaze, so I tried to change the subject.

"Do you mind if we start over?" I extended my hand. "I'm Ryan Olson." My hand hung in the air until I realized that she didn't intend to shake it.

"I can't believe this," she said bitterly, as if someone had played a cruel joke on her.

"The girls seem to know each other," I pointed out. "Do they go to school together?"

She hesitated, debating her next words. "We started attending St. Luke's earlier this year. This is…umm, well, this is—"

I interrupted, "I think the word you're looking for is 'ironic.'"

"Don't patronize me," she snapped.

"Didn't mean to. Sorry for my poor attempt at humor."

"Believe me, there is nothing funny about this."

Tearza's almond-shaped eyes continued to bore into me, but they softened as she glanced over at my girls. They were cave black—soft, unconditional, best-friend eyes. Finally, she nodded in the direction of my girls. "They're absolutely darling."

"Thanks," I smiled. "Fortunately, they got their good looks from their mother."

"I can see that," she said wryly. "So what did they inherit from you?"

I shrugged and looked at my feet. "Gracie has my eyes and Sarah my height. The rest is all about their mother."

"Mom, come on," the taller girl begged. "Let's pick out our ice cream."

Tearza put her hand on her daughter's shoulder. "This is my oldest, Marci."

Marci was about the same height as Sara but with dark eyes and the same light, Asian skin of her mother. Out of habit, I started to extend my hand, but quickly dropped it because Marcie ducked behind her mother.

"What's your favorite ice cream?" I asked Marci.

"Chocolate chip cookie dough," she mumbled without looking at me.

"Mine too." I smiled and then nodded toward Tearza. "What's your mom's favorite?"

Before Marci could respond, Tearza said, "Excuse us, we must be going." She put her arm around Marci and moved toward the ice cream case.

Sara tugged on my pant leg and pulled me over to the ice cream case. She pointed at her friends and explained. "Marci's my age and Ella's in Gracie's class. Isn't that funny?"

"Funny?" I said.

"We're best friends."

"I see that. Life's full of coincidences, isn't it?" I spoke louder than I needed to.

Tearza looked up but didn't change her expression as she helped her daughters choose ice cream flavors. Once they made their choices, Tearza reached into her pocket but came up empty. She thrust her hand deep into her other pocket with the same result and then frantically checked both pockets again.

"Anything wrong?" I asked.

Tearza's face turned red as she tried to explain how she'd accidently left her money at home in a different pair of jeans. I didn't make a big deal about it and offered to buy. It was a chance to smooth things over.

After everyone got their ice cream, the girls sat down at a table near the window to enjoy their treats. Tearza and I sat at a separate table and I watched the girls talk while Tearza nervously licked her cone.

"Why are you smiling?" Tearza asked, shifting her gaze between the girls and me. "Still gloating?"

"Hardly," I said. "Actually, I was thinking about my girls. All of a sudden, they look so grown up. They used to sit in here with me, usually with Gracie on my lap, but that's all changed."

"That's girls for you," Tearza said.

"I know, but it makes me lonesome."

"Why?"

Stalling, I played with my napkin. Finally, I confessed, "I don't know."

"Change is hard."

We awkwardly slurped ice cream for a few moments. Finally, she said, "So, how long have you been a partner?"

"I'm not yet, but I'm working on it."

She licked her cone and stared out the window. "That must keep you pretty busy."

"Busy is an understatement. It's been a challenge to balance work and raise the girls by myself."

Tearza stopped eating. "You're a single parent?"

"Yeah—divorced about two years ago." Embarrassed, I tried to change the subject. "By the way, what do you do?"

My cell phone went off and I glanced at the number on the screen. "Sorry, I have to take this. It's my office." I excused myself and walked outside to take the call.

We never resumed the conversation. On the way home, I mentioned to Sara, "You seem to enjoy those girls."

"They're great."

After I drove a couple more blocks, Sara tapped me on the shoulder. "How do you know their mom?"

"I don't." I paused. "Well, I do, sort of. We met a few months ago regarding her husband's business."

"What does their dad do?" Sara asked. "They never talk about him."

"Didn't they tell you?" I said.

"Tell us what?"

I glanced in the rear view mirror at the girls. "They lost their dad two years ago."

"What happened?" Sarah asked.

"He died of a..." I debated what to say. "...of a heart attack."

The car got very quiet. Gracie reached for her blanket and Sara stared out the window. Nobody spoke the rest of the way home.

◆ ◆ ◆

Work the next day was a marathon. I spent the afternoon rotating between three conference rooms for various depositions, document revisions for my associates, and coordination of client meetings. It was after seven when we finished the last meeting and I was beat. It had been a long day. Several lawyers decided to go out for a drink, but I politely declined and went back to my office. A few minutes later, Travis, one of my associates, poked his head in.

"Come on, Ryan. You can't work all the time."

"Sorry, you go ahead. I have to finish this letter and get home to my daughters."

"When was the last time you went out?" Travis asked.

I rubbed my chin. "Umm, let's see."

"If you can't remember, it's been too long."

"You're probably right."

One of the other lawyers joined in. "We heard you used to party with the best of them."

I shook my head. "Don't believe it."

"That's not what Andy told us. He claims that when you were fresh out of law school you had a fun group of associates that used to go out quite often."

"The older he gets, the bigger the story."

Travis persisted. "Come on, don't you have a nanny? Call her and say you'll be a little late." He picked up the receiver on my phone and wiggled it.

"Okay, but a quick one. I'll be right with you. I have to call home first."

After my divorce, the first three nannies were disasters, but the girls adored Betty, a short, plump woman who waddled when she walked, smelled like cotton candy, and wore bright, red lipstick. At around sixty, she spoke so slowly that I constantly fought the urge to finish the sentence for her. She was a perfect combination of Mary Poppins and Mother Goose—tough when needed, but sweet as pecan pie the rest of the time. Betty dearly loved my girls and was very protective. But with me it was different. She didn't trust me and we disagreed on a number of things. She constantly suggested ways for me to spend more time with the girls. Although she made me feel defensive, she was careful not to cross the line in our lively discussions about all the time I devoted to work.

Betty gave me the green light to coming home late, so I grabbed my briefcase and joined the others at our local watering hole. It had been two years since I'd been there and it hadn't changed a bit. It had the comforting smell of damp wood soaked in years of stale beer mingled with sawdust lightly scattered across the floor. Even though it was early, the place was already hopping.

I worked my way through the crowd to Travis's table in the far corner. Someone produced a chair and someone else plunked a beer in front of me. Once settled, we all raised our thick mugs and with a cheerful clink the night was on.

Another round of beers arrived and I had to admit I was glad they had talked me into having some fun. Travis poked me in the arm and nodded toward the door.

"Here she comes."

I was surprised to see Tiffany, one of my co-workers, enter the bar. She was a tall, striking blond with high cheekbones and dangerous, deep blue eyes.She created an electrifying effect whenever she entered a room, even at the office. She waved at us from the front door. Walking toward us like a model on a runway, she caused every man in the bar to watch her all the way to our table.

"Why's Tiffany here?" I asked.

"Ed invited her. He's in love with her, along with every other guy in the office." He took a good pull from his mug and wiped the foam off his upper lip. "Normally, she never comes to these things, but she changed her mind when she heard that you agreed to join us."

"Bullshit."

"It's true," Travis insisted. "We've voted you the luckiest guy in the office because you get to work with her all the time." He shook his head from side-to-side and smiled. "And what about all the trips you take together to New York City? Yah, baby!"

"It's strictly business."

He laughed. "If you say so."

Tiffany finally made it to our table.

Ed offered her a seat next to his, but she stood over me waiting for Travis to move over. "Thanks, but I think I'm fine right here," she told Ed.

"Hi Tiffany," I said, then poured a beer and set the mug in front of her.

She shook her head solemnly. "Would you mind ordering me a Belvedere martini, extra dry with three olives?"

"You don't drink beer?"

She leaned over and whispered in my ear. "Sorry—it's not good for my figure."

I choked on my beer. "I hadn't noticed."

She winked and tapped my thigh under the table. "You're so sweet."

An hour and a few more drinks later, I glanced at my watch and remembered Betty and the girls.

Tiffany could sense my need to move my chair back. She pulled a toothpick out of her martini and tantalizingly put an olive in her mouth. "See, this wasn't so bad," she said. "We should do this again."

The noise and music was extremely loud. "What?" I asked, as I leaned closer to her.

Grinning, she yelled above the noise, "You need to get out more often."

"Maybe you're right, but it's hard to stay out with the girls waiting at home."

"That must be tough." She sipped her martini. "I don't know how you do it."

"Neither do I." I shook my head and sneaked another look at my watch. All at the table cheered when I bought them a round of shots but jeered even louder when I announced that I needed to leave.

I left to pick up my car, but about a half block from the bar I heard someone call my name. I turned to see Tiffany waving at me.

"Wait up," she yelled.

"Did you forget something?" I asked.

"Yes," she said, surprising me with a kiss.

At first I balked. "We aren't supposed to—you know—date."

She grinned. "I know. That makes it even more fun, don't you think?" She tilted her head and gave me a pouting look. "Tell me you didn't like my kiss."

I looked to see if anyone had seen us. "We could get fired for this."

She grabbed my hand and led me toward the parking garage. "I have a great bottle of wine at my apartment that I've been saving."

I looked at my watch. "I need to get home, Tiff. My babysitter will kill me."

Tiffany didn't let go of my hand. "Come on, loosen up. My place is just around the corner. We won't be long."

An hour and a half later, I made it back to my car. I was so tired from the long day that I could barely keep my eyes open. I hoped the girls were in bed. I walked into the kitchen and announced, "I'm home."

Predictably, Betty was sitting at the table with her arms crossed. "You're late," she snapped.

"I thought you said it was okay if I went out for a drink."

She glanced at her watch. "You said one drink, not several."

"I had to go back to the office to finish something," I lied.

She crossed her arms. "Why didn't you call me?"

"Just lost track of time a little."

"Remember our conversation last week—or the one before that?" She started to pack a purse the size of a beach bag. "I warned you."

This was the last thing I needed after such a brutal day. "Come on, Betty, don't do this. It's the first time I've gone out with the guys in ages."

"This has nothing to do with a drink or two." Betty put her hands on her hips. "You're always running late."

"You know the reason. If one of the partners asks me to work late, I have to stay."

"I don't give a hoot about your partners!" Betty paused and gave me a sharp look. "How many babysitters have you gone through before me?"

"Two."

"Only two?" she said even louder.

"Well, it might be three, but the last one wasn't my fault."

"Oh really!" Betty snorted. "I know you have to travel on business, I get that part, but when you're home all you do is work. The girls never see you anymore—it's like they have a ghost for a father."

Suddenly she stopped talking. Sara and Gracie were standing in the living room doorway holding hands, not saying a word, just watching us. Cooper joined the girls and sat quietly next to Sara with his tongue hanging out. The only sound was muffled voices coming out of the TV in the other room.

Sara's eyes didn't blink as she said, "What's going on? You're yelling at each other."

"No we're not," I assured her.

Sara looked at Betty holding her coat and bag. "Are you leaving us?"

Betty gave me a dirty look and quickly moved toward the girls. "No, honey, I'm not leaving you. Your daddy and I were having a discussion—that's all."

"That's what my mom always said," Sara said, gripping Gracie's hand harder.

"Go on." Betty gently prodded them. "Why don't you sit in the living room and watch television. I'll come in to kiss you goodnight before I leave."

Sara slowly turned away with Gracie in tow but glanced back at me.

"Thanks, Sweetie, I won't be long," Betty said.

Once they were gone, Betty turned her full fury to me. She threw her jacket on the back of chair and motioned me to sit at the kitchen table. "I can't do this anymore," she said. "I don't want to hurt the girls, so I'll stay for another week to give you time to find someone else."

Shit, I thought. *Not again.*

"What should I tell the girls?"

"That's your problem. Make something up so they don't think I'm abandoning them. Tell them I have to take care of my daughter's new baby because she has to go back to work."

My mind went blank. I couldn't think straight. "There must be something—"

She cut me off, "No, we've been over this too many times."

I was out of ideas. She was determined to quit, so I gave up. "I understand."

"No you don't." Disgusted, she stood up, picked up her things and slammed the door on the way out.

◆ ◆ ◆

Two weeks passed since Betty had left. Sara was barely speaking to me. I couldn't find another nanny to replace Betty right away, so I enrolled the girls in an after-school latchkey program. To cover the evenings, I arranged to have a young woman who was attending college nearby pick them up from latchkey, make them dinner, and help them with their homework until I got home. The girls hated it, but I didn't have any other choice.

After another grinding day in court, it was late when I got home and the girls were already in bed. Gracie was asleep but had kicked off her covers. I pulled the comforter tightly around her neck and kissed her on the head. Then I leaned over Sara. She was awake, but instead of reaching up to kiss me, she turned away and faced the wall.

"I hate you," she whispered.

"It's not my fault."

"I miss Betty."

"I know."

She punched her pillow. "She would've stayed if you didn't work so much."

"That's not fair."

Sara started to cry again. I gently turned her over so I could see her face. I wanted to tell her I was sorry, but I didn't know how.

"But we loved Betty." The tears streamed down her face and her lips quivered.

I sat down on the edge of her bed and stroked her hair. "I'm sorry honey. But there's nothing I can do about it."

Chapter 2

Tearza

I finished writing checks for the bills that I could pay. My severance money ran out five months ago. Although I've sent out a dozen resumés, I haven't received one positive response. Unless I'm willing to move out of state, there aren't any jobs here in my field.

I plowed into a list of to-dos before the girls returned from a friend's house. The day was a sprint until I tucked the girls into bed. I was almost asleep when I heard my bedroom door open. I rubbed my eyes, bewildered, while Marci and Ella stood in the doorway holding hands.

I looked at the clock. "What time is it?"

There was an awkward silence as we all stared at each other.

"Come here." I patted the bed. "What's wrong?"

Neither said a word but looked at the floor.

"Are you scared?"

They both nodded.

"Hop in with me." We snuggled under the comforter and talked until they drifted off to sleep.

I constantly worried about the girls. Ever since Jim died, each of us had struggled in a different way. Ella lost some of her spunk and played with dolls for hours by herself. Marci harbored a silent rage that would erupt at the slightest provocation. I tried to help, but I could barely function myself, just going through the motions of making it through each day. Everyone said that time would heal the pain—but it didn't.

Even though it was a Sunday, Marci was the first to wake up and to my surprise she asked, "Can we go to church today?"

"Church? Why?"

"Our new friends, Sara and Gracie—they go every week."

"I don't think that would be a good idea."

"Why not?"

Why not? I thought. *Because I can't forgive God yet? Because I have a hole in my heart the size of the Grand Canyon?*

Marci insisted. "Mom, everyone else in my class goes."

"Okay, let's try it."

"Can we sit with Sara and Gracie?"

"We'll see."

We arrived late and settled into the last row in case I wanted to leave early. I felt strange because the last time I had attended mass was for Jim's funeral. The girls pulled out a book to read and I silently listened to the opening hymn. St. Luke's was an old-fashioned Catholic church. Tiny alcoves glowed with dozens of candles perpetually burning for hope and faith. Mass was served passionately by an old Benedictine priest. He looked like Santa Claus with a twinkle in his eye, generous round tummy, and quick laugh.

Once Father had started his homily, I noticed he didn't have any written notes, which made me hopeful for a quick sermon. Big mistake. After a minute or two, I could tell we were in for a long one. My mind drifted until I heard him utter the words, "Better, not bitter."

Grabbing onto those words like a life jacket, I prayed as he made the sign of the cross.

Marci suddenly squeezed my hand. "Feel better?"

"Why, do I look sick?"

"You're smiling."

I thought of my grandmother and realized that guardian angels come in all sizes.

◆ ◆ ◆

I spent a long, restless night worrying about the start of another busy week. I woke up Monday in a fog and carried a cup of coffee into the family room. Standing next to the window, the intense early morning sunlight soothed me. Patches of daffodils were beginning to emerge, reminding me of the spring flowers in the fields above our farm. I kept thinking about a vivid dream from the night before. Mom and I were painting together in our summer kitchen and I was so happy.

After finishing my coffee, I walked over to a storage closet I hadn't been in since Jim had died. It was dark inside and smelled of wood, old canvas, and oil paints. I flicked on the light and everything was there—just as I had left it two years ago.

Old habits return quickly. I set the easel next to the window to catch the best light and picked up my brush, but for some reason I stopped and rearranged everything again. Finally, I sat down on the stool and stared at the canvas, but the white space just stared back. I tried closing my eyes, as my mother had taught me, to allow images to appear in my mind, but nothing came—no color, no images, only emptiness. I began to cry and eventually gave up.

Later that day, I left my accountant's office very depressed. Reluctantly, I was accepting that we had to move out of the house because I couldn't afford it.

Back home, I scoured the want ads for an apartment within my limited budget. I noted a few possibilities, then gathered up a map and a large cup of coffee. I yelled to the girls. "Come on, we're going apartment hunting again."

"Mom, why are you smiling?" Marci asked as we walked to the car in the driveway.

I pointed to the sun. "I love spring."

"You're funny," Marci said as she turned and raced Ella to the car.

Not funny, just weird, I thought.

The girls knew exactly what to expect since we had looked at apartments on the previous two Saturdays. However, this time as I got into the car, Marci said, "Mom, I have this feeling—today we're going to find our new home."

"I hope so, honey, because this process is wearing me out."

After two hours searching without any luck, our Suburban looked as if we lived in it. Unfortunately, most of the apartments were either too big and expensive or too small and in disrepair. I was extremely discouraged as we rounded a curve.

Marci yelled, "There it is! That's the one!" She pointed at a man pounding a For Sale sign into the front lawn.

"Honey, that's a house, not an apartment."

"Slow down," she insisted.

Situated on a corner lot, the house had a large yard that backed up against some woods. It was a charming older home with a cottage in the back that looked like some enchanted dwelling you might see in a Disney movie. The cottage was white with a rounded roof shaped like a mushroom. I half-expected to see Sleeping Beauty and the Seven Dwarfs sitting in rocking chairs on the front porch.

At my daughter's insistence, I pulled over to the curb.

The man stopped working on the sign and said, "Can I help you?"

I rolled down the window. "I'm sorry to bother you. We were driving by and my daughter admired your house."

"It's not mine. Mr. Jacobson owns the house. My name's Bob and I'm his realtor."

"I'm curious. How much are they asking?"

"You'll have to ask the owner. I don't think he's decided yet."

We heard the sound of an eggbeater getting louder and louder. It came from an old, yellow Volkswagen pulling into the driveway.

Bob motioned to me. "Good timing, here he comes. Let's go ask him."

"No thanks," I said, but the kids had already jumped out of the backseat, running toward the cottage and ignoring my pleas to come back.

Furious, I turned off the car, As I went after the girls, the car door of the VW swung open and a tall man unfolded out of it like a giant Gumby.

He noticed how I stared at him. "I know," he said, caressing the Beetle with his right hand. "I look funny driving this, don't I? Actually, it's Mary's car, but I love it."

He stepped forward and shyly extended his hand. I sensed something familiar about him, but I couldn't put my finger on it. He appeared to be in his seventies with wavy silver hair and blue eyes. I gulped at the huge hand he offered, and I expected his skin to feel rough and calloused, but to my surprise it was as soft as a baby's.

He smiled with his eyes. "I'm Jerome Jacobson, but everyone calls me Jake."

"I'm Tearza," I said, then gestured toward the girls in the backyard. "And these are my girls. We're looking for an apartment to rent. I'm curious—how much are you asking for the house?"

Mr. Jacobson eyes twinkled. "Could I offer you and your girls some fresh lemonade in the house? I made some this morning."

Ella appeared from the side of the house. "I love lemonade," Ella said.

"Ella Marie," I scolded.

He grinned. "Then you'll love mine."

"Come on, Mom," Ella begged.

"Okay, but only for a minute."

"I see you've met Bob."

The man who again was forcing the sign into the ground waved at us.

As Jake led us inside his home, the screen door squeaked like the one on our house back on the farm. While we waited for the lemonade, my eyes wandered around the living room. The house was simple and everything in it had some connection to his family—the pictures on the walls, old trophies the children had won, photos of grandchildren, a cozy, hand-made quilt that was thrown across the couch.

Jake sat down and passed out glasses of lemonade. "My children want me to sell the house," he said sadly. "They think it's too much for me to take care of."

I felt guilty taking his time and drinking his lemonade. "I'm sorry, but we just can't afford to buy a home right now. I didn't mean to waste your time."

He ignored me and continued speaking. "They think I'm becoming a cranky old man."

I didn't know what to say.

Suddenly, he stood up. "I have an idea. I'd like to show you something."

"No, that's okay. We should be leaving."

"Please, I need a woman's opinion."

I hesitated before asking, "About what?"

"A garden," he said.

Jake led us down the hall toward the kitchen in the back of the house where he paused for a second and showed me a picture of himself and his wife when they were young.

"You have so much to look forward to," he said softly, then gently set the picture on the counter. "I envy you. You and your husband have your whole life ahead of you."

I wanted to cry, but I didn't say anything.

He led us outside and pointed to a small cottage behind the house. "At one time, this was a large estate and the domestic help lived in the cottage. This—" he spread his arms wide to highlight a large, overgrown garden plot— "is Mary's happy place."

"What did she plant in the garden?" I asked.

"Phlox, veronica, bee balm. Over there she had petunias, salvia, and marigolds. And see the rose bushes? They were her pride and joy."

"I love working in the garden," I confessed. "Actually, I was deciding on my annuals for this spring but then realized that I'd have to wait until we found our next home. I'd love to get her opinion on some changes I've been considering."

Oddly, Jake didn't respond. I wasn't sure if he heard me. My dad was hard of hearing too, so I didn't risk embarrassing him by repeating myself. "Tell me more about the cottage. It looks beautiful."

"Let's take a look, shall we?" Jake grinned and led me to the cottage. He opened the door and turned on the lights. "It's bigger than it appears. It has three bedrooms and two bathrooms. Needs a little paint, but other than that it's in great shape. My niece and her husband lived here for two years while they were in graduate school."

He motioned for me to sit down again and the girls jumped on the couch next to him. He smiled at the girls and turned to me. "How long have you and your husband been looking for a house?"

Suddenly, the girls stopped fidgeting and looked at me expectantly. Bob silently joined us in the room, obviously interested in our conversation.

"As I mentioned earlier, we're not looking for a house. I lost my husband unexpectedly and we have to sell our house and find an apartment. Finances are a little tight right now."

He grimaced, which sent shivers through me. I immediately knew he had lost his wife too. It all made sense now—the noisy yellow Beetle, the messy kitchen, and the untended garden.

"I… I lost my Mary several months ago," he whispered. "I feel like I'm betraying Mary by leaving our home. I've had a hard time letting go."

All I could offer him was a timid, "I'm so sorry."

"How about you?" he asked, surprising me.

"What?"

"Don't you find it hard to let go?"

I nodded, rubbing the wedding band I still wore.

He looked at my hands. "Life has its own agenda, doesn't it? I worked so hard to save money for my retirement. We sacrificed so much over the years anticipating all the exciting trips we'd take together. And now this. I never imagined losing Mary before we had a chance to enjoy our dreams."

I couldn't bear to look at him.

"Feels like we've been robbed, doesn't it?" he asked.

"Of everything," I said as my eyes grew moist.

He paused, pulled a white hanky out of his back pocket and handed it to me. "It's clean."

I tried to smile as I dabbed my eyes. "I'm sure it is."

He blushed, realizing how silly that sounded. "Can I ask you something? Would you ever consider renting the cottage?"

Bob suddenly cleared his throat, an intentional interruption.

Jake turned and shot him a stern look, then turned back to me. "What do you think?"

"But I thought you were selling the house?"

"I wouldn't have to sell if you rented my cottage. My kids live out of town and they hate that I'm alone here."

Bob took a step closer to Jake and said, "Maybe we should talk about this first, Jake. I don't think you should rush into anything. We should call the kids."

"I don't need to talk to the kids," Jake snapped. He leaned toward me. "What's your budget, may I ask?"

I felt my face turning red. "Twenty-five hundred a month."

"Really, what a coincidence." Jake slapped his thigh. "That's what Bob estimated a new buyer might get for renting the cottage."

Bob's face went white. "I know I said that—but it was only a guess."

"Let me worry about that."

Bob frowned. "But the city will require some code changes. That'll cost you."

"The rent will cover it," Jake answered.

"I really think you should consult with the kids," Bob tried again. Jake ignored him.

"Mr. Jacobson, are you sure?" I asked.

"It's Jake. And yes, I'm positive."

The girls leaped off the couch, screaming. Marci's crazy hair flopped around her while she shouted at me at the top of her lungs. "I told you. Mom. I knew we'd find a home today."

Jake interrupted us before we could celebrate any further. "Excuse me, but there's one more thing."

My heart stopped. I didn't think we could take another disappointment.

"You recall earlier, how we discussed your passion for gardening. I want you to promise that you'll restore the garden. It meant so much to Mary and it would mean a lot to me."

I looked at this kind, gentle man and his misting eyes.

"If you can promise me this one small concession," he said, "then we have a deal."

I couldn't believe what had happened. I couldn't hold back any longer, so I jumped up to give him a big hug. The girls joined us and we stood together for a long time, half-crying for joy.

"Jake, you have no idea. We can never ever thank you enough for your kindness."

"You just did," he said, "and that's more than enough for me. This is a good place. It still has a lot of love to give. That's the way my Mary would want it."

◆ ◆ ◆

Once I got home, I started to panic. I wanted to make sure that I didn't make a mistake with the lease agreement. I stared at the phone in the family room for a long time trying to work up the courage to call Ryan for help. I finally picked up the phone, half-hoping he wouldn't be there. It was after dinner and they might be out for the evening.

"Hello?" he answered.

"I hate to bother you, but I need some advice," I said. "I'm not sure if I've made a big mistake, but I found a small place to rent."

"That's great," he said.

"The owner's an older gentleman and he's never rented to a stranger before. He asked if I knew anyone who could draft a lease agreement. So, I thought of you. Would you be willing to help me? I'll gladly pay for your time."

"Don't be silly. My expertise is litigation, but I've done a few real estate deals. When do you want to review the lease?"

"Any time that works for you."

"I could do it now if you want. I'll bring Sara and Gracie along to play while I put together the lease."

"Thanks, that would be great."

"What's your address?"

"It's 1250 Lakeshore Drive."

"Perfect, just ten minutes from us. See you soon."

Sprinting around the house, I threw everything into drawers and closets to hide the mess. I quickly did the dishes and was putting on a pot of coffee as the doorbell rang. Ryan's girls waved at me through the window of the front door and I motioned them in.

"Thanks for coming on short notice."

"No problem." Ryan sniffed the fresh coffee. "By the way, my billing rate is two cups of coffee per hour."

"Thank goodness, because by the time I finish paying rent, that's about all I can afford."

"You have a beautiful home. I'm sorry that you have sell it on account of me."

"Don't be." I paused. "It's actually not your fault."

"Does that mean you forgive me?"

"Let's not go that far." I wagged my finger in his direction. "I want to see how good you are at drafting this lease first. Then I might reconsider."

I walked him into the family room and put a fresh log on the fire. We sat on the couch and he pulled a lease out of his briefcase. He asked some questions and began to mark up a standard agreement. After a few minutes, the coffee was done.

"What do you like in your coffee?" I asked.

"Bailey's or Irish whiskey," he deadpanned without looking up.

"Sorry—no Baileys, but we always have Irish whiskey. Maiden name's O'Sullivan—right off the boat."

He glanced at my Korean face with a look of surprise.

"Yeah, I know— before I was married, I got the same reaction from everyone when I used my maiden name. I was adopted as an infant from Korea. I'm so grateful for my parents. They made sure that I was as proud of my Korean legacy as my place in their family. I loved understanding where I was born, but I'm as Irish as they are. In fact, I can chug a beer faster than my father and brother."

"I agree—chugging beer is an essential life skill." Ryan chuckled. "Really, that explains everything." He laughed again. "On second thought, I better skip the Irish whiskey. I want to make sure you get your coffee's worth."

I fetched the coffees and sat across from him. I watched him work, making notes and changes on each page. He periodically adjusted his glasses and unconsciously tapped his pen on the table while he concentrated. Finally, he turned the last page and reached for his coffee. "There you go," he said, handing me the marked-up agreement, "That was easy."

So much like Jim, I thought. Jim always made everything look easy.

"Easy for you, but I have no clue what all this means," I confessed. "Other than the fact I'll be signing my life away if I go through with this."

"Renting isn't a big deal. If you want, we can go through the entire lease line by line and by the end you'll be an expert." He motioned for me to join him on the couch.

Our shoulders touched when I sat down and for some reason I had a hard time focusing on the words. I moved slightly away, mad at myself for feeling like a dumb schoolgirl. *What am I doing, fraternizing with the enemy?*

Suddenly, four girls burst in from the other room and a Nerf ball sailed past my shoulder and knocked over Ryan's coffee, spilling it all over the lease. I leaped off the couch, ran for some paper towels and frantically tried to wipe up the spill, but the coffee had soaked several pages. I felt embarrassed until Ryan touched my arm. "No worries, these are standard forms and my revisions are still legible. It'll be easy to print off a new set to revise…if you approve."

"I'm sorry—I thought everything was ruined. I'm a little nervous about this whole thing."

"Do you like baseball?" he said.

"What?"

"Baseball, you know—a wooden bat and white ball."

I blushed. "I suppose, but I don't follow it. Marci's crazy about baseball, though."

"So is Sara," Ryan said. "Would you like to go to the game on Saturday?"

The question stunned me. "I don't know," I stammered.

"Don't you like the Cubs?"

"No, it's not that." Quickly, I figured the cost of the tickets and food for the three of us. I didn't have any money to spare this month.

"Then…what?" he pressed.

"I already have plans," I said a little too fast.

He looked confused. "You haven't forgiven me yet, have you?"

I didn't know what else to say.

"Well, maybe some other time," he said quietly.

"Sure, that would be great," I said, embarrassed again.

We both looked away for a second. I continued to swab spilled coffee and he gathered up the pages and stuffed them in a folder.

"Okay, I'll finish the lease tomorrow, get it printed off and then you can sign it." He stood up and reached for his briefcase. "Congratulations. Can't wait to tour the cottage. Sounds really cool."

"Thanks," I reached out to shake his hand. "I couldn't do this alone." He leaned over as if to attempt a hug, but he stopped. I flinched when I noticed Marci staring at us from across the room.

"Don't worry," he said, "things will get better for you and the girls. I'm sure of it." Then he whistled for Sara and Gracie to join him in the car.

◆ ◆ ◆

A week later, the girls and I finished packing up and I walked through our old house one last time. The girls were already settled at the cottage. The last van was packed and waiting for me. I thought about Jim—and about letting go. I found myself standing in our empty bedroom, my heart feeling as bare as the space. I could almost hear our babies sleeping in the next room, and I ached for the tenderness of Jim as we made love in our king-size feather bed. *How could I say goodbye to this house and all the memories it held? Would Jim think I betrayed our love—our life—by moving on?* I sank to my knees and sobbed.

◆ ◆ ◆

Jake was waiting for me on the porch with a big smile as I pulled up with the moving van. He brought me into the kitchen where a vase of beautiful flowers sat in the center of the table.

"Welcome to your new home," he said.

I smelled the flowers and then picked up the note. It said, *Your home is where your heart is.* I gave him a hug. "Jake, you're so sweet."

He spent the afternoon helping me direct the movers to the correct rooms. Jake pointed to a large box labeled *Paint.* "Where do you want this box to go? In the garage?"

"No, just leave it."

"Nonsense, I got it." Jake lifted the box. "This doesn't feel like cans of paint."

"It's not."

"What is it?"

"Art stuff."

"I didn't know that you paint."

"I don't."

"I'd like to see your paintings some time."

"No. I don't think that would be a good idea," I said louder than intended.

Jake set the box down. "I'll check on the guys and see how they're doing with the rest of the furniture." After the movers left, Jake handed me a two-page list of all the critical things I needed to know about the cottage.

Standing in the middle of a living room filled with unpacked boxes, I reviewed his long list of handwritten notes, but I could barely read the scribbling. "Jake, I don't understand half this stuff."

"You mean my handwriting?"

"I don't know a water softener from a water heater. Jim always handled the house."

"Don't worry. My phone number's right at the bottom, and you know where I live. Oh, I almost forgot. In the refrigerator is my own special chili." He blushed and shoved his hands in his pockets. "I made it earlier today because I knew you wouldn't have time to cook with the move and everything."

"Thank you."

He shrugged. "It's a little spicy."

"I'm sure it's wonderful."

"I have to leave, but call if you need me."

"I promise."

What a blessing. I thought gratefully. *Nobody in the world could've made this move easier.*

◆ ◆ ◆

The phone startled me—my very first phone call in our new house. The caller ID displayed Mom's number.

"Congratulations on your new house!" Mom said. "We can't wait to see it."

"It's a cottage, not a house, but thanks." I switched the phone to the other ear so I could continue stirring Jake's chili on the stove. "I'm really nervous about the payments. It was more than I planned on spending, but we fell in love with it."

"Dad and I are very happy for you," she said. "How're the girls?"

"Pretty good. They have good days and bad ones. They spend a lot of time with Sara and Gracie. Darling kids, unfortunately their mom moved away shortly after the divorce two years ago."

"Sweet Mother, that's awful."

"I don't know exactly what happened yet."

"What's the dad like?" she asked.

I tasted the chili and added some salt. "You don't waste any time, do you? He's a lawyer. You know the kind—preppy, a partner wanna-be. You are what you drive."

"Tearza Marie, you're so judgmental."

"Wonder where I get that from."

"I'll pretend I didn't hear that. Sounds like he has potential."

"To you, if he's breathing, every man has potential."

She laughed so hard I had to pull the phone away from my ear. You could hear her laugh in a crowd of a hundred people, and it was infectious. Everyone loved her when she got the giggles.

"How did you meet?" she asked.

I explained our first awful encounter at his office, and then later at the ice cream store. "I wanted to belt him, but I restrained myself. His girls were with him."

"Restraint? Hello, do I have the wrong number?"

"I know. To make matters worse, after we picked our ice cream I went to the counter to pay and I didn't have any money, so he paid. So embarrassing."

"You must've been mortified. What does he look like?"

"Frankly, he could be a clone of Robert Redford. Sandy hair, tiny sun freckles across his nose—looks like he just stepped off a sailboat." I stopped talking long enough to cover the chili pot and let it simmer.

"But you wouldn't like him—he's the complete opposite of Jim."

"Not exactly your type?"

"Correcto mundo." I paused. "However, behind his glasses—he has killer eyes. You know, those sleepy, sad, blue eyes that make your knees weak."

"So, what else don't you like?"

I burned my hand on the chili kettle and silently winced. I continued talking as I ran cold water on my fingers. "I'm glad the girls like each other so much. Remember what it was like to have your best friend at that age?"

"At any age," Mom said.

"Here's a funny coincidence, it turned out the girls do a number of the same activities."

"What are the odds?"

"They spend so much time together that we see them weekly."

"But I thought you didn't like him?" she said.

"I know, but once I got to know him…"

"I've heard that one before."

"Mom!"

"Sweet child of mine, you do whatever you think is best." She paused. "Honey, your dad's calling from the barn. I'll call you tonight."

A few minutes later, the phone rang again. I was sure Mom had forgotten to tell me something. "Did you forget something?"

"I don't think so," a man's voice said.

Shocked, I asked. "Who is this?"

"I think you're the one forgetting something."

I recognized Dylan's voice, Jim's best friend from college, then suddenly remembered the half dozen voice messages he'd left on my phone.

"Hi Dylan. I thought you were my mom."

"That's okay. At least I finally caught you."

"Sorry about not returning your calls, but things have been a little crazy around here."

"You survive the move?"

"You're so sweet—but how did you know I moved?"

"Ali told me."

I didn't respond.

"Is everything okay?" he asked.

"We're fine."

"Anything I can do to help?"

"No, but thanks."

"Once things settle down, I'd love to take you to lunch," Dylan said.

"That would be nice." I tried to figure out a graceful way to get off the phone. I had no interest in having lunch. "Sorry, gotta to go. Marci's beeping through on the other line."

"Okay, but don't forget."

I felt guilty lying. "I promise."

Chapter 3
Ryan

Andy, our managing partner, assigned me two new clients, which is great, but it forced me to work late almost every night. Some of the partners understood why I needed to spend more time with my daughters. Others, like Jamison, didn't care, and I felt more pressure than ever. I worried about the firm's concerns over my situation as a single parent. Was I committed? Would I be able to handle big cases? I was determined to work even harder over the next few months. My frequent absence was hard on the girls, but I was sure they'd understand when they get older how my sacrifice was for them.

After dinner, our kitchen table often doubled as my office, and this evening was no exception. On purpose, I'm sure, Gracie placed her math book on top of the contract I was reviewing.

"I don't get it," she complained.

This was the third time in the last half hour that one of the girls had interrupted me.

"Did you read the book first?" I asked.

"I tried," Gracie said, "but I still don't get it."

I glanced at the clock then looked at Sara for help, but her head was buried in a reading assignment.

I explained to Gracie, "You have to learn to figure this out for yourself. I won't always be here to help you."

Sara's face shot up from her book. "What do you mean—you won't always be here?"

"I didn't mean it that way."

"But that's what you said."

Gracie started to cry and went back to her seat. Cooper walked over and put his head in her lap.

"I'm sorry," I said meekly. "I'm so far behind in my work." I realized that my complaining was falling on deaf ears. "Gracie, come over here." I pushed my work into the middle of the table. It would have to wait until after the girls went to bed. At the office I could control my schedule, but at home I didn't have a clue.

Sara often helped Gracie with her homework when I was too busy. A typical firstborn, she was organized and mature beyond her eleven years. I was concerned that she had taken on too much responsibility for someone her age. Sara had struggled more than her sister with the pain of the divorce because she was old enough to understand.

Even though they were only eight and eleven, the girls were sure they knew what was best for me. Dominated by two little ladies whom I adored, I couldn't complain too much. Everyone was concerned about me. My parents and friends tried to set me up. Even my office co-workers arranged blind dates for me. The women they suggested were fun and nice, but I always found a way to avoid a second date.

It was different with Tiffany. For some reason, she didn't seem to be looking for a long-term partner any more than I was. Although she thought my girls were cute, she made it clear that she had no interest in becoming a suburban housewife. She had set her sights on a position with a prestigious law firm in exciting New York City. I understood her ambition and that I was just a stepping-stone—no, more likely just a diversion. No one knew about our secret rendezvous. Dating associates was strictly prohibited, which was okay because I wasn't serious about her anyway.

As an example of my friends' failed attempts to set me up, my assistant Susan called last night to introduce me to a college girlfriend who had recently moved from Seattle. Even though it had been months since my last real date, I really wasn't interested.

"Please take her out," Susan begged. "She doesn't know a soul in the city."

"Don't do this to me."

"Come on," she whined. "I'm on my knees."

"How do I know that? Send me a photo."

"Trust me."

"Do you remember the last one you set me up with?"

"How did I know she worked weekends in a tattoo parlor?"

"That was the least of my problems that night."

"Stop, that's as much detail as I need to know. Remember, I work with you. This one's beautiful."

"And?"

"She's rich."

"And?"

"And what? Isn't that enough?"

"You know what I mean."

"All right, she might be a little high maintenance."

"That's all?"

"Well, she has a loud laugh."

"How loud?"

"You might want to go to a busy restaurant."

"Great."

"Does that mean you'll do it?"

"No, it means I don't know how I ever got stuck with you as my assistant."

She didn't respond.

"I suppose you're pouting now," I said.

Stymied, I could only keep this up so long and she knew it. Susan learned how to get what she wanted from the master. Clair and I used to have a great time when we were with Susan. The two of them were inseparable, but that was a long time ago—before Clair got sick.

Finally, I asked, "Exactly how bad is her laugh?"

Susan gushed, "Thank you, thank you. I owe you one."

I dreaded the date as soon as I said yes.

◆ ◆ ◆

When date night arrived, the girls were despondent. They hated the thought of me dating. Even though Clair had left us two years ago, they held onto the dream that someday she'd come home.

I checked my watch—in ten minutes the babysitter would arrive. As I walked into the living room, Sarah burst out laughing.

"You aren't wearing that, are you?"

"What's the matter? I wore this on my last date."

"Well, remember what happened last time. You were home before Gracie and I even went to bed."

Sara grilled me about every woman I considered dating. Who was she? What did she do? Had she been married before? If so, did she have any kids? Did she smoke? Would Gracie like her? She would persist until I begged for mercy. I assured her I'd never date a woman she didn't approve of, but that was never enough for Sara. In her mind, nobody would ever replace Clair.

Quickly, I switched pants and put on a different shirt. Satisfied, I checked the mirror one last time and walked back downstairs. I glanced at my watch and knew I'd late for my blind date. I half-debated cancelling, but I was tired of sitting home alone night after night.

I picked up my coat and handed the babysitter my phone number as the girls tried to push me toward the door. They kissed me twice and told me how good I smelled.

Twenty minutes late, I picked up my date, but she didn't seem to mind. I had decided to take her to a Mexican restaurant Clair liked to visit. The place was a little cheesy—cheap posters of bullfights covered the walls and fast Mexican music played in the background— but the food was always good.

We sipped our margaritas, nibbled on chips and fresh guacamole, and tried to make small talk. I could smell my date's heavy perfume from across the table and she giggled too much at almost everything I said. She was beautiful and from appearances seemed wealthy— fancy clothing, heavy gold jewelry and a rock on her right hand the size of an almond. She also seemed confident on the outside, but I sensed desperation and loneliness inside. I quickly downed a second margarita hoping it would help my mood, but it didn't.

I flinched when she reached across the table, touched my hand and said, "Did I tell you how I met your Susan?" She began a long story, but I wasn't listening.

As I glanced over my date's shoulder, I saw Tearza across the restaurant having dinner with a girlfriend. I couldn't take my eyes off her as she smiled, tilted her head and leaned forward in conversation. Her fingers played with the rim of the margarita glass as her tongue licked the salt off her full lips. I was surprised that I noticed such a detail.

My date interrupted my gaze with a snort that I swear sounded like a horse. "Did I tell you about my trip to Mexico over Christmas?"

"No, you didn't."

"Wow!" She rolled her eyes. "Ever hear of the Blue Marlin in Cabo?"

"Afraid not."

"Well, let's say we won't be welcomed back there anytime soon."

She started another boring story about herself. I thought about ordering a shot of tequila but realized it would be another big mistake. My cell phone vibrated, and I glanced down at the number on the screen. It was Jamison. He always had some crisis requiring my intervention.

I apologized and went outside to take the call. On my way back, I bumped into Tearza walking toward the restroom.

"Hi." I didn't know if I should shake her hand or hug her. Like a dope, I didn't do either but simply stood there feeling like a shy sixteen-year-old with braces.

"What're you doing here?" she asked.

Pointing toward our table, I said, "I'm having dinner with a friend of my assistant."

Tearza looked around me, straining to see where I sat.

"Your date's beautiful."

"She's not a date, not really." I tried to change the subject. "What a coincidence we're at the same restaurant."

"Yes, it is." She smiled shyly and tucked her hair behind her ear. Her smile and tiny dimples made me forget my next thought until I blurted, "You look like you're having fun."

"Too many margaritas. I'm such a lightweight. Hope I don't need an attorney before the night's over."

"That wouldn't be the end of the world, would it?"

"Maybe not." She raised her left eyebrow, then turned and continued toward the ladies' room.

Back at my table, I made up an excuse that a client emergency demanded my immediate attention. Within a minute, I was mercifully on my way home. But I entered the house in the middle of a catfight between Sara and Gracie.

The babysitter was sitting in the living room eating popcorn and watching television, oblivious to the screaming. She looked up and asked, "You're home early. How was your date?"

Ignoring her, I said, "Who's winning upstairs?"

"Hard to say—it's World War Three, I tried to get them to stop, but they wouldn't listen to me."

"Don't feel bad. They don't listen to me either."

The babysitter grabbed her coat and I paid her, then walked upstairs to the battle scene. The argument grew louder and then I heard a big rip.

"*Th*ara, I hate you!" Gracie screamed. She had a slight lisp that only flared up when she was excited or upset.

Sara held a fluffy, pink bunny tail in her hand, while Gracie cradled the rest of the Easter Bunny costume in her arms.

"Stop fighting!" I ordered. "Now speak."

"Look at my costume, Gracie said. "I'm *th*upposed to wear it for our Easter egg party at *th*chool tomorrow." Her lisp became worse when she got angry.

It was nine o'clock and I pondered my options. Gracie cried all the way down the hall to her bed, stopping periodically to yell at Sara. I was desperate, so I called Susan hoping she knew how to sew a tail back on a bunny costume and repair a rip in the seat. All I got was her voicemail.

"Tearza knows how to sew," Sara said.

"How do you know?"

"She made Ella's costume. I saw her working on it at their house."

I wondered if Tearza was home from the restaurant. Anyway, I called her in desperation and sighed with relief when she answered.

"Hi, it's me, Ryan."

"Yeah, I recognize your voice."

"I have a big problem."

"How big?"

"Well, put it this way. I temporarily stopped World War Three."

"I'm impressed."

"But it'll start again soon if I don't get a bunny tail sewn back on a certain someone's costume for the Easter party at school tomorrow."

"Let me guess. A certain someone fought with another certain someone and the tail got pulled off?"

"Familiar?"

"Very," she said. "We're still up. Can you bring the costume to my house?"

"I'll be right over. Can you give me directions? Not sure I remember the address to your cottage."

After a ten minute drive, Tearza met me at the door.

"I love your place," I said, stepping inside.

"Thanks. I still have boxes to unpack, but it's starting to feel like home."

I held up the damaged costume. "You're saving my life."

"You're my good deed for the day." She took the costume and led me into a spare bedroom filled with rolls of cloth and bags of white stuffing material. A large sewing machine sat on a table covered with a dozen thimbles of colored thread and an assortment of needles.

"Wow, what's all this?"

"My sweat shop. I used to sew to make extra money in college." She picked up Gracie's costume and assessed the damage. She put the costume on the sewing machine and started to hum as she pushed the pedal.

"I didn't know you were so talented."

"There's a lot you don't know about me," she said while watching the needle going up and down.

"How did you learn?"

"All good girls from Wisconsin know how to sew."

I stepped closer to the sewing table and leaned over her shoulder to watch. She pushed the pedal of the sewing machine with her foot as she guided the costume back and forth.

"Small world," Tearza said. "I can't believe we were at the same restaurant tonight. Did you have fun on your date?"

"I did Susan a favor."

"Some favor. Do you often personally sacrifice yourself like that?"

"Only for Susan."

Tearza pulled the costume off the machine and held it up. It looked good as new.

"I don't know how to thank you," I said.

"No worries." She stood up and handed me the costume. "You handled everything on my lease—this is the least I can do in return." She stopped me when I got to the door. "It's nice to have help, isn't it?"

"You don't know."

"I think I do."

"You've made Gracie one happy camper."

Chapter 4
Tearza

The sweat stung my eyes and dripped off my nose into the freshly turned soil. I finally stood up after two hours of hoeing and spading to measure my progress. Mary would be proud. I'd kept my promise to Jake and the garden was slowly taking shape. I bent over and ripped out the last patch of weeds and perennials. Out with the old, in with the new. Nothing smelled as good as freshly tilled earth.

"I like it," a familiar voice said from behind.

Ryan stood on the edge of the garden. I had been concentrating so hard on the garden I didn't hear him approach. He looked handsome—strong shoulders, summer tan, white shorts, teal blue soccer shirt. Quite a package.

"It's not ready yet," I replied. "I still have a lot to do before I can plant."

He smiled and pointed. "I meant your hat."

"Oh, this." Embarrassed, I took off the floppy, wide-brimmed hat and wiped the sweat from my brow. "Mom gave it to me years ago." I looked at my watch. "Oh, my gosh, I completely lost track of the time."

"No problem, I'm early," he said. "You look like you have a natural green thumb."

"How can you tell?"

"Let's see—the red rubber boots, muddy knees, face and hands black with dirt—and still smiling. I'm taking a wild guess, but this must be a happy place for you."

"Actually, I made a promise to someone."

"Lucky someone," Ryan said, as he walked into the middle of the garden where I stood.

"Give me three weeks, then you can be the judge."

"Deal." Ryan picked up the garbage can full of dead weeds and carried them to the edge of the driveway. I followed behind dragging a hoe and a shovel.

"Hey, any progress on the job hunt?"

"Not good," I replied.

"Don't worry, something will come up."

Ryan set the empty can down and shoved both hands into his pockets, kicking the gravel under his feet. "I've been meaning to talk to you about what happened last week. I wanted to apologize for being late to pick up the girls. I got on a conference call and I couldn't get off."

"It's all right," I said. "The girls were worried when you didn't come on time."

"I know. It won't happen again. Sara read me the riot act."

A red Porsche pulled into the driveway. I was surprised to see Dylan. I gulped, remembering that I had never called him about lunch.

Ryan looked at the approaching car. "You stay here. I'll grab the girls and take them to the park for a couple of hours." On his way back to his Suburban with the girls, he and Dylan said a polite hello to each other.

"Dylan, this is a nice surprise," I said.

"Who was that?" Dylan asked.

"Oh, Ryan—just a friend." I took off my hat and gardening gloves. "He's Sara and Gracie's dad. His girls are Marci and Ella's best friends."

"I see." He stared at the Suburban driving away. "I heard you got a new place. This is nice."

"It'll do for now."

It was hard to know what to say. So much had transpired since we had seen each other at Jim's funeral.

"How are you?" we both said at the same time.

"You first," I said.

He smiled. "No, you."

"Me? Fine, I guess." I wiped dirt off my knees. Dylan's face was directly in the sun, so I put my hand over my eyes to block the bright light. "And you? I heard you and Jill went through some hard times."

"That's almost over. We've basically called it quits. But we can't seem to figure out how to end it yet."

"I'm sorry. You know how much I think of you both."

"It's okay. We never should've married in the first place. At least we didn't have kids, so that makes it easier." He rubbed his hands together and looked away from me. "It's not anyone's fault. We aren't mad at each other. Sad, maybe, but not mad."

"What's next?"

"I don't know yet. I've been thinking about moving back to my hometown. I admit that I've never liked living in the city. That was Jill's idea. Guess I'm a small-town boy at heart."

I nodded. "I can relate to that. Do you have time to visit?"

"Don't want to interrupt your gardening."

"I need a break anyway. Come sit with me for a while."

We walked back to the cottage and I brought some iced tea out to the porch where we sat down.

He looked out over the garden. "Ali said she gave you my letter."

"I know. I've been meaning to call you. It's just that…"

"You don't have to explain."

"The eulogy you wrote was beautiful," I said. "Jim would've loved it."

We didn't look at each other for a few minutes. Dylan stared at his glass of tea. The condensation dripped in long streaks. He wiped his wet hands on his pants as I tried to think of a way to make him understand.

"Can I do anything for you?" he said.

"I'm fine."

"Really?" He tilted his head and looked at me out of the corner of his eye. He started to say something else but changed his mind. "How are the girls?"

"Not good. They fight over nothing and Marci's having trouble in school. Unfortunately, she's inherited my Irish temper."

Dylan laughed.

"Ella breaks my heart whenever she talks about all the things her girlfriends do with their dads."

Dylan put his hand on my knee. "I know how hard it must be for them not to have a father. I lost my dad when I was young." He paused and looked out over the garden. "Jill and I didn't have kids, but I know I'd be a good father if I had the chance."

I squeezed his hand. "I know you would."

He looked at me with hopeful eyes. "What I mean is…I could take them to do things. Stuff that normal fathers do with their daughters."

"That's so sweet of you. I'll keep that in mind."

He looked disappointed. "I'm trying to help."

"I know. Thanks for the offer." I tried to change the subject. "Tell me about work and your parents."

That seemed to break the ice and we launched into a nice long talk.

Finally, he looked at his watch. "I should let you get on with your day."

"Dylan, why did you come today?"

"I don't know. I walked through town this morning and saw a painting in the window of a store that reminded me of your art."

"What a coincidence."

"You think so?" Dylan set his glass down. "Are you still painting?"

"No."

"Why not? You were so good at it. You used to paint so often before—" He caught himself and stopped. "Sorry."

"It's okay."

"Tell me about the man who left with the girls."

"Marci and Ella's best friend's dad?"

"What does he do?"

"A lawyer."

Dylan shook his head. "That's the one profession Jim always hated."

"This one's different."

Dylan scratched a fashionable, day-old beard. "Really."

"He's—"

Dylan interrupted, "Can I ask you something?"

"Sure, anything."

"The guy in the Suburban."

"Ryan? For heaven's sake, no. Why?"

"Because all you've talked about since I got here is about this guy and his daughters."

"I didn't realize that. We do things together with the girls."

"Huh." He turned to face me, opened his mouth, but stopped.

"What?"

"Nothing."

"Come on. Tell me."

"You know what they say about lawyers. They'll steal your wallet and then break your heart."

I didn't know how to respond. "Is that the Gospel according to Dylan?"

He laughed and shook his head. "Nope. Saw it in a movie." He stood up. "I really enjoyed seeing you again, but it's time to go."

"Thank you for coming," I said.

"Call if you ever need someone to talk to."

"I will."

◆ ◆ ◆

It started to mist softly as I drove to pick up the girls at the park. The rain made me sleepy. I missed the time when the girls were young and the days were ours to follow the sun, rather than the crazy schedules we now kept. On those rainy afternoons, Jim would gather the girls into his arms and take them to the porch to read their favorite storybooks. Sleepy and cuddled under a pile of warm blankets, their dreams and mine were soon filled with fairy tales. We have a similar porch at our new cottage, but it wasn't the same without Jim. I still cherish those quiet, rainy afternoons, because it's only there—in my dreams—that Jim and I could be together again.

In the car, I brooded over my recent conversation with Ryan about my work situation. I passed a sign advertising spring flower tours at our arboretum. It reminded me of the flowers we picked on our recent bike ride with Ryan and the girls. I had a revelation. It was so obvious: flowers. I couldn't believe I hadn't thought of it earlier. Ryan reminded me how flowers were my happy place. Maybe I could find a job working with flowers.

I found a job at Forever Green, a small flower shop near our cottage. My hours were ten to three, so I could get the girls off to school and be home before they got off the bus. I went outside to tell the girls who were playing in the backyard.

"I have some good news. I got a job."

Ella stood up in the sandbox and walked toward me. "A job? Why?"

"Well, I need to make money."

"Sara says her dad is never home. Will that happen to us?"

"I'm not working the same hours as a lawyer, if that's what you mean."

"Sara doesn't like it."

"Like what?"

"He's always working."

"I promise. It won't be like that. It won't be any different than when I worked at the university."

Marci stuck her hands deep into her pockets and shrugged. "I like it the way it is now. I don't want you to work."

"Are we poor?" Ella asked.

This was not the reaction I had expected. "No honey, we're not poor. But we do need to make money, as your dad used to do for us." Marci wouldn't look at me. "Come on, it'll be all right. I need to do this for us. Don't you understand?"

"Will we be alone?" Ella asked.

"What do you mean?"

Ella looked at Marci. "Who'll take care of us?"

"I will. We don't need a nanny. I'll be home to get you on the bus and here when you come home." *It had sounded so easy when I discussed it with Ryan.*

I gathered them in my arms. "Come here, you two. Nothing will change. I'm only working while you're at school."

Ella asked, "What will you do at the flower shop?"

I told them about my job with flowers and we all felt better the more we talked about it.

◆ ◆ ◆

My position at Forever Green soon became my dream job. After a week of training in the front of the shop, the owner paired me with Amber, one of the experienced girls, to show me how to make the flower arrangements. Amber walked me into the back of the shop and reached for the first flower order of the day.

"I don't know how you do your flowers," Amber said in a husky, smoky voice and waved her arms around like a mystic. "Good—bad—happy—sad—you have to feel it before you can make it."

We stood in front of a large square table that gave us plenty of space to spread out. Cutting shears, colored ribbons, tissue paper, wire, and tape covered the table, along with a mixture of different types of greenery and flowers.

Amber was about my age, but we had taken different paths in life. She had backpacked around the world, lived in Las Vegas and New York City, and had recently moved here from Telluride. She wore a small silver ring in her left eyebrow. A little rough around the edges, she was nevertheless attractive, but not pretty. I was quite sure there were more piercings, but I was too afraid to ask.

Amber asked several questions about me while she selected flowers for someone's birthday. Strangely, though we were quite different, she was easy to talk to, almost like we were old friends. To my surprise, I ended up telling her my life story over the next twenty minutes.

"What about you?" I finally asked.

"Me? I'm working two jobs, divorced, and chained to the house with two kids." She looked up from her flowers. "Sounds pretty pathetic, doesn't it?" She pointed her scissors at me. "But I haven't given up."

"On what?"

"Love, of course." Before I could respond, she continued. "I know this sounds crazy, but there are still times when I miss him."

"Whom?"

"My ex." She chewed on her lower lip and drew a heart in a small pile of black dirt that had spilled on the table. "Tearza, do you think we'll ever fall in love again?"

I didn't know what to say.

Amber noticed my stare. Embarrassed, she smacked herself on the forehead. "Listen to me. What do I know about love?"

She held up a pink lily to the sunlight streaming in. Turning the flower carefully in a circle, she whispered in a strange voice, "Like the Dalai Lama once said, 'Women are the true seeds of compassion.'"

"What does that mean?"

"Forgiveness."

She saw me flinch. "You know—it's our flaw. We're really good at forgiving everyone else, but not ourselves." She lifted the sweet flower to her nose, inhaling deeply. "Look at me. I'm a poster child for the flaw. I've forgiven my ex-husband so many times I can't count... but not me." She shrugged and resumed cutting more flowers.

"How do you know these things?" I asked, amazed.

She leaned close to me.

"Sometimes you only learn things when you least expect it."

"I don't understand?" I said.

"Years ago, I met a Buddhist priest in Seattle of all places. I'll always remember his eyes—gentle, like the sea at dawn. I was in trouble, searching for answers. He simply repeated an old adage, but one that I hadn't heard before—'The teacher comes when you're ready.' I can't explain it, but it's so true. Still gives me goose bumps."

She tied a pink ribbon around the vase. "Well, this one's done. You can take it up front." She patted me on the arm and headed out the back for a smoke.

Amber had to make a delivery, so it was my turn to make a flower arrangement on my own. I pondered the next order, a wedding anniversary. Easy, I thought. All I had to do was think of Jim and the flowers he'd sent to me over the years. Twenty minutes later, I triumphantly carried my first creation to the cooler in the front of the store.

Amber spent the rest of the afternoon teaching me about life and how to make a dozen more arrangements. It was almost five o'clock when I carried the last order to the front and placed the flowers in a safe spot. The girls were at Ryan's house with their nanny after school, so I could work until closing.

As I shut the foggy glass door, I heard a familiar voice. "Miss, could you please help me?"

I turned, surprised to see Ryan. His blue polo shirt matched his eyes.

"I wanted to stop by and see how you liked your new job. Also, I need a nice flower arrangement for Susan, you know, my assistant. It's her birthday this week."

"I'd love to help you, but since I'm a beginner you should work with one of the more experienced girls."

"No, I'd rather work with you," Ryan assured me.

You can always tell something about people by the flowers they pick. I was secretly pleased at the flowers Ryan suggested. No white carnations for him, only spring flowers with lots of color.

"I didn't think hard-core attorneys liked flowers," I teased.

He put his hand on his chest. "We do have hearts, you know."

"My, my, aren't we sensitive today?"

"Okay, I'm a softy, but you can't tell anyone or I'm toast in the litigation business." He bent over, picked up a long-stemmed red rose from a vase and handed it to me.

"See, we're not so bad," he said.

"That'll be five dollars."

He smiled. "Best money I've spent today."

He followed me around like a puppy as I moved from cooler to cooler picking flowers for Susan's arrangement. "So, what are your favorite flowers?" he asked.

"That's easy—gardenias and daisies. I love the fragrance of a gardenia. I wore one in my hair for our wedding. And the yellow daisies grow wild in the fields above the house back on the farm."

"I bet you looked beautiful."

"What?"

Ryan blushed. "I mean the gardenia in your hair. I bet it looked beautiful."

"How about you?" I asked. "Do you have a favorite?"

"Lilies of the valley—because they smell good," Ryan said shyly.

"They're pretty, but they don't last very long."

"Seems like some of the best things never do."

We continued to discuss the flower arrangement and then Ryan stepped closer to examine the flowers I had selected. I could smell his cologne as I sorted through the best flowers and tied them into a bouquet.

"Are you okay?" he asked. "Your face is flushed."

"It's hot in here, don't you think?"

Not waiting for an answer, I quickly moved to the counter, took a deep breath and started to ring up the order.

Mary, the store owner, followed Ryan out of the store and locked the front door. "That's enough fun for one day," she said. Then she turned around and walked back to the front desk where I was still cleaning up.

"Leave that for tomorrow," she insisted.

"I'm almost done," I said.

Mary closed out the register and put the day's cash in a zippered pouch. "Tearza, how do you feel about your job with us?"

"I have so much to learn," I said.

"That'll come. Be patient." She smiled. "You're doing great. I know it may not feel like it yet, but you're a natural with flowers."

"Thanks, it's been challenging but I love it."

"Learning a new job is a piece of cake compared to losing your husband."

I nodded. "Nothing prepared me for the speed of all the changes in my life since Jim died."

The store was empty, except for the two of us.

"I know what you mean," she said slowly.

"You do?"

"Chaos is the best way to describe what happens when you lose a spouse."

"You read my mind," I said.

"I lost my husband five years ago." Mary sighed. "For months, I felt like a deer frozen in the headlights of an oncoming truck. I didn't know a debit from a credit, term insurance from a term paper, or probate from a good debate. With three children, it took me a long time to settle into my role as a single working parent."

"I'm so sorry," I said. "I didn't know."

Mary picked up her car keys and her purse. "What's been the hardest for you so far?"

"Besides losing Jim..." I hesitated. "I'm lonely. I hate the change in friendships, never getting calls to go out with other couples, eating alone when the girls are gone, and driving to the kids' games and school activities by myself."

Mary flicked off the lights and we went out the back door. She locked up and put the keys in her purse. Halfway across the parking lot she stopped. "You know, it gets better over time."

"Everyone says that." I frowned. "I'm not so sure."

Mary looked up at the night sky. I followed her gaze and noticed how the full moon was exceptionally bright.

She whispered, "Can you feel it?"

"Feel what?" I said, as I continued to stare at the moon.

Mary's face glowed in the moonlight. "The energy."

"I don't feel anything anymore...only emptiness."

"Not even for your girls?" Mary turned, reached over, and hooked her arm under my arm.

"Of course. I love them," I said defensively.

"Love is the purest form of energy." She stared at the moon as we walked. "No beginning, no end."

"What do you mean?"

"Love isn't a singular experience. It's universal. Once I accepted that, I found my husband again. Found him everywhere—

in everything." She squeezed my arm tightly as we slowly walked toward our cars. "Smell the flowers, listen to the wind, dance on moonbeams." She let go of me, then twirled around and around with her arms stretched out, as if she were dancing with her husband. Suddenly, she stopped, blew a kiss to the moon and gave me a hug.

"Goodnight, Tearza."

She walked away into the shadows of the parking lot.

I thought about our conversation all the way home. After the kids were in bed, I turned out the lights and mindlessly watched TV in my bedroom—another night alone. I glanced out the window. The moon looked like a giant white spotlight. I kept thinking about what Mary had told me. How can I change the way I feel? She made it sound so easy in the parking lot.

Finally, I turned off the TV, picked up a book and tried to read, but the phone rang. I glanced at the clock—ten o'clock. Who would be calling at this hour?

"What're you doing?" Mom asked.

"Had to work late. I put the girls down and was trying to read."

"You sound tired."

"I can't sleep."

"Me neither." She paused. "Something about a full moon. It gives me the monkey brain every month."

I laughed and thought about her in the kitchen with a day-old cup of coffee reading the local paper for the third time or rummaging through old scrapbooks of us kids when we were young. Dad would've been asleep for hours. For a long minute, neither of us spoke. We found comfort in knowing the other one was on the line. Ever since I'd left home, we'd always had some weird telepathy that went beyond the bits and bytes that connected us by phone.

"So, what did you do this weekend?" she finally asked.

"I did six loads of laundry, then cleaned the bathrooms. Let's see, that's about it for fun."

"You need to get out more."

"Please, don't start on me again."

She pressed, "What about Marci and Ella's friends, Sara and Gracie. Isn't their dad nice? I know you've changed your mind about him since you've gotten to know him."

"No." I tried to figure a way to say this correctly. "He's more like a good friend. Besides, I'm not his type."

"So, you've forgiven him for being a good lawyer?"

"Sort of."

"There must be someone."

"Mom."

"Whatever. It's your life, I guess. What do I know?"

"Exactly," I said.

"I'm curious, what type do you think he likes?"

"For God's sake, you don't quit, do you? Well, certainly not a farm girl from rural Wisconsin. He works every day with a smart, professional woman, named Tiffany. She's a lawyer at his firm. I doubt he's sitting around the house reading magazines at night. I saw him at a restaurant last month with a different woman—gorgeous, and she wore jewelry that would have made Elizabeth Taylor jealous."

"He doesn't know what he's missing."

"Trust me, he doesn't even think about me."

"I would if I were he. He should wake up and smell the petunias."

"It's coffee, Mom, not petunias."

"Coffee, petunias, whatever. Give me his number. I'll talk some sense into him."

I laughed and glanced at the clock. "Mom, what would happen if I did go out with someone?"

"You mean Ryan?"

"Anyone."

"I'm sure you'd have a good time."

"But how would Dad feel about it?"

"Since you were a child, you've been cursed with the O'Sullivan genes of thinking about everyone else but yourself. For once, think about what would make you happy."

I didn't know what to say.

"Are you still there?" Mom asked.

"Yes," I said.

"Are you okay?"

"I will be."

"That's my girl."

"Goodnight, Mom. Love you," I hung up the phone. She could drive a saint to drink, but I had the greatest mom in the world.

I rolled over in bed and looked out the window. Orion's Belt looked so close you could almost touch it. My days were fine because I stayed busy. But at night, after the girls were asleep, the past haunted me. Even after two years, I'd put my arms around my pillow pretending it was Jim. In the dark, I would push my face deep into the pillow to search for the faint smell of his cologne. Then I would lick my lips trying to remember the sweet taste of his toothpaste as we kissed each other goodnight under the covers. If I squeezed my eyes tightly enough, I could almost feel the warmth of his chest with his arms wrapped around me while we slept.

That's when I prayed the hardest.

The next morning, I grabbed my coffee and started sorting yesterday's mail. It was too depressing, so I set the bills aside. UPS had left a small package at the front door, but I hadn't open it. Later that afternoon, I tore the tape off the box and pried open the flaps. Inside was a book, *The Art of Happiness* by the Dalai Lama.

I was mystified because I hadn't ordered this book. I didn't know much about the Dalai Lama, but happiness had certainly been a fleeting goal for me over the last two years. As I browsed through the book, a small envelope fell out. The note read, "Happiness starts with those who love you."

Oddly, there was no signature. I turned over the note and wondered who would have sent me a book like thus.

Chapter 5

Ryan

A flash of headlights passed through the kitchen window. As I rose from my chair, the crunch of tires on my gravel driveway suddenly stopped. I peered out at the tan Buick parked next to the house. I opened the screen door and stepped into the cool evening air, cursing when I saw my stepmother behind the wheel of the still-running car.

I tapped on the window. "Hey Stella, what're you doing out here?"

She turned off the car and rolled down the window. "Nothing." She glanced at Dad asleep in the passenger seat. "We needed a minute."

"What took you so long?" I asked. "I expected you two hours ago."

"We had to make a couple of stops." She poked my father in the arm. "Billy, wake up. We're here."

My father was a tall, barrel-chested man with a belly so large you couldn't see his belt. He was a shadow of the straight-jawed, buzz-cut, strong-shouldered man of his former Marine Corps days. Stella jabbed him a second time. Dazed, he looked around and slowly got his bearings. Once he found the seatbelt buckle, Billy had to rock back and forth to get out of the front seat.

He stumbled trying to stand up but caught himself by grasping the door handle. As he straightened, he stared at me, "It's been awhile."

Neither one of us attempted to shake hands or hug.

I glanced at Stella and then back to my father. "We should go in. The girls have been waiting."

"I brought you something from Jimmy's Smokehouse." Billy reached back into the front seat and grinned as he held up a stained, brown paper bag. "Stella made me stop to get your favorite beef jerky."

"Oh, thanks," I mumbled as I removed their suitcase from the back seat. "Let's get your things inside."

As we entered the kitchen, Sara and Gracie ran up and flew into his Stella's arms. I was shocked at how Stella had aged since the last time we were together. Her straight brown hair was streaked with grey, and she walked with a slight limp. The bright blue eyes I remembered now looked dull and sunken.

"My goodness," Stella said, clasping her hands to her face. "Look how tall you've become since we saw you last."

The girls stepped away and twirled in a circle. "Grandma, do you like our new Cinderella pajamas?" Sara asked. "Dad bought these for us to celebrate your visit."

"You look beautiful in pink," she said.

Billy stretched his arms out and shouted, "Hey, what about me?"

The girls hesitated and then slowly approached Billy. He tried to hug them, but after a few seconds the girls pulled away and went back to Stella.

"Wow, what a difference a year makes." Billy said. "They have really grown."

I frowned. "Try *two* years."

Stella quickly grabbed the girl's hands. "Come on, show me your room."

In their room, Sara pointed to a framed photograph of her fifth-grade class. "Grandma, look, I'm in the back row next to my best friend, Marci."

"My, my, Sara, you're the tallest girl in your class." Stella smiled. "I can't believe how much you look like your mother."

Sara blushed.

Gracie touched Stella's arm and held out a drawing. "Grandma, do you want to see the picture I made in my art class?"

"Of course," Stella said, "I want to see all of your pictures."

Gracie grinned, looking like a jack-o-lantern missing a few teeth. She's the antithesis of Sara. With wild, curly dark hair that bounced around her head when she laughed, she's a tornado trapped in a third-grade body. Gracie's the only person I know who has the unique ability to laugh and cry virtually at the same time. Sara is Gracie's rock and hovers over her like she's a newborn.

After reviewing their "wall of fame," Stella sat down in a large rocking chair and patted her lap for them to join her. "Would you like me to read a story?"

The girls clapped their hands and hopped onto her lap. Cooper tried to muscle his way into the chair to, but Sara pushed him away and picked up *Goodnight Moon*. "This is my favorite book," she declared. "Can you read this to us?"

"What makes this book so special for you?" Stella asked.

"It's the only book I remember Mom reading to us before she left."

Stella frowned and waved for me and Billy to leave. "I'll put the girls to bed. You two get something to eat."

Billy shrugged and nodded toward the kitchen. "Let's have a drink."

An hour later, Stella walked into the kitchen with puffy eyes.

"How did it go?" I asked.

"Great, but I fell asleep reading to the girls." She yawned and stretched her arms in the air. "What are you guys doing?"

Billy ripped off a piece of tough jerky, gnawed on it for a second, and then pointed it at me. "Junior's trying to give me a lesson on politics."

Stella noticed the half-empty bottle of scotch next to the crackers, cheese, and salami. She frowned and said, "Rehashing old grudges again?"

I side-stepped her remark and said, "I'll fix you a drink. The usual?"

Stella nodded, sat down and lit a cigarette. "What were you talking about?"

I rolled my eyes.

Stella reached for her gin and tonic. "Not the damn war again. You haven't spoken to each other for two years and you're back arguing over the same bullshit?"

"All about God and country." I scoffed.

"Don't you talk like that!" Billy growled. "You should be grateful for the others who fought for your freedom while you sat in a cozy college classroom and slept in a nice bed every night."

"Are you serious?" I shook my head. "Take the Afghanistan war. It's a repeat of Vietnam all over again. You were a colonel during Vietnam. Why didn't you do something to stop that senseless war?"

Billy sucked a quarter inch off his cigarette and then clenched his teeth.

I couldn't help but add, "Our government's doing it all over again. The stupid military is spending ten million dollars a month fighting a losing war in Afghanistan."

Billy pounded his hand on the table. "Watch your damn mouth. You've never served a day in your life. While you sit here drinking scotch with your buddies, others are getting their asses shot off in the Middle East."

"Here we go again," I said, pretending to play a violin in the air.

A shadow appeared in the kitchen doorway. Sara clutched her blanket. Her tangled, long hair hung over her eyes. Stella quickly motioned to Billy and me to stop talking. "Honey, how long have you been standing there?"

Sara shrugged and rubbed her eyes. Barefoot in pink pajamas, she squinted as she shuffled into the bright kitchen light.

"What's wrong, sweetie?" I asked.

"Gracie had bad dreams and wet the bed again."

Billy shook his head in disgust. "Does Gracie still wet her bed? For Christ's sake, she's ten years old!"

"She's only eight," I corrected him.

"Whatever." He waved his arms. "Get the girl a mother. That's what she needs."

"Brilliant," I said. "Maybe I'll order one from Russia. I hear they're having a clearance sale."

"Well, you already tried that once with that women from the Caribbean or wherever. How did that turn out?"

"Stop it!" Stella glared at Billy then swept Sara her into her arms. "Gracie's a normal, sweet child. Some kids do that. She'll outgrow it."

"I'm telling you," Billy said, shaking his finger at me, "the girl has problems."

Sara tried to explain. "Gracie only wets when she gets afraid and has bad dreams."

"My dear, what's making Gracie afraid?" Stella asked. "You shouldn't have bad dreams at your age—only good ones."

Sara shook her head and twisted a long strand of hair. "It's not only Gracie. I have them too."

Stella hugged Sara and pulled her closer. "It's okay, sweetheart. Tell grandma what makes you so afraid?"

"Sometimes—" Sara stared at the floor, "—we hear things in the dark."

Stella glanced sideways at Billy. "It's okay. You're not the only one who hears things in the dark at night."

I stood up. "I need to change Gracie's sheets and put Sara back to bed."

When I returned from the bedroom and sat down, Stella held an empty glass and Billy had disappeared. I asked Stella, "Would you like another drink?"

"Sure, why not."

"Is Dad in bed?"

Stella nodded. Separated by more than the thirty-six inches of oak, we played with our glasses and didn't speak for a long time.

Finally, Stella shook her head. "Why does it always have to end this way with you and your father?"

"Ask him."

"He's drunk, so I'm asking you."

I shrugged.

"I give up." Stella rubbed her temples. "You two are so much alike it's scary." She pulled out another cigarette, lit it, blew out the match, and dropped it into a metal ashtray.

For as much as I tried to disown my father, it was clear that we did share many of the same characteristics—tall with big hands familiar with hard work, and possessing broad shoulders, blue eyes, and a strong face accustomed to getting things our way. This was in sharp contrast to my stepmother who was so tiny she had to sit on a pillow to drive a car. She was a chain-smoking, skittish woman with pale skin that begged for sunlight.

Stella took a long drag on her cigarette, leaned back and exhaled, watching the smoke swirl toward the ceiling. She lurched forward with a sudden, racking cough and held her hand to her chest.

"You've got to quit smoking," I said. "Those things will kill you."

"Don't lecture me," Stella said.

"How do you put up with it?" I jerked my thumb toward the bedroom where Dad was sleeping.

Stella reached into her pocket for a handkerchief and dabbed at the corners of her eyes. "It wasn't always like this. He was so handsome in his marine uniform when we first met." She started to say something more, but then stopped.

We stared at our drinks. At last, I cleared my throat. "I hate the way he treats you."

"He doesn't mean it."

I leaned back in my chair and sipped my scotch. "Yeah, right. You said the same thing about the way he treated Clair."

"You've never tried to understand him."

"You're kidding, right? Try to understand him? That's a joke." My anger grew with each word. "Here's what I don't understand. The only time in my life that Dad hugged me was when I left home for college. Not once do I recall that he ever told me he loved me."

"Don't use that old excuse again. You're as much to blame for your fucking relationship." Stella flicked the ash off the end of her cigarette. "Sorry for my French, but you and your dad drive me crazy at times."

I didn't respond.

"I knew him before he fought in Vietnam," she said. "He's a good man, but he endures emotional and physical pain that you'll never understand." She took another drag, letting the smoke work deep inside before letting out a long sigh. Finally, she leaned forward and crushed the cigarette in the ashtray. "It's getting late. I've decided to drive back home in the morning."

"Aw, come on. Don't do that," I said. "Besides, it's Mother's Day tomorrow. We planned on attending church together with a nice brunch at home afterward. The girls will be so disappointed."

"I know," she paused, "but I think it's better this way."

"Better for whom?"

"Look, he's going through a very difficult time."

"When isn't he?"

"This is different. I've never seen him like this before." She paused, tapping her fingers nervously on the kitchen table. "Did you know that Billy's the one who insisted we drive down for Mother's Day? He was very agitated on the way here because he said he had something important to discuss with you."

"Why now? He hasn't stepped foot in our house for more than two years."

"I don't know. He wouldn't tell me." Stella slowly gathered her purse and cigarettes then leaned over and kissed me on the cheek. "See you in the morning."

◆ ◆ ◆

I woke up early the next morning to the steady drumbeat of rain. Stella and Billy were almost finished eating breakfast. Billy slept in his clothes and smelled of stale cigarettes and booze. He barely looked up and his right hand trembled as he ate a bowl of Wheaties.

"Mom told me that you're driving home."

"After breakfast," Billy grumbled.

I looked at Stella. "What do I tell the girls?"

"Make something up. You're good at that," Billy said.

"I had a good teacher."

Stella raised her eyes heavenward. "Both of you, stop it! I'll talk to the girls before we leave." She moved her gaze at me. "Do the girls still ask about Clair?"

"Of course." I lowered my voice. "It killed the girls when Clair left us. The worst part is not knowing from day-to-day whether she's dead or alive. I can only hope that she finds a program that works for her issues."

Dad shook his head. "I told you not to marry her. The girls needed a real mother and she was never that."

I bristled. "Thank you—Oh Wise One—for your insightful observation. And by the way, how are you doing with your AA program at the VA?"

Stella jumped up, exasperated. "That's enough! I'm going to say goodbye to the girls." She gave Billy a stern look. "Why don't you pack the damn car?"

The girls were still sleeping, so Stella walked into their bedroom to kiss them goodbye. I followed Billy out to the car. The rain had finally stopped.

Billy took a deep breath of damp, morning air, then reached into his front shirt pocket for a cigarette. "I'm sorry for last night," he said without looking at me. "I know I can be...well, you know."

"Dad, get some help. If not for you, do it for Stella." I kicked the gravel next to the car. "The girls need you. Stella needs you."

The screen door slammed and Stella struggled with her red suitcase. Billy wrestled it into the backseat as Stella stopped to give me a kiss.

"Be good," she said, as she wiped lipstick off my cheek. "Call when you get a chance."

"Happy Mother's Day," I said.

Stella smiled and walked around to the driver's side. She paused for a second and glanced over the roof at me. Her lips moved, but she turned away before I could make out the words. Then she stepped into the car and they drove off.

I went inside and picked up the kitchen until it was time to wake the girls for church. I walked down the hall and peeked into the room they had shared since they were babies. Even though they had twin beds, they always ended up in the morning tightly spooned together. It never took much coaxing to get Gracie out of bed, but Sara usually woke up cranky. I tickled Sara's feet, but she rolled over and groaned, "I don't want to go to church."

"Why not?"

"It won't be the same without Grandma and Grandpa," she said. "Grandma woke me up to tell me they had to go home, but she didn't say why."

I tried to pull her covers off. "They had a neighbor who needed help." Sara grabbed the edge of the blanket and pulled it back over her. "Come on. You have to get up."

"No!"

"Be ready in twenty minutes," I said, losing my patience.

"I hate you," Sara said, as she rolled away from me.

Cooper, the faithful weathervane to Sara's heart, rose from the corner of the room, trotted over to her bed and poked his wet nose under the sheet. She gave him a shove. "You go away too."

We are in for a long morning, I thought.

♦ ♦ ♦

The priest began by inviting all the mothers to stand. Then he asked all family members to extend their hands over their mothers as he read a prayer. Now I realized why Sara was so crabby this morning.

During the blessing, the girls squirmed and fidgeted. Gracie stared at dozens of mothers as they stood around us but Sara wouldn't even look up and just kept rapidly flipped through the church songbook until the prayer was over. To our left, I spotted Tearza glowing as Ella and Marci stretched their hands over her and then smiling as she recognized us. She cared so much for my girls and knew how Sara and Gracie struggled without a mother, especially today. After the service, we hurried out of the church because I didn't want to talk to anyone. Poor girls—they had suffered for something that was not their fault.

At home, I decided to make my Stella's Sunday brunch specialty—upside-down French toast smothered with butter, freshly whipped cream, and lots of syrup. Cooking always made me feel better. While I sliced the French bread, Sara grabbed a soccer ball and motioned Gracie outside. On her way out, she looked at me and said, "Did you call Grandma yet?"

"Thanks for reminding me."

The girls flew out the backdoor while I finished making brunch and then called home. "Happy Mother's Day," I said.

"Thank you," Stella said. "How was church?"

"Okay." I picked eggs out of the refrigerator with my free hand. "Mother's Day is hard on them. They miss Clair. I see it in their eyes every time another mother does something for them. Especially Tearza—she's so different from Clair, but the girls are drawn to her... something I can't describe, but it's there."

"Have you heard from Clair?"

"Got a postcard last month. She promises the girls she's coming home, but then breaks their hearts," I said angrily.

"Maybe she needs more time."

"Why?" I sensed a weird tone in her voice. "Do you know something?"

"I know she loves the girls."

"And you," I said, "she always loved you."

"She felt insecure around you dad, but I loved her like a daughter."

"It's been two years now. I guess this is what we can expect."

"Have faith," she said softly. "Maybe things will get better."

The timer on the oven went off. "I have to run," I said and then hung up as the girls barreled into the kitchen.

After breakfast, the girls asked if Ella and Marci could come over. An hour later, Tearza walked in with the girls, her eyes slowly scanning several piles of junk.

"Sorry, I said sheepishly. "I know it's a mess, but I didn't have time to clean up from this morning"

"That's okay." She stared at the dishes stacked in the sink and then grabbed a dishcloth. "Looks like you could use some help."

"Please don't. I can get that later."

Before I could stop her, she started washing and humming to herself. I placed the dishes in the dishwasher as fast as she rinsed.

"Do you always sing to yourself when you do the dishes?"

She blushed. "They're silly songs that my mother used to sing to me while she worked in the kitchen. Frankly, I don't even know I'm doing it half the time."

She periodically brushed her hair back behind her ear leaving soap bubbles stuck there.

"What are you looking at?" she said, smiling.

"Nothing. I tried to imagine you at home on the farm."

Later, Tearza sat at the kitchen table and played with the dish towel, and neither of us spoke. Cooper laid his head on her lap and she gently stroked him, saying, "Like getting a hug from your best friend."

"You look a little road weary. Is there anything wrong?"

She shrugged and turned to see if the girls were within earshot. "Just missing my job at the university. I love working at the flower shop, but my research on climate change was exciting and I really felt I was making a difference."

In most ways, Tearza was the opposite of my ex-wife who was a wild love child who never outgrew the sex, drugs and music of her college years. Clair also wanted a career and was never content settling down, living in the suburbs, going to coffee with the other moms, or joining the PTA. We had tried to salvage our marriage, but each intervention for her depression and alcoholism pushed us further apart. It wasn't until I understood that Clair couldn't change that I finally stopped blaming her for our failed marriage.

"Thanks for helping me clean up my mess," I said.

"Hope you didn't mind. Growing up on the farm, old habits die hard."

I leaned against the sink and waved my arm in a wide circle. "As you can see, I'm still working on my domestic side. Thank goodness you can't see the bedrooms."

Tearza laughed. "We all have our little secrets, don't we?"

I pulled two wine glasses out of the cupboard. "Now we can celebrate."

"Celebrate what?"

"Mother's Day!"

Tearza hesitated, then said, "It's a little early," but then she smiled as she held up her index finger. "Okay, but just one."

We took our glasses to the porch to enjoy the sun.

"Ah, just what I needed," she sighed and sipped her wine. "What a nice way to spend Mother's Day."

"I never asked you, but how did you end up in Chicago?"

"I had a job offer to conduct research on climate change at Northwestern University."

"How did you meet Jim?"

"His company helped create a brochure for a conference I hosted at the university. His firm provided all the printing at below cost. I always accused him of rigging the bill so I'd fall in love with him." She took a deep breath. "We were so young back then."

"How do you like Chicago?"

"It was difficult at first. I miss the slower pace of my hometown, knowing each other's business, the Dairy Queen, Molly's sweet rolls— and calling everyone by their first names. But mostly, I miss my family." She looked up at the sun. "What about you?"

"Me? I left home with a backpack full of dreams and a nickel in my pocket. I got a small scholarship and worked nights as a bartender to pay my way through college."

"Then what?"

"I was accepted into Columbia Law School."

"In New York City?"

I nodded.

"Wow, you must be smart,"

"Hardly, but I made up for my lack of intelligence by working hard."

"Something to prove?"

"No, I made a promise to someone."

"How did you like New York City?"

"A long story, but I never attended Columbia."

"You're kidding! What happened?"

"Couldn't afford it. I had a mountain of college loans, so I ended up at law school in Madison on a partial scholarship. After I passed the bar, I was offered a job in Chicago."

"Do you regret it?"

"What?"

"Not having lived in New York and attended Columbia?"

"Dreams come and go," I said. "I never thought that I'd ever have another chance to see New York, but now I'm travelling there on business a couple times a month." I turned to Tearza. "And you? Do you regret leaving your hometown and moving here?"

"Sometimes." She tucked a strand of hair behind her ear. "But then again, Marci and Ella would've never met Sara and Gracie."

"Then your regret is our blessing."

Tearza smiled and neither of us spoke for a while. Finally, I cleared my throat. "You mentioned something earlier about maybe getting a research position again. How's the search going?"

"Terrible. All the federal funding for my kind of research has been cut."

"How did you become interested in climate change?"

"On the farm, everything depends on the weather. A small change in the temperature or precipitation can be disastrous. Besides, I have a passion for getting my hands in the dirt. We had a huge garden for the sweet corn, tomatoes, and other veggies. And we had a garden full of my mother's favorite flowers. I inherited her love for flowers, and our garden became my happy place."

Her napkin fell on the floor next to me. She leaned to pick it up, close enough that I could smell her perfume.

"I think that the single most important thing you can do for the girls," I said, "is to make yourself happy, because if you're happy the girls will be happy."

"I wish it were that simple." She leaned back.

"Sara signed up for baseball. Would Marci like to play? We could carpool."

"Maybe." She glanced at her watch.

"Can I ask you something?" I said. "What's your mother like?"

"Hmmm..." Tearza smiled. "She'd trade her soul for a bar of milk chocolate, she snorts when she laughs, and she sings like a frog in church. But she loves her Jesus." She paused when she sensed me staring at her.

"She sounds wonderful."

"What about your mother?"

I stared into the bottom of my wine glass. "Never really knew her. Stella's my step-mother."

"What happened? Divorce?"

"No, she died giving birth to me. I never heard what really happened because Dad refuses to discuss it." I didn't want to talk about this, but Tearza cocked her head showing she wanted to know more, so I continued. "I don't know anything about my real mother. It's a blank hole in my life. I don't know what her voice sounded like when she sang to me. I don't know what she would've smelled like when she read bedtime stories. I don't know what it would've felt like to have her be the first thing I saw when I woke in the morning. I know it sounds silly, but sometimes I lay awake at night wondering what her laugh would sound like. Was she funny? Did she have many friends? Was she kind? Did she love me?"

Tearza's eyes started to glisten. "I'm so sorry."

"My dad hates me. Every time he looks at me, he sees her. He never got over that I was the one who survived instead of the love of his life."

"Oh, Ryan," she paused. "I can't believe your father, or any father, would feel that way about you."

"My father tried to erase any memory of my mom. He destroyed everything that reminded him of her." I stood up. "Wait, I'll be right back."

I went inside and then returned with my wallet. I pulled out a small, slightly bent photo and showed it to Tearza. "Her name was Charlotte. This is the only photo I have. I found it in the bottom of a chest in our attic when I was young. Dad must've missed it when he was in a drunken rage one night and burned everything that was my mom's."

Tearza held the faded photo close. "She's beautiful."

I put the photo back. Embarrassed, I added, "Well, now you know everything about me, for better or worse."

The phone rang and Sara yelled from inside. "It's for you. It's Grandpa."

"Tell him that I'll call him back later."

Sara came back, "He says it's really important."

"Go take your call," Tearza insisted.

I walked into the house and picked up the phone. "Hello."

"Are you busy?" Dad slurred his words.

"I need to take the girls to the store," I lied.

"You didn't call your Stella."

"Yes, I did. We talked earlier."

"Are you calling me a liar?"

"No, maybe Stella didn't tell you."

Dad mumbled something incoherent. Then I heard the phone hit the floor and Billy cursing as he tried to pick it up again.

"Are you okay?" I said.

"I've tried to tell you," his voice cracked. "I wanted to tell you how sorry I am for all the years of... you know...everything. That's why we came to see you." He sobbed. "I thought I could, but I can't...I can't explain it. I don't know how."

Suddenly, the connection went dead. I hung up, and when I turned around, Tearza was standing in the kitchen with our empty wine glasses.

"Are you okay?" she asked softly.

"Sure, why?" I looked away.

"You sounded upset on the phone."

I slumped into the kitchen chair and stared at the floor. "It's hard to…"

Tearza waited, but I didn't offer any more explanation. Finally, she glanced down at her watch.

"I should get Marci and Ella back home."

"That would be a good idea."

Tearza hesitated for a second, then pulled out the chair next to me and sat down. "It's none of my business, but do you want to talk about it?"

I chuckled nervously.

"What's so funny?"

I shook my head slowly and ran my fingers through my hair. "I swore I'd do things differently when I had children. I didn't have a father or a mother like other families. I thought I could fake it on the father side. But without the girls having a real mother, I'm failing at both."

"First of all, that's not true." Tearza touched my arm. "And second, you're doing the best you can."

"But it's not enough," I said.

"What do you mean?"

"What if I've totally screwed things up for my daughters and they don't even know it yet?"

"They're beautiful girls," Tearza said. "Trust me, they'll be fine."

I rubbed my hands over my knees. "They need a mother."

Tearza rubbed her left ring finger. "I understand."

"I'm sorry. It's just that I've made some terrible mistakes."

"You think you're the only parent who has regrets?"

I lifted my head. "But you seem so—"

"Perfect?" She held her hand up for a second with her palm facing me. "You tell me what's perfect. We're like the millions of fireflies in the alfalfa fields on warm summer nights at the farm—all desperately circling around in the dark trying to find each other."

I blinked hard several times.

"You're not alone," Tearza said.

I looked up and Tearza patted me gently on the arm. "You have Marci and Ella." Then she paused and smiled. "And you have me."

I hung my head. "I'm so embarrassed. I don't know what's wrong with me right now."

Tearza put her arm around my shoulder and gave me a squeeze. "I know."

I pushed my chair away from the kitchen table. "Thank you."

Tearza glanced at her watch. "I didn't realize it's so late." She gathered her purse and keys but then turned around. "You know, sometimes our regrets can turn out into our best blessings, but…" she paused.

"But?" I waited for her to finish.

"My grandmother told me that suffering sometimes requires patience and time to reveal the blessings that come out of our pain."

◆ ◆ ◆

The rest of the day flew by. After dinner, I found Sara and Gracie brushing their teeth. Gracie stood on a stepstool with toothpaste foam all over her lips making funny faces in the mirror. The girls didn't see me so I watched them for a minute.

"You need to practice your speech therapy," Sara said, as she brushed her teeth.

"But I don't want to," Gracie replied.

"Come on, Gracie. Sally sells seashells."

Gracie took a deep breath and then burst into giggles. "*Th*ally *th*ells—"

"No, Sally!"

"*Th*ally." Gracie stopped and hit herself in the forehead. "I'm such a dummy."

"No, you're not. You try too hard."

Gracie pointed at the mirror with her toothbrush. "Will it ever get better?"

"Sure, we have to practice. Try saying Sara instead of Sally."

"*Th*ara—I mean Sara *th*ells *th*eashells down by the seashore!"

They looked at each other in the mirror and Sara clapped. "See? Better! At least you got Sara right."

After they finished brushing I herded them into the bedroom, kissed Sara goodnight, then tucked Gracie into her bed. They smelled like bubble gum toothpaste and baby shampoo.

"I need to get a drink of water," Gracie said.

"No." I said.

"I have to give Cooper a hug goodnight."

"You already did. He's right next to Sara."

"I didn't kiss Sara."

"Gracie!" I implored.

Gracie tried to continue. "But—"

Sara giggled from her bed.

Almost out of patience, I asked, "But what?"

She looked at me doe eyed. "I didn't kiss you goodnight."

"You're incorrigible," I said.

119

"What's that?"

"It means I love you."

"Good." She kissed me on the cheek and plopped down on the pillow. I smiled as I pulled the covers up to her chin. She looked like a street urchin with wild hair and sparkling dark eyes. I lay with Gracie until she stopped rubbing the satin along her upper lip. *She's so beautiful,* I marveled.

I tried to get up quietly to leave but Sara stopped me. "Dad."

"I thought you were asleep."

"Why do you have to go to New York all the time?"

"It's my job, sweetie." I reached over to give her kiss. "I have to go there because that's where our biggest client is located."

"But I don't like it. Can't you do something else?"

"Like what?"

"I don't know. Anything so you can stay at home with us." She sighed and rolled over and hugged her pillow. "Do you have to go this week?"

"No, not this week."

"Good, I hate it when you're gone."

I kissed her on the ear. "Go to sleep now."

I looked back at Gracie. I thought she was asleep, but she was still awake. She had wrapped herself in her favorite blue blanket while staring at a picture of her mother on the bed stand.

"What's wrong?" I asked.

She shook her head and rubbed her lips with the satin edge of the blanket.

I tried again, "Gracie—"

"I can't remember what she looks like," she said.

I knew what she needed and reached for the family photo album next to her bed. I began flipping through the pages of pictures, but she stopped me and buried her head in the pillow. I ran my hand down her hair and waited.

After a few minutes, she lifted her head. "Do you think Mom still loves me?"

"Of course she does. She loves you forever."

"Sara doesn't think so, because why else would she leave us."

"Look at my eyes." I stroked her hair and lifted her chin. "She left because of *me*—not you."

"But she never called us, never wrote to us…"

I wiped the tears off Gracie's face and glanced at Sara who pretended to be asleep. After Gracie finally drifted off, I picked their clothes off the floor and hung them in the closet, and then checked their backpacks to make sure they had what they needed for school. Inside Sara's bag, I found a handmade Mother's Day card with a poem written in red crayon.

From where I dream
stars can sing and
the moon is blue.
From where I dream
I have wings and
I can be with you.

Sara sat up when she heard me rummaging through her backpack. "What're you doing?"

I held her card in the air. "You wrote a beautiful poem for your mother."

"That's private. You have no right!" Then she flopped back down on the bed.

"What's wrong?" I asked.

"They made us draw Mother's Day cards at school." She sniffled. "But I don't have a mother." She pulled covers over her head and yelled, "Stupid project!"

"Honey, I know it's hard. Can I save the card for Clair? Maybe she'll come back someday."

"No, throw it away!" She half-choked on tears. "I'll never have a mother."

I was out of words so I left and came back twenty minutes later. As stepped back into the bedroom, I sensed that she was still awake.

"Honey, can't you sleep?"

"No."

I sat on the edge of the bed and pulled her comforter up to her neck. "Talk to me."

"Gracie's night light is too bright."

Confused, I said, "Sweetie, her night light isn't on." Then I glanced at the window. Light from a full moon flooded her bed, painting it a pale blue.

Sara sat up and looked at the trees swaying in the wind and making shadows on the wall. Suddenly, she turned away and said, "Dad, close the curtains."

"Why? You always love looking at the moonlight."

She rolled over. "Not tonight."

"Sara, please don't worry." I kissed her on the cheek.

I walked over to the window. The moon was so bright that you could almost read a newspaper by it.

"Daddy?" Sara whispered.

"Yes, honey."

"Where's my mother?"

I stared at the Milky Way for a long time and then closed the curtains. In the dark, I wiped my eyes and said softly, "Somewhere in your dreams."

◆ ◆ ◆

Saturday, my first day off in three weeks. I drove Tearza and the girls to the beginning of a three-mile bike trail that looped through a nature preserve about a half-hour from our house.

Tearza looked up. "Beautiful day for a bike ride."

"Awesome. I love spring."

The girls were ready to ride and yelled for us to stop talking.

"Do you want to lead the way?" Tearza asked.

"I'll bring up the rear."

"Try to keep up." Tearza laughed and took off. The girls peddled like mad to keep up with her. Giggling and laughing, their ponytails swung in the wind.

Halfway around the loop, we stopped for a rest. Small patches of wildflowers adorned both sides of the bike path. I stretched out on the grass while Tearza helped the girls pick a small bouquet of flowers to take home—yellow daisies, pink lady slippers, buttercups, irises, foxtails, sticky willys and pussytoes.

"How do you know the names of all these flowers?" I asked.

"The same ones grow wild in the fields on our farm. My mom taught me their names when I was young." Tearza beamed as she pointed out more wildflowers and explained something about each one.

"I've never seen you look so happy," I said. "It must be the flowers."

Tearza blushed. "Do you have a favorite?" she asked.

"Besides lilies of the valley, the only other one I know…" I pointed, "…is that evil one next to your foot."

Tearza bent down to pick up a handful of dandelions. "You don't like these?"

"Not really."

"I think they're cute and yellow's my favorite color."

"They're weeds!"

"But everything has a purpose."

"Not these—unless they were created to torture me. They invade my yard every spring with a vengeance."

"They may not be very pretty, but they have a secret" Tearza said. "They can divine true love."

I laughed.

"You don't believe?" Tearza stepped closer. "Pay attention." She twisted the stems into two yellow bunches and waved to Marci and Ella. "Come here and show Ryan how this works."

She handed the flowers to the girls. They knew what to do and held the dandelions under the chins of Sara and Gracie.

"Watch." Tearza pointed. "If their chin turns yellow, that means they love each other." Marci and Ella giggled as they rubbed the flowers under the chins of Sara and Gracie. Tearza pointed to the yellow marks. "See? They love each other."

Sara looked at Tearza. "Does it work for all flowers?"

"Nope, only dandelions."

Gracie yelled at Sara, "Our turn!"

Off they ran to pick more flowers. While they were gone, I decided to adjust the seat on my bike. I felt a tap on my shoulder from Tearza who was holding a large dandelion.

"For me?"

"Close your eyes," she instructed.

Something cool tickled the skin under my chin.

I quickly opened my eyes. She was intently looking up at me. "Well…?"

"Too bad," she said, as she dropped the dandelion on the ground.

"Why?"

She looked deeply into my eyes. "Because if you don't believe, then you'll never know."

The girls rushed up to us, each carrying a large handful of wildflowers.

Tearza pointed to her bike. "Put them in my basket. When we get home, I'll show you how to save the flowers by pressing them in books."

After we finished the bike ride, we went back to our house for lunch.

The girls clumped their flowers into four separate piles on the kitchen table. Sara ran into the other room and grabbed four books for pressing them. Tearza picked up a book Gracie had selected, *A Christmas Memory*, and held it up in the air. "I love this book!"

"No kidding?" I said. "Me too. That's my favorite Christmas book."

Once they had finished placing the flowers between the pages, Sara asked Tearza, "How long do we have to wait?"

"We can check them in a month or so."

I gathered the books. "I'll keep them in my study until they're ready."

Tearza looked at her watch. "Oops."

I walked her to the door. "What an interesting morning. I learned something new today."

"So did I," she said.

After she left, I wondered what she had meant.

Summer

Chapter 1

Ryan

I stepped outside with Cooper for his morning walk. His nose went straight in the air, sniffing the warm southern breeze. The morning air smelled like honeydew melon. He looked at me and I felt it too—summer had arrived.

School was finally over, and the girls were excited for summer vacation. They spent the morning discussing all the things they wanted to do and I suggested we go to the bookstore to find a few books for summer reading. Of course, the girls insisted we bring Marci and Ella along, so we picked them up along with their mother. On the way to the bookstore, Tearza opened the window and stuck her hand out in the wind like a child.

"Are you sticking your nose in the wind next?"

"Maybe." She laid her head back on the seat.

"Cooper would be jealous. You're sitting in his spot."

She turned her face to the sun and closed her eyes. "I love summer."

"Me too."

Suddenly a car honked. I had drifted toward the center line as I looked at Tearza.

She shot me a look. "Should I be driving?"

"I'm in complete control."

She pretended to double-check her seatbelt. "By the way, how did Susan like the flowers I put together for her birthday?"

"She wants to send all her friends to you."

A few minutes later we arrived at Zadie's, and Tearza took off her sunglasses. "This place looks cute," she said.

I licked my lips. "Wait until you taste their cupcakes. Hmmm, heaven."

◆ ◆ ◆

Zadie's was built like a Hobbit's hut covered with green ivy. The reading room always smelled of burning wood and sweet things baking in the kitchen. Hand-painted murals covered the walls beneath large wood beams that crisscrossed the white ceiling. The coffee shop became my home-away-from-home, the one place where I could work without the interruptions I couldn't avoid at the office.

Each girl selected one of Zadie's famous cupcakes and retreated to the corner of the bookstore to sink into squishy red and green beanbags to read. Meanwhile, Tearza and I crawled onto a large, over-stuffed couch. We sat there quietly for a few minutes drinking coffee and listening to the Crusaders playing jazz overhead.

"How was your week?" Tearza finally asked.

"Terrible," I said. "Several long meetings in New York with high-maintenance clients."

"Do you go there often?"

"Yes, lately. Our biggest client has their headquarters in New York City.

"Do you go by yourself?"

"Most of the time. We don't have an office yet, so we collaborate with another firm in Manhattan. Sometimes other associates come with me depending on the case."

"What do you think of New York City?"

"Love it. Love everything about the place. It's so—" I tried to think of a way to describe it, "—alive!"

"I'm not cut out for New York City."

"You have to experience it to really appreciate it. You should take a trip there sometime."

"Not likely. Chicago's urban enough for me."

"New York's very different. You'll fall in love with the sounds and smells—and the food. I've turned into a Mets fan to spite the Yankees."

"Is it hard on the girls when you're gone?"

I evaded a direct answer. "All this travel is just temporary. When I make partner, I'm convinced the travel will slow down. They can send some other junior associate."

"When will that happen?"

"Later this fall, I hope. If it doesn't happen soon, I'll move on. In the meantime, I do struggle with balancing work and home. Frankly, the girls haven't totally dealt with losing Clair. They fought nonstop while I was gone this week." I took a sip of coffee. "Their grief gnaws away at their hearts and I don't know how to fix it. On top of that, they hate me for losing Betty."

"Is there any way to get her back?"

"Not likely." I sighed. "I'm at a loss as to what to do. It has affected Sarah the most. She withdraws into her room and has no patience for Gracie anymore."

Tearza glanced at the girls. "I'm worried too. Marci and Ella won't talk about their feelings after losing their father."

Ella rushed over to Tearza with a children's book. "Look at this."

Tearza saddened as she looked at the cover of *Amy Goes to the Farm* and then handed it back to Ella who carried it to the corner to show Marci.

"What was that about?" I asked.

"I had a sister named Amy. We lost her when she was sixteen."

"I'm so sorry."

Tearza spoke in a low voice. "In the span of several seconds my whole world crumbled. Amy, my little sister, was driving home from high school and crashed into a ditch. An ambulance took her to the hospital in Madison which was forty-five minutes away."

"You must've been terrified."

"The uncertainty during the drive from Chicago was excruciating because no one had any information about the accident. At the hospital, the bad dream turned into our worst nightmare. We rushed into the lobby but I didn't see any of the family there. The receptionist said her name wasn't in the system. Then I remembered I'd given her my married name, Regan. When I gave her Amy's last name, O'Sullivan, she pulled out a note my brother had left for me. It simply said, 'Come home to the farm.'"

Tearza stopped talking and her lower lip quivered. "I knew what those five words meant."

I wanted to reach over and hug her—do *something*. As I started to move closer, laughter erupted from the girls. Tearza wiped her eyes and gave me a thin smile.

"I wonder what made those goofy girls giggle so hard."

"I guarantee you it's either Ella or Gracie."

She took a deep breath and resumed her story. "Funny how some things stick in your mind. Dad had been a rock for us during the days before the funeral, but we worried about him. On the way home from the cemetery the day of the burial, we stopped at the top of the hill above our farm. Below us an army of neighbors were spread out across the fields planting Dad's crops. My brother turned off the car and we all got out. Dad swayed in the wind as he looked out at the farm. Suddenly, he knelt like a broken man in the tall green grass alongside the road. I put my arms around him to pick him up as he kept repeating, 'Can you believe it? Can you believe it?'"

"You have incredible neighbors," Ryan said. "What they did for your family reminds me of my grandmother's favorite quote, 'We can do no great things, just many small things with great love.'"

"Who said that?"

"Mother Teresa."

Tears fell down her cheek and I handed her a napkin. "That's twice for me," she said.

"What is?"

"Losing someone I love."

Now I was the one fighting back tears. "Come on, let's get the girls," I suggested.

Although everyone acted as if nothing special happened—something had changed.

◆ ◆ ◆

Mondays are always the worst. I barely finished answering my messages before sprinting to court. My first case put my whole day behind schedule. Even though I skipped lunch, I was hours behind. Back in the courtroom, my cell phone vibrated in my pocket for the second time in less than a minute. The first message was a text from Tiffany wanting to meet for a drink after work. The second was from Tearza—"*Where are you?*"

I had forgotten to pick up the girls for their baseball game. I quickly texted Tearza and asked if she could take the girls and I would get there as soon as possible. Tiffany would have to wait.

Jamison sat to my right and another of my associates, Travis, sat on my left. When the judge paused to ask the defendant's lawyer a question, Travis passed me a note. "Is everything okay?"

I wrote back. "Baseball starts in ten minutes."

He replied under the table. "I've got you covered. Go."

Suddenly, a loud voice from the bench interrupted us. "Am I missing something important?"

"No, Your Honor," Jamison said.

Travis and I shook our heads and a minute later I left the courtroom and drove as fast as I could to the baseball game. I arrived in the fourth inning. Tearza was sitting in a lawn chair along the third base line thirty yards from the other parents.

"Sorry I'm late. How are we doing?"

"Losing again, down 8-2."

"Why're you sitting way out here?"

"I didn't feel like chatting." She tilted her head toward me. "What happened?"

"The trial lasted longer than expected."

Tearza was quiet for a minute and then said, "I know your work's important, but I need to count on you. Maybe carpooling doesn't work right now." She crossed her arms. "Maybe we should wait until work slows down a bit for you."

"It won't happen again. I promise."

"Promise?" Tearza leaned forward as if to say something else but stopped.

"I know I screwed up, but I don't want to stop carpooling."

The parents cheered as one of our girls scored a run. Tearza shielded her eyes from the sun. "All right, you win. Let's see how it works."

The game was almost over—one more at bat by our team. Tearza sat up in her chair and said, "Here she comes."

Marci walked up to the plate, glanced at Tearza, and took a couple of practice swings. Three pitches and she was out. Disgusted, she threw her batting helmet on the ground and walked slowly to the bench.

"It's painful to watch," Tearza confessed. "She's struck out every time over the last three games. I've never played baseball so I'm clueless how to help her."

"I can see part of the problem. Would she mind if I offered a few suggestions?"

"I'll ask her after the game."

We lost by six runs. Marci walked up to us dragging her bat on the ground like a dead possum.

"Good try," I said.

"I stink."

"Ryan has some suggestions, if you're interested." Tearza said.

Marci looked disgusted. "It's no use—I can't hit." She glanced at me and frowned. "I don't know what I'm doing wrong."

"You're stepping in the bucket before the ball is barely out of the pitcher's hand."

"What does that mean?"

"Means you'll never hit the ball."

"What do I have to change?"

"You have to wait for the ball to come to you."

"Then what?"

"This is the hard part. You have to want to step into the ball, not away from it."

She threw her glove onto the ground. "I can't."

"Why not?"

She stared at her glove. "Because I'm afraid."

"Yeah—I know it's scary, but you can't expect to make solid contact when you step away from what you fear. You'll miss by a mile. It's true for everything—not just for hitting a baseball. Would you be willing to try?"

She wiped her nose on her sleeve and sniffled. Then she nodded

I took off my suitcoat and tie. "Okay, grab a bag of balls from your coach and meet me at the backstop behind home plate. I'll be with you in a second."

"Thanks for helping," Tearza said.

"Don't thank me yet."

"Maybe I should take a lesson from you too."

"You want to learn how to hit a baseball?"

"No, I want to learn how to stop stepping away from the things I fear."

"Are you coming?" Marci yelled from the backstop.

I picked up Marci's bat and walked over to her. "Turn around," I said, pointing at the backstop.

"Why do you want me to face away from the field?"

"So, you can hit into the fence." I knelt down about five feet in front of the fence with a dozen balls. "I'll toss it into the strike zone from the side. Pretend the pitcher has already thrown the ball. Then step toward the ball with a hard, downward swing."

She missed the first two. "See—?" she said, dejected.

"Remember to step forward, not sideways," I reminded her.

She licked her lips, squeezed the bat and smacked the next five in a row.

"Well?" I asked.

She beamed. "That's amazing!"

After another fifteen minutes of practice, she had it down. Finally, she stuck out her hand and said, "Thanks, Mr. Ryan."

Tearza started to gather her chair and cooler. "Can I make you and the girls dinner tonight as a small thank you?"

"Ah, I'd love to, but I have a big case to prepare. Can I have a rain check?"

I felt guilty telling a lie, but Tiffany had already made plans for a rendezvous this evening. I rushed home to feed the girls and get them ready for bed before the babysitter arrived. Tiffany was providing the wine if I brought the steaks to put on her patio grill. As I walked into her place, I realized I'd forgotten the charcoal.

"Hey, Tiff—I need to go get some charcoal."

Tiffany was wearing tight, pink shorts and a white, almost-see-through top. "I'll ride along. I need some mushrooms for the steak."

As we strolled through the store, I saw Tearza at the end of an aisle. Frantic, I grabbed a box of mushrooms and headed to the shortest checkout line hoping Tearza wouldn't see us. Three carts were ahead of us.

"What's wrong?" Tiffany asked. "Your hopping around like a three-year-old."

I tried to laugh it off. "Just can't wait to try the ribeyes I brought."

We made it to the register just as the tape ran out. *For God's sake, of all times!* I thought. "Listen, I have to make a quick phone and check on the girls," I told Tiffany. "Can you grab a bag of charcoal and finish checking us out? I'll meet you in the car."

"No problem."

I glanced around the store as I left and didn't see Tearza. That could've been a disaster.

Chapter 2
Tearza

I had finished selecting the fresh produce for the week and as I started toward the dairy I recognized Tiffany's high-pitched voice on the other side of the aisle. I peeked around the corner and saw Ryan picking up a box of mushrooms. I couldn't believe he had lied to me about working to avoid having dinner with us. Worse, he had lied about Tiffany. He didn't see me, so I rushed into the restroom so he wouldn't know that I'd seen them together.

I could never trust someone who doesn't tell the truth. I had a sad heart as I drove home. He's a handsome single guy, but we aren't dating so why should I feel as if I've been dumped? He has every right to see other women. I really like him, but this certainly changes things. Brings me back to reality.

◆ ◆ ◆

June was always my favorite month. Jim and Ella's birthdays were within days of each other, so we had double the fun. Today was Ella's golden birthday, a special celebration when your birth date is the same as your age. Our birthday tradition always started with breakfast in bed. For Ella, that meant candy for breakfast —tons of it. Unfortunately, the poor child had inherited my sweet tooth.

To make Ella's birthday extra special, Marci suggested surprising her by turning breakfast in bed into a pajama party with Sara and Gracie. Marci coordinated all the arrangements with Sara. At eight o'clock, Ryan pulled up with his girls who looked cute in their pajamas as they carried their presents in. Ryan came around from the other side of the Suburban and stopped when he saw me in my pink Nike running outfit.

"Aren't we supposed to wear—" He pointed to his blue flannel pajamas and fuzzy slippers.

"Well, well, look at you." I circled around him. "Fancy pj's, baseballs, bats—the whole baseball theme really works for you."

He glared. "Sara!"

Sara giggled as she ran past him.

I grabbed his arm and steered him into the house. "Ella will love this."

"Here." Ryan handed me a box from the bakery. "If you promise to put on your pajamas and stop teasing me, I'll let you have a raspberry scone with almond frosting."

I agreed and quickly changed into my pink pajamas. Ryan whistled when I emerged from my bedroom. "Now we're talking."

We gathered in the hall outside Ella's bedroom, then marched in singing "Happy Birthday" with her presents and a breakfast tray. Pretending to be asleep, she rubbed her eyes and pushed her tangled hair away from her face. Her eyes grew huge as she bit into a large truffle and tried to talk with dark chocolate dribbling down her chin.

The girls spent the rest of the morning arguing over which chocolates were the best and playing with Ella's new toys. After Ryan left to take Sara and Gracie to swimming lessons, I asked Ella, "Okay, birthday girl, we have the whole day ahead of us. What would you like to do?"

Ella wiped some chocolate off her chin and then announced, "I think we should go camping."

At first, I balked—too many memories. We hadn't camped since Jim had died, but Ella insisted. After struggling to come up with a good excuse not to go, I finally gave in. Somehow, she knew we had to do this together.

I went out to the garage to assemble our camping gear. I found it packed away as Jim had left it—waiting for our next camping trip: fishing poles, a dark green tent, four brown sleeping bags, cooking stove, two lanterns, and a small hatchet. I carefully went through all the equipment and set it in a pile on the floor. I sat by myself in the garage for a long time thinking about Jim. I wasn't sure whether I could go through with this. Jim wouldn't be there to tell scary ghost stories around the fire, teach them how tie a good fishing knot, or skip a flat rock way out into the lake.

Ella called loudly from the open garage door, "Mom, where are you?"

"Over here."

"We've been looking all over for you. We're ready to go."

"Sorry, I was sorting through our camping stuff."

A few hours later, we loaded everything into the Suburban and headed to our favorite campsite along the western shore of Lake Michigan. We struggled, but finally got the tent set up so the fun part of camping could begin. I gathered wood, while the girls went for a walk. I was busy setting out food for our dinner when they came back a half hour later.

"Where did you go?"

"Down to the shore," Marci said.

"What's in the bucket?"

"Small pretty rocks for your garden."

"You're so sweet. So, what else did you do?"

Marci set the plastic bucket on the picnic table. "I showed Ella how to skip rocks."

"That must've been fun."

She looked so sad. "Not this time," she said. "It's not the same without dad."

"I know, sweetie." I hugged her. "Come on, you can help me light the fire."

After supper we made gooey s'mores and told scary stories. As the fire died down, so did our voices. The burning logs drew us closer together. Hypnotized by the glowing embers swirling smoke into the black night, none of us spoke for a long time.

Marci quietly laid four of the larger smooth stones in front of her crossed legs, rearranging the order a few times. "What are you doing," I asked.

"Nothing."

"Are those stones you found on the shore?"

She nodded. After a moment, she pointed to each one. "Me, Marci, you...and Dad."

I didn't want the girls to see me cry so I went to fetch more wood.

After another long silence, Ella finally spoke. "Mom, is there really a heaven?"

Her question surprised me because Ella rarely spoke about Jim.

My eyes stung as I tried to answer. "Of course there's a heaven."

"Is Dad there?"

"I believe he's watching us from the stars right now."

Ella shivered. "How can you be so sure?"

Marci was somewhere far away with her own thoughts about her dad.

"Do you remember the last trip we took to the ocean?" I asked.

Both girls nodded.

"Do you remember how we sat on the beach at the end of each day to watch the sunset?"

Perplexed, they waited for me to go on, so I did. "Remember watching a beautiful boat sail into the orange sunset? Remember how she sailed away from us and got smaller and smaller until Marci yelled out, 'There it goes' as it disappeared over the horizon."

Their eyes brightened. They were back in that moment again with their dad and me on the beach.

"I'll tell you a story about sailboats that's been told many times around the campfire like this one. Are you ready?"

They moved closer to me.

"Where do you think the sailboat went? We can't see it anymore, but is it really gone?"

Ella unfolded her arms. "It's still sailing. It's a big ocean. We can't see all of it."

"Exactly," I said.

Marci listened to Ella but didn't say anything. She continued to poke a stick into the fire.

"Your dad's like that sailboat. Even though he's sailed out of our view, we remember everything about him. He hasn't changed. He's not gone, but we can't see him."

After waiting for the image to sink in I added, "Think of your dad as that sailboat. He's passed beyond where we can see him, but with our faith we know he's still there. He's with Aunt Amy now, and even though he misses each of you dearly, he's happy because he's in heaven."

Marci sniffled and zipped her jacket more tightly around her neck.

"Marci, talk to me. You haven't talked about your dad since the funeral."

Marci wiped tears on the sleeve of her jacket. "You wouldn't understand."

"Maybe not. There're many things I don't understand about what's happened to us, but we need to trust each other."

Marci hesitated, then mumbled something.

"What did you say?" I asked.

She whispered more loudly, "Dad never said goodbye."

My voice deserted me.

Marci jammed her stick deep into the fire, sending a large plume of sparks into the air. "See, I knew you wouldn't understand!"

"Honey, that's not true." I wiped my own tears away. "None of us got to say goodbye."

Marci pulled up her knees and hugged them tightly as she stared at the glowing logs. She idolized Jim. She was his sidekick, his buddy. They were soulmates. He was the person who always read to her in bed, told her stories in the moonlight—and the last one to kiss her goodnight.

Finally, she spoke again. "It's so unfair."

"I know, honey."

"Why did Dad do that?"

"I don't know," I said softly.

"Why didn't you stop him?"

"I had no idea he was so depressed."

Ella turned to Marci and asked, "What did she mean? What is 'depressed?'"

Marci ignored her question and stared at me. "How could you *not* know?"

I closed my eyes and sighed. "I've asked that every day since he died."

The girls continued to poke at the embers as I lay on my back gazing at the stars. A big summer moon hovered above the treetops. A shooting star blazed across the sky.

Marci pointed. "Did you see that?"

"You get to make a wish," I said.

Ella excitedly said, "I think that was Dad!"

A few minutes later, I poured water over the fire and put away the food. We all crawled into the tent and I zipped up the door. The tent smelled like old canvas and bug spray. We slid into slippery sleeping bags and listened to a serenade of crickets and frogs interrupted occasionally by a solo from a hooting owl.

"Goodnight, Mom," Ella said. "Goodnight Marci."

"Don't let the bedbugs bite," I said, reaching out to hold their hands.

Maybe it was the fresh air, the pines rustling in the wind, or the moonlight casting shadows across the ceiling of our tent, but for the first time in almost two years I slipped into a deep, dreamless sleep.

Chapter 3

Ryan

I thought about Tearza and the tense discussion we'd had when I didn't pick up the girls on time for the game. It wasn't my fault that I was stuck in court. But lately, Tearza had seemed rather distant. I hoped she didn't feel bad that I ducked her offer to make dinner. Lately, no matter what I did for anyone, it never turned out to be enough. I was always disappointing someone.

I got up early and the girls were still asleep. I had just started making chocolate chip pancakes when Sara and Gracie marched into the kitchen wearing their pajamas and holding magazine pictures of Old Faithful. They exchanged a nervous look, then Gracie nudged Sara.

"What's up?" I asked.

She carefully placed the pictures on the counter. "Tearza took Marci and Ella camping for their summer vacation." Sara bit the corner of her lip. "We were wondering—would you ever take us to see Old Faithful?"

Caught off guard, I said, "Maybe."

They both looked crushed, assuming that "maybe" really meant "no." In truth, I was concerned about missing work—that, and I'd never taken a trip alone with the girls before. What if they didn't have fun? What if I disappointed them, again? My crestfallen girls stared at me, waiting for a response.

I clapped my hands together. "Okay, let's do."

Gracie jumped on my lap and gave me a big hug.

"You know, I was almost your age," I explained, "when my dad took me on a trip like this. Let's look at your pictures and start planning our getaway."

♦ ♦ ♦

A few days later, Tearza called after spending the Fourth of July on the farm. "I heard about your upcoming vacation," she said. "You're a brave man, all alone with two busy girls and no back-up."

"Care to join us?"

"I can't, but you can always call if you need me."

I laughed. "Thanks. That makes me feel sooo much better."

"Don't worry. You'll have a wonderful time."

"I'm just not sure how to keep them busy for an entire week."

"You sound like you've never done this before."

"I haven't."

The phone went silent for a few seconds, and then she said, "Really?"

"Yeah, really."

"Why don't you come over tonight and I can help you plan some activities. I have a cousin who lives near there and we used to visit."

"You're a lifesaver."

♦ ♦ ♦

Two weeks later, we packed the car with homemade beef jerky, Pez, gummy bears, miniature Snickers bars, and Sara's homemade chocolate chip cookies. As I was pulling out of the driveway, Gracie suddenly yelled, "Stop! I forgot my blankie." Thank goodness she remembered it or we could've had a disaster on our hands.

We were about a mile from home when Sara tapped me on the shoulder. "We have to go back."

I hit the steering wheel with my hand. "What now?"

"I forgot my backpack."

We turned around and headed back to the house. She had trouble finding one of her DVDs, and by the time she was back in the car Gracie had to use the bathroom. I looked at my watch. *This might be a really long vacation just leaving the city,* I thought.

Finally, we were off and the city disappeared in the rearview mirror. The girls fell asleep and I thought about how fast they were growing up. Since Clair had left, I had spent too much time thinking selfishly about me. Was I cut out to be a partner? Was it worth the sacrifice? After five years, I didn't feel any closer to reaching that goal. The clients and courts controlled most of my schedule and the girls took up the rest.

As I continued to drive, I thought about Tiffany and Tearza. On paper, Tiffany was everything I had always thought I wanted in a woman—beautiful, smart, and sophisticated. Maybe she's a bit too high-maintenance, but we liked many of the same things.

I tapped my fingers on the steering wheel. *So, what's wrong with this picture,* I thought. I glanced at a basket of goodies that Tearza had made for us. She was so different from Tiffany. I was confidant and in control with Tiffany, but with Tearza I was way out of my comfort zone.

A day later, we finally arrived at Yellowstone. In the shadow of the Grand Tetons, our log cabin was nestled twenty paces from a beautiful creek that meandered through a majestic forest of old growth trees. The air was cool and fresh and smelled of sweet pines. The girls explored our cabin for a few minutes and then ran to the creek. They threw off their shoes, rolled up their pant legs and waded into the water.

Sara waved at me to hurry. "Dad come on. This is great."

Pointing to my cell phone, I yelled, "I have to check in with work."

She thrust her hands on her hips. "Sure, you always say that."

I started to dial in but had no bars—no service. I panicked because I couldn't be out of touch with the office for a whole week.

Sara watched me fumble with my phone. "What's the matter?"

I held up the phone. "No service."

"Whoo-hoo!" Sara danced in a circle. "Gracie, did you hear that?"

Sara makes me laugh. I fretted about work for the first two days, but by the end of a third day of hikes, swimming, and horseback riding I had almost forgotten about the office. Every evening after dinner we read books and played board games. The last thing I remembered each night was the soft crackling from the fireplace and the soothing sound of the creek through open windows.

On the fourth day, a rusty green truck pulled up to our cabin. A tall man in blue jeans and cowboy boots stepped out carrying a large Fed Ex envelope. He was the owner of the small ranch where we were staying.

"This just arrived," he said as he handed me the package. "I thought it might be important."

"You're kidding. How would anyone know how to reach me way out here?"

He spit in the dust, then readjusted the chew inside his lower lip. "Don't know that."

I opened the package and cursed.

"Bad news?"

"It's work."

"Oh." He watched the girls collecting a pile of pinecones and nodded. "None of my business, but whatever's in that envelope can't be as important as those girls." He winked. "You know, mail gets lost all the time around here."

I stared at the envelope.

He grinned and spit again. "Well, I'll be going." With that he drove off.

He's right, I thought. *This can wait.*

The rest of the week flew by. All too soon, we headed back to Chicago. While the girls slept on the drive home, I was painfully aware of how much I'd missed by working so much.

Gracie woke up and yawned. "Where are we?"

"Almost home."

"Dad, how come we never took vacations before? This was really fun."

"We did once. You were a baby and too little to remember."

"Did Mom come with us?"

"Yes honey, before she got sick."

"Good." Gracie rubbed the satin on her blanket along her face. "I'm glad, even though I can't remember. Can we do it again?"

"Absolutely."

Heartburn crept up my throat. I swallowed hard wondering if Clair was actually coming back this summer.

◆ ◆ ◆

Sunday morning came too fast. I still hadn't unpacked from our vacation. I spent most of the morning fooling around with the girls, extending our vacation as long as possible.

The doorbell interrupted a serious game of Go Fish and Tearza walked in with her girls.

"Hey, stranger, I expected to find you dressed in jeans and cowboy boots."

"I did buy a cowboy hat, but the girls think I look like a dumb city slicker." I smiled and motioned for them to sit at the kitchen table. "Would you like to see some of our pictures?"

"Absolutely. Do you have one of you on a horse?"

"Very funny."

We started to view the pictures but the doorbell rang again. I yelled for whomever it was to let themselves in.

Tiffany's voice called out from down the hall. "Are you ready yet?" She stepped through the doorway, saw Tearza and girls, and said, "I'm sorry. I didn't know that you had company. Am I interrupting something?"

"No, we were looking at pictures of our trip," I said. "What brings you to the neighborhood?"

"Don't you remember?" She pointed to her watch. "We scheduled lunch because we have to prepare for our trip to New York this week."

I smacked my hand on my forehead. "Oh man, I completely forgot."

Tearza watched Tiffany frown and cross her arms, then she extended her hand. "I'm Tearza," she said politely.

I stood up. "Sorry. This is Tearza and her daughters, Marci and Ella. They're best friends with Sara and Gracie."

"Nice to meet you," Tiffany said coolly. "I've heard so much about you."

"Really?" Tearza said flatly, then glanced at me. "That's nice."

"Tiff, can we meet tomorrow morning?"

"Sure, but it'll have to be first thing."

Awkward could not describe the three of us silently standing together. Finally, I said, "Would you like to sit down with us? How about a cup of coffee?"

"No thanks. I'll catch up tomorrow." The two women shared a quick look, then Tiffany swiveled like a model on a runway and walked out.

"She's stunning," Tearza said quietly.

"Stunning, no—but over-dramatic, yes."

We dove back into the photos, but Tearza clearly was focused on the New York trip that Tiffany had blurted out. After a few minutes, Tearza asked, "Another trip to New York next week?"

"It's just an overnight."

"The third trip this month."

"I know. Business is booming out there."

Tearza fingered several little medallions hanging from a bracelet. She avoided my eyes when she said, "So Tiffany goes to New York with you. You never mentioned that."

"Well—Travis and some of the other lawyers go with me too." I squirmed in my chair. She studied me, waiting for a better explanation. "I never mentioned it because it's just business."

"I see," she said, obviously unconvinced.

"How often does Tiffany—?"

Gracie interrupted us, thank goodness, and jumped into my lap. "Are you guys going to talk all day or can we look at the pictures?"

Tearza and the girls left mid-morning. Maybe I was imagining it, but Tearza seemed upset about Tiffany. The rest of the day was a blur as we unpacked from our trip. Why was Sunday night always such a battle?

Chapter 4

Tearza

Today was the big day of the Hanna Montana concert. The girls hadn't slept a wink because they were so excited. I picked up Ryan and the girls in the Suburban.

"How about this." Ryan pointed at his watch. "Ready right on time!"

"I'm impressed." I said sarcastically. "Did Sara play a joke by setting your watch a half-hour fast?"

He laughed. "Come on, at least I'm trying."

On the way to the concert, I glanced at an invitation I'd left on the dashboard of the car. I hadn't decided whether to attend the annual dinner for the Special Olympics. It would be depressing to wander around the silent auction tables by myself. So much of my social life with Jim had revolved around couples. After he died, I had slowly lost touch with many of our friends because it felt awkward to be a single. Nevertheless, I really enjoyed the Special Olympics and the old friends I'd see at the dinner, so I decided to take a chance.

"Ryan," I said tentatively.

"What?"

I suddenly lost my courage and said, "Where do you think we should park?"

"I know a good spot two blocks from the auditorium."

The concert hall was full of excited kids. When Hanna finally took the stage, the auditorium exploded. Ryan put Gracie on his shoulders so she could see better. After a few songs, he did the same for Ella.

At the intermission, I asked Ryan how he liked the show so far.

He laughed. "At my last concert, Led Zeppelin played and I wore a jean jacket, a puka shell necklace, and we held up Zippo lighters."

"Hard to envision you in a jean jacket."

"Probably good that those times are way in the past."

"I had you preppy in a Polo shirt, short hair, and penny loafers."

He chuckled. "Remember, I grew up in northern Wisconsin, not Lake Forest. Try long hair, cowboy boots, and a rusted pick-up truck."

"My, my, and look at you now."

Hanna Montana came back for a second set and the place erupted with screaming kids again.

On the way home, I thought about the Special Olympics dinner again. With only three more blocks until we reached Ryan's house—it was now or never.

"Ryan, would you consider coming with me to a fundraiser dinner next week for the Special Olympics? It's a black-tie event, but it's fun and not stuffy. It's kind of a couples thing and I'd love to have you as my guest."

"A couples thing?" he asked. "Hmm, if I agree to go does that mean we're a couple?"

I stated to blush, so I looked out the window—too late to take it back.

"Well, no. I mean, we'd go together, but no one would assume we're a couple."

Ryan looked over his shoulder at the backseat. "Okay girls, did you hear that? Your mom asked me to go to a couples thing. Think I should I go?"

Ella and Gracie yelled at the same time. "Yeah, go!" They could see their cheers embarrassed me, so they really poured it on. Everyone except Marci started to chant, "Mommy has a boyfriend, Mommy has a boyfriend."

"Thanks a lot," I said, looking at Ryan who was laughing as hard as the girls. "See what you started?"

He wagged a finger at me. "I didn't start it—you did."

I tried to sound disinterested. "Is that a yes or a no?"

Ryan scratched his chin and finally announced with a dramatic pause, "Yes."

The girls cheered and I turned around to glare at the girls in mock anger. Everyone grinned except Marci who just stared out the window. I wondered if I'd made a big mistake. Marci carried a sadness about her that worried me. One minute she acted so distant, lost in her own little world, but in the next moment soda could spray out of her nose when she laughed at something Ella did. I knew she had some reservations about Ryan. I hoped this didn't make things worse.

◆ ◆ ◆

The next morning, a loud knock on the front door startled me. The deliveryman grinned as he handed me a large bouquet of flowers from Forever Green. I held the flowers in my arms like a baby, opened the top of the wrapping paper and inhaled deeply. They smelled like the fields behind our farmhouse.

It had been years since I had received flowers from anyone. *They must be from Mom*, I thought. A small card was tucked into the flowers with the inscription: *Would you please join me for lunch next Monday, 12:00 p.m., at Anthony's Restaurant?*
Fondly, Dylan.

My heart sank because I couldn't think of a way to refuse him.

On Monday, I spent all morning fretting about my lunch. I arrived at Anthony's early, checked my make-up in the mirror, locked the car, took a deep breath, and walked in. Sunlight streamed through the floor-to-ceiling windows and green planters separated tables covered in white linens. Debussy emanated from ceiling speakers and fabulous smells wafted from the kitchen. Dylan spotted me and stood up as I approached his table.

"Hi Dylan—great to see you again." We gave each other an obligatory hug and I asked, "How are you?"

"Good." He motioned for us to sit down. "Thanks for coming."

"My pleasure." I tried to sound interested. "How nice of you to invite me."

Neither of us knew what to say so we nervously consulted the menu.

"I hear the halibut is wonderful," I said to break the ice.

"I'm having the mussels. No one makes it better than this place."

We set the menus down and I said, "Ali told me the divorce was final. I'm sorry."

Dylan shrugged, then tried to smile and change the subject. Raising his glass, he said, "But look at you—you look great!"

I heard a familiar voice call my name. Ryan was halfway across the room waving at me.

"Dylan, can you excuse me for a second? I need to say hello and then I'll be right back."

"Take your time," he said.

My heart skipped a beat as I greeted Ryan. He looked so handsome with his summer tan, open-collared linen shirt, light brown slacks, and sockless loafers. He reached out to kiss me on the cheek and the smell of his cologne made me dizzy.

"This is a nice surprise." He pretended to look around. "Are you meeting anyone I know?"

"I doubt it. Just having lunch with an old friend."

He nodded. "That's nice. What's his name?"

"It's Dylan," I said.

Ryan looked surprised but recovered quickly. "My mistake. Isn't he the guy I met at your cottage when I was picking up the girls?"

"Yes—Jim's college roommate."

"Good friends are food for the soul, aren't they?"

"What about you? Whom are you meeting?" Suddenly, I heard Tiffany's voice behind me.

"Sorry I'm late. I got stuck on a conference call. You know how those things go."

She was dressed in a spectacular navy pantsuit with her blond hair held up high by a pretty hairclip. Ryan gave her a kiss on the cheek and then put his hand on my arm. At the same time, I looked down at my out-of-date shoes and four-year-old summer dress and felt like a thrift-shop mannequin.

"Tearza, do you remember Tiffany from my house when we got back from vacation?"

"How could I forget?" I said politely with a much bigger smile than necessary.

Tiffany extended her hand. "Good to see you again." Her teeth were so white they looked painted.

Before I could respond, Ryan stepped closer to me and nodded toward Dylan. "Care to join us?"

I stammered, "Uh, no, but thanks anyway. I...I really should get back to my table. Tiffany, nice to see you."

Flustered, I stepped away and almost fell over an empty chair. Ryan started to reach for me, but I pushed his hand away and walked quickly back to Dylan's table.

How could this happen? How could I have been so stupid? I looked back at the beautiful, professional woman seated with Ryan. We come from very different worlds. I worked in a flower shop, my nails hadn't been touched in months, and my clothes were probably mismatched. I was out of my league here.

And then I realized my foolishness. *How could I be jealous? Ryan and I don't even date.*

I wanted to run out the back door, but I couldn't do that to Dylan.

"What's wrong?" he asked. "You look like you as if you saw a ghost."

I needed to figure out how to handle this situation. "I need to ask you a few things," I said firmly to Dylan. "Did you send me the Dalai Lama book without a note?"

He looked confused.

"Why did you invite me lunch?" I asked.

"I thought that—you and I—maybe we could spend more time together, that's all. I enjoy being with you."

I shook my head. "Oh, Dylan."

Suddenly he sensed his mistake. He played with the silverware in front of him, obviously hurt. Without looking me in the eye, he said,

"I've been fond of you ever since we met. I took it as a funny twist of fate when your mother called a couple of months ago asking about you."

"Wait a second—Mom called you?"

"She told me she worries about you and asked if I'd seen you lately. She said you seemed so unhappy, so lonely, and never did anything for yourself."

"I'm sorry Mom got you into this. She means well, but this isn't what I need right now. This can't work."

"Why not? Remember what great friends we used to be?"

The waiter interrupted our conversation to announce the specials, which gave me a moment to breathe. I couldn't believe this discussion. Dylan was sweet and attractive in a teddy bear sort of way, but nothing more.

"Look, don't blame your mother for this. I wanted to see you. She just opened the door a crack. You don't know this, but while you were dating Jim, I warned him that he'd better marry you or I would."

I didn't want to hurt his feelings, but I had to stop this now.

"Dylan, look at me. We've been friends since college and you know how much you mean to me, but I can't do this."

"At least think about it?" he pleaded. His right foot started tapping frantically and he raised both hands in the air. "I'm such a fool. I don't know what to say."

"You don't have to say anything."

We both stared at the table and then around the room, avoiding eye contact until the waiter came back to take our order.

"Did I mention that I might be moving back to my hometown?" Dylan asked. "I miss my family and I never really liked the big city. Going home would give me a fresh start."

I couldn't think of anything else to say and neither could he. I realized the rest of the lunch would feel unbearable for both of us. "Dylan, I know this is hard, but can you please forgive me and let me reschedule lunch with you in a couple of weeks?"

"Sure, give me a call when you can." He was overly gracious.

I gave him a quick hug and hoped that I wouldn't bump into Ryan on my way out.

Chapter 5

Ryan

I pulled the two loops and cursed. The black bow tie looked like a third grader had tied it. The printed instructions from the tuxedo shop were just a series of cartoons drawn by some idiot. After my fourth attempt, I ran out of time.

Sara stepped into the bedroom and pointed at her wrist. "Dad, hurry up."

I cringed. This was one time I didn't want to be late. Frustrated, I pulled the tie off and hoped Tearza could help me. I stuffed the directions to the dinner in my pocket and raced out the door.

With a bit of luck, I hit every green light to Tearza's and ran up the steps picking Cooper's hair off my black tuxedo. Tearza opened the front door in a floor-length, strapless black dress. Simple, yet elegant. She had pinned her hair up and wore a small gold chain with a beautiful angel pendant.

"I must have the wrong house. I'm supposed to pick up a princess," I said.

"Why may I ask? What's the occasion?"

She stepped closer and her perfume hit me like a drug. I managed to say, "The king has invited her to his ball."

"I'm not a princess." She grabbed the edge of her dress and twirled around in a slow circle. "But I happen to be free tonight."

"Well, I guess you'll do. However, you have to complete one test before I can accept you." I held up my bow tie. "We don't wear these where I come from."

Tearza laughed. "No problem. Jim could never tie one either."

◆ ◆ ◆

Even in a tuxedo I felt under-dressed as we walked into the hotel filled with dozens of elegant couples milling around the lobby. A small string quartet played as Tearza pulled me toward a marble staircase and through the doors of the main ballroom.

The room was filled with hundreds of people dressed in tailored tuxedos and elegant sequined gowns. I stopped and slowly turned around in a circle.

"What's wrong?" Tearza asked.

"Nothing."

She grabbed my hand. "Stick with me."

A waiter walked by with a tray of wine and I selected two glasses for us. Without thinking, I drank half of mine in one swallow.

"Your face is flushed," she said.

I pulled at the neck of my shirt. The stupid tie choked me like a dog collar. "It's not the champagne, really."

She escorted me deeper into the room. "Don't worry, this will be fun."

A pretty woman in a long, red gown shrieked and ran toward Tearza with her arms wide in the air. "Tearza, it's great to see you. I'm so glad you came." The woman and her companion gave her a group hug. "It's been too long."

Tearza pointed at me. "This is my friend, Ryan." The two of them waited for an explanation. "Ali, I told you about Marci and Ella's best friends. Well, this is Sara and Gracie's dad."

She turned to me and explained, "This is my best friend, Ali, and her husband David."

"You have the belle of the ball tonight," David said. "You're a lucky guy."

"Thank you—I know."

The women put their heads together to catch up with each other, and David said to me, "Tearza's quite the girl. We love her." He eyed me the way I would scrutinize a potential date for my daughter. "Did you know Jim?"

I shook my head. "But I heard he was a special person."

"Special would be an understatement. The nicest guy I ever met." He sighed. "One of a kind."

Tearza stepped between us. "Sorry, David, but you've had him long enough. We're off to dance."

"We are?" I said.

She grabbed my hand and dragged me toward the music.

On the way to the dance floor, another couple stopped us but the interaction was quite different.

"We're so sorry about Jim," the woman said. "You must be devastated."

Tearza didn't respond and didn't introduce them to me.

"How are the girls?" the woman asked.

"About what you'd expect."

"We must get together soon," the woman said before walking away.

I asked Tearza, "How do you know her?"

"Her daughter's in Marci's class. Victoria's such a fake. She only pretends to like me because Jim used to play golf with her husband. During a lunch at her snooty country club, she said foreigners, illegal immigrants, and minorities were leeches who ruin our country. She looked at me, and said, 'Oh, but not you dear.' Then she had the audacity to continue her tirade as if I weren't there. Such a bitch."

I laughed. "Wow. Miss Potty-mouth. And I thought you were such a nice girl."

She leaned close and whispered, "There's a lot you don't know about me." The sweet smell of gardenias made me dizzy and her hair tickled my nose. I closed my eyes and took a deep breath.

She pulled away and smiled. "Come on, let's dance. You do know how, don't you?"

"I suppose you want to lead."

She laughed. "Well, here's the deal. You can lead, but if my feet get bloody, you may have to swallow your pride."

I felt a tap on my shoulder. I turned to see Dylan behind me.

"May I cut in?" he asked.

Before I could respond, he grabbed Tearza's hand and led her away to the music. Tearza gave me a helpless look, while I gave a hand signal it was okay

Tearza looked beautiful as Dylan twirled her in a circle. One song turned into two. Then, as the third song began, I tapped him on the shoulder and said, "Sorry, but this is our song."

He hesitated for second and then made a dramatic bow. "Thank you for the dances."

As he walked away, Tearza said, "I didn't know we had a song."

I hesitated because the song was The First Time Ever I Saw Your Face by Roberta Flack. "We can sit this one out if you want," I said.

She locked onto my eyes. "Shall we dance or stand here?"

I held out my hand and shuffled around.

"Do you always stand three feet away?"

"Just afraid I might bloody your feet. It's been a long time."

She stepped closer and we moved in a small circle.

"You're not so bad."

"Me or my dancing?"

She didn't answer, just leaned into my shoulder.

Impulsively I asked, "Remember our conversation at Zadie's about New York? Would you ever consider visiting New York City with me?"

"No, and I don't think I'd like it. All that noise, cabs honking, crime, police sirens—sounds scary." She lifted her head off my shoulder. "Why do you ask?"

"It's not like that anymore. New York is different than twenty years ago. Quite safe."

She put her head back on my shoulder again. "I'll take your word for it."

"Would you ever consider going there with me?"

She flinched and stopped dancing just as another couple started to hug her. She never answered my question and we didn't have an opportunity to dance again. One couple after another made a point to say hello as we moved throughout the event. After a while, I felt like an escort rental. But Tearza loved the attention and I watched her relax for the first time in months.

On the way home, she turned toward me. "Thanks for taking me tonight. I know it was probably hard for you."

"You have very nice friends," I said. "And I learned a lot about Jim. He was quite a guy."

Tearza stared out the window while I drove. "The president of the Special Olympics asked me to chair the event next year. Would you ever consider co-chairing it with me?"

"Sure, that would be fun." I instinctively lied knowing I'd be living in New York City next year.

She sat up in the seat. "Really? You'd do that for me?"

I smiled. "I'd do anything for you."

"Thank you!" She kissed me on the cheek. "You're the best."

I don't think so, I thought.

Ten minutes later I pulled into her driveway and walked her to front door. We turned and faced each other. Neither of us knew what to say. Her red lips were smudged from kissing friends. The evening breeze blew a strand of hair over her right eye. I wanted to brush it back, but she tucked it behind her ear. We stood quietly in the moonlight until Marci flicked on the porch light and opened the front door.

"How was it?" she asked.

"Great." I stepped slightly back from Tearza. "Your mother was a celebrity tonight. Everyone wanted to talk to her."

"It wasn't me. All my nosy girlfriends wanted to get the scoop on my handsome date."

"Your date?" Marci asked.

"No, nothing like that." I quickly added.

"What did you tell your friends?" Marci insisted.

Tearza looked at me, then back to Marcie. "That he was Sara and Gracie's dad."

That was my cue to leave, so I said goodnight and walked to my car. Tearza had told me a little about Jim before, but after the way everyone gushed over him, I realized there was no way I could compete with the perfect ghost of her husband.

◆ ◆ ◆

The next morning Susan followed me into my office and set a cup of coffee on the desk. She stood over my shoulder waiting. "Well?"

"Well what?"

"Last night?"

"Slept like a baby."

"Don't make me angry. I grew up with a brother twice your size. I can make your life miserable. What did she look like?"

"Beautiful."

"Did you dance?"

"I tried. You would've been proud of me. I only stepped on her feet a couple of times."

"You're playing with fire here."

"What do you mean?"

She scowled at me. "Does Tiffany know you went to the fundraiser ball with Tearza?"

"No."

"You've been seeing each other for at least a couple of months. Not counting the trips to New York."

"It's only casual. We're not really dating per se. She's cool with that."

"Tell that to *her*." She leaned toward me. "I dare you."

My cell phone rescued me. I looked at the incoming phone number. "Sorry, it's Jamison."

"We're not through yet," she warned.

The rest of my day was a blur of crises and catch-up. No time for anything else—never any time for me. I was almost ready to head home when Susan reminded me, "Don't forget to pick up Gracie's birthday present. I'll bet Sara and Gracie are excited about their mom coming home for the birthday party."

"Yes, we haven't seen her in more than a year."

"How did she sound on the phone?"

"Much better than before. I'm a little nervous because of what happened on her last visit, but hopefully she's in a good place right now."

"Think she'll show?"

"She better or the girls will be crushed. I worry because she doesn't have a cell phone, so it's impossible to call her and confirm."

I rushed home to decorate for the party. Tearza was tending the girls so I could get everything ready. She decided to bake Gracie's favorite cake—double chocolate angel food with fudge frosting. I prayed that Clair would show up.

When Tearza arrived with the girls, she surveyed the room. "Great job with the decorating."

"I hope Gracie likes it."

"Are you kidding, it's all of her favorite things." Tearza picked up a handful of Skittles. "I love the purple ones best. I forgot to ask you the other night, how did your lunch go at Anthony's? What a coincidence to bump into you."

"Was fine."

Tearza changed the subject. "What did you decide to make for Gracie's birthday dinner?"

"Baby dill pickles, black olives that fit on her fingers, garlic toast, and tomato basil soup."

"Fancy," she said.

The birthday party opened with a game of Rummy Royal, and Marci was the big winner. After the girls left to play in the other room, Tearza looked at her watch. "Anything from Clair?"

"I told her the party started at five-thirty."

"It's six-thirty. Should we start dinner?"

"Let me ask Sara."

I walked into the family room where the girls were playing video games. "Sara, it's getting late. Do you think we should start dinner?"

Sara looked at the clock. "Did you hear from Mom?"

I shook my head.

"You told her five-thirty, didn't you?"

"Maybe we should start with appetizers."

"Not yet," Sara insisted.

I walked back into the kitchen and sat down with Tearza.

"What if she doesn't show?" Tearza asked.

"I don't even want to think about it."

"You said she completed her treatment program and that she's working?"

"Yes—sounded the best I've heard her since she finished the chemical dependency program."

"Do the girls wonder if she'll ever come back and live here?"

"Earlier, yes. But she's been gone so long they've given up on that possibility."

Suddenly, Tearza got up, poured herself a glass of water from the sink and stood looking out the window until she finished the drink. "It's almost seven. Maybe we should get started," she said, definitely changing the subject. Finally, we started the party with appetizers.

After a few minutes, Sara sniffed the air and jumped up from the kitchen table. "I forgot the garlic toast!" She ran to open the oven door where smoke already billowed out. Sara looked at the burnt garlic toast, set the pan on the stove, burst into tears, and ran to her bedroom.

I started to go after her when Tearza put her hand on my shoulder. "Let me go," she said. "Stay with the girls and enjoy your appetizers. We'll replace the garlic toast with something else."

Tearza came back thirty minutes later with her mascara smeared.

"Are you okay?" I asked stupidly.

Tearza nodded and took a deep breath. "Sara will be fine—give her a few minutes. She'll be back for cake."

"The toast isn't important."

"It's not the toast."

Sara walked in the room sniffling with red eyes.

"Are you okay?" Gracie asked.

I stood up, but Tearza clapped her hands together.

"Let's do the cake," she said.

"Are you ready to make a wish?" I asked Gracie before I lit the match.

Gracie put her hands over the candles. "Shouldn't we wait a little longer for Mom?"

Tearza stepped next to Gracie and put her arms around her. "Why don't you make your wish, then we'll save a big piece for your mom?"

After we sang "Happy Birthday," Gracie looked at the clock one more time, drew a big breath, and blew out her candles.

Clair never showed up or called.

Finally, Tearza said she and her girls had to go home. I stopped her at the door.

"What happened in the bedroom?"

"Sara thinks the divorce was her fault."

"Oh God." I dragged my fingers through my hair. "What should I do?"

"Let it go—for tonight anyway. We can talk again in the morning. She's a wonderful young girl."

"I know."

◆ ◆ ◆

Despondent—that was the girls over the next two weeks. We barely spoke to each other. All of us seemed to go through the motions. I had just taken Cooper outside to play when I got a phone call from Stella.

"Dad and I want you to come up to the lake before school starts," she said.

"Really? Why?"

"Can't you just say yes once in a while? Why make such an issue out of a simple invitation?"

"Because he hasn't invited us since Clair left."

"Don't say anything, but Dad wants to talk to you about some things."

I brought it up to the girls. Although I worried about Dad and his state of mind, they were excited to spend time with Grandma at the lake. Two weeks later, we drove north to Dad's cabin. While the girls slept, my mind drifted to Tearza. After the Special Olympics dinner, I had been wondering if I could ever live up to Jim's high standard.

I knew Marci didn't like the idea of me or anyone else replacing her dad, but I didn't want to replace Jim. I wanted Marcie—and Tearza—to accept me on our own terms.

Even though the girls were crazy about Tearza, the woman confused the hell out of me. She was everything they could want in a mother, and she loved them dearly. But I wasn't sure how she felt about me. On the other hand, there was Tiffany. She was everything Tearza was not. The girls, particularly Sara, didn't like her at all, but she was fun and loved New York City. She'd probably move there in a heartbeat. But, I realized, I didn't love her.

We pulled off the highway onto the long dirt road that led to the cabin. The car had barely stopped moving when the girls jumped out and sprinted to the kitchen to see Stella. I unpacked the car while Dad grabbed three fishing poles off the porch and yelled, "Come on, girls, let's catch some sunnies and have a fish fry tonight!"

Carrying coffee cans, the girls flew off the porch and followed their grandpa to the garden to dig for worms.

Stella called to me from the porch. "Honey, the car can wait. Let's visit first. I want to hear all about you and the girls." She brought out two glasses of iced tea and we sat in white rocking chairs watching Dad and the girls fish off the dock. Every minute or two, a squeal broke the silence as one of the girls caught a fish, which kept Dad busy baiting the hooks.

"You know we're very proud of you," Stella said. "By the way, how's Tearza?"

I smiled. "I just got here and you're already digging into my love life."

"It's a stepmother's prerogative."

"Tearza and I—it's complicated," I said. "She invited me to a fundraiser and we had a great time. It wasn't a date, exactly—more like two best friends out for an evening."

"Did you have fun?"

"It's so easy to be with her. She's a fantastic mother and Sara and Gracie love her. But some things are hard."

"What do you mean?"

"She always talks about Jim."

"That's only natural, don't you think?"

"Sure, but this guy sounds so perfect. Not only how she talks about him, but everyone we met at the Special Olympics dinner described him in such glowing terms." I stopped because Gracie pointed and yelled at me to look at the big sunny she had caught. I waved back. "How can I compete with her dead husband?"

"You can hold your own." Stella patted my hand. "She sounds wonderful. We look forward to meeting her."

"Probably not anytime soon. We needed a break—I'm so mixed-up. I really like her but I can't figure out where I fit in—or *want* to fit in."

"What's holding you back?"

"I'm not holding back."

"Oh, really?"

"Really," I said a bit too defensively.

She stopped rocking. "What are you afraid of?"

I thought for a few second. "What if I screw up again?"

"You won't."

I closed my eyes, and when I opened them Stella was still watching me.

I needed to change the subject. "Well, at least I've finally made Dad happy," I said.

"What do you mean?"

"The managing partner hinted that the firm may make me partner at the next meeting."

"It's what you've always wanted, isn't it?"

"I know how important it's been to him."

"To him?" she asked.

"You know how hard he pushed me in school—and all the way through law school. Well, I finally did it."

"You've got it all wrong. I love you dearly, but don't blame your father for your choices."

"I didn't mean it that way. It's just—"

Suddenly, Stella leaned forward. "Listen now, this is very important. You're the only one who can make yourself happy—not me, not your dad, nor anyone else. You may not believe it, and he may not show it in the way you want, but he only wishes for you to be happy." She tapped her fingers rapidly on the arm of the chair. "Did you know your father always wanted to be a lawyer?"

"You're kidding. Why didn't he?"

She looked out over the lake. "Life's full of choices. Some you get to make yourself and others are made for you."

Confused, I asked, "What?"

She slowly turned her gaze toward the water. "You know I love you, but the older I get, the less patience I have for people who make excuses for their unhappiness. Regrets are another excuse for not taking a risk." She stood up, kissed me on top of the head, and then whispered, "Just remember, *you* get to choose."

The screen door squeaked as it closed behind her.

After I unpacked the car, I changed into shorts and went down to the dock. Water is like a drug for me. I'm attracted to it like a bug to a light on a dark night. Early evening was always my favorite time. I sat on our old wooden dock and dangled my toes in the warm water. The wind had died down, the lake was flat as glass, and a loon called out in the distance. I breathed in the sweet smell of pine and relaxed for the first time in months.

Wooden boards creaked under the weight of approaching footsteps. Dad smiled, carrying two glasses of scotch. He groaned slightly as he sat down next to me.

"Old bones," he said rubbing his knees. "Not as flexible as they used to be."

"It hasn't affected your elbow. You can still get that glass to your mouth without any problem."

"When that goes, take me for a long ride and drop me in the middle of the lake with a cement block tied to my leg."

For a long time neither of us spoke. Most of my childhood memories were filled with anger and pain. I appreciated the silence without the usual conflict.

A loud crash came from the house and the girls erupted into laughter. Dad shook his head. I imagined Stella holding court in the kitchen as they baked cookies.

Finally, Dad broke the silence. "Stella said you seem a little blue. How are the girls feeling?"

"Okay," I said. "But it's overwhelming at times. I never know if I'm doing enough. Sarah's adjusted better to losing Clair. Gracie was too young to remember when Clair was struggling." Once I started talking, I couldn't shut down the words—they just kept coming—and Dad listened.

"It's funny how Gracie has really latched onto to Tearza," I said. "I used to be the center of her universe, but now she jumps into Tearza's lap whenever she gets the chance. Sara's another story. She's growing up so fast it's scary. I can't tell if her mood swings are because of me or the normal things that girls go through at that age."

Dad stared out over the lake and sipped from his glass. "It must be tough at times."

"It's hard enough to be a good dad, much less a mother too."

"You're doing a great job with the girls. They're growing up with your love, I'm sure that's enough."

I looked at Dad as he stared across the lake. This was the first real conversation we'd had in years. We sat together quietly for a long time.

"What about your friend?" Dad asked. "Stella gave me specific orders not to come back to the house until I weasel out some information about your Tearza."

"First of all, she's not *my* Tearza. We've become very good friends. She's fun and the girls love her, especially Gracie."

"Are you dating?"

"No. I can barely keep my head above water between work and the girls." I shook my head. "I don't have the time or the stomach for more drama."

"Meaning...?"

"I had enough of that with Clair."

While I made small circles in the water with my bare feet, two sunnies swam up to check out my toes.

"I'm having second thoughts about the law firm," I said. "The work keeps piling up and they're pressuring me to travel more. I should make partner this fall. I assumed that things would slow down if I had more control, but I'm worried it might become worse. It's not what I expected."

"What did you expect?"

"Easy street."

"I can't tell you what to do, much as I'd like to, but some of the biggest decisions in my life seemed no-win at the time. As I got older, though, I started to draw a line between the dots and finally realized it wasn't a coincidence. The Big Guy upstairs was guiding me, even if I didn't understand it."

"My life looks like a scattergram of dots," I admitted. "I don't even know where to begin."

Dad swirled his glass in circle before taking another sip.

"I'm sorry," I said.

"For what?"

"For me."

"You..." He squinted into the setting sun. "You're not a regret." Suddenly he stood up. "You're a..."

"A what?" I waited.

He stood up without finishing the sentence and walked away. I'd learned over the years that he would shut down every time I tried to bring up my mother. If I pressed him to talk about her, he would just get angry. I felt I'd never understand him.

Stella shouted for me to come in because the girls wanted to start their favorite games. I moved to the porch as the girls grabbed their flashlights and rounded up the neighbor kids to play capture-the-flag in the dark.

After the games were over, the girls were sweating so we finished with a late-night dip in the lake. Everyone gathered on the dock to swim out to the raft. A half hour later, we were all lying on the raft looking at the stars and talking in the dark. The raft gently rocked and the summer moon slowly rose like a gigantic snowball.

"It's called a Blue Moon," I explained.

"Looks white to me," Sara said.

"It only happens when there are two full moons in the same month. An Indian legend says you get to make a wish." I turned to Gracie. "What's your wish?"

"To have a pony," she said.

"Sara?"

"I'm not telling." She turned her head toward the moon then asked me, "What did you wish for?"

I tried to remember the last time I had made a wish for anything, but I couldn't.

The full moon cast a surreal, shimmering white reflection on the water. Amazing how something like this could happen twice in one month—almost like a second chance to get it right.

I wondered if I'd ever get a second chance. And if I did, would I screw it up again?

♦ ♦ ♦

Dad woke us up the next morning with a call of "*sol er ruppe*," which means "the sun is up," the start of a traditional Norwegian salute to start the day. The girls giggled as they each lifted a glass of orange juice to the morning sun. He led everyone in the poem, which ended with all of us yelling, "*Skol!*" Then we raced to down the juice in one gulp.

On long car trips, our family tradition was to play the audiobook of *Charlotte's Web*. A beautiful reminder about family, friends, and the true meaning of love, the story made us cry every time we listened to it. I knew why Wilbur so desperately wanted to have a friend, someone to love. I understood why he became so afraid when Charlotte died. He felt she could never be replaced. How can you go on when you lose someone that special?

But Charlotte didn't have any regrets. She loved Wilbur even though she knew that he would experience the pain of losing her when she died. Love and loss can be great teachers. Through love we learn how to overcome loss. Through loss, we learn how to better love someone. It's a paradox that it sometimes takes a tragic loss to discover a deeper love—a love we otherwise would have never known. Charlotte gave Wilbur the gift of understanding this. Although the pain of losing her was real, her love became endless, renewed each spring through her children.

The car was quiet after the story ended. The girls had fallen asleep and I didn't feel like turning on the radio. Driving down the deserted two-lane highway, I felt like Wilbur waiting for my spring to come—waiting for my new friends—waiting for my second chance to love again.

My mind drifted to my mother. *How ironic,* I thought. *The only two things I possess of my mother is a small photo and her name—Charlotte.*

Chapter 6

Tearza

I endured another long, sleepless night. Feeling foggy, I stood in front of the bathroom mirror staring at my bare neck and realized how much I missed my necklace. Sara had become so upset at Gracie's party that I gave her the angel pendant my grandmother had given me when I got married. She needed it more than I did. Nevertheless, ever since that night, I constantly touched the spot where it used to rest. I still needed my guardian angel.

Glancing at the clock, I saw that I was going to be late for work again. When I finally arrived, I sensed something was terribly wrong. The shop was too quiet and Amber was standing behind the counter with red eyes. The owner Mary waved for me to join her in the office. She closed the door, motioned for me to sit down.

"Tearza," she said, "you know how much we adore you."

My heart sank as I knew what Mary was going to say next. "Let me make this easy on you," I said. "I know that business is terrible, but I want you to know how much I like—no, how much I *love* it here. You gave me a great opportunity. I can't tell you how much I appreciate that."

Mary leaned forward and put her head in her hands. "I've tried to figure out some way to avoid this, but I have to cut expenses or I'm out of business."

"How soon?" I asked.

"Two weeks."

I quickly did the math. This was a horrible time to be looking for a job. "It's not your fault," I said, and then we hugged.

"I'm so sorry. I wish I could do more."

"I know. Don't worry about me—I'll be fine."

Amber was waiting for me by my car. I shook as we cried together with my face buried in her shoulder. Finally, we pulled apart. "Things happen for a reason," she said.

"I guess."

"I had a dream about you last night."

"Was it good?"

"Dreams can only be bad if you allow it."

"I'm not sure I understand."

"When bad things happen to me, I tell myself 'it's only a dream,' and then I can deal with it. Something positive always follows. I've learned to be patient for the good things to be revealed."

"If you say so."

Amber's eyes narrowed. "I'm weird but believe me—I know this."

All I could do was nod and wipe my eyes. I took the long way home after stopping at the grocery store. I'd always found comfort in food.

As I pulled up to my garage, Jake was standing on a ladder changing light bulbs on the porch. He got down and walked over to the car.

"How's my favorite gardener?" he said through the car window.

"Fine."

He looked at me strangely. "You don't sound fine."

I got out and grabbed the groceries.

"Here, let me help you," he said.

He pulled the bags from me and we walked into the house. "Can you believe how fast the summer went?" He wanted to talk, but I didn't.

"Yes," I answered lamely.

"Are the girls excited about starting school soon? They love it there, don't they?"

"They do."

"We sent all three kids through St. Luke's and they had a wonderful experience."

"It's been a blessing, especially because of what the girls have been through."

"Well, I need to finish changing the lights." Jake hesitated at the door. "As long as I'm here, is there anything else you need?"

"How about a miracle?"

"That might take a little more time."

"How much time do you have?"

He looked at his watch and smiled. "I suppose I could put off my nap for a while." He pulled up a chair, sat down and folded his hands.

I didn't trust myself to look at him, so I put away groceries while we talked. "I lost my job today."

"Oh, no."

"To be honest, I'm really worried. They gave me two weeks of extra pay, but if I don't find a job, we can't afford to stay here."

Jake crossed his arms. "I never did it for the money."

I held back tears. "I mean it, Jake. If I don't get a job soon, I'm broke."

"I understand," he said quietly. "We'll work something out."

"Jake, I can't promise anything."

"I know."

"And you don't care?"

"Like I said, I didn't do this for the money."

"Why would you do this?"

He scratched his chin. "Life's a mystery. It can give you everything you need and then take it away just as fast. I learned the hard way that regrets can teach you to love or teach you to hate."

"I don't understand."

"It's never easy, but we get to choose." He took a deep breath. "I was a poster child for hate and self-pity after Mary died. I almost drank myself to death and drove my family away. I didn't think I could go on without my wife until I had a dream that changed my life."

He stood up and walked behind me, kissing me on the top of the head like a loving father would do. "Maybe someday I'll tell you my dream—when you can understand it."

I thought of Amber reminding me that good things usually come from bad. "Can you do me a favor?" I asked.

"Anything."

"Please don't say anything to the girls or anyone else. There may be a lot of things that have to change, and I need to figure out a plan first."

"Let me know if there's anything else I can do to help."

"You've done more than you'll ever know."

He walked to the door and held it halfway open. "Things will work out. I know it's hard but have faith."

Faith is all that I have left, I thought.

The screen door closed. Alone, I put the last of the groceries away and sat down to calculate my finances.

◆ ◆ ◆

After two weeks of searching job listings and calling friends, I didn't have one opportunity. I had submitted nearly fifty resumés to various agencies and universities to see if I could resurrect my research project on climate change, but I came up with a big fat zero.

After a walk to clear my head, I listened to a voice message from Ryan. I panicked because I had completely forgotten they were coming over for dinner tonight. Tonight's menu headliner was Mom's Tater Tot Hot Dish—salty and crispy tater tots tucked over cream of mushroom soup mixed with peas and hamburger. I needed comfort food tonight.

Later, Ryan entered the kitchen with his girls. The top of his shirt was unbuttoned, his tie was pulled loose, and his hair was a mess.

"Rough day?" I asked as I filled a Pyrex dish.

"Brutal." He slumped into the closest chair. "Are those tater tots? Growing up I lived on hot dish, succotash, and tuna casseroles. The girls will love this."

"Some kids don't like the old-fashioned food we grew up on."

"And how was your day?" Ryan asked.

I tried to act nonchalant. "Can't think of the right adjective."

"Whoops, one of those?"

"You could say that." I pulled fruit slush out of the freezer. "More like a bad couple of weeks."

"What's wrong?"

I wiped my hands on my apron repeatedly. "Nothing."

"You sure?"

"Actually, could you take the girls to the mall without me?"

"We can switch and do it another night."

"No, the girls would be too disappointed."

"Okay, if that's what you want."

After they left, I called friends networking for job possibilities, but nothing came of it. I was worried because it was almost eight and Ryan should've been back with the girls. I tried his cell but only got his voicemail. By eight-thirty, I was grabbing the car keys when I heard Ella's crazy laugh coming through the front door. The gang rushed into the kitchen carrying bags. Ella dug into hers first and pulled out an American Girl doll.

"Look what we got!" she squealed, pointing to Marci, who showed off her doll too. Ryan stood behind them grinning.

I was so furious I could barely speak. "Where have you been? You never answered your phone."

"Sorry, I had it on silent mode at work and forgot to turn it back."

"What took you so long?"

Marci spoke first, "Ryan spent a long time talking to some blond woman in the mall."

"Really? And who was that?" I asked Ryan.

Ryan fidgeted with his phone for a second. "Tiffany. Sorry, we got a little side-tracked on an issue for one of the cases we're working on."

"I thought you went to the mall to walk around for a short time and get a little treat?"

"We did, but you know me." Ryan looked sheepish. "I'm mush when it comes to saying no to the girls."

Marci held up her doll. "What do you think?"

"That's really nice, but they have to go back."

"What?" Ella said.

"Don't argue with me!" I sounded angrier than I was, or maybe not.

Ryan started to speak, but I cut him off. "Girls, why don't you go into the living and watch some TV. I need to talk to Ryan."

They left and I shut the door. "What do you think you're doing?"

"Listen, I only—"

"You have no right."

"I don't understand."

"I can't afford that stuff!"

"But it's my treat."

"No!" I stomped my foot, then felt embarrassed about it. "That's not the point."

Ryan looked down and didn't say anything.

I threw a dishtowel across the room. "I can't compete with gifts like that."

"It's not a competition, Tearza."

"You're the big lawyer with the big bucks. You have no idea…"

Ryan's face turned red. Finally, he looked up. "I wanted to make them happy, and you're making a federal case out of it. I'm sorry if I made a mistake. I should've called you first. I'm not Mr. Perfect. I'm not *Jim*." He squinted as if to say something else but then turned around.

"Come on girls, we have to go!" he yelled.

Sara shouted from the family room, "But we just got here!"

"Don't argue. Just do it! And bring Gracie." He led the girls out the front door.

"Ryan," I called after him.

He didn't answer or look back, just walked swiftly out the door. I kicked a wastebasket and papers flew out as it hit the wall. I cursed at the mess and was picking up the garbage when Ryan reappeared in the kitchen.

I was in no mood for a peace conference. "What now?"

"I can't find my keys." Scowling, he circled the kitchen until he found them on the counter. He started to leave but stopped. "I just don't get it."

"You don't get it, is right." I picked up the scattered papers, afraid that if I looked at him I might explode. "You don't have to worry about things. Not like I do."

"Like what?"

"Like work, like money, like paying the rent."

I slumped into a chair.

"What're you talking about?"

"I was laid off today. I need a job right now or we're in deep trouble—something you never have to worry about as a big shot lawyer."

"Oh, God," he said, then looked up at the ceiling. "What happened?"

"Business is bad. They had to lay somebody off." I hoped that the girls were not listening. "I'm the new kid at the shop, so the first to go. I've applied to every flower shop in town but nobody's hiring."

"I'm really sorry."

"Sure, you're always saying you're sorry about something," I snapped.

"Come on—I didn't know."

"Because all you ever talk about is your work, your big cases. When was the last time you asked anything about me or my work?"

Ryan glared at me. "That's not fair."

"Not fair? I'll tell you what's not fair. Try the fun of a single mom with two girls to raise, no job, and dead broke? How's that for not fair?"

"Have you tried applying somewhere other than at flower shops?"

"No," I said sarcastically, "I just sit around and wait for companies to call."

"I'm only bringing up other possibilities."

"Which doesn't help."

"Okay, if that's the way you want it." He shook his head and then left without another word.

Feeling sick, I tried to clean up the kitchen but didn't get too far when Marci appeared in the doorway.

"What was that about?" she said, fidgeting with her hair.

"Nothing."

"Pretty loud for nothing."

"Time for bed."

"Did you have a fight?"

"No, a misunderstanding."

"About what?"

"Do I have to ask you again?" I said sternly.

"But Mom…"

"Marci!"

"Was it about us?" Marci asked.

"What? No."

"About Ryan?"

"No, honey, it's not you or Ryan. I can't explain it right now. Please take Ella and go to bed."

In truth I was furious with Ryan, mad at the situation, and mad at myself. The phone rang and I answered a call from Ali.

"Tearza Marie, we loved meeting Ryan at the Special Olympics Event. He's adorable."

"I'm glad you called."

"Why?" she asked.

"Because you're my angel."

"Good, but if you ask my husband, he may have a different opinion."

"You're the perfect couple."

"Hah, glad you think so, but we have our moments. We all do. You had a few with Jim, right?"

I didn't respond.

"Every couple has differences once in a while. We've had some doozies. That doesn't mean we don't love each other. I always felt better after a good argument."

"I never felt good after Jim and I argued."

"Honey, I don't want to wreck your memories, but remember when Jim and one his buddies left work early to go bowling and ended up drinking way too many beers?"

"Yeah, I remember."

"Well, if I recall correctly, you were hosting a dinner party at your house that night and Jim showed up tipsy and two hours late?"

"I remember."

"I learned a few new barnyard words from you that night."

"Very funny."

"Nobody's perfect, not even Jim. Need I bring up more examples?"

"But Ryan makes me so mad sometimes. It's frustrating because at times I just don't understand him."

"That's good. It means you care enough about him to be mad."

"I worry that if we argue like this now, what would it be like if…" I hesitated.

"If what?"

"If we were together all the time, would it be better, worse, or more of the same?"

"You can't know until you try," Ali said. "So, what's the problem?"

"I think that I've made a terrible mistake. I should've never let myself get into this situation. It's not fair to the girls."

"The girls?"

"I could ruin everything."

"For Ryan or you?"

For a second, my temper kicked in again. I was too angry to respond.

"Are you still there?"

"Yes."

"Why are you so upset?"

I tried to think of a way to explain. "I don't know. I'm so confused."

"Trust your heart."

"I wish I could. I don't trust much of anything anymore. Sometimes I think that I should just marry Dylan."

"What? You must be kidding."

"He could solve all my problems. I'd have the flexibility to resume work on a full- or part-time basis. Or never go back to work and become a stay-at-home mom. No more money issues. He mentioned that he would like to move back to his hometown. That would put me only forty-five minutes from my family."

"Tearza, are you crazy, girl?"

"He's a kind man and he'd be a good father to the girls. The girls really need that in their lives."

"Nice speech, but aren't you forgetting one small thing?"

"He doesn't smoke or run around like some guys do."

"No, you left out the most important part."

"What's that?"

"You don't love him, so how could you marry him?"

"Not everyone marries for love. Do I have to mention some of our college friends?"

"I won't even respond to that comment. You're one silly girl, but I love you anyway." Ali made a kissing sound over the phone. "I have to go, but let's get together for lunch next week."

◆ ◆ ◆

Three days later, we drove to the farm to spend some time with my parents before school started. It was dark by the time we got there. Dad was already in bed, so I tucked the girls in and talked with Mom for a while before falling exhausted into my old bed.

Mom was in the kitchen long before I woke up. I wandered downstairs following the aroma of fresh coffee and sat silently at the table with a cup.

Mom turned away from the stove. "What's wrong? You haven't said a thing since you came down."

"Nothing. I'm enjoying you."

"Would you like some breakfast?"

"Coffee's fine."

She smiled. "Now tell me about—"

I interrupted because I knew her next comment. "I heard Dad bought a new cow."

"Tearza."

"Mom, don't. Please."

"You're blushing."

"Do we have to talk about it now?"

"I'm your mother."

Mom doesn't give up easily, so I decided to get it over. "Well, Ryan's certainly different. The whole thing's kind of complicated."

"What's so hard about two people who like each other?"

Before I could explain, a waterfall of emotions flooded my heart. I suddenly let go of two years of bravery—two long years of time alone. After a good cry, I felt better, but I had a bone to pick with her before I could explain the situation with Ryan.

"Mom, did you call Dylan and try to set us up on a date?"

"No, why?" She turned away from me.

"Mom, you know how terrible you are at cards. Look at my face."

She went to the refrigerator and began searching for something.

"Listen," I said, "I know you mean well, but you have to stop doing things like this. This only makes things worse."

Mom turned around holding string cheese in one hand and summer sausage in the other.

"It's six-thirty in the morning, Mom. Are you working on a new diet?"

She looked at her hands and we both burst out laughing.

"Oh Tearza, I want you to be happy, that's all."

She wiped her hands on her apron and slumped into the nearest chair.

"I'm sorry," she said.

"I know." I put my arm around her. "Let's take our coffee out to the summer kitchen."

The summer kitchen was just five steps from the house. Originally built to keep the main house from getting hot when you cooked in the summer, it now doubled as a sunroom and painting studio for my mother. I loved the small, cozy space, painted white with a high peaked ceiling and tall windows facing the sunny south. I set the coffee pot on a small table and we snuggled into our chairs.

I nodded toward Mom's easel. "What are you working on?"

She turned her head around. "Oh, that. I'm stuck. It's been sitting there for a month."

I surveyed the half-finished summer landscape of the river valley below the farm.

"Having some trouble finishing it?"

"I can't get the color right—the morning light."

"Is there a wrong color? It changes as fast as the sun rises."

"I can't make up my mind."

"It looks beautiful so far."

"Let's get back to Ryan," she said. I wasn't sure if she was really that curious or just didn't want to talk about her painting.

"Okay, you win," I said. "It's not like we have a romance or anything, but it feels like we've known each other for a long time."

I explained how we met and carpooled, then added, "It's incredible how natural it feels for all of us to be together."

"But no romance, right?"

"I've decided we should be friends and leave it at that."

"I'm curious," she asked. "How do the girls feel about him?"

"Ella adores Ryan, but the jury's still out with Marci. It's not that she doesn't like him, but she doesn't want anyone to ever replace Jim."

"That's normal. Do you think she can ever separate Jim from Ryan?"

"I don't know—maybe over time. Maybe she's afraid of betraying her dad."

"What about you?"

"What *about* me."

"Tearza!"

"I'm afraid too, I guess."

She touched my hand. "Honey, what's holding you back?"

"Ryan seems married to his work. Jim worked hard, but he always put our family first."

"Always?"

I thought about the long hours Jim worked before he died—and our last argument.

"Not always, I guess."

"Work can be hard to balance when you're single. You know that better than anyone."

"But it's already cost Ryan one failed marriage."

"People can learn from their mistakes."

"It's not just that. You should see the women he dates. Not exactly girls off the farm."

Mom frowned. "You'll have to explain that."

"Well, for example, there's a woman he sees from his work. She's a successful lawyer, former model, and rich. How do I compete with that? Like I said earlier, it's complicated. He's different than anyone I've ever met."

Mom patted my arm. "You're lucky to have special people like that in your lives."

"I know, but can I risk becoming another casualty? It's probably best if we just stay friends, that way nobody gets hurt."

"Are you sure about that?"

I didn't answer. It was time for breakfast, so we walked back to the kitchen. While mom started the eggs, I picked up a hot, gooey roll fresh out of the oven and brought it back to the table. I crossed my feet up beneath me, debating how to break my news to her.

"There's something else I need to tell you."

Worried, Mom set her spatula on the counter and waited.

"I was laid off at the flower shop."

"Oh no, what happened?"

"The economy happened. I need to get another job in a hurry. You know, with the rent and everything." I pulled apart a piece of the sweet roll, took a bite and licked the sugar off my fingers. "I really loved that flower shop."

"I know you did."

"It was something…"

"What?" Mom asked.

I bit my lip. "…something I was really good at outside of my job at the university."

"Another job will come up, I'm sure."

"I hope so," I said, "but I'm scared."

"Don't worry. I'll talk to your dad."

"No, you have your own problems."

Mom leaned close. "Honey, look at my eyes—don't worry about the money."

"It's not that."

"Then what are you afraid of?"

I whispered, "Every time I find something I love—I lose it."

Mom put her arms around me and kissed my ear. "I have a good feeling that when school starts you'll find a new job, and you and Ryan will work everything out."

"We'll see," I said, more to appease her than anything else.

The men finally came in from milking, so I quickly took my plate to the sink and went for a long walk in the woods above the farm.

◆ ◆ ◆

The next day began with a trip into town for the start of the summer festival that took place the same week every year. The town blocked off Main Street and a polka band played at one end, a country band at the other. Between them, vendors filled the sidewalks with corn dripping in butter, brats, hot dogs, krumkake, lutefisk, cotton candy, snow cones, homemade pies, and warm cookies. Since everyone knew everyone, I gave the girls a couple of dollars and they disappeared into the crowd.

At the end of the day, we all gathered on the front porch and talked about our time at the fair. I felt so different now with Jim gone. I constantly caught myself waiting for him to join us on the porch or sneak up from behind me and bury me with hugs and kisses as he always did.

Our porch overlooked a long field of alfalfa that fell away to the river below. As the sun set, the temperature dropped, and a fog rose like a white blanket from the river bottom. The girls played a card game on the porch while Mom, Dad, and I sat in rocking chairs.

Suddenly, Dad called for the girls. "Come quick! The fog's out, and you know what that means."

"The leprechauns come out to play," the girls squealed.

He shook his finger at them and smiled. "That's right. Be careful in the fields tonight so they don't play any tricks on you."

"Okay, Grandpa," Marci grinned.

At dusk, the fields came alive with lightning bugs. It started slowly, then the field exploded into as many twinkling lights as the Milky Way, or so it seemed.

The girls grabbed Mason jars and leaped off the porch, darting back and forth to capture the glowing insects. Before long, they came back with their little jars full of blinking bugs. Marci decided to be a queen and pulled the lights off the bottom of the bugs and stuck them on her forehead like a crown. They blinked on and off while she announced, "Look at me! I'm a beautiful queen."

"Marci, that's gross," I said.

Mom scolded me, "You should talk! You were the worst at their age."

Not to be outdone, Ella made two quick bug bracelets and decorated her T-shirt with blinking bug lights, screaming even louder, "Look at me too, I'm a beautiful fairy!"

As the evening air cooled off, a light dew settled on the grass and Mom brought out blankets to keep us warm. We talked and watched the silhouettes of the kids as they chased lightning bugs under the stars. Despite how much had changed and how much time had passed, so many things remained the same.

Closing my eyes, the evening breeze caressed my cheeks and I considered taking off my shoes to run barefoot in the fields. I could almost hear my sister Amy yelling at me to hurry up. My parents sat close together on the porch, holding hands and gently rocking. They watched the girls but remained silent, content as if my childhood were yesterday.

"Watching them run reminds me of Amy," I said.

"I remember," Mom added. "You were the one who always helped Amy catch her lightning bugs."

Marci yelled from the field as the evening deepened. "Grandpa, I have something for you." She stepped into the porch light with two Mason jars and handed one to dad. "This one's for you."

Dad stared at the jar for a long time, then unscrewed the cap and held the jar high in the cool night air.

"What are you doing?" Marci asked.

"Letting go," he said.

"Why?"

He pointed out to the fields. "Do you see all those blinking lights? It isn't fair to keep these little critters in a bottle. They're just circling around in the dark trying to find each other—trying to stay connected."

When the last lightning bug flew out of the jar, he sullenly headed toward the front door.

"What's wrong?" Mom asked.

He didn't answer. He went inside and the porch screen door closed quietly behind him.

Alone with Mom, I asked a question I had wanted to ask for years. "We talked many times about Korea. You always made sure I appreciated the history and culture of my birth parents. I don't recall that I ever asked *why* you adopted me? Ben was your biological baby. Why did you decide to adopt me instead of having another baby?"

She smiled. "I had a traumatic birth with Ben. They told me later the damage to my uterus was too great to have another pregnancy. We always wanted a large family, so after months of prayer and discussion, we decided to adopt. We went to Catholic Charities and they helped us apply. Three years later, our prayers were answered—with you."

She rose off her chair and knelt in front of my chair, wiping tears off her cheeks. "I'll never forget the day we picked you up in Seoul. You were the most beautiful baby I'd ever seen." After a moment, she laughed. "And then ten years later…whoops…surprise! I found out I was pregnant with Amy. She was a miracle."

I loved Mom's laugh. The sound of her joy filled my heart.

"Honey, we always encouraged you to find your parents."

I stopped her. "You *are* my parents."

"Thank you—but I mean your biological parents. You need to make a journey to Korea and fill the part of you that is missing. I understand your fears. We discussed this when you were in college. I'll give you the contact information to the adoption agency in the morning and they can connect you with the right agency in Korea."

Mom noticed how I shivered.

"What if I find out something terrible about my biological parents?"

"There's always that risk, but at least you'll know." She smiled. "Trust me, dear—it's time."

She leaned close to kiss me and then followed Dad into the house. I sat on the porch for a long time counting the many blessings in my life.

The next day, I checked my voicemail before we headed back. One was from St. Luke's, probably about how to transfer our student records to the public school. I hadn't told the girls they couldn't return because I was still holding out hope for a miracle.

I returned the call and Jerry, the principal, answered, "I have good news."

"What's that?"

"You don't have to move to the public school."

"What're you talking about?"

"An anonymous donor paid the tuition for next year."

"Do you mean for both Ella and Marci?"

"Yes. But before you ask, he wants to remain anonymous."

"That's so generous, I don't know what to say. But Jerry, really, I don't need charity."

"It's not charity, Tearza. It's a gift."

"But I didn't earn it."

"That's the definition of a gift, isn't it?"

"I'll have to get back to you."

Nobody knew about my situation but my parents—and Ryan. He had some nerve, if it was him! First, he bought the American Girl dolls, and now he was paying my daughters' tuition. I walked into the kitchen.

"Mom, did you discuss my situation with Dad?"

"Yes, why?"

"Did he pay for our tuition at St. Luke's?"

"No. We'd love to, but we couldn't do anything like that right now. Why do you ask?" she said.

"Never mind." Then I walked outside for better reception and called Ryan.

"Hi, Tearza," he said. "How's the trip?"

"I need a straight answer from you," I blurted out.

"Uh, sure, what do you want to know?"

"The truth."

"About what?"

"Did you pay for our tuition at St. Luke's?"

"No."

"Don't lie to me, Ryan. This is critical between us."

"I'd never lie to you. Besides, after the way you went after to me for buying those dolls—I may be slow, but I'm not dumb."

I was totally confused. There was no other "he" who knew about my predicament. Then I remembered Jake.

"Ryan, I'm sorry, but I have to go."

"After all that?"

"I think I made mistake."

"Oh, really?" he said sarcastically.

"Sorry, I'll get back to you."

I'm such a fool.

Fall

Chapter 1

Ryan

Summer was almost over, and school opened in two weeks. Gracie bounced up and down on the bed while Sara and I reviewed the school supplies she needed for their first day.

Sara yelled, "Gracie, stop it!"

Gracie stuck her tongue out and kept jumping. In fact, she started flapping her arms like a bird with each ascent. "Watch—I can almost touch the ceiling."

"Careful, I don't want you to fall off," I said.

Annoyed, Sara turned to the clothes laid out on her bed. "What do you think?" she asked me.

"They look fine to me. Cooper, what do you think?"

Cooper's head popped up from Sara's bed.

"Very funny," she said. Sara had lost her little girl face and grown three inches.

"Go ahead, try your clothes on," I said. The football game started in a few minutes and I was anxious to watch the kick-off, but Sara didn't move. She was just staring at me.

"What?" I asked.

"You need to leave for a second."

"Are you kidding? I've dressed you since you were a baby."

Sara put her hands on her hips and shared a look with Gracie.

I shook my head and said, "Okay, if it'll make you feel better. Come on, Cooper, the women need their space."

"Cooper can stay," Sara smirked.

I went into the hall alone to wait until called back. When I returned, Sara stood in the middle of the room, her skirt too short and sweater much too tight.

"I can see we have a problem." I said.

Sara nodded in agreement. "I've outgrown everything, and so has Gracie."

Gracie started to snicker. "She's just a baby."

Sara took two steps and kicked Gracie in the stomach. Gracie doubled over and screamed as she tried to catch her breath. "I hate you!"

"Serves you right!" Sara shouted. Before I could stop her, she pushed Gracie onto the floor. I grabbed her by the arm, but she yanked it away.

"What's wrong with you?" I said.

Sara started sobbing but managed to squeeze out, "Everything."

Gracie took a swing at Sara and missed.

"Okay, that's enough! Sara, move over to your bed right now. And Gracie, come over by me and sit down."

I looked at Sara. "Speak," I demanded.

Sara just shook her head. "Why? You don't care."

Confused, I asked, "Care about what?"

"Me." The tears streamed down her face. Then she pointed at Gracie. "Us."

"Of course I care about you two."

"No, you don't. You work all the time. You go to New York and leave us with babysitters who are mean to us. When you have free time, you spend it with the stupid woman Tiffany instead of us."

I looked at Gracie and she nodded agreement. Suddenly the sisters had a truce and I seemed to be the bad guy.

"Why didn't you tell me about the babysitters?"

"Why should I? If you cared, you wouldn't have fired Betty."

"I didn't fire Betty."

"Then why did she leave?"

I didn't have a good answer.

"See...?" She burst into tears again.

I sat down on the bed. Finally, I couldn't take it anymore. "Listen, I'll call Betty tomorrow. Maybe we can work something out."

"Really?" Sara stopped crying and sat up. "You'd do that?"

I wiped her face and gave her a hug. "I can't promise she'll come back, but I'll try."

"I'm sorry about what I said. I don't hate you, not really."

"I know, sweetie." I brushed the hair out of her eyes.

◆ ◆ ◆

The next day I invited Betty to lunch. She was reluctant, and it took all my lawyer skills just to convince her to meet. I had a big job ahead of me.

I arrived at the restaurant early and practiced a prepared speech. My hands were sweaty and cold. I looked at my watch. After twenty minutes, I began to think she had stood me up but finally she entered the restaurant and she gave me a polite hug.

"Thanks for meeting," I said.

She sat down, folded her hands tightly together and waited.

"How are the girls?" she finally asked.

I tried to smile. "Good."

Betty didn't say anything.

"The truth is, not really."

She didn't move or change her expression.

"They miss you dearly."

She sighed. "I miss them too."

I took a deep breath. "Would you ever consider coming back?"

"Ryan, I've been hard on you and I'm old enough to be your mother, but whether you like it or not, I need to tell you a few things. If you don't want to hear me out, then we can have a nice lunch and I'll leave." Her face softened slightly. "Your girls desperately need you. Sara had trouble in school last year and the girls fight over the smallest things. You have to make some big changes soon or you'll regret this for the rest of your life."

She stared at me, waiting to see if any of this was sinking in.

"I'm sorry. I want to be a good dad, but I really like being a lawyer too. I feel pulled in ten directions at once most of the time. When I'm at work, I feel guilty that I'm not at home with the girls. But when I'm with the girls, I constantly think about all the things I should be doing at work."

"Has anything changed with your work?" she asked.

"Nothing really. I'm hoping I get promoted at my annual review next month. Most of the partners like me, but a few are concerned about my family situation. They want to know if I'm committed to the firm. You know—being a single dad and all."

"And are you—" she paused, "—committed?"

I hesitated. "I really don't know anymore."

Betty didn't say anything for a moment but fingered her car keychain with a picture of her family on it. "That's the first honest thing I've ever heard you say about your job. Maybe that's a start." Slowly she looked up. "Ryan, are you happy?"

My cell phone chirped. The screen said it was one of my biggest clients and I debated whether to answer it. Betty's eyes narrowed as she watched me read the screen.

Squirming, I set the phone on the table. "Betty, I'm *so close*! My firm's giving me bigger and bigger cases. Everything will be better once I make partner, I think. No more financial pressure. And I'll have more control over my work schedule."

"You didn't answer my question."

"I love being a lawyer."

"I'm sure you're a good lawyer, unfortunately you have a small window to get this right or you'll ruin everything."

"It's not that bad."

"I'm pretty sure it is."

This time my phone vibrated—an email message. "Sorry," I said, then put the phone in my pocket.

"Being sorry doesn't help."

"I'll change. I promise. The girls really miss you and they need you." I pressed my hands on the table. "And I need you. Please, one more chance?"

There was a long pause until finally Betty threw her hands up in the air. "I may regret this—let's start with your work schedule and we can go from there. I do have a few conditions."

"Sounds like blackmail."

She almost laughed. "Last spring, Sara was interested in playing fall soccer. I suggest you sign her up and attend her games. Better yet, you could coach her team. Sara would love that."

"Anything else?"

"Gracie."

"What about Gracie?"

"She loves to dance. "Sign her up for dance class. They meet every Saturday morning."

"No problem. I can arrange to have someone take her."

"No, my second condition is that you take her."

"And sit with all the other moms?"

She thought for a moment, then said, "Your penance." Her lips may have curled upward just a bit.

"Is that it?"

"For now."

Begrudgingly, I nodded. *She's one tough cookie,* I thought.

Over lunch, I brought her up to speed on the girls. Betty agreed to start on Monday, and I couldn't wait to get home to tell the girls. Finally, some good things were happening again.

The next morning, I had a difficult conversation with my boss Andy, made even harder by the way he began. "You've been a real machine over the last several months, Ryan, and the firm really appreciates it."

"That's great." I cleared my throat. "But right now, I really need to take some time off."

"We're really swamped, you know that. A vacation's not a good idea right now."

"No, not a vacation. Fact is, I need to spend more time with my daughters. I'd like to coach Sara's soccer team."

Andy stared at me and then looked at the calendar.

"We go to trial on the Anderson case in four weeks. That's your big opportunity."

"I know, but I can work at home at night."

"Ryan…" He stalled. "I just don't know."

"The girls are having problems and really need me right now."

Andy got up from his chair and put one arm around my shoulder.

"You know how fond I am of you, and how much I care about your girls."

I nodded, waiting for him to finish.

"This will not go well with some of the partners—I'm sure you know that. Everyone is sympathetic about your situation these past two years, but we have a business to run. Every time you've missed work, the other guys had to pick up the load. Most understand, but some are starting to grumble."

"Like Jamison? He doesn't have kids." I started to go on, but Andy waved me off.

"Don't worry. I'll run interference with Jamison." He looked me in the eye. "You're a damn fine young lawyer. One of our best."

"Thanks."

"Give me a couple of days. I think I can smooth things over to make coaching happen." Andy winked. "We have big plans for you." He patted me on the back and walked me to the door.

Relieved, I rushed back to my office and made a list of all the things I needed to do. First, continue my arrangement with the evening babysitter so Betty could leave at a regular time. Second, sign Sara up for soccer and offer to coach. Third, buy a soccer ball— and last, trade my precious BMW for a large Suburban, an official team car.

A week later, I honked as I drove into the driveway with my new Suburban. Surprised, Betty whistled as she walked out of the house holding hands with Gracie.

I stood outside the car. "So, what do you think?"

They both circled the vehicle.

"What happened? You loved that BMW," Betty said.

"It's the *new* me."

I ran my hand across the hood. "Zero to sixty in fifteen seconds flat. Only slightly different than my Beamer."

"Hah." Betty laughed. "Niiiice."

Gracie jumped into the backseat and started pushing buttons. "Does it have a DVD player?"

"Yeah, hang on. I'll show you in a minute."

Betty hopped into the front seat and tapped my hand. "I'm proud of you. Come on, Andretti, let's go for a ride."

◆ ◆ ◆

After agreeing to coach, I hung up the phone with the soccer director and wondered if I'd made a big mistake. I had never coached a youth team, much less a team of young girls. Armed with a briefcase full of soccer drills, I woke up in the middle of the night sweating over the first practice. I couldn't sleep, so I sharpened pencils, revised the practice schedule twice and prayed that nobody would ask me questions about soccer strategy.

At the field, we got out of the Suburban and I couldn't find my whistle. I frantically looked on the floor and under the seats.

Sara asked, "What are you looking for?"

"My whistle."

"You mean that silver thing hanging from your neck?"

I reached down and felt the chain.

She rolled her eyes. "Dad, relax—you worry too much."

As we walked toward the practice field, Sara reminded me, "Make sure you turn off your cell phone. It's embarrassing, because it goes off all the time."

Not trusting myself to leave it turned off, I ran it back to the car and put it into the glove compartment. When I returned, I was surprised to see Marci and Tearza standing with a small group of parents at our designated field. Sara and Marci hugged and then ran over to the other girls, leaving me alone with Tearza. At first, we didn't look at each other, just watched the other parents and kids running on the field.

Finally, Tearza broke the silence. "This is a surprise."

"What are the odds?" I said.

"Yeah," she repeated, "what are the odds?"

An errant soccer ball rolled up to Tearza and she kicked it back.

"Pretty good kick. Maybe we should sign you up."

"I don't think so. By the way, have you seen our coach yet?"

A woman suddenly grabbed my arm and interrupted us.

"I noticed your whistle," the woman said. "Are you the coach? I wanted to make sure we're on the correct field."

"Yes, I am." I shot a glance at Tearza. "We'll get started in a few minutes. We're waiting until everyone has arrived."

The woman smiled and walked away. Tearza cocked her right eyebrow up and said, "So, I guess this means that I must be nice to you."

"We all have our crosses to bear."

"Some are heavier than others," she said under her breath.

"What's wrong? Are you upset with me?"

A mom waved at Tearza, trying to get her attention from a short distance away. She waved back and said, "Excuse me for a second. I need to say hello to a friend."

The first practice reminded me of my first case as a rookie attorney. I blew my whistle to start the practice, silently hoping that I could bluff long enough to gain some experience and not look like a total fool. Over the next two weeks, we lost the first four games, and I was worried. Our last defeat was a blowout and the parents had started to grumble. On the way home, I asked Sara, "Are you having fun?"

"Sure."

"Are the other girls?"

"It's not your fault we haven't won yet."

"Tell that to the parents."

Sara shook her head. "Don't listen to them. They're just being adults."

The next game was an even worse defeat than the last one. I had a team meeting with the girls to cheer them up. Afterward, I started to collect the balls and other equipment when a dad approached me. He was built like a former linebacker and not smiling.

"I'm Jill's dad," he began. "Why isn't she playing more? She's the best player you have and we're getting killed out there."

"I have to play everyone. At this age, it's supposed to be a participation league."

"Are you kidding? Look at the other teams. They don't do that. They want to win."

"So do I."

"Yeah, I noticed your daughter plays a lot." He scowled, pulled a toothpick out of his mouth and threw it on the ground. "Look, Mac..."

"It's Ryan."

"Have you ever played soccer before?" He glared and took another step toward me. "Have you played any sports before?"

At that point, another dad stepped between us. He was five inches taller than both of us and put his hand on the man's shoulder.

"Give him a break—he's doing the best he can. Our girls aren't very good, that's the reality."

"But he should—"

The big man leaned over him with a menacing smile. "Give it a rest, okay?"

The man fumed for a second then walked away in a huff.

"Sorry about that. He's a nut. I've been on another team with him and he drives everyone crazy."

"Thanks. I thought for a second he wanted to fight."

"He's all talk. You'll get used to it." He held out his hand. "By the way, I'm Jason, Molly's dad."

"Nice to meet you. Molly's quite the athlete."

"Listen, Molly thinks you're the greatest."

Jason helped me gather up the rest of the soccer equipment. "I don't want you to take this wrong, but would you like a little assistance with the coaching? These girls can be quite a handful all alone."

"That would be awesome. To be honest, I don't know what I'm doing."

He gave me a big grin. "I hadn't noticed. I played a little soccer in college, so I could give you some ideas." We agreed to get together in a few days.

Tearza and I rounded up the girls and walked off the soccer field together. We chatted about soccer, homework, dance lessons, and our predicament with over-scheduled girls. We commiserated about how difficult it was to get the girls to all their events, especially when their schedules conflicted.

"I have an idea," I said as we got to the parking lot. "I'm at every practice and game anyway. Maybe we should carpool again."

"What about your work schedule? We had trouble during the baseball season."

"Yeah, I know, but I cleared it with my managing partner so I shouldn't have problems like that."

◆ ◆ ◆

The next day, I confronted the issue of new clothes for the girls. Although I dreaded the idea of shopping, last year was pretty easy. Back then, of course, Sara and Gracie had been young enough that they didn't care much what we bought. This year, I expected everything would be different.

"I have an idea," Sara said. "I talked to Marci this morning and they're shopping for school clothes this afternoon. Maybe we should ask her mom if we could go with them."

I was still feeling bummed out by Tearza's coolness to me. "She's probably too busy," I suggested.

"That's so dumb." She rolled her eyes in a way reserved for women who are completely exasperated with men. So, I called Tearza.

She picked up and I said, "It's me."

"Hi, me. How are you?"

"Good." At first, I thought we had been cut-off, but then I heard noise in the background. "Are you still there?"

"Yes."

Out of desperation, I blurted out, "How was your trip to the farm?"

"Exactly what I needed. And how was your trip to the lake?"

"The same," I said, expecting her to say something—anything. The silence on the other end was killing me. She probably understood my guilty feelings and was determined to make me suffer.

"I have a favor to ask."

"Anything—you know we are here for you," she said sarcastically. "The same way you are there for us." Bullseye.

"Tearza, you have to let me explain."

"I do?"

Sara was standing next to me, listening with a perplexed look on her face.

"Please, can we talk about this later?"

She didn't answer right away, but finally she said, "Why did you call, Ryan?"

"Sara mentioned you might take the girls shopping for school clothes today. Is there any chance we could tag along? For some reason, Sara doesn't trust her father's taste in girl's fashions."

"No problem. We can talk then. Would it work for you to pick us up in an hour or so?"

At two o'clock, I walked up to Tearza's house. She opened the door and I greeted her with, "Madame, your limo's here for your shopping spree. Where will it be today—Rodeo Drive?"

"I was there yesterday. Macy's will be fine, thank you." She wore just a hint of a smile. "How was the trip to your parents' cabin?"

"Perfect. The girls spent so much time in the water they sprouted gills."

Tearza looked behind me. "Where are the girls?"

I pointed to the Suburban and Sara waved from the window. Tearza rounded up Ella and Marci and we drove to the mall.

"The girls really missed Marci and Ella while you were gone," I said.

Tearza turned around and glanced in the backseat. The girls were watching a movie with headsets. Satisfied that they couldn't hear her, she settled back into the front seat. "I'm really sorry about—well, you know—the last time at my house." She twisted a long strand of hair with her right hand. "I had no right to be upset with you. It's your life."

"Let me explain."

"No need—it's none of my business."

"Tearza, look at me."

She shook her head.

"Please, I need to see your eyes."

She quickly wiped away a tear. "I had just had a really bad day and…well, let's say it was a surprise."

"It's not the way it looks with Tiffany."

"Oh really? What am I supposed to think?"

"Not what you're thinking." I tried to think of a way to explain. "Meeting Tiffany at the mall was a coincidence. She wanted to talk about a case, and I couldn't figure out a way to excuse myself without acting rude. She's quite a talker and our discussion lasted longer than I thought it would. Please understand—we're not in a relationship."

"What do you call it then?"

I was surprised at the limits of my vocabulary.

Tearza pressed on. "What kind of relationship does Tiffany think she has with you?"

"She's a big girl."

"I'm not so sure."

We turned off the freeway and approached the mall. I decided to turn the tables. "You never explained your bad day."

"I was upset about losing my job and I took it out on you. Don't forget—I was raised in an Irish family."

"I hadn't noticed."

She smiled for the first time since we went sideways. "Liar. Forgive me, OK?"

"Deal." It was as if the dark cloud that had been hanging over us had disappeared. "How's the job search?"

"Not good."

"Don't worry. The perfect job will materialize."

"It better hurry or I'm in trouble."

The girl's department was busy with mothers and daughters doing the same thing we were. I walked with Tearza until she suggested I wait in a chair by the dressing rooms. I must have dozed off for a moment because suddenly all four girls marched past me with stacks of clothes.

"You have to be patient, but I think we selected some great stuff," Tearza announced triumphantly.

It had already been more than an hour and they hadn't yet tried on one piece of clothing.

Loud laughter came from the dressing rooms as the girls changed. It felt good to hear them laugh again and have fun.

Finally, Tearza peeked out and said, "Get ready. We have a big fashion show for you."

I clapped. "Bring it on!"

Gracie came out first in a cute little jumper. I motioned for her to come over for a hug. Next, Sara stepped out and I was stunned. What had happened to my little girl? A few minutes ago, she had entered the dressing room goofing around with Gracie, but she emerged as somebody else. She smiled shyly as if she knew something had changed.

Ella was next. She blushed as she twirled and held her arms out like a little princess. Finally, it was Marci's turn. When she emerged from the dressing room, she had transformed just as Sara had. I was shocked at how our babies were growing up.

Tearza beamed. "They look pretty good, don't they?"

"I hardly know what to say."

Tearza walked over and put her arm around Sara. "We still have a few more clothes to try on, but then we'll be right out."

While Tearza was in the dressing room, I asked the clerk about a pretty outfit on a mannequin I had seen Tearza admiring.

"Did she say she liked it?" I asked.

"She did, but she said she'd have to pass on it for now."

"If you have it in her size, would you ask her to try it on for me?"

She winked. "Wonderful idea."

The clerk guessed Tearza's size and brought the outfit to the dressing room. I could hear Tearza putting up a fuss and the girls begging her to try it on. Finally, the clerk came out and gave me the thumbs up.

The girls bounded out of the dressing room to watch Tearza model the outfit. Gracie jumped on my lap and gave me a big hug.

"Thanks, Dad, this has been great."

"You're welcome, honey. You looked beautiful."

The dressing room door slowly opened and Tearza stepped out in a soft black turtleneck, camel-colored skirt and black boots. Her black hair was slightly tussled from pulling on the sweater and her cheeks were flushed from the heat of the dressing room. No one said a word as we all stared at her.

Tearza looked embarrassed. "Well, how do I look?"

Not trusting my voice, I took a sip of water from a cup on the table and choked.

"You're beautiful!" Sara yelled out.

Tearza blushed even more.

"Thanks," I said, "we'll take it." I handed over my credit card. "I'll pay for it."

"No," Tearza said.

"This is the least I can do. Please—let me do this?"

For a second, I thought she'd refuse again, but then she nodded and returned to the dressing room to help the girls.

When got to the parking lot, I stopped Tearza and said, "Thanks again for helping us."

"My pleasure, really."

"The girls had a lot of fun, but I felt like a third wheel."

"Why?"

"Watching you with the girls. Each year I realize they need me a little less."

"That's not true."

The girls ran thirty yards ahead to the car.

"Thank God I have Sara and Gracie," I said, watching them laugh. "I'd be lost without them."

Tearza set her bags on the ground. "Listen, there's one other thing I need to discuss." She paused. "I'm sorry I accused you of paying for the girls' tuition when I was at the farm."

"Don't worry about that."

"It never occurred to me that Jake might have paid the tuition."

"I've already forgotten it." I opened the rear door to load the bags into the back and waved. "Let's go, girls."

On the drive home, while approaching a major intersection, Gracie suddenly yelled, "Stop the car!"

I slammed on the brakes. Everyone lurched forward and Tearza spilled a soft drink on her pants. I looked in all directions but didn't see anything. I turned around and looked at Gracie for an explanation.

She sat in the backseat behind Tearza waving at someone. A homeless man with a cardboard sign approached us. Tearza looked at me with concern. As he got closer to the Suburban, I reluctantly lowered Tearza's window.

The man's clothes were soiled and hung loosely on his thin body. His hair was matted from sleeping on the ground. He leaned his head near the open window and turned toward Gracie.

Boldly, Gracie asked, "What does your sign say? I can't read your handwriting."

"I work for food," he answered quietly.

Gracie looked at him perplexed. "What kind of work do you do?"

This launched a litany of questions about the man's life and family. Finally, she stopped, and an awkward silence filled the Suburban until she yelled, "Daaad."

I knew what she wanted, so I dug into my pocket, pulled out a ten-dollar bill and handed it to the man. Cars honked impatiently behind us.

"Sorry, we have to go," I said.

"God bless you sir." Then he smiled at Gracie. "Wait a second," he said to her, "I want to give you something." He reached into his dirty pants pocket and pulled out a shiny penny. "Young lady, this is my lucky penny. I want you to have it. Someday, when you need some luck, hold the penny next to your heart and make a wish."

He slowly backed away and we left him standing there holding his sign up for the next car.

"Wasn't he the nicest man?" Gracie said to no one in particular.

We drove along in silence.

"Gracie, you did a wonderful thing back there." I silently wished I could see the world as she did.

Gracie spoke softly. "He doesn't have anyone."

Sara asked, "He doesn't have what?"

In a sad voice, Gracie said, "I think he's all alone. I just don't understand it."

"Understand what?" Sara asked.

"Why people who love each other leave and go away," She reached for her blue blankie and rubbed the soft satin along her face.

Chapter 2

Tearza

The transition from summer to school were always the worst. The girls didn't want to go to bed at a decent time, hated their homework, and despised getting up early to catch the bus. The only activity that Marci enjoyed was playing soccer on Ryan's team. They had a terrible team, but Marci didn't care as long as she was with Sara, her best friend.

Thank goodness, the girls finally won their first soccer game. They were ecstatic. They hugged, squirted water at each other, and high-fived for at least ten minutes. Marci and Ella wanted to celebrate by getting homemade custard ice cream with Sara and Gracie, so I asked Ryan if he wanted to join us.

"I don't know," he said. "I haven't been back to that shop since the last time we met you there. It'd be like returning to the scene of the crime."

"I don't think you were convicted—just accused."

"Should I retain someone to represent me?"

I smiled and crossed my arms. "Only if you have something to hide. However, I do have the power to make pardons in exceptional cases."

"Okay, I give up."

The girls grabbed our hands so we would stop talking and we packed into the Suburban to get ice cream.

After numerous tastes, the girls finally selected their favorites and sat on a picnic table near us. Even though Ryan and I had spent more time together over the last couple of weeks, this was the first chance we'd had to talk at length alone. I felt uncomfortable when he asked about my husband, and he was hesitant to discuss his divorce, but I suppose he had his reasons.

"How does Marci like soccer so far?" he asked.

"She loves it."

"What about you?"

I laughed. "I'm a soccer mom in training. At times, I feel overwhelmed with all the responsibilities of a single parent. I'm learning how to be a sports trainer, accountant, nurse, financial planner, and—"

Ryan stopped me and pointed a thumb at himself. "Me too! I'm trying to learn how to cook, braid hair, and clean the bathrooms." He laughed and took off his glasses.

We both stopped talking at the same time. His eyes made me catch my breath. They were stunning, a deep ocean blue. Everything went into slow motion and the sound around us stopped. For some reason, articulating all the new things we shared as single parents made me realize how far I'd come since I had lost Jim.

I asked, "It's hard, isn't it?"

"What?"

"You know—everything."

He stopped eating his ice cream. "With the girls?"

"Especially the girls. I doubt everything I do. I never dreamed that I'd have to do this alone."

He nodded.

"Whoops, you dripped," I said.

He looked down at his shirt as I dunked a napkin in my water glass and dabbed at the spill. "Pre-spot this stain before you throw it in the wash."

"Pre-spot?" he asked.

"Don't tell me you've never pre-spotted your clothes."

"I thought that you didn't have to do that with Tide."

"Oh, boy." I rolled my eyes.

"Hey, you don't have to rub it in—we barely know each other."

We both laughed and I appreciated how good it felt to talk to another adult, to enjoy a real conversation, instead of having discussions about Barbie dolls or unicorns.

Ella grinned at me with a chocolate ring from her chin to her nose. Ryan had to leave for a meeting, so we finished our ice cream and left together.

Back home, Marci said she had an assignment due through the internet via Ed-Line. She knew how to go online without my help. I was such an idiot when it came to computers. The girls scattered to start their homework and I had just sorted dirty soccer uniforms when the phone rang—my daily call from Mom to check on us and deliver the latest news from the farm.

Mom's voice sounded odd, so I asked, "Is something bothering you?"

"No, why?" she mumbled.

"Come on."

"I called to see how you're doing. You seemed so quiet the last couple of times we've talked."

"The girls are fine. Don't worry about them."

"It's not the girls."

I sighed. "Mom, you're a world-class worrier. Between you and Grandmother, you've bought enough prayer candles to light the moon."

There was a long silence.

"Honey, you don't sound happy. I'd feel so much better if I could see your face," she said.

"I'm hoping we can make it home for Thanksgiving."

"What have you been doing lately?" Mom asked.

"The usual—hauling kids from one event to another."

"You should get out more, maybe start dating. I hate the thought of you sitting alone night after night. You're way too young for that."

"We've gone over this, Mom."

"I know, but I can't help it. It's been—"

"Stop it," I cut her off and an angry silence filled space. "I'm sorry, but I have to go and get the girls ready for bed."

"Don't be mad at me."

Marci yelled from her bedroom. "Something's wrong with the computer! I can't get Ed-Line to open up."

"Hang on, I'll be right there," I yelled back. "Sorry Mom, I have to go."

"Tearza, I love you."

"Love you too—I'll call tomorrow."

I sat down at Marci's computer but Ed-Line didn't open for me either. I exhausted the few ideas I had, but nothing worked. The more I tried, the more agitated Marci became. She was a good student, and her schoolwork was important to her.

Finally, Marci exploded. "Mom, this is important! I have to turn this in by tomorrow."

"I'm trying—I just don't know what to do and the school's closed."

"Dad would know what to do. He always knew how to fix my problems."

"I'm not your dad!" I shouted.

Marci was furious with the computer and me, and I was behaving like a schoolgirl instead of a mom.

"Marci, I'm sorry," I said. "I'll call Ryan. I'm sure he knows how to log on for Sara and Gracie."

Her eyes got wide. "No!"

"Why not?"

She turned away. "You wouldn't understand," she said, stomping out of the bedroom and slamming the door.

Damn these dumb computers. Damn the temper she inherited from me. I finally gave up on the computer and put the girls to bed. It was late, but I couldn't sleep, so I got out of bed and peeked into the girls' bedroom. Ella was sleeping on her back with her hands behind her head as if she were looking up at the sky on a beautiful day. Next to her, Marci was curled up in a ball and hugging pillow.

They're so beautiful, I thought.

Dozens of family photographs covered the walls of our hallway—our "hall of fame." Next to the girls' bedroom was a photo of Jim and me taken outside on the night before he died. Marci had taken the photo before we had left for a sunset walk. I remembered how we walked arm-in-arm around the lake oblivious to the next day. We had struggled over the past few months of our marriage, but I thought we had all the time in the world.

CHAPTER 3
RYAN

The first few weeks of school were hectic, but gradually we settled into a routine. I tried hard to be home for supper so I could be with the girls and catch up on their day. Normally, I couldn't get a word in edgewise with Gracie at dinnertime. She liked to hold center stage—but not tonight. She seemed unusually subdued. I glanced at Sara who noticed the same thing.

"Gracie, honey, are you feeling okay?" I asked.

She shrugged her shoulders and pushed her peas around the plate. By the end of dinner, her forehead was soaked in sweat and her cheeks were flushed. She hadn't smiled or said a word since sitting down. I knew she had a fever, so I carried her to bed and put towels on the floor along with a cake pan and a wet washcloth. I surveyed the bedroom one last time and geared up for a long night. My bedroom was next door so I could hear if anything got worse.

What a great time for Betty and Susan to be out of town, I thought.

A few hours later, the sound of crying woke me up. I thought it was Gracie until I recognized Sara's voice. They were both sick.

As I stood up, my bedroom started spinning. I sat down, teetering on the edge of the bed. "You've got to be kidding me," I said out loud.

Thank goodness the bathroom was only ten steps away. I barely made it before throwing up. I washed my face and hurried back to the girls' room because they were both groaning. Gracie had already thrown up in her bed, so I wrapped her in a comforter and I changed the sheets. Sara was shivering in her bed and begging for more blankets.

This was big trouble. I weighed my options because I knew couldn't keep this up all night. I thought of Tearza, but I didn't feel comfortable calling her in the middle of the night.

I tried rocking Gracie to sleep, but she threw up all over both of us. Desperate and feeling I was out of choices, I called Tearza. She answered the phone with that same worried voice we all have when you receive an unexpected call at two in the morning.

"I'm in trouble," I said.

"What's wrong?" Tearza asked. "You sound terrible."

"We're all sick with the flu. I can't take care of the girls by myself." Before I could explain, she stopped me.

"Say no more. I'll be right over. Let me pack up Ella and Marci. We'll be there in fifteen minutes."

Tearza came into the house like a general summoned to the front. She put Ella and Marci in the spare bedroom, then turned her attention to Sara and Gracie. She quickly changed their wet pajamas, stroked Sara's sweat-soaked hair and then rocked Gracie to sleep in a big blanket. Both girls melted into her arms.

Finally, Tearza turned her attention to me. "How do you feel?"

The room was starting to spin again. "Fine," I lied.

"You're sweating like you're in a sauna," she said.

"Sorry I haven't been much help."

"I'm putting you to bed."

She held my arm and steered me to my bedroom. I protested, but she ignored me and got me into bed. Drifting off to sleep, I vaguely felt a cool washcloth on my forehead, and in my delirium thought I was kissed on the cheek, the kind of kiss my mother gave me when I was sick.

♦ ♦ ♦

Dazed and confused, I looked at the clock—nine o'clock. Weakly, I climbed out of bed and walked into the girls' room. It was empty and their beds were made. I tried to focus for a second until I heard Gracie's familiar laugh down the hall. I found all four girls in the kitchen eating breakfast while Tearza did the dishes. She turned her head when she heard me and smiled. "Girls, look who the cat dragged in."

They giggled as I shuffled to the kitchen table.

Tearza said, "Gracie was so worried about you she wanted to give you her blanket."

Still foggy, I sat down and rubbed my head. "What happened?"

Tearza described the rest of the night. "I wasn't too worried because my girls had the same thing last week. Sara and Gracie woke up the next morning feeling fine."

As she talked and rinsed the last of the dishes, the morning sun made her glow like an angel.

She caught me staring at her. "What's wrong? Do I look funny with these yellow latex gloves on?"

"You look fine. Thanks for saving us last night."

While the girls ate their breakfast, they worked on a puzzle in the middle of the table. Tearza walked over and started to braid Sara's hair. Suddenly, she whispered in Gracie's ear and pointed to a puzzle piece. She grinned, quickly grabbed the piece, and put it in the right spot.

It seemed so natural to have Tearza in my kitchen—almost as if she'd always been there.

For a moment, I let myself pretend that I would wake up to this every morning. I probably still had a fever.

Chapter 4

Tearza

In an odd way, I looked forward to school starting again. For most people, January was the beginning of the New Year. But for me, it was always September. While growing up, the new school year presented me with a fresh start for everything—new clothes, new shoes, new backpack, and the anticipation of what the coming year would bring.

Thankfully the first few weeks of school were uneventful. Everyone seemed to adjust to the new schedule except Marci. It was a daily battle to rouse that grumpy sleepyhead from bed every morning.

Jake had been away on vacation since school had started. When he returned, I confronted him about the tuition. Not surprisingly, he pretended that he didn't know anything about an anonymous donor and refused to discuss it. Every time I tried to bring it up, he'd change the subject or simply walk away until I finally gave up. In the meantime, I focused on finding a job with no luck, but I filled in at the flower shop whenever someone was sick or on vacation.

I was busy making an after-school snack when the school bus rumbled by the house. I watched the girls wave goodbye to the driver and run up the driveway. Their backpacks landed in a heap on the kitchen table, and Marci handed me a form for joining the Junior Girl Scouts.

"That's great," I said. "I was a Girl Scout at your age."

"There's only one problem," Marci explained. "We want Sara and Gracie to join too, but they don't think their dad will let them."

"Why not?"

"You know—he's really busy."

"Would you like me to talk to him?"

They both said yes at the same time, so I called Ryan.

"I know they'd love to join," Ryan said, but his voice sounded odd.

"Is there a problem?"

"Well—what would I have to do?"

"Nothing at all. I can drive them."

"Okay," he said, "but under one condition. You let me make dinner for everyone on the night of the first meeting."

◆ ◆ ◆

Two weeks later, after our first scout meeting, I pulled into Ryan's driveway and adjusted the mirror to check my appearance.

"Come on Mom," Marci said. "You look fine. You've been looking in the mirror now for five minutes."

"I have not!" I finished touching up my lipstick. "Okay, let's go."

Ryan had made spaghetti and garlic cheese bread, my girls' favorite meal. After we ate, I complimented him on his cooking. He blushed and said, "I owe everything to Sara."

Sara wrapped her arms around his neck and squeezed. Then she said, "Spaghetti's one of the few things he knows how to make. Trust me, he's a horrible cook. We never let him in the kitchen except to set the table and wash the dishes."

Pretending to pout, he said, "Unfortunately, it's all true."

After dinner, Ryan walked us to the car and I drove away feeling different—but not sure why.

A storm had rolled in while we ate dinner, and the rain poured down on us during the drive home. Straining to see, I adjusted my windshield wipers to full speed and thought about the dinner.

From the backseat, Marci asked, "Mom, what do you think of Ryan?"

"What do you mean?"

Ella giggled and poked at Marci, who said in a flat voice, "We saw you staring at him during dinner."

"I wasn't staring at him," I said. "You're imagining things."

"You don't look at other men that way," Marci insisted.

Marci hadn't spoken about Ryan like this before. I wasn't sure how to answer.

"Well, he's good to Gracie and Sara. I like his quick laugh. I believe he's a kind, good father. What do *you* think of him?"

In the mirror, I watched the two of them look at each other. Finally, Ella said, "Mom, you act different around him. You laugh—like at dinner."

"Marci, what about you?"

Before she could answer, the car abruptly filled with blue and white flashing lights. A police car was pulling me over.

Panicking, I tried to remember what I was supposed to do when stopped by the police. As a person of color, I was terrified by any encounter with law enforcement. I sat perfectly still and put my hands on the wheel where the officer could see them. I looked in the rearview mirror. The officer wasn't coming yet, so I reached across the seat to pull my driver's license from my purse.

A loud rap on the window startled me. "Slowly pull your hands out of the purse and place them on the steering wheel," a stern voice instructed. The officer held a flashlight in his left hand and had his right hand on his holster.

Ella shrieked.

"Open your window and hand me your driver's license," he commanded.

My hands shook so badly I dropped the license twice.

"Relax, ma'am." He shined his flashlight around in the car. Ella and Marci were terrified.

The officer pointed the light on the girls and smiled. "Don't be afraid, girls. I need to talk to your mom for a minute."

He looked at my license and frowned. "Where do you live?"

"Around the corner. Why?"

He looked at the address on the license. "Are we going to have a problem?"

"Of course not. Why?'

"Let's try this one more time."

I hit my hand on my forehead. "My address is 840 Rainbow Lane. I moved recently and haven't had time to change the address on my license."

"Believe me, the last thing I wanted to do was to pull you over and get out in this rain, but you passed me on the freeway."

"You're kidding! I didn't see you. I must've been distracted."

"With what?"

"Talking to the girls."

The police officer looked at the girls. "About what?"

"Mommy's boyfriend," Ella blurted out.

Marci corrected her. "He's not her boyfriend."

"Uh-huh," Ella insisted.

The rainwater dripped off the brim of the officer's hat as he leaned a little closer to the window.

"Which is it?" he asked.

I didn't answer.

"Distracted, huh?" He folded his notepad and tapped his flashlight in his hand for a second. "Tell you what. I've decided to let you off this time with a warning, but you better get this boyfriend thing figured out before someone gets hurt." He might have smiled a bit before walking away.

The girls didn't say a word, and I couldn't stop shaking until we got home. The news in Chicago was full of beatings and arrests gone awry with people of color. At the same time, there wasn't enough coverage of courageous actions by policemen and women who put their lives on the line every day.

Too agitated to sleep, I went into the kitchen to make a hot, lemon-honey drink. It had stopped raining, so I took it outside on the porch. Everything outdoors seemed as unsettled as I was. Our prevailing winds came out of the west to northwest, but tonight the wind was coming from the east. That didn't happen very often, but when it did, it always meant that change was coming.

Chapter 5

Ryan

For a few minutes, I leaned against a backyard oak breathing in the rich smell of fall. Swirling in the October wind, the leaves were turning the lawn into a tapestry of red and gold. I loved this time of year. It always made me quicken my pace, thinking of all the things I needed to accomplish before fall turned into winter.

The temperatures had climbed back into the seventies for a few days. I hurried to winterize the house because this was probably our last reprieve before we said goodbye to warm weather for many months. I finished blowing out the sprinkler lines and putting away the last of the garden hoses. Tomorrow, I planned to take the girls to Petersen's to pick out the perfect Halloween pumpkins.

Marci, Ella, and Tearza joined us on our trip to the pumpkin patch. It was a picture-perfect day—blue sky, warm sun, no wind. On the drive, Tearza and I agreed the girls could pick any pumpkin they wanted so long as they could carry it to the car.

The car had barely stopped rolling before the doors flew open and the girls disappeared into the long fields. While they searched for special pumpkins, Tearza and I followed behind and she described how they used to grow their own pumpkins on her farm.

Suddenly, Tearza stopped and grabbed my left hand. "What's this? I didn't notice your bandage in the Suburban."

"Nothing." I tried to pull my hand away.

She held on and examined my left thumb. "Did you cut yourself?"

"Maybe."

"How did you do that?"

"Last week I was watching a cooking show with Sara. The cook had this cool metal thing she used to slice potatoes and veggies."

Her eyes got wide. "You mean a mandolin?"

"Violin, mandolin, something like that."

Tearza laughed—such a beautiful sound, the way a child giggles uncontrollably over nothing but for the pure joy of it. I loved her laugh.

"Stop." I put my hand up. "Sara talked me into buying one. How would I know they were dangerous? I ended up in the ER for two hours. Damn near sliced my thumb off."

"I'll have to talk to Sara. No running with sharp scissors or sticks for you."

Our conversation drifted to school and I admitted how nervous I was about the upcoming school conferences. "Everything's different when you're a single parent, don't you think?" I slid my good hand into my pocket. "I'm never sure about the girls."

"Me neither," Tearza said.

"I'm not much of a mother," I confessed.

Tearza stopped and faced me. "And I'm not much of a dad." Then she reached up and pulled at the collar of my jacket that was half-rolled under. Her black eyes swallowed me. "We're quite the pair, aren't we?" she said.

"What if I'm wrecking—"

"Don't." She put her finger to my lips. "You're a great dad."

"Hmmm."

"Look." She reached down and picked up a small pumpkin hiding under some vines. "Perfect." She smiled and handed it to me.

I spotted the girls in the distance. "We'd better catch up."

"Thanks. By the way, how's work these days?" she asked.

"I'm working almost full-time on the Benderson account."

"That's good, isn't it?"

I nodded.

"They're your firm's biggest client. Isn't that what you wanted?"

"I always thought so."

"What do you mean?"

"Nothing."

Gracie yelled and waved at us. Apparently, she had found her pumpkin.

"I'm being paged," I said, grateful for an excuse to change the subject. We hurried over to Gracie.

"Great job," I said. "This one's a beauty."

She beamed.

"But can you carry it? Remember, that's the deal."

Her smile disappeared. "I don't know—it's heavy," she said.

Gracie bent down, gritted her teeth and made a herculean effort to lift the giant pumpkin. Unfortunately, the pumpkin didn't move an inch. Sara came running over and tapped Gracie on the shoulder. "Wow, this is perfect."

Gracie was almost in tears. "It doesn't matter. I can't carry it."

Sara frowned at me. "Come on. The two of us can lift it and carry it to the car."

"Dad won't let us."

Sara put her hands on her hips and stepped toward me. "You said we could buy any pumpkin as long as we could carry it to the car, right?"

"Yes, but—"

Sara interjected, "You didn't say we had to carry it alone—you said we had to carry it to the car by ourselves."

By now Marci and Ella had joined us. All four girls stared at me waiting for an answer.

"Oh, I see what's happening." I crossed my arms. "No fair. Four against one."

"Life isn't fair," Tearza said, struggling to keep a straight face.

"Five against one." I glared at Tearza. "A conspiracy."

They stood silently in solidarity.

"Okay, you win this time," I said.

The girls cheered.

On the way back to the car, Tearza said, "Your daughter's pretty sharp. She out-smarted you with your own words."

"Story of my life."

"Maybe she should follow in your footsteps and become a lawyer."

I laughed. "Can you imagine an opposing attorney across from her in a courtroom? The judge would love her, the jury—putty in her hands, and then she'd eat you alive. I'll never forget the toughest lawyer I ever met. She was a peanut, beautiful, and had the cutest smile as she cut my client to pieces before anyone knew what happened. I once asked her how she was so successful in the hard-nosed business of litigation. She batted her eyes, innocent as a saint, and said, 'They never see it coming.'" I shook my head. "Lord help the poor guy who attempts to marry Sara."

After paying for the pumpkins, we drove to our favorite apple orchard where we ended the day with a hayride, hot cider, caramel apples and a bag to take home. The four girls fell asleep on the way home and we marveled at our blessings in the backseat. After a day like this, I was ready for winter.

At bedtime, Gracie lay there staring at a picture of Clair. This was my favorite time to talk with the girls, but tonight something clearly was wrong. Earlier, Gracie had seemed agitated and insisted in sitting on Tearza's lap and holding her hand.

I slid into bed with Gracie as she hugged her blanket. I sensed fear bordering on panic.

"What's wrong?" I asked.

She didn't respond, only pulled my arm tighter around her waist. "Honey—"

"I can't remember what Mom looks like," she said in a tiny voice.

I reached for the photo album by her bed but she stopped me. "That's not what I mean." Then she started to cry.

Sara was in bed staring at the clouds painted on the ceiling. She looked determined to force her memories of Clair permanently into her mind.

A year had passed since the girls had last seen Clair. I understood how they wanted to remember the lines on their mother's face, her sweet smell in the morning, her gentle voice singing a lullaby, her soft touch, her loving smile when she kissed them goodnight.

I stroked Gracie's hair and said, "Close your eyes, both of you, and think of something you used to do with Mommy."

Both girls squeezed their eyes shut.

After a minute, I whispered, "Whenever you miss Mommy, close your eyes like that. She'll come to you no matter where you are."

They both opened their eyes at the same time, looking at me suspiciously.

"Go ahead—just try it. Close your eyes again and wait."

Gracie shut her eyes and then squeezed my hand. "There she is," she said softly.

Sara didn't say anything, but a tear ran down her face.

"Sara?" I asked, hoping she would speak, but she just shook her head and pulled herself into a tight ball. Cooper stood up and pushed his nose into Sara, but she wouldn't respond. He whimpered and then settled onto the floor. No one spoke until sleep replaced the girls' pain with dreams.

◆ ◆ ◆

The next day was busy and I had to meet a client for dinner, so I dialed my assistant. "Susan, please check the calendar. Who has the kids tonight?"

She looked at the calendar and said, "No activities tonight. Betty has them. Did you look at the clock? You've only got twenty minutes before you're supposed to meet the Bendersons."

"Thanks. The Johnson letter is done. Can you revise it and put it on my desk tomorrow?"

"No problem, but you better leave now because Jamison will throw a hissy fit if you're late."

I still had a few minutes to call the girls and make it to dinner on time. I dialed home, someone picked up, but all I heard was giggling.

"Gracie, is that you?"

"Hi, Dad. Wait a second." Gracie yelled at Sara to stop.

"No, don't go. I don't have time—" The phone went dead. I looked at my watch again—two more minutes before I had to go.

"Sorry, I had to punch Sara."

"Honey, what're you doing?"

"Drinking beeer and whoodka."

"Oh, really. What's your big sister doing?"

"Watching TV and smoking cigars."

Betty jumped on the phone. "As you can hear, everything's under control here. I think Gracie's had too many chocolate chip cookies."

"Save some for me. I'll be at Charlie's Restaurant with clients. Hoping to duck out early and be home by eight. Does that work?"

"Got you covered."

"Tell Sara not to inhale."

I sprinted from my car into the restaurant. The Bendersons were already seated, but Jamison wasn't there yet.

"Thank you for joining us," I said, as I sat down. "Have you been waiting long?"

"We ordered drinks but didn't know what you wanted."

Right on cue, the waiter approached with their drink order.

"Jamison should be here any minute. You know how he runs late all the time."

"Oh really?" I heard a familiar voice from behind me. "Like someone else I know?" The waiter placed a dirty martini on the table next to me—Jamison's favorite. I was a dead man.

Mr. Benderson reached for his drink and held the glass high in the air. "This ought to be an interesting evening."

During dinner, we had long discussions about a range of business issues. Just as after dinner drinks were served, I heard a familiar laugh over the restaurant noise. Tearza was sitting with her back to me across from a man about our age. The handsome guy appeared to be telling her a funny story. It was obvious they weren't strangers. I cringed at the thought she was dating someone. I wondered who he was.

"So, what do you think, Ryan?" a voice said. I turned back to my table and found everyone staring at me.

"Sorry, I missed what you were saying."

Jamison cleared his throat. "A lawsuit of this magnitude can be a huge problem and awfully expensive. We need to analyze all the implications of their case against us before we respond. We may be able to settle without a trial." He took a sip of wine before continuing. "In spite of his choirboy looks, Ryan's really good at this type of work."

I put on my best smile and nodded while silently cursing my stupidity. I knew that I'd hear about this tomorrow. The evening couldn't get any worse. First, arriving late, and then seeing with Tearza with a strange man, and now this. I just wanted to get home.

After dinner, Jamison followed me to my car. "Ryan, I want to see you in my office first thing in the morning. You acted like you were on another planet tonight. Damn it, you say all the right things, look the part, but you're all show!"

He stomped off before I could respond. Jamison had chewed me out before, but this time I was really worried. I tried to invent plausible excuses for my behavior to get me off the hook, but I couldn't think of any.

The girls were in bed by the time I got home. I was too agitated to sleep, so I settled in at the kitchen table to catch up on work. I read the first page of a deposition twice before giving up—I just couldn't focus on it. All I could think about was Tearza with another man. I wished she had been having dinner with me. If only I had the courage to ask her for a date.

After a mostly sleepless night, I went to work feeling grumpy. Susan gave me a cup of coffee and handed me a message. "Andy wants to see you in his office as soon as you get in."

"Andy? You mean Jamison."

"No, Andy."

"Oh, boy," I said.

"What happened last night?"

I shook my head. "I better get this over with."

Outside Andy's office, I straightened my tie, knocked on the door and poked my head inside. "You wanted to see me, sir?"

Andy didn't look up from a document he was reading, but he waved me in. His jaw was tight, as if he had bitten on something hard.

"Close the door," he said. "We need to talk."

My heart sank. In all the years here, I'd only seen his door closed once.

Andy played with an unlit cigar and slowly looked around the room. The walls of his office were covered with plaques, awards, and photos of him with everyone from past clients to the President of the United States. He handed me an old photo from his desk.

"Guess who these guys are?"

I stared at the two young men in cheap black suits with their arms around each other. Their ties were loose and they each held a bottle of beer.

"I don't recognize either one."

"That's me on the left when I had hair. And on the right, that handsome guy is Carl Benderson. He was my first client, and in that photo, we were celebrating the day he started his business." Andy rubbed his shiny bald head. "It seems like yesterday. Who would've guessed I'd end up the managing partner and he'd become our firm's biggest client?"

The suspense was killing me, so I decided to get this over. "I'm sorry about last night. It was irresponsible of me."

"Is that why you think you're here?"

I didn't answer.

He chuckled. "You're right. Jamison wants your head. I should take you to the woodshed, but that's not why I need to talk to you." He stood up and looked out the window. "The Benderson lawsuit got delayed. It'll be rescheduled toward the end of the year."

"That's actually good for us," I said. "It'll give us more time to prepare."

He smiled, which relaxed me. "We had our monthly partner meeting last week while you were gone." Andy extended his hand. "They're considering making you a partner at our annual meeting next month."

I shook my head in disbelief. "I don't know what to say."

"I know how you feel. I remember when they told me the same thing twenty-two years ago." He paused and winked. "Here's the best part. Our business in New York City is growing much faster than anyone expected. As part of strategic planning, we're considering opening a permanent office there. We haven't made a final decision, but since you've been traveling there more than any of us, you'd be the perfect partner to lead the New York office."

I didn't know how to respond.

He laughed. "Speechless?"

"Exactly." I had to sit down. "When would you want me to move? I'm not sure I can uproot the girls anytime soon."

"As I mentioned, we haven't made a final decision yet, but we'd give you plenty of time to make arrangements."

"I'm serious—I don't know what the girls will say. Their best friends are here. They love their school." I didn't say anything about Tearza.

"Girls are flexible at their age. They'll be fine. In a couple months, they'll have a new set of best friends. Anyway, let's not worry about a move now. There are a lot of things that would need to fall in place before we proceed with a permanent office." Andy stepped up and gave me a guy-type hug. "I wanted to give you the good news before we made the formal offer. Again, congratulations. We have so much confidence in you."

I nodded and headed for the door feeling numb.

"One more thing." Andy turned his head and sighed. "Ryan, I'm retiring."

"What?"

"I wanted you to know before the other partners because I'm putting you in charge of the Benderson case. You're the only one I trust to manage their account."

"I'm not sure I'm ready. Maybe you should assign one of the more senior partners."

"Believe me, you're ready. Otherwise, I wouldn't give you my best client and personal friend."

"Why now?"

"Why now…?" He pointed to a sprawling green spider plant on a corner table. "See that plant? It's over twenty years old. My wife gave it to me when I first moved into this office. It was just a little shoot in a tiny pot. Over the years, I've learned that if I don't re-pot the plant every few years it stops growing. In fact, it gets weak and loses its color."

"I don't understand," I said.

"I need to re-pot myself. I'm wrapped in such a tight ball that I can't grow anymore. I need to find a bigger container."

"But you're the managing partner."

"This is only a part of my life." Andy smiled and we stared at each other for a moment.

"This is such a shock," I said.

"Well, don't say anything until I tell the others."

"Who's taking over the firm?"

"Jamison."

I cringed.

Andy saw my response. "I know. Everyone will roll their eyes, but I need him to handle the firm right now. The economy's in the tank and our firm has grown fat and lazy over the last couple of years. He's agreed to stay in the role of managing partner for two years then retire."

I stood up to shake his hand. "I'll miss you."

"Thanks, but nothing will change between us. Our future meeting won't occur in this office but somewhere fun. By the way, I heard you spent most of the night watching some cute girl instead of paying attention to our clients."

"Well, not really."

"Who is she?"

"A friend. Our daughters are best buddies."

"What's her name?"

I looked at my watch. "I should return to my office."

"Not so fast." He folded his arms, blocking the door.

"It's Tearza."

"How did you meet her?"

"She was in our office once."

"And?"

"And Jamison negotiated the purchase of her husband's printing business. The situation was tragic. The owner committed suicide and left Tearza alone with two young girls."

Andy rubbed his chin as if recalling a tense meeting.

"You stopped in the conference room for a few minutes," I said.

"Not the pretty young lady in the blue polka-dot dress?"

I nodded.

"I remember now. How did things turn out for her?"

"Not great, but ironically we've become good friends."

He grinned. "Are you dating?"

"No way."

"You should be. I've been happily married for more than forty years. I know the look, and you have it. People around the office refer to you as the high-school boy in puppy love." He winked. "Have you asked her out yet?"

I shook my head.

"What're you waiting for?"

"Good question. Let's see." I pretended to make a list. "One, she ended up with a paltry sum of money after the sale we so brilliantly negotiated. Two, her deceased husband was Mr. Perfect. Three, she's beautiful, funny, and has eyes that could melt a chocolate bar—way too good for a boy from Northern Wisconsin. Four, she has two beautiful daughters, one of which is worried that I plan to steal her mom. Five— did I mention that she hates lawyers?"

"That's it, really? Trust me, ask her out." Andy looked at his watch. "Now, get out of here and leave the door open."

I rushed home, cooked dinner, and put the girls in bed. The house was quiet and the euphoria had worn off. I pulled out one of my business cards and tried to imagine "partner" beneath my name. On the refrigerator was a crayon drawing of Betty the girls had drawn this morning with a big smiley face and the words "We love you." *How could I explain a move to New York to them?*

I needed to talk to someone, so out of desperation I called Dad.

In a hoarse voice he said, "What time is it—is everything okay?"

"Were you asleep? Sorry, I forgot how late it was."

"It's okay. What's going on?"

"I have a big decision to make and I can't do this one alone."

The phone went silent for several seconds. "You're asking me for advice?"

"I know. Hard to believe, isn't it."

"Do you need money?"

"It's not about money." I paced around the kitchen. "Anyway, I was told the firm will make me a partner at their next meeting."

"Congratulations. You told me that at the lake."

"You don't sound very excited."

"I'm very happy for you," he said in a monotone voice.

Why does he always make me feel this way?

"So, what's the problem?" he asked.

"I can't explain it. I should be thrilled, but I'm not."

"Correct me if I'm wrong, but isn't this what you always wanted?"

"Of course, it's always been my dream—but now I'm not sure I can accept."

"Why not?"

"They want me to move to New York City to run a new office. It's like, 'Hey, good news, you won the lottery. But the bad news is you have to give up your family to get the money.'"

"New York isn't so bad."

"It is when you're a single parent."

Dad tried to sound reassuring. "The girls will be fine."

"It's not only the girls."

"Is it about that woman Stella talks about? What her name? Teresa or something—?"

"Her name's Tearza."

"I didn't think you were dating?"

"We're not."

"Then what's the problem? This decision should be a lay-up. Look at all you've sacrificed to get this far. It's your big chance for the brass ring."

"So, you think I should take it?"

"Absolutely."

"Even if the girls are upset?"

"In a heartbeat. You can't pass up that kind of money. Listen, take it from me—if you turn down this offer you'll regret it for the rest of your life."

"I don't know. It's not just about the money anymore. I've made some progress with the girls. They love Tearza, and her girls are their friends. They'll hate me for this."

"So…" Silence. "Have you decided?"

"I'm not sure—I don't want to make another big mistake."

"You'll do the right thing."

Our conversation didn't help. I felt more frustrated than ever. When I hung up, Gracie stood in the kitchen doorway holding Sara's stuffed golden retriever by its scruffy ear. Her hair looked like a wild bird's nest and her pajamas dragged on the floor as she shuffled toward me.

"I can't sleep."

"Was I talking too loud?"

"No, bad dreams. Can you lay with me for a while?" She walked over and put her head on my shoulder. "Do you ever get scared?"

"We all do at times, even grown-ups. When I was your age, I'd hug your grandma as hard as I could, and all the bad dreams would go away."

"But I don't have a mother."

I pointed at my heart. "But you do have a father."

She put both of her arms around my neck and squeezed me.

"Daddy, I love you," Gracie whispered and kissed me on the neck.

The second she said those four beautiful words I found my answer for Andy.

◆ ◆ ◆

The month flew by and the partners completed their November meeting. I was invited to join them in the board room. I dreaded the meeting because I couldn't figure out a way to reject their offer. Everyone stood up and applauded as I walked in.

"Welcome—we have a lot to discuss." Andy pulled out a chair next to him.

My heart pounded as I looked at the faces of all the partners.

"Ryan, on behalf of the other partners," Andy said, "I want to invite you to become the next partner in our beloved law firm. It's a great honor, and you've earned it."

How could I explain my decision to Andy?

I took a deep breath. "I don't know how to say this, but—"

Andy raised his hand and gently chided me. "The first thing a new partner needs to learn is to let the old man finish his speech. You've been the best senior associate our firm's ever had. As a reward, we're doubling your salary, providing you with a leased Mercedes—" He paused to let all this sink in for a moment. "And in addition to the Benderson account, we're giving you the Grady account. As you know, they are one our fastest growing clients."

My mind raced. This was a reward beyond my wildest dreams.

Before I could respond, Andy walked over to a group of twelve glasses of champagne on a credenza. He picked up two glasses and handed one to me. The other partners reached for glasses and gathered around us. "Let's toast to our new partner," Andy said.

Andy winked and I nodded back. *With his help, this might work,* I thought. Now I had to figure out a way to tell the girls—and Tearza.

◆ ◆ ◆

Even though school had started two months ago, the girls hadn't fully adjusted to our new schedule. Every night after dinner, I begged them to do their homework, sometimes threatening them. One evening, as I was doing laundry, I was walking toward the girls' bedroom to pick a load of whites. Along the way, I glanced at the whiteboard on the hallway wall displaying the girls' schedule for the next day—jam-packed as usual. I made a mental list of all the things I had to:

- Pack two lunches
- Sign the school authorization form for Sara's field trip
- Send a check for their gym outfits
- Fill out their latest immunization dates—if I could find their records
- Give Cooper his heartworm pill
- Pick up Gracie's medicine at the pharmacy
- Drop off clothes at the drycleaners
- Remember Sara's piano lesson after school

The girls were wrestling in front of the TV. "Turn off the TV!" I yelled. "And start your homework now."

This was my life, I thought wearily. The same kinds of things day after day. I couldn't remember the last time I'd done something for myself.

After I let the room, I heard yelling again followed by a loud thump. The girls were in a fierce tug-of-war over the remote control.

"What's going on?" I asked as calmly as possible.

Gracie's shoulders shook. "*Th*ara's being mean to me again."

I grabbed the remote. "Sara, is that true?"

Sara didn't respond at first, then burst into tears.

"You don't understand! You never do. And you always take Gracie's side." Sara glared at me defiantly,

She was right. I didn't understand her most of the time. I told Gracie to turn off the television and put on her pajamas. Still angry, I went into the kitchen and the phone rang.

"Hello," I said abruptly.

"Ryan?"

A chill went down my spine. It was Clair.

"It's me," she said.

"Clair? Is this your idea of a sick joke?"

"No," she said quietly.

My voice shook. "You never showed up for Gracie's birthday. Do you know what you've put the girls through?"

"Sorry—you need to understand, I couldn't—"

I cut her off, "Understand? You might start with some kind of explanation, and it better be good."

"It's just…" She suddenly stopped speaking.

"What happened to you?" I asked. "Why didn't you come for Gracie's party?"

"It's a long story. You have every right to be mad." Then she abruptly changed the subject—she was always good at that. "How are the girls? I bet they've grown so tall. I probably wouldn't even recognize them."

I calmed down because I knew she'd hang up on me if I kept unloading on her. "Are you kidding? They look exactly like you. Why didn't you at least call?"

"It's complicated," she paused for several seconds. "I was in the hospital again."

"How do you feel now?"

"Better."

"Do you want to talk to the girls?"

There was a long pause before she said, "I don't think so."

"They'd go crazy if they knew you were on the phone."

"Tell me about each of them."

"Well, Sara is a little mother hen. She's losing her baby face and becoming a delightful young girl. She's the one who keeps everything together for us. You'd be so proud of her."

"And Gracie?"

"A whirlwind— a tiny tornado who leaves a trail of wonderful debris no matter where she goes. More energy than the sun. She makes Sara and I laugh all the time—when she's not fighting with Sara."

"I knew you'd take good care of them. By the way, who does the cooking?"

"There you go again—and we were having such a nice visit." We laughed together for the first time in years. "I haven't gotten any better in the kitchen."

There was a prolonged silence. I was afraid she was gone. Finally, she said, "So, does my big-shot lawyer still drive a BMW and wear monogrammed shirts with gold cuff links?"

"I traded all that in for a silver Suburban, a whistle and a clipboard."

"You're coaching?"

"Yes."

"What about work?"

"I'm in recovery."

"At least we still have something in common."

Silence again. I had so many questions, so many things I wanted to say, but nothing came out.

At last, I spoke. "I finally made partner."

"You're kidding! I thought you just said you were in recovery."

"I am, in a way."

"Well, congratulations. It's what you've always wanted."

"Yeah, but it's different than I thought. I'm sorting through the new role."

"Don't let your work hurt the girls."

"You have no right to say that," I said angrily.

"I know. I'm sorry."

I heard a faint car honk on the call.

"Listen, I have to go," Clair said. "I wanted to know that you and the girls were okay. Please let Gracie know how sorry I am that I missed her birthday."

"Wait—do you remember what you said to the girls the last time you put them to bed?"

She didn't respond.

"They still kiss you every night in their dreams."

She hung up. I debated whether to tell the girls but suddenly I remembered I had left Sara in the "penalty box." Gracie was asleep. In the other bed, Sara was lying on top of her sheets with arms and legs sprawled in every direction. Cooper, her guardian angel, was in a ball at her feet. I tiptoed in, sat on the edge of her bed, and watched her. When the phone rang, I flinched. Clair again? I raced to the kitchen and picked up the receiver.

"Did I catch you at a bad time?" Tearza asked.

"No, this is fine," I paused. "I can't believe you're calling."

"Why?"

"I don't know."

"I'm returning your call."

"I didn't call you."

"I got home a few minutes ago, and Ella said I should call you."

It was a small miracle. Tearza's voice was like a ray of sunshine.

"Ryan, is everything all right? You sound kind of funny."

"I'm fine." I took a deep breath. "Can I ask you something? Do you have anything going after we drop off the girls at their music lessons?"

"Hah, you should see my to-do list!"

"Oh, okay."

"Why do you ask?"

"Nothing."

"Are you sure?"

"Well, I was just wondering if you were free for lunch."

"You mean just us?"

"Just the two of us."

"Any special reason?"

"I thought—you know, we rarely get to talk. We're always running so hard with the kids."

"Isn't that the truth? Good idea. I'd love to have lunch."

"Great, I'll see you tomorrow."

◆ ◆ ◆

The next day I paced the kitchen and checked the mirror for the tenth time. Finally, Tearza's car pulled into the driveway.

"Where do you want to go to lunch?" she asked, as I climbed in. I could hardly take my eyes off her.

"Have you tried Tutto Bello down by the river?" I asked.

She shook her head. "Heard great things about it, though. What does the name stand for?"

"*Tutto bello*—everything beautiful. It's a tiny restaurant but has a nice setting, and an amazing little store with some of the best cheese and Italian wine in the city. I want to show you the shop before we eat because it's so unique."

We arrived fifteen minutes later. In the shop, I felt dizzy from the powerful aromas of garlic, marinated olives, cheeses, and salt-cured meats. The arched doorways and hand-troweled stucco walls made you feel as if you were in Italy.

The owner stood behind the counter humming to Italian opera music. His white apron covered a generous tummy. He waved to us, and as I began to show Tearza around the shop he strolled over and in a thick Italian accent said, "*Buon giorno!* How may I help you and your beautiful bride?"

Tearza blushed

"She is beautiful," I said, "but unfortunately she's not my bride."

He stared at Tearza for a moment while tapping his thick finger against his large nose. "My mistake, although I have a sense for these things."

"We're having lunch in the restaurant, but I wanted to show Tearza your shop first," I explained.

"Tearza. I love the name. It's the name of my oldest daughter, and she's beautiful like you. In Hebrew, her name means 'she's my delight.'" He rubbed his chin for a second. "I have an idea. Let me make a picnic lunch and you can take it down to the river. It's a gorgeous day. Shouldn't waste it inside."

"Perfect." I said.

While Franco put together our picnic, Tearza noticed the back wall covered with dozens of pressed flowers in frames.

"Look at these beautiful arrangements," she said. "No two are alike. Like snowflakes"

A short, pleasantly plump woman shuffled up to us from the back room. She reminded me of my grandmother with beautiful silver hair and olive skin that belied her age.

"Can I help you?" she asked shyly in an Italian accent.

Tearza moved slowly along the wall. "Did you make all of these?"

"Yes, my mother had a small flower shop in Sicily. She taught me."

Franco joined us and said, "I see you've met my wife Sofi." He kissed her on the cheek. "She's very talented."

Still marveling at the flowers, Tearza said, "They're beautiful, like your wife."

"Even in this bad economy," Franco said, "they go out the door as fast as she can put the arrangements together."

Sofi blushed and she said something in Italian to Franco. He laughed, grabbed her from behind and tried to give her a hug. She slapped his hands and tried to push him away, but she snuck a wink at Tearza. "Thinks he's twenty."

"Sofi, where do you get your flowers?" Tearza asked.

Franco interrupted. "She has a beautiful garden in the back."

"And you do this all by yourself?"

"*Si, si,*" she smiled. "It's my happy place."

"Did you say happy place?" Tearza stepped closer to Sofi. "That's what I call my garden."

"The work is too much," Franco explained as he put his arm around his wife's shoulder. "I want her to retire. My daughter used to help until she left for college. Now Sofi is alone."

"I try some young girls, but they didn't have—" Sofi struggled, searching for the right words. "My English not so good. Franco, *passione*?"

"Passion," Franco responded.

"My mamma believed people touched with passion for flowers was a gift from God." Sofi tapped her heart. "I no can explain." Then she stepped close to Tearza. "Dear, let me see your hands." She turned Tearza's palms up, then squinted while carefully tracing the lines of Tearza's hand with her index finger. Finally, she let Tearza's hands drop and smiled. "*Capiche*?" she said to Tearza.

Tearza looked bewildered.

"You grow up on farm?" Sofi asked.

Stunned, Tearza asked. "How did you know?"

"We are tied to our land. Like God, it never leaves you."

Franco tapped me on the shoulder. "I think the women need a minute alone."

"But what about our picnic?" I said.

"Trust me. Come, I'll make you a cup of espresso."

A half hour later, Tearza returned to the front of the store with a strange expression.

"Are you okay?" I asked.

"Perfect." Tearza smiled and then nodded to Franco. "I start on Monday."

"What do you mean?" I asked.

Tearza beamed. "Sofi's invited me to become her apprentice."

"You're kidding!" I turned and shook Franco's hand. "I'm so glad we stopped in. Who would've ever guessed?"

Franco twisted his bushy mustache and then crossed himself, looked toward the ceiling and kissed a silver medallion he wore around his neck. "It's *destino*—fate."

I thought we were ready to check out with our picnic lunch when Franco shook his head while muttering under his breath in Italian.

"What's wrong?" I said.

"Aren't you forgetting something?"

"What's that?"

"A romantic picnic in my country always includes a good bar of chocolate and a bottle of wine. Here." He threw his hands in the air. "You kids don't know what you're doing. Let Franco help you."

He put a large bar of milk chocolate in a bag and then pulled out a bottle of wine from behind the counter. It didn't have a label, but he gently held it in his hand like it was one of his children. He handed the bottle to Tearza and said, "This is a special wine for a special woman. It's from my grand-uncle's vineyard in Sicily. It's soft, luscious, and full of fruit with a long smooth finish—like you."

Tearza smiled and her cheeks grew red under his intoxicating spell.

"Hey, Franco, who's going on this picnic," I protested, "you or me?"

He gave Tearza another wink. "I'd say it's up to the beautiful woman."

"I love it when men fight over me." Tearza said, patting her heart.

Tearza gave Franco a hug. "I'll see you next Monday."

He smiled and waved. *"Ciao, mi bellissimo angioletto!"*

As we walked out the door into the sunshine, Tearza said, "Does he act like that all the time?"

"You have a strange effect on people."

"What did he say in Italian?"

"You're his beautiful little angel."

She laughed. "You guys are all alike."

We walked down to the river and I opened the wine. My initial nervousness disappeared as we talked and nibbled our way through our little feast. Lingering over chocolate, I poured the last of the wine into Tearza's glass.

"That went fast," I said, holding up the empty bottle.

"Best wine I've ever tasted." Turning to face the sun, she closed her eyes for a minute. Several strands of hair fell across her face. She slowly opened her eyes and caught me staring at her.

Embarrassed, I started to gather the remains of our lunch.

She said, "Leave that. Let's go for a walk before we have to pick up the girls."

We strolled along a narrow path that followed the meandering river. As we rounded a curve, we came upon a young couple on a soft blanket on the opposite bank. Suddenly, he wrapped both arms around her and gave her a long, hard kiss—the kind that seems to never end. Mesmerized by their passion, we couldn't take our eyes off them.

We rounded the bend in silence, walking closer and closer until our hands accidently brushed against each other. Finally, I reached for her hand and it fit perfectly into my palm. I squeezed her hand and leaned down to kiss her, but she stepped back and pulled her hand away.

"We better get back," she said and then spun around and walked quickly away without waiting for me.

Confused, I hurried to catch up. "What's wrong?"

"Nothing."

I had to break into a trot to catch up to her. "Did I do something?"

"It's not you." She abruptly stopped in the middle of the path. "It's me."

Maybe I'm not good enough—not like Jim, I thought.

She ran both hands through her hair and looked out over the river. "I don't think I can handle something like this."

"Handle what? We're friends, aren't we?"

She looked at me, scared. "I know. I don't want anything to ruin that."

"But we could—"

She glanced at her watch. "My gosh, look at the time. Their music lesson's over!"

We ran back, threw everything into the car and raced to the girls. They were standing on the sidewalk waiting for us along with one of their teachers.

Tearza jumped out of the car. "Sorry I'm late. I'm so embarrassed you had to wait for us."

"We haven't waited long," the teacher said. "See you next time."

In the car, Ella asked, "Mom, where were you? We waited and waited—Oh. Hi, Ryan."

Marci leaned forward from the backseat. "Why are you here?"

"Ah, umm," I stuttered.

"Car trouble," Tearza quickly interrupted. "I had trouble starting the car and Ryan helped me. He wanted to ride along to make sure I didn't have a problem—right, Ryan?"

"Right," I said, wondering why she had lied to the girls.

Chapter 6
Tearza

The alarm went off at six-thirty. An intense dream lingered in which I was a child again, and dawn had just broken on the farm. Like a duckling, I followed Dad to the barn to help him milk. The morning dew felt cool and wet on my bare feet. I was so happy.

The dream ended abruptly, and I got out of bed, pulling my robe tightly around me and padding into the chilly kitchen. An early frost etched the corners of the windows. I lit a fire in the family room and sank into Jim's favorite chair, worried about the school conferences later today. I was confident that Ella was doing well, but was concerned about Marci.

At school, I greeted the other parents as we waited for our conferences. I hated attending these sessions alone. The other parents had no idea how lucky they were to have each other.

Ms. Anderson, Marci's teacher, waved at me. I took a seat in front of her desk and she opened Marci's file. "We've had a few challenges this quarter," she said. "Her schoolwork is excellent, but Marci has a pretty quick trigger."

"What do you mean?"

"Let's say she doesn't let others push her around." Ms. Anderson smiled and doodled on a notebook. "Since we conferenced last spring, we've kept a close eye on her. The causes vary, but there are times when she just explodes. Other times, though, she gets very quiet and withdrawn. The kids have learned the hard way to stay clear of her when she's in a bad mood. I didn't mention this to you earlier because it doesn't happen all the time. She always seems to shake it off pretty quickly, but you need to know that it's definitely there."

I shifted nervously. "Marci's been through a lot."

"I wanted to discuss one other thing." The teacher turned her eyes away. "Has she mentioned any problems with certain kids?"

"I'm not aware of any. Why?"

"You know how cliquey girls can act at this age."

I shrugged, urging her on.

"A certain girl calls her names."

I leaned forward. "What kind of names?"

"She told Marci, 'Go back to Korea.' We've tried to stop that kind of talk, but some kids are subtle in how they can hurt others. And they pick up stupid things on television."

My blood boiled. "Let me take a wild guess. Her mother's name is Victoria."

"I'm sorry. We'll monitor Sally very closely. This will not be tolerated in my classroom. We think Marci will be fine, but before you go I have to tell you a funny story. Marci has a cute tendency to get words mixed up. We read a story in class one day and I stopped to ask the class if anyone knew the word 'moxie.' Marci raised her hand and said, 'Maxi pads—they're on TV all the time.' I thought she was kidding until her classmates all nodded in agreement. Marci was so proud that I didn't correct her. Tearza, these precious moments are the reasons I teach. I wish I could keep them this way forever."

I almost cried. Marci had lost so much of her innocence since Jim had died. Now, at that difficult age of straddling childhood and her teens, she was experiencing the harsh reality that life wasn't always fair. These are hard lessons that transcend the fact that she recently turned twelve.

Chapter 7

Ryan

Tearza drove all the girls to their November Girl Scout meeting. It gave me a few rare hours to myself before they came home. I had just opened a beer and put my feet up when the phone rang.

"Am I interrupting you?" Andy asked.

"No, of course not," I lied.

"We had a meeting and decided to proceed with the office in New York. I know it's short notice, but do you think you could make the arrangements to move there shortly right after the holidays? We thought it might be easier to transfer the girls to their new school before the next semester starts in January."

My heart sank.

"Are you still there?'

"Yes, sorry. This all so sudden."

"I know, but we have a number of new cases in New York that need attention right away."

"Can we talk about this tomorrow?"

"Sure," he said, "But buckle up. This is your big chance."

I chugged my beer and debated having another when I glanced at my watch. The girls would be home soon, so I cleaned up the house and cleared the dinner dishes. Cooper's ears perked up, alerting me to their arrival. He trotted over to the kitchen door and barked as the four girls and Tearza barged into the kitchen.

"Did you have fun?" I asked.

They all answered at the same time, then laid out drawings they had made on the kitchen table. Marci walked to the kitchen door and pointed. "What're these pencil marks on the door frame?"

"Dad measures our height," Sara explained.

"Cool."

Pushing away from the table, I grabbed a pencil. "Everyone up against the wall. We'll mark each one of you tonight." I winked at Tearza. "And then we'll see how fast you grow."

I measured Marci first. "You're the same height as Sara."

She grinned. "That's a coincidence."

Tearza ran her fingers along the lines. "They're twins."

"One more," I said to Tearza. "It's your turn,"

Tearza protested, but Sara gently pushed her against the wall and told her to stand straight. I aligned the pencil along the top of her head, our eyes met, and I froze. She was exactly the same height as Clair.

"What's wrong?" Tearza asked.

I pretended to draw a line. "Nothing."

Tearza walked away and motioned to the girls. "Show Ryan your drawings."

The girls argued about who should be first, but Sara quickly stepped in. "I'll go first. All your pictures are better than mine anyway." She held up a picture of a turkey that looked more like a peacock.

Next came Gracie. She showed us a stick figure of a pilgrim and a Native American with oversized heads that looked like pumpkins. We all clapped, and Gracie beamed.

Marci and Ella engaged in a stare-down over who would be next. Finally, Marci held up a picture of a large table covered with a traditional Thanksgiving dinner.

Now it was Ella's turn. Her eyes darted back and forth between her drawing and the other girls. She fingered her drawing for a few seconds, unconsciously brushed a hair from her eyes, and then slowly held it up. It was a crayon picture of a red barn, a big turkey, and six stick figures holding hands. Ella stood perfectly still while holding the picture with growing desperation.

"It's home on the farm!" she blurted.

"Who're the people holding hands?" Gracie asked.

"It's us. See—Gracie, there you are," Ella said pointing at a small figure, "and then Sara, Marci, and Mom."

"Who's holding hands with your mom?" Sara asked.

"Your dad," Ella said with a quick glance at Tearza.

It suddenly became very quiet. Gracie walked over to the drawing and looked closer. "I don't know," she said, then pointed to the figure. "That doesn't look like my dad. He's much taller."

Ella leaned over and touched the paper. "I can fix it. I'll make the legs longer."

Tearza said, "Honey, you don't need to change a thing." She put her hands on my shoulder and I flinched. "It's perfect, isn't it, Ryan?"

"Ella, thank you for including me," I said. Then, noticing that Marci was staring at me, I changed the subject. "Who'd like more milk and cookies?"

They all yelled at once.

"I forgot that I left the cookies from the grocery store in the Suburban. Be right back."

As I started for the garage, the phone rang.

"Tearza, can you grab that for me? Just take a message."

When I returned, I asked, "Who called?"

"A real estate agent from New York."

I stopped with the bags of cookies in my hand. "What did he say?"

"He was returning your call." She stared at me. "He had the information you needed on the apartment market in New York."

I turned away because I get red in the face when I'm nervous. "Oh, right—a friend of mine might be moving to New York. Since I travel there a lot, he asked if I could help him out."

Tearza watched me carefully. "You're a good friend."

I avoided looking at her and quickly set the cookies on the table.

After a few minutes, Tearza gathered all the pictures and said, "It's late. I need to get the girls home."

Tearza and her girls scurried to the front door. I thought they were gone when suddenly Tearza poked her head through the kitchen door.

"Did you forget something?" I asked.

"Are you traveling to your parents for Thanksgiving?"

"Not this year. They're heading to Florida early."

"You're alone?"

"Yes."

"I wonder..." Tearza hesitated, biting the corner of her lip. "Would you like to join us for Thanksgiving this year?"

"You mean...at the farm?" I asked, surprised.

Tearza's smile vanished. "Look, I—"

"We'd love to go to the farm with you," I quickly added. "It'll be a great chance to meet your family."

She smiled. "Good, I'll call you tomorrow."

After Tearza left, I second-guessed myself. *What would her parents think? Was Tearza acting nice since we planned on a quiet Thanksgiving? What about Marci?*

♦ ♦ ♦

We headed out Thanksgiving morning blessed with beautiful weather. In the car, Tearza explained, "Mom's the glue in our family. Dad's a little quiet, but that doesn't mean he doesn't like you. He's actually very funny but in a subtle, dry way. Now my brother, Ben, he's another story. He can be intimidating, but really he's a big teddy bear. And I almost forgot, watch out—he's also a big teaser."

After three hours, we pulled off the main highway and switched to a dusty gravel road, which cut through long fields of harvested corn. As we emerged from a long curve overlooking the valley, Tearza shouted, "This is it. We're home."

I made a right turn and slowed before reaching the top of a steep hill.

"Wait, pull over for a second." Tearza pointed out the window. "Sara, Gracie, look down below—there's our farm. That's where I grew up."

It felt as if I'd been here before. From the hilltop, the view stretched out like a Van Gogh canvas. In the distance, the river meandered below us. White farmhouses dotted the valley. A thin black road followed the ridgeline and disappeared into the horizon. A small, white church sat quietly on the top of the adjacent hill. Its majestic steeple could be seen for miles. Everything was the way Tearza had described it to me.

"I always feel like I'm looking at this for the first time," Tearza said, gazing over the farmland.

I drove the car down the hill and turned into the driveway. A half-dozen young cousins sat on top of a wooden pole fence and behind them an older couple slowly walked toward us. Tearza waved out the car window as I honked the horn.

"There's Mom and Dad."

Tearza's mom shyly announced, "I'm Eve, Tearza's mom. It's so nice to finally meet you."

Tearza's dad extended his hand. "I'm Jack."

I greeted them, and then Eve reached out and hugged Sara and Gracie. "We've been looking forward to your visit. Marci and Ella talk about you all the time. Let's go down to the house. I made some fresh monkey-bread to tide you over until lunch. Have you ever eaten monkey-bread? No? Well you're in for a treat—it's my specialty."

Tearza's home was a typical two-story farmhouse set behind a screen of green pines that blocked the prevailing northwesterly winds. A tall windmill, covered in vines, stood guard. A red barn with two tall, silver silos was a short walk from the house. In the distance, black and white cows dotted faded green pastures surrounded by tilled ribbons of fields where corn, oats, soybeans, and alfalfa had grown. The view took my breath away.

The house was filled with a dozen cousins, aunts, and uncles who greeted us as if we were long lost relatives. Sara and Gracie disappeared into the other room, while I was passed around like a newborn from aunt to aunt, each sizing me up for approval. Eventually, I ended up in the kitchen sampling an assortment of homemade goodies.

My small, stoic Norwegian family was a big contrast to Tearza's big Irish Catholic family. It took time for me to acclimate to all the noise and commotion, but the girls bonded quickly with Marci's cousins. They sat at the kitchen table eating snacks and talking and laughing as if they came here all the time. Holding a cookie in each hand, Ella jumped up and announced they were taking Sara and Gracie out to the barn to play.

I balked. "I'm not sure that's a good idea."

"Ryan, it's all right. They know which areas are safe," Tearza assured me. Then she turned to Marci. "I'll yell when it's time to come in for dinner."

The girls scrambled out the door.

While the women worked at getting Thanksgiving dinner together, Eve provided a running monologue of the latest news about friends and neighbors. Tearza looked over at me while licking whipped cream from an egg-beater. She waved one at me, but I shook my head. I was content to watch.

The girls were only gone for a few minutes when Tearza's brother Ben, filled the kitchen doorway. He was so tall that he had to duck to get under the doorframe. I gulped and stood to introduce myself.

"We've heard a lot about you and the girls," he said. "Ever been on a dairy farm?"

"The closest I ever get to a cow is when I buy a carton of milk."

He didn't even give me a faint smile. Instead, he motioned toward the door. "Let's go before the women put us to work. I'll show you around." He grabbed a handful of cookies.

Tearza pointed a large wooden spoon at him. "Don't be too long. We're almost ready."

Ben slowed down before we got to the barn, which was empty. "As you know, Ryan, it was devastating for Tearza when she lost Jim." He kicked some mud off his boot. "She's endured more than anyone should."

"I know that."

"Then you know I'd do anything to protect her from any more pain." He stared at me like a rattlesnake shaking its tail. "Do we understand each other?"

I nodded.

"Good." His eyes softened and he waved his hand. "Come on, I'll show you Dad's pride and joy."

We walked through the milk house into the lower barn thick with musty air. In the corner, an old radio played country music to keep the cows company. Black and white Holsteins occupied two long rows of stalls separated by a long cement runway. I gingerly sidestepped the puddles of urine and manure and learned to move quickly if a cow lifted her tail, signaling a blast from its dinner.

I noticed a small placard tacked onto the wood beam above each stall. "What's that for?" I asked.

"Name, rating, and production numbers. Dad breeds Holsteins. Everything rated above a ninety qualifies as an excellent cow. These are his babies. He's proud that most of them are rated excellent." Ben patted one on the rump. "Ever milked a cow?"

"Never been in a barn."

"Would you like to try it?"

I tried to act nonchalant. "I'm not sure."

"Anybody can do it. Here, I'll show you."

Before I could refuse, he arranged a milk bucket and a stool for me to sit on. "Reach under and grab one of the teats, then squeeze as you pull down."

I sat down and leaned into the side of the cow. Her skin was surprisingly warm, and the short hair felt rough against my cheek. I tentatively grabbed a teat and pulled. The cow jerked her head toward me, kicked hard and gave out a loud bellow. I jumped back and Ben laughed.

"She won't hurt you. She's chained in."

The cow and I stared at each other for a moment. She was irritated because I was interrupting her meal and I was scared she would kick me into next week. I pulled and squeezed several times, but nothing came out. I kept trying, determined to show Ben I could do it. Finally, I looked at him with embarrassment.

"Guess I'm not cut out for this."

"One more try—just squeeze harder," he insisted.

I gave it one last hoorah, squeezed really hard, and the cow bellowed as if she were giving birth. At that moment, Tearza entered the barn.

"What in the world is happening out here?" she yelled at her brother. "We can hear someone torturing that poor girl all the way to the kitchen."

Tearza placed her hands firmly on her hips and glared at him. Then she turned to me. "Ryan, there's no way you're can obtain any milk out of that cow. "She's dry! This is my sick brother's way of welcoming you to the family."

Ben threw his head back and laughed. "Jim fell for the same thing," he said, slapping me on the back so hard I almost fell off the stool. Then he turned to Tearza and gave her a hug that lifted her off the ground. "Tearza, you still love me, don't you?"

Back on the ground, Tearza squeezed his hand before giving him a big shove. Turning to me, she said, "See what I have to put up with?"

By the time we returned to the house, the kitchen looked like a wedding reception without the band. Ten adults occupied the kitchen table, eight kids shared two card tables and two grandchildren sat strapped in highchairs. Once everyone was seated, Tearza's dad said grace. For the first time since we'd arrived, the house was quiet.

After grace, Jack continued. "Since this is the first year that Mother's not with us, I want to pass on something important. As you know, Mother gave the same Irish blessing to us every Thanksgiving since I was a child. Now, after ninety-four years, she's in heaven and I know she's standing at the Lord's Table this very minute reciting to God the very same poem." His voice cracked. He stopped for a few seconds and then cleared his throat. "So, I've asked Marci if she'd be kind enough to carry on Mother's tradition."

Jack sat down and Eve rubbed his hand. Marci slowly walked over to Tearza's dad. She smoothed the edges of her blue dress and tucked her hair behind her ears like Tearza often did. She glanced one last time at a card with the poem, then put her hands behind her back recited it in a voice that didn't match the young girl I had brought from Chicago. Her voice started out small and simple but gathered strength until we all felt the presence of Marci's great-grandmother. When Marci finished, there wasn't a dry eye in the kitchen. Overwhelmed, everyone began to hug each other.

Jack stood up one more time and raised his glass. "I'm not done yet. Before we begin our meal, I want to make a toast. To Mother—and to the passing of the family blessing to Marci!"

We all raised our glasses and the mood immediately changed from tears to joy. I smiled at Tearza. She wiped her eyes and smiled back.

All the nephews began reaching for the food at the same time. Suddenly, Jack pounded his fist on the table, which made everyone jump. "Some of us have forgotten their manners!" he said. "We have one more tradition. We like to give our guests the opportunity to give the Thanksgiving prayer."

Everyone looked at me. I panicked because I didn't know any good prayers. My mind raced all the way back to Sunday school, but I went blank. What could I say about Thanksgiving that didn't sound completely dopey? Then I remember thinking about Tearza and the girls on the drive down.

I stood up, setting my napkin on my chair. "If you think about it, *Thanksgiving* is the perfect word for this holiday. The word 'thanks' represents all the blessings that God has given us during the past year. And 'giving' is all about love. I've only been here a short time, but as I look around the table at your beautiful family, I see the love you give to each other. That's what makes this time of year and Thanksgiving so special. Amen."

Ben smiled then whispered, "Short, but nice."

Jack kissed Tearza's mom, faked a stern look at his nephews, and said, "Now we can eat."

It was every person for themselves. Ten conversations filled the room at the same time. Eve moved constantly between the tables and the long kitchen counter beaming while making sure everyone had exactly what they wanted.

After dinner, Tearza and I walked up the dirt road to the top of the hill where it was quiet and peaceful. She led me to the large walnut grove where they gathered nuts every fall, the pond where they captured frogs, and the ravines that served as secret hiding places during her childhood. Eventually, we made it to the barn.

"I want to show you the hay loft. It's full this time of year. We spent hours playing in here when we were kids." Tearza pulled back the large, red wooden doors.

Magical was the only way to describe the upper barn as she closed the door behind us. Startled at our presence, barn cats dove into hiding places. Several pigeons swirled inside the barn until they settled back in the upper rafters. We stood perfectly still, not wanting to disrupt the peace as we waited for our eyes to adjust to the dim light. Tearza took my hand and pulled me to the center of the barn. It smelled like hay, balls of twine, dust, old wood, and oil from an old tractor in the corner. I looked around, trying to imagine Tearza as a child at play in this space.

Tearza carefully climbed up the bales, leading me to the top of the loft where it leveled out. We sat down, facing each other. Through a crack in the wall above us, a shaft of dusty sunlight shone like a spotlight on Tearza. She reached for my face, took my glasses off, and brushed the hair away from my eyes.

"Close your eyes," she said.

I flinched.

"I won't hurt you," she said softly as she moved closer.

"What about the girls?"

"Shhhh."

I shut my eyes and sensed something brush against my cheek. Then it happened again. Curious, I opened my eyes for a split second. Her eyes were closed and she was giving me a butterfly kiss with her eyelashes. I shut my eyes again as she softly kissed one eye, then the other. I sat perfectly still, powerless to move, until I tasted something soft and sweet. I licked my lips, like a bee drunk on honey, while her lips swallowed mine. Suspended in time and space, I had no idea how long we kissed—it could have been five minutes—or a lifetime.

"You're a pretty good kisser," Tearza teased me. "Who was your teacher?"

"An older woman took advantage of me."

"Tell me about her."

"I was fifteen. She was sixteen and very experienced. All I can remember was that she tasted like bubble gum." I gently pushed Tearza onto her back in the hay.

"Did she teach you everything about love?" Tearza said.

"I was a slow learner who needed a lot of practice."

"I bet."

I looked down at Tearza. Her hair was full of straw and her eyes were closed. She didn't move for a moment, then arched toward me, lifting her lips to mine. Suddenly, she stopped.

She stared at me and whispered, "Maybe we'd better get back. Everyone will wonder what happened to us."

"Are you okay?"

She kissed me again and quickly climbed down to the barn floor. It was already dusk, so we hurried across the yard to the house. Eve was busy cooking when we walked into the kitchen.

"There you are. We were about ready to send out a posse to find you."

"I was showing Ryan the farm."

"It's so beautiful out there, so peaceful," I added a little too quickly.

"Glad you enjoyed it," she said. "Sit down while I get you some coffee and a cherry bar. They're still warm."

Eve stood up and put her hand on Tearza's shoulder, while pulling two long pieces of straw from Tearza's hair. "Looks like somebody made it to the barn."

We both blushed. In a panic, I looked at the girls to see if they had noticed. Fortunately, they were engrossed in a card game. I tried to change the subject by asking, "Who's winning?"

Sara looked up from her hand. "We're not sure. Marci's trying to teach us how to play euchre."

Gracie threw their cards on the table. "It's too hard."

Tearza turned to her mom. "Where's Dad? Has he started chores yet?"

"He went out about fifteen minutes ago."

"Ryan, if you don't mind, I want to give Dad some company while he milks." She pointed at me. "Ryan, maybe you can play with the girls."

"But I've never played before," I confessed.

"Marci can teach you," Tearza insisted.

After a few hands, I picked it up pretty quickly. Marci and I won the first game.

We set them on the next game and Marci screamed, "Bumpo!" Then she hit me on the arm. "Ryan, come on, you have to yell 'bumpo' if we win by setting them."

We high-fived and yelled "bumpo" together a second time while Ella howled in protest.

While Eve shuffled the next hand, she said to Marci. "You two are quite the team."

Marci smiled at me.

What a nice surprise, I thought.

◆ ◆ ◆

After a couple of days, it was time to go. Standing next to the car, we delayed the inevitable departure with small talk and long embraces. The girls repeatedly hugged their new "cousins," excitedly plotting the next visit. I finally started the car. Eve was crying, and Jack turned away, pretending he had something in his eye. With a last wave goodbye, we were finally off.

"What did you think of the farm?" Tearza asked.

"The girls loved it."

"What about you?"

With my eyes on the road, I babbled on for the next five minutes. When I finally looked over, Tearza was sound asleep. I glanced in the rearview mirror, and so were all four girls. I smiled because we hadn't even hit the blacktop yet.

So, this was what it might be like, I thought. *If only I could be so lucky. But now what? I'm such an idiot. I'm falling in love with a woman whom I'm leaving in January.*

Chapter 8

Tearza

There was no time to savor our Thanksgiving on the farm because Christmas was right on its heels. The day after we got back, I decided to pick up spruce tips and a Christmas tree before the good ones were gone. I was almost done arranging the spruce tips and pinecones in my outdoor flower boxes when my cell phone rang.

"Tearza, I think your mother broke her wrist," Dad said.

"What happened?"

"She tripped walking up the hill to her car. The doctor said she might need surgery. I know it's asking a lot, but I'm not good with doctors. Could you drive down and meet with them?"

"When?"

"They want to discuss things late this afternoon."

"I could be there by three-thirty at the earliest.

"That would be great. Thanks, honey."

I called Jake and arranged for the girls to stay with him until Ryan got off work.

The drive back to the farm gave me three hours to myself. The land whispered to me as I got close. Like a salmon migrating back to its birthplace, I was being pulled home by some irresistible force.

The meeting at the hospital went fine. No surgery was needed, just a soft cast for two weeks. We brought Mom home and propped her on the couch in front of the television. It was getting late in the afternoon, so Dad kissed Mom and left to start milking.

I decided to help Dad with the chores. As a child, I was the one who always got up at dawn with him. It was our special time.

The wooden door creaked as I stepped into the milking parlor. The cows all turned their heads, wary of the intrusion. I couldn't see Dad, but I heard him yell "Hello" from the other side of the barn. As if time had stopped, the smell of sweet hay, the taste of gritty dust, and the sounds of cows moving in their stalls were exactly the way I remembered them from my childhood. Nothing had changed but me.

For as long as I could remember, Dad always wore the same brown overalls, dirty boots, and faded Badger's cap. But as he glanced at me, I noticed how he had aged. His thick curly hair had grayed, and his once broad shoulders had lost their breadth. The eyes and voice were the same, but the wind had hardened his face into deep, fractured lines.

I guess time hadn't stopped.

Dad stopped milking and walked over to me with his hands in his pocket. He kicked the limestone dust on the cement floor with his muddy boot as if he wanted to tell me something, then grinned when one our favorite polkas came on the radio. Suddenly, he held out his hand. "Shall we?"

He led me up and down the runway, swinging and twirling with the music until the song was over.

"You know, the best times of my life were knowing you were safe and asleep under our roof. I miss you and can't tell you how happy I am you came home."

I didn't know what to say. Dad was like the land—hard, stoic and tough on the surface, but beneath that earthy crust he was soft, forgiving, and nurturing.

"I know this sounds silly, but do you believe that dreams can come true?" I asked.

"Of course. Almost every night, after your mother and I finish chores and walk back to the house, we look up at the Milky Way and make a wish." He scratched the rump of his favorite cow and grinned. "Sometimes two wishes."

"What do you wish for?" I asked.

Dad's eyes twinkled. "That's simple—for you kids to be happy."

"Happy?" I leaned against him. "I can't figure out what happiness is anymore."

He hugged me. "What do you wish for?"

I thought for a long time, then said, "I want the girls to be happy." I stopped, not knowing how to explain the conflict in my heart. "Dad, you haven't mentioned anything about Ryan."

"What do you want me to say?"

"I don't know. Do you like him?"

He grunted and averted his eyes.

"Come on."

Dad shoveled the last of the feed from an old wooden barrel.

"That's between you two."

"Wisely said, man of few words."

He shrugged. "I don't know about these things. I was lucky enough to marry your mother." He took off his cap and scratched his head. "Maybe you should ask her."

"I want to know from you."

"Why?"

"Because of Jim."

"We all think about Jim," he said. "Every day—and the same with Amy."

The balk tank turned on with a loud click. Dad stared out at a half-dozen deer grazing on the hillside. Finally, he said, "Jim's part of you and part of us. He always will be. But honey, you can't live in the past."

Neither of us spoke for a moment.

"Life's full of choices," he said.

"Maybe for someone else."

"We can't choose what happens to us, but we can choose how we respond to what happens to us."

"I'll try to remember that when I write my bills next week."

"Don't you see? If we project ourselves as a victim, then nothing positive comes back to us. We either continue the pity party or we can choose to be happy, thankful for what we have, and it all comes back to us many times over."

I raised my head off Dad's shoulder so I could see his eyes.

"What?" he asked.

"I love you."

"I know, sweetie. Oh, before I forget, I have something for you." He pulled out a letter from his back pocket.

"What's this?"

"I found this on my mother's dresser after she died. It was addressed to you, but she never got a chance to mail it."

"Why would she send me a letter?"

"I don't know."

"Other than a birthday card, I've never received a letter from Grandmother."

"She was never much for letter writing."

A cow bellowed.

"I better finish the chores," he said.

I took the letter and sat in a pile of hay in the corner of the barn. I slit open the envelope and pulled it out. The note smelled just like her—sweet. Her handwriting was shaky and crooked, so I had to read it slowly.

> My Dear Tearza,
>
> I'm 94 years old and outlived two husbands. I've suf-
> fered and loved. I've experienced the joy of birth and
> the heartache of death. I've watched you courageous-
> ly carry on since you lost Jim. Nothing can change
> that, but I want to share a letter that my first husband
> gave to me a few days before he died of cancer.

I unfolded the yellowed letter attached to her note.

> Dear Ellie,
>
> I worry about you. I see it in your eyes—all the fear,
> anger, and pain. Soon I'll be gone, and I want you

to know something. Our love belongs to the infinite stream of the universe. We can't possess it or own it. We can only belong to it. Through our love, we are connected to everything; therefore, our love knows no beginning or end.

I want you to be with me when my time comes. To get a glimpse of what I see when I dream—to see where I'm going. I'll always be a part of you. You need not be afraid. I've simply used up this body. Like a snake, I will rub against death and shed my old skin to renew, grow, and begin again.

So much to learn, so much to experience, so much to dream.

When I'm gone, listen for me like a song in the wind. Look for me in the wildflowers along the path in the woods above our house. Smell me in the spring lilacs. Feel me on your face in the summer sun.

Dream with me in the moonlight.

I'll always love you, but you can't stop living. Let love find you like a gift. You have so much yet to give.

Love you always,

Allen

I carefully returned the letter to the envelope and watched Dad. After every milking, a dozen barn cats waited for him to bring them a fresh pail of milk. Those goofy cats would sing like crazy and make Dad laugh. He loved his animals and the barn—this was his happy place.

Dad noticed I had finished the letter. "She was quite the woman."

I nodded. "I miss her."

"Me too."

He had a few more chores, so I decided to walk back to the house and check on Mom.

♦ ♦ ♦

It was late when I finished cleaning the kitchen. Mom and Dad were in bed early. I decided to give a quick call home to talk to the girls. I was so grateful that Ryan could watch them for me during this emergency trip. After I talked to Ella and Marci, Ryan came on the phone.

"How's your mom?" he asked.

"Fine, but a bit uncomfortable. Did you find everything okay in the house?"

"Yes, Marci was a big help. But I learned something new tonight," he said.

"Really?"

"Marci took me into your closet to get some extra blankets. It was full of paintings. I didn't know you were an artist."

"That was a long time ago."

"Do you still paint?"

"No."

"Why don't you?"

I didn't know how to answer that question.

"You're really good. If I were you, I'd take it up again." Silence. "Are you still there?"

"Yes, sorry." I said. "Thanks for taking care of the girls. I'll be home by noon tomorrow."

"No problem. Give your mom a hug from us."

Dad was sleeping in the spare bedroom to give Mom more room. The lights were off, and I slipped into bed with her for a few minutes. She was still awake and put her arm around my shoulders.

"How does your wrist feel?" I asked.

"Sweet mother, I'm fine," Mom said. "Thanks for coming home, I haven't had a chance to talk to you about our Thanksgiving. I want you to know how much we like Ryan and his girls." She stroked my hair and kissed my ear. "Tearza, you seem different—like your old self again."

"I'm glad to be home."

She smelled like warm chocolate chip cookies and we fell asleep whispering to each other.

◆ ◆ ◆

At dawn, I was lying in the darkness of my bedroom disoriented and unsure. Was this real or one of my recurring dreams? It was my second morning home alone without Jim or the girls and I didn't want to get up yet. I wanted to stay right where I was for a little while longer.

As my mind gradually let go of the night, consciousness returned with the familiar smell of clover, fresh cut hay and lilacs; the sound of a tractor rumbling in the distance; the smell of coffee brewing in the kitchen.

My body stirred, responding to some mechanism hidden deep inside. Daily life on the farm followed the sun, but I'd lost that ancient, circadian rhythm when I moved to the city. In the hustle and bustle of my over-scheduled, over-regulated life, I seldom took time to appreciate a sunrise, hear the birds wake up, take a nap in the sun, or watch the sunset create a new masterpiece.

Our house groaned in the wind like all old farmhouses. At the end of the hall, my parents' old spring mattress squeaked as Dad rolled out of bed. A few minutes later, his shadow passed my door and the wooden steps creaked as he went downstairs. Below my bedroom, an old grandfather clock chimed five times. Each day, I remembered, was a life cycle. You learned to live—to love—and to accept.

A few minutes later, Mom followed Dad downstairs. I could hear her puttering around the kitchen in a morning routine as predictable as Dad's. My favorite chair waited for me when I joined them in the kitchen. By the time Mom gave me the day's first cup of coffee, the sun was peeking through the kitchen window. I loved watching Mom in her old bathrobe and fuzzy slippers preparing breakfast for the men when they came in from milking. My stomach growled, responding to the smell of frying bacon and cinnamon rolls rising in the oven. Mom hummed and sang softly to herself as she baked. I knew all the songs by heart because they were simple and she sang them to me as a child.

I missed the certainty that came from the routine of such mornings. As if I had never left home, I slowly surrendered to the reassuring rhythm of the life I used to have. Mom and I spent the next two hours paging through old scrapbooks—a wonderful stroll through our lives. When she turned the last page, Mom handed me the stack of scrapbooks.

"Take them home with you," she said. "Cherish them and create your own. Memories are gifts—Christmas presents that you can unwrap and open over and over."

December

Chapter 1

Ryan

I shivered as I padded barefoot across the wooden floor to the bathroom. Winter had snuck up on us during the night. Our first snowfall, usually in December, always came as a surprise.

I decided to clear the snow off the sidewalk before making breakfast, so I stepped outside and was greeted by dazzling sunlight and millions of tiny diamonds sparkling off the untouched snow. Cooper romped and rolled in the white powder like a new-born puppy, barking for me to join him.

By the time I was done, the girls were at the kitchen table and writing busily.

"What are you working on?" I asked.

"Our wish-list to Santa," Sara said.

Gracie set her pencil down. "Dad, what can I ask for?" She reached for her blanket and rubbed the satin edge on her face. "What if I ask for something that I don't think he can fit in his sack? Will he think that's bad?"

"There's no such thing as a bad wish. That's the whole point. If you believe, then anything's possible."

Gracie looked doubtful until Sara gave her the thumbs up. I sat next to her with a cup of coffee and opened the newspaper.

A few minutes later, Gracie tapped my shoulder and handed me her stubby pencil. "Have you made *your* list?"

"Grown-ups don't make lists for Santa."

"Why not? Don't you believe?"

"Can't a guy read in peace?" I resumed reading, but I felt her staring at me. I lowered the newspaper slightly and she was still waiting for an answer.

"Well?" she asked.

"Of course I believe."

Sara pushed a piece of paper across the table to me. "Here's your chance."

Why not? I thought. I hadn't made a wish, any wish, for a long time. "You win," I said.

Sara said, "Come sit between us while you make your list."

They quickly moved over to make room. Sitting between my two favorite people in the world, I picked up the pencil and pondered my Christmas wish.

"What's wrong?" Gracie asked. "You're not writing."

"I'm thinking."

"Maybe you should start with something you've always wanted," Sara suggested. "The rest will come easy."

She was right. After a few minutes, I wrote five things on my list.

Gracie finished first. Her eyes twinkled because she was up to something.

"I'm not done yet," Sara said.

Gracie folded her letter to Santa and handed it to me. "Make sure Santa gets this."

I started to open her list, but Gracie yelled, "Dad, you can't look!"

"Why not?"

"It's private," she said. "Promise you won't peek?"

"I promise."

A loud knock interrupted our conversation. Tearza and the girls walked into the living room with a basket of cookies.

"The girls wanted Sara and Gracie to help decorate the Christmas cookies."

"Perfect," I said. "I'll clear the kitchen table."

The girls spent the next two hours licking butter cream and candy sprinkles off their fingers. After they were settled at the table, Tearza motioned for me to join her in the living room.

We sat on the couch and I asked, "What's up?"

"I had a long talk with my parents when I was back home. I've decided to go to Korea to meet my birth parents."

"Wow. That's a serious decision. When do you leave?"

"Next week. Can the girls stay with you? I'll be back in six days."

"Absolutely," I said, but then paused. "But I'm wondering what happened to make you decide to find your parents?"

"It's hard to explain. I love my parents here. I never felt adopted, but I always wondered, you know. I have a hole in my soul—a piece of me that's missing. I didn't want to search for my biological parents because I didn't want to hurt the parents who raised me." She rubbed her hands together. "While I was at the farm, Mom raised the issue, and she insisted that now was the time."

"You're a brave woman."

"I'm scared, though. What if I find out something terrible about my past? What if my parents were drug addicts or criminals?"

"That's a risk, but does it really matter? You are who God made you. You have a wonderful family who loves you more than anything in the world." I grabbed Tearza's hand. "At least you'll be able to fill that gaping hole with *something*. We'll be waiting right here for you."

Tearza leaned over and hugged me. "Thank you."

◆ ◆ ◆

Two weeks later, we stood at the exit gate for international travelers. Tearza was arriving home from her adventure in Korea. The girls had made large welcome home signs, and they screamed with joy as Tearza walked through the gate with her luggage.

We hadn't communicated since she had left, so I was anxious to find out what happened. "How was the trip?" I asked

She smiled softly. "Not what I expected, but good." The girls were all trying to hug her at once. "I'll tell you later."

At home, the girls finally decided to go to their room to play. Tearza made coffee in the kitchen and we sat at the table.

"Well...?" I asked.

"I never met my parents."

"You're kidding. What happened?"

"The adoption agency in Korea had the wrong information. They thought I was someone else. They tried to locate my records, but apparently they had lost most of their old documents in a fire several years ago."

"You must've felt devastated. What did you do?"

"I was stunned. The emotional buildup was immense, and then... and then to realize that I would never know about my past was—yes, it was devastating. Funny how life works. As long as I was in Seoul, I signed up for a tour that took me all over Korea. This is the crazy part— the other Korean travelers "adopted" me when they found out why I was in Korea. I learned more about Korea than I ever imagined. I came to love them...and my birth legacy." She sighed. "It was wonderful."

"This is an amazing story."

She smiled again. "I had an epiphany on the flight home. I found a magazine in the seat pocket that had reviews of various new books. On the first page was a quote from T.S. Elliot that blew my mind."

"Do you remember it?"

"I'll never forget it. Elliot wrote, 'We shall not cease from exploration. And the end of all our exploring will be to arrive where we started and know the place for the first time.'"

Elliott's words provoked something in me too.

"That's what my mother tried to tell at the farm before I left. Oh, do I love that woman."

"Tearza, I'm so happy for you. What a blessing." I hugged her again. "Let's find the girls."

◆ ◆ ◆

The following week was a blur. For the last two years since Clair left, I dreaded Christmas; although we'd picked out our tree, I'd found it too painful to unpack Clair's Christmas decoration boxes. But for some reason, this year felt different.

After a short discussion, Sara, Gracie and I decided to have a tree decorating party. The girls gathered the apple cider, Skittles, cookies, and popcorn while I retrieved the boxes of ornaments from the basement. I strung the lights while the girls danced around the tree singing old Christmas songs with Alvin and the Chipmunks. Then we draped the tree with glass icicles and hung angels all over it. Twinkling with tiny white lights, our Christmas tree was a scrapbook of love from friends and family. Each ornament had a special meaning. In the bottom of a box, I found my favorite ornament nestled in a bed of white tissue—two white-feather angels tied together on a long thread. I held the angels up in the air and gently blew to send them in flight.

Gracie watched the angels swing in air. "Can I hang those?"

"Sure, but be careful—they're delicate."

Gracie carried them to the tree as if she were holding a butterfly. "Who gave you this ornament?" she asked over her shoulder.

"They're from Mary Jane. She made them to celebrate our first Christmas together with your mother."

"Who's Mary Jane?"

"A sweet woman—my second mom. Unfortunately, she died before you were born."

"They're so pretty."

"This was also Clair's favorite ornament."

"Really? Then they need a special place in front." Gracie moved two ornaments from the center of the tree and hung the angels. "There—what do you think?"

"Perfect. Clair and Mary Jane would love it."

Sara picked up a pretty glass cross. "Who gave us this one?"

The answer was on the tip of my tongue, but sadly I couldn't remember. There were several others I couldn't recall either. Clair knew every single one.

An hour later, the bottom half of the tree was decorated as high as the girls could reach. We stood back to admire our work.

"Pretty good," I said.

"Now what?" Gracie said.

"What do you mean?"

"No school tomorrow. Can we go skating?"

"Sure, but first I have to check my messages."

"Do you have to?"

I nodded and Gracie frowned.

"What's the matter?" I asked Gracie.

She fidgeted. "We won't go skating. You always have messages."

I put my phone away. "You're right, no messages! Let's go skating."

Gracie hugged me.

"I have an idea. Maybe I should give Tearza a quick call to see if they're free."

"Yes!" Gracie clapped.

Tearza answered and I explained why I had called.

"I'm sure Marci and Ella would love to go skating, but I can't go," Tearza said.

"Why not?"

"I don't know how to skate."

"I can teach you."

Tearza hesitated. "I'm willing to try, but I don't have any skates."

"What size are your shoes?"

"Seven," she replied.

"Clair's skates were sevens. I'll pick you up about six-thirty bringing skates."

♦ ♦ ♦

It was a perfect night for skating. The temperature was near zero but there was no wind and the clear sky shimmered with stars. While the girls went into the warming house to put on their skates, Tearza grabbed my collar and gave me a quick kiss.

"What's that for?"

"Your first present for the Twelve Days of Christmas."

"Does that mean I've been a good boy?"

"Depends. You still have eleven days left."

"While I was growing up, Stella always gave me presents for the Twelve Days of Christmas." I pulled out a metal folding chair from the back of the Suburban. "Two kisses for the second day?"

"You'll have to wait and see." She smiled, then pointed at the chair. "What's that for?"

"This is how most of us learned to skate."

Tearza shook her head. "I'm too old for this."

I chuckled. "You'll be fine."

The frigid air made my nostrils burn as we came out of the warming house. Several couples gracefully glided in circles around us. Little kids ran around, more on floppy ankles than on skates, chasing each other in games of tag. The older boys played keep-away with a hockey puck on the far side of the rink while small groups of teenagers milled around, pulling on each other, holding hands or doing crack the whip.

I held out my arm to Tearza. "Here we go. Let me help you over to the ice."

Tearza cautiously shuffled her skates in tiny baby steps.

"Now stand there and don't move while I get the chair."

"Move? You've got to be kidding." She held her arms out for balance. "Just hurry."

I returned with the chair and set it down in front of her. She gripped the top of it and took her first tentative steps. After pushing off several times, she began to get her balance.

"This must look ridiculous," she said. "A grown woman with wobbly ankles standing over a metal chair on the ice."

The girls skated around us as Tearza gradually took more steps. Suddenly, she let go of the chair and skated off in a long wide circle. Her arms flapped as she tried to keep her balance. On her way back, she went down with a thump. Sitting there on the ice, she laughed harder than I'd ever seen.

I offered to help her stand up. "Are you okay?" I asked.

"My ego's bruised more than my bottom-end." Her deep black eyes glistened beneath the black wool hat pulled down on her head. I helped her up and she let go to brush the snow off her pants. But she lost her balance and went down again. This time she held onto my arm as she stood up and straightened her hat.

We took a few more turns around the rink, arm-in-arm, until the girls skated over again.

Sara said, "I think we should go."

"Why?" I asked.

"Marci can't feel her feet."

Marci looked at Tearza. "Is that bad?"

"Your skates might be too tight, you've grown so much."

Marci started to cry, so Tearza bent over to unlace her skates and I stopped her.

"Not here," I said. "I'll carry her to the car." I picked up Marci and gave her a piggy-back ride to the Suburban. "Don't worry, honey, everything will be okay, I promise. I'll take good care of you."

Fifteen minutes later, we were back at Tearza's cottage. I carried Marci into the bathroom and set her on the counter.

"Your feet will hurt as they warm up," I explained. "Has this happened before?" She shook her head. "They'll sting for a few minutes, but then like magic the pain will disappear."

"Are you staying with me?" she asked.

"I'll be right here."

I took off her jacket and filled the sink with warm water for her feet. "Ready?" I asked.

She nodded and gripped the edge of the counter.

"It's okay if you feel like crying."

"Do you ever cry?" Marci whispered, staring at me with sad eyes.

"I can cry with the best of them."

Steam fogged up the mirror as Marci's feet touched the warm water, she threw her head back with a look of surprise and terror. At first, she dug her fingers into my arm and wailed, but after several seconds she stopped.

"It's gone, isn't it?" I asked.

"Yep, just like you told me." Marci wiped the tears from her eyes and gave me a big hug.

"What's that for?" I asked, surprised.

"For helping me," she whispered with her head on my shoulder. I hugged her back. Then without another word she slid off the counter and ran down the hall to join the others.

Tearza walked into the bathroom. "Looks like Marci survived."

"She's great."

Tearza moved very close to me and whispered in my ear. "And so is someone else I know."

We returned to the kitchen and I said, "I'm having a birthday party for Sara next weekend and she wants you to come for dinner and cake."

"What can I bring?"

"Only your silly girls."

◆ ◆ ◆

The following week was the worst since I became partner. I was like a circus performer spinning a dozen plates at once but knowing they would soon all come crashing down. Everyone looked to me to solve their problems.

Finally, it was Saturday. I woke early to clean the house before Betty came to take the girls to their skating lesson. It gave me a few precious hours to shop for Sara's presents and decorate the kitchen. I was setting the table when a call from Jamison flashed on my screen. He only called on weekends when he had problems. Reluctantly, I answered.

"I need you to go to New York," Jamison barked.

"Whatever happened to 'hello' or 'how are you?'"

"Very funny. I don't have time for this."

"I can't go to New York, but why?"

"The judge moved our case up to next week. I need you to get there and start finalizing the trial documents."

"I could go tomorrow," I offered.

His voice was stern. "I need you to be there by tonight."

"We're celebrating Sara's birthday today. I'll catch the first flight out tomorrow."

"Ryan, I'm not asking you."

"I can't keep traveling back and forth to New York on short notice like this. A couple times a month is one thing, but this is turning into a commute."

"I agree with you, commuting doesn't work. I know we discussed your transfer to occur after the New Year, but I need you out here now."

"What?" I gasped.

"Our lawyers in the New York office lack leadership. I planned on discussing this with you earlier, but I've been too busy."

"What about the Sara and Gracie, and their school?"

"Kids are resilient. Listen, you wanted the big cases, the money and the corner office. Well, this is your chance, or maybe not."

"What are you saying?"

The call dangled in the air. I could hear Jamison breathing on the other end.

"Ryan, do I have to spell it out for you? Just be on that flight."

He hung up before I could respond. I stared at the phone in my hand. Since Andy had retired, Jamison had been a disaster as the managing partner. Drunk with power, he had alienated almost everyone in a matter of weeks. Our New York office was a mess. He didn't like me, but he needed me. I slammed the phone down on the table and kicked one of Cooper's doggy toys across the room. *What should I tell Sara?* I wondered.

I decided to call Tearza. "I have terrible news," I said. Jamison called and ordered me to take the two o'clock flight to New York today."

"Today? Well, tell him you can't."

"I tried."

"Sara will be crushed. Is there any way to avoid the trip?"

"Afraid not."

"Oh Ryan, this will be bad."

"Can the girls stay overnight with you? Betty can take them tomorrow and I'll be home later Monday night."

"Of course, but Sara..." there was a long pause, "are you sure about this?"

"I'll talk to her as soon as she gets home. Betty took them to their skating lesson."

"We'll be over in a few minutes."

◆ ◆ ◆

Sara and Gracie walked in from their lesson and threw their skates on the kitchen floor.

Sara admired the birthday decorations. "Nice job."

My cell phone rang again, but I didn't answer. "There's something I need to talk to you about."

Sara stared at my phone. "What?"

"I have fly to New York today."

Her eyes darted back and forth. "After the party, right?"

"I have to catch the early flight."

Sara ran down the hall to her bedroom and slammed the door. Gracie stood next to me in shock. Her eyes said it all, narrowing like a laser into my heart. Finally, she shook her head and walked slowly into the living room to watch TV.

Tearza knocked and walked in with Sara's presents. I explained what had happened and then made the walk of shame down to Sara's bedroom.

I tapped on the door. "May I come in?"

"No!" she yelled.

"Please, I need to talk to you. Tearza's arrived with Marci and Ella. We can still have a great birthday party. Then afterward, you and Gracie will stay at Tearza's house until I get back."

I was greeted by silence.

"Sara, please."

"Go away!"

"I don't have a choice. Do you understand?" She didn't respond, so I gave up and went back to my bedroom to pack. Tearza stood in the middle of the room waiting for me. She folded her arms and frowned.

"Do you really have to go?"

I continued to throw clothes into my bag.

"What did Sara say?"

"She won't let me in the room."

"I'll talk to her. When do you have to leave?"

"Soon."

Tearza then sat down on the edge of the bed as I finished packing. Finally, I stopped and sat next to her.

"This isn't what I expected," I explained, rubbing my head. "I'm damned if I go, but I'll lose my job if I stay."

"What do you mean?"

"There's something else too."

Tearza squirmed and held her breath.

"I've been transferred to New York."

Her eyes shot up. "When?"

"Originally, they wanted the transfer to occur after the holidays so I could start the girls in the next semester at their new school. But now they want me in New York before Christmas."

"Ryan, you can't do this to the girls."

"It's not my idea."

Her voice rose. "Tell them no."

"It's not that simple."

"Why?"

"Because…"

Her eyes grew big. "Because you want to do it."

"It's a big promotion. I'd manage the entire office."

"Who cares? You can't just uproot the girls. And what about Marci and Ella?" She stood up and pointed at me. "Don't you care about us?"

"Of course I do."

Her voice quivered as she stood up and faced me. "Then don't take the promotion."

"I can't talk about this right now." I looked at the clock next my bed. "I have to finish packing."

Her shoulders shook. "So that's it?"

"No, I'll call you tonight and we can talk more about it."

Back in the kitchen, Tearza wouldn't look at me. After I lit the candles, Gracie insisted that Sara make a wish before we sang Happy

Birthday. Sara squeezed her eyes shut, took a big breath and blew as hard as she could. I looked at Tearza, then Sara, and felt like a total loser. The room was quiet as Sara opened a few presents. I looked at my watch, kissed the girls, and Tearza walked me to the door.

"I'll make sure Sara has fun while you're gone," she said coolly.

The taxi honked but we just stood there, each waiting for something the other couldn't give. "Thanks, Tearza. I don't know what I'd do without you," I finally said.

Tearza did not answer.

It snowed all the way to the airport. By the time I got to the check-in counter, half the flights were canceled or delayed. Our gate was crammed with passengers. To kill time, I started a new crossword puzzle but found myself stuck on one last word of five letters—"a gift not earned." I thought about Christmas and birthdays, but nothing came to me. I noticed that half the stranded people were working on puzzles. Next to me, an older man was focused on a newspaper crossword puzzle. His glasses hung so far off his nose they defied gravity.

He sensed me staring and looked up.

"I'm terrible at this," I said.

"At my age, you use it or lose it."

I pointed to my puzzle. "I'm stuck."

He smiled. "Happens to me all the time."

"It's the last word in the whole puzzle. Five letters—'a gift not earned.'"

He set his newspaper down. "Do you want the answer?"

"Do you know it?"

He nodded. "I'm sure you do as well. You only need a reminder."

"I give up."

He leaned forward and said, "Grace. A blessing bestowed upon us by God. A gift you can't earn."

"Grace is the name of my daughter."

"Then you understand." He winked and smiled. "See, you knew the word all along."

I wrote the letters in the boxes, staring at the word like a fool.

He peered over his glasses at me again. "Too easy?"

"No." I shook my head. "Too hard."

"Sometimes, the obvious thing is the easiest to take for granted."

I've taken far too many things for granted, I thought.

An agent announced that our departure would be delayed another half-hour. I decided to call Sara before we boarded.

A girl's voice answered, "Hello."

"Gracie?"

"No, it's Sara."

"You sound so much alike these days. I can hardly tell you apart."

"You want to talk to Gracie?"

"No, did you finish eating yet?"

"Almost."

"Sara, I'm sorry I'm missing your party. I didn't want to leave."

"I know."

I said, "I love you," but the overhead speaker drowned me out with another announcement.

"What?" she said. "I can't hear you."

It was no use. "Honey, they're boarding now. I have to go, but I'll call you when I get to New York."

I walked down the ramp following a family with two young children. They stopped suddenly because the youngest had fallen.

"Are you okay?" the big sister asked, obviously concerned.

"I broke it." Almost in tears, the little one pointed to her Minnie Mouse backpack and held up the strap that had ripped off.

"Don't worry—you're more important than a stupid backpack," the big sister said as she helped her little sister up and carried the backpack for her. As they walked on, the little girl suddenly pointed to her big sister and said, "I love you, Buckaroo."

Big sister smiled and said, "I love you too."

I quickly returned to the gate entrance. The agent said, "Sir, is anything wrong?"

"Everything," I said, then left the terminal.

Outside, I took a deep breath and noticed it was snowing harder than before. The cold air energized me as I stood in line for the next taxi. After a twenty-minute wait, it was finally my turn. The taxi driver wore a ski hat pulled down to his eyes. He stepped out of the cab, placed my luggage in the trunk, and I gave him Tearza's address.

"Got it." He gripped the steering wheel tight as the wind whipped the snow.

Settling in, I took off my coat and selected the weather app on my phone. A major ice storm was bearing down on us from Canada.

The driver peered at me in the rearview mirror. "Our weather people crack me up."

"Why is that?"

"The storm's already here and they were predicting it for tomorrow. I have no idea why we live here."

I looked at my watch. The girls should be at Tearza's by now. I reached for my cell phone to call Sara but then decided it would be more fun to surprise her.

Chapter 2
Tearza

Ryan's taxi turned the corner and disappeared. I should've known better than to let myself think he really cared about me. I'm such a fool! I packed the girls' overnight bags and drove back to my house. Before long, the storm was a howling blizzard. I wondered if Ryan's flight would take off on time.

The girls settled in the family room under a pile of pillows, blankets, sleeping bags and stuffed animals. I started a movie, kissed each one and moved to the kitchen. It was the first week of December, last call for sending out Christmas cards. Even though I didn't have time, I always made a special point of writing a personal note on every card. For some of us, it was the only way we stayed in touch.

I began the first card. Satisfied with the note, I automatically signed it "Love you—Jim, Tearza, Marci, and Ella."

Sad beyond words, I stared at our names. It had been two years and I still couldn't get used to Jim not being with us. I crumpled up the card and threw it in the wastebasket. The Christmas cards would have to wait.

I didn't feel like joining the girls, so I called Mom and we talked for more than an hour. I glanced at the clock—Ryan would be in New York by now. Odd that he hadn't called. Maybe he was waiting until he checked into the hotel. The ice storm had descended on us so quickly that in just a few hours thick ice glazed the trees and power lines.

Another hour passed without a call from Ryan. Something seemed wrong and I began to worry. As I was making tea, I noticed that Ella had left her favorite book, *The Gingerbread Man,* on the kitchen table. She was five when we'd first read the book to her. It seemed like yesterday when the girls helped us make gingerbread men cookies. We dressed the girls in a couple of Jim's old T-shirts and then laid out all the ingredients on the counter. Ella, our little sugar bug, ate the cinnamon candies off each cookie as fast as Marci put them on. It drove Marci crazy, but that's what sisters do.

I remembered how Marci stood in front of the oven door when the cookie sheet made a popping noise from the heat. She was sure that the gingerbread men were trying to get out. I looked at Jim and we both had the same idea. Jim distracted the girls while I pulled the pan out and hid the cookies in the girls' bedroom. Then I put the empty pan back in the oven and waited for the timer to go off. When I opened the door, the girls screamed, "They got out! They got out!" Ella was almost hysterical with excitement. Both girls ran around the kitchen counter looking for the gingerbread men until they eventually found them under their bed.

Ever since that precious day, it had become our annual tradition to start the holiday season by spending an afternoon reading Christmas books and baking cookies. Nostalgic with Christmas memories, I changed my mind about the tea and treated myself to a cup of white chocolate cocoa with a squirt of almond. As I waited for the cocoa to heat up, I was watching the snow fall when the phone rang.

The caller ID displayed "Olson." Relieved, Ryan was finally calling from New York. "Hey, you made it," I said.

"Tearza it's me, Billy—Ryan's dad."

I gripped the phone. "Billy—What's wrong?"

His voice trembled. "Ryan's been in a car accident."

My cup shattered into a million pieces as it hit the floor. *This can't be. Please, God, not again,* I thought as I leaned against the kitchen counter.

"We got a call from the highway patrol. No details yet, but they took him in an ambulance to the Chicago Hope trauma center."

"That's not possible. He's in New York on business," I said numbly. "He called Sara from the airport before he took off."

"Are you sure?"

"Yes, the girls are with me until he gets back."

"That explains why they called me. They couldn't get an answer at his home. Apparently, they found my business card in his briefcase. When they saw the same last name, they called me hoping I was a relative."

I felt as though I might faint. "Oh, God."

"Can you get to the hospital?" he pleaded

"Of course. I'll leave right away."

The call started to break up. "Tearza…pray for Ryan…we'll…" The line crackled and went dead.

The girls had fallen asleep while watching the movie, so I woke Sara to tell her what had happened. "Honey, I don't want you to worry, but your dad's been in a car accident. I'm sure he's fine, but I have to go to the hospital to check on him."

Sara rubbed her sleepy eyes and her voice quivered. "Is he hurt?"

I couldn't lie. "I really don't know, sweetie. Jake's coming over to stay with you until I get back."

Sara started to get up. "I'm coming with you."

I leaned over and gave her a hug. "No, I need you to stay here with Gracie so she doesn't get scared."

Sara unhooked her necklace with the little angel, the same one I had given to her when she was so upset that her mother hadn't come to her birthday party. "Give this to Dad."

Gracie woke up at the sound of our voices. "What's going on?"

I quickly explained. She leaped out of bed and opened a tiny purse she kept on her dresser, handing me a shiny penny.

"I don't understand," I said.

"Don't you remember?"

I shook my head.

"The homeless man on the street with the sign? He said this was a magic penny and that I could make one wish."

My eyes filled tears.

"Take it to the hospital." Gracie said. "Remember, the man said to put it next to your heart and make a wish and it'll come true." She wrapped her arm around my neck. "Make Dad safe."

"I'll do that. Thank you."

"Promise?"

"I promise. Your dad will be fine."

I stuffed the necklace and penny into my pocket and turned away so they couldn't see me cry. "Don't worry. I'll call you as soon as I know anything."

When Jake arrived, I grabbed my purse and bolted for the car. My hands shook so badly that I couldn't insert the key into the ignition, but after the third attempt I finally started the car. Frantic, I hit the gas too hard, backing out of the driveway and shooting across the icy road into the neighbor's snowbank. I screamed at my stupidity and hit the steering wheel with both hands. "Not now, damn it. Not now."

I rocked the car back and forth until the tires caught some traction, then raced to the hospital as fast as I dared in the icy conditions. Entering the emergency room, a familiar, nauseating smell from the past whisked me back to the day of Amy's accident.

I gave the information desk Ryan's name and she said he wasn't in the system. I started to panic, but then she said, "Found him. He's in the intensive care unit, room 136."

Another world existed beyond the heavy doors of the ICU. On the wall behind the central desk, I searched for Ryan's name on a large whiteboard. A nurse looked over at me. "Can I help you?" she asked.

"I'm here for Ryan Olson. We got a message," I took a breath, "that he'd been in an accident."

She glanced at my empty ring finger. "Are you family?"

"Yes— I mean, no. Not really, but I'm like family." I stuttered, not expecting the question.

"We're not allowed to give information to anyone but immediate family." She peered closely at me, while she adjusted her glasses. "If you aren't family, what is your relationship to him?"

My mind raced—good question.

"My name is Tearza Regan. I'm a close friend," I blurted out.

"I can check with the doctor, but I can't divulge any information. It's hospital policy."

With no patience for this nonsense, I gripped her arm. "Look, I need to know Ryan's condition, and I need to know now."

A doctor noticed the commotion and walked over. "Miss, please calm down."

"I'm sorry, but I'm a close friend of Ryan Olson and his parents called me about a car accident. They asked me to find out his condition as soon as possible."

"I tried to tell her it's against policy," the nurse said to the doctor. "She's not family."

The doctor took off his glasses and looked at the nurse. "Can you get me his chart?"

"Please, doctor," I said, "I know I'm technically not a relative, but I need to know if he's okay."

"What's your name again? Tearza?" He glanced down at a beeping pager on his belt. The nurse handed him the patient file and he scanned it for a moment. "Okay—my name's Dr. Petersen, please follow me."

My heart pounded as we walked toward Ryan's room. Before, I was only worried, but now I was scared. We passed by one dimly lit intensive care room and I flinched. Through the partially open door I could see an old man in bed with his eyes closed. A ventilator made a rhythmic noise as it pushed another breath into his tired body.

The doctor stopped outside the door. "This is all we know so far. They found him in an upside-down taxi that had slid off the interstate near the airport. Good news that he was wearing a seatbelt. The bad news is that he has a severe head injury, although we don't know the full extent. He's in a coma and we have no idea how long he'll remain like this." His voice trailed off. "We've done all we can for now." He spoke about brain injuries for a minute and then reached for his card with his pager number. "Call me if you need anything." His beeper went off again and he excused himself. I wondered how often he delivered a similar message to loved ones.

Terrified, I crossed myself as I slowly opened the door to Ryan's room. To my surprise, except for a bandaged head, he looked as if he were taking a nap. A nurse checked his vitals and made several notes in his chart.

"How is he?" I asked.

"The same. No change since they brought him in." She patted me on the arm. "I'll be here all night. Let me know if you need anything."

After she left, I pulled up a chair next to his bed. I didn't know what else to do, so I began to rub his arm and hold his hand—anything to let him know I was here.

"Ryan, I don't know if you can hear me, but I'm here. I'll be waiting for you when you wake up."

I quickly called Ryan's dad and told him the situation. Four hours later, there were three soft taps on the door. and I waved in Ryan's parents. Stella gasped when she saw him and fell against the metal safety bars with a bang. We grabbed her arms and helped her into a side chair.

"Oh God, look at my baby," she kept repeating as she stroked his hands. Billy stood behind her wiping his eyes on his sleeve.

"What did the doctors say?" Billy's voice was barely audible.

I tried to assure them. "The brain scan looks good, so the doctors are hopeful,"

"How long will he be like this?" Billy asked.

"He may wake up any minute or..." I shrugged. "They don't really know."

Billy burst into tears and looked at Stella. "I never got the chance to say I'm sorry."

His words hung in the air, his pain hard to watch.

Stella said, "Billy, they say that people in a coma can still hear. This is your chance."

Billy sat on the edge of the bed and leaned close to Ryan's head and whispered, "I'm so sorry for the way I've shut you out of my life..." His voice was in and out from what Stella and I could hear from across the room. "...she was so beautiful. Tall, with long blond hair that she always twisted in one hand if she was thinking about something. You have her soft eyes and her smile. Charlotte loved to laugh and dance."

Billy dropped his head on Ryan's arm, too choked with tears to go on. Several seconds later he resumed, "She loved music and would sing the "Bye, Baby Bunting" to you every night while she was pregnant." He whispered in Ryan's ear for a long time, pausing only to wipe away tears.

I held Stella while Billy continued to speak to Ryan. She cried as hard as Billy. After several minutes, Billy kissed Ryan on the forehead.

Stella said, "We need a coffee and some fresh air. Can I bring you anything?" Before she left, she reached into a bag and pulled out a square package wrapped in brown paper. "Give this to him when he wakes up."

We took turns sitting with Ryan but finally his parents decided to go back to my house to relieve Jake and console the girls.

Alone with Ryan, my heart started to pound again. He hadn't moved since I had arrived and fear was setting in. I reached into my pocket for a tissue and felt Sara's necklace and Gracie's penny. I pulled them out, kissed the angel and gently attached the necklace around Ryan's neck. As I leaned close to Ryan, I held the lucky penny next to my heart, squeezed my eyes shut and I prayed for a miracle.

The phone rang and I picked it up. It was Mom, one of my guardian angels.

"How is he?"

I burst out crying. "How did you know I was here?"

"I called your house to chat and your friend, Jake, answered the phone and told me what happened. How is Ryan?"

"In a coma."

"And you?"

I started to cry again. "I'm so afraid."

"Honey, don't go there."

"What if he…?"

"Don't think about that."

"I can't help it. I love him."

"I know."

"You do?"

"I knew it the minute I saw you together when he came to the farm. I saw it in your eyes."

"I can't take this all over again."

"What do you mean?"

"Nothing."

"Tearza, talk to me."

"We argued."

"Everyone does sometimes."

"You don't understand. We argued before he left. He told me he was transferred to New York."

"Oh dear."

"I was so mad."

"What did he say?"

"We didn't have time to finish the conversation because he had to leave for the airport. He said he would call once he got to New York. Mom, I've never told anyone this before, but the same thing happened with Jim. We argued over some stupid thing and he stormed out. I never said goodbye, or I love you. He was so upset. It was my fault that he committed suicide. I'll regret it until the day I die."

There was a long pause, then my mother said, "Listen to me. That was not your fault. You can't carry that around with you forever."

"What if Ryan doesn't wake up? I never thought I could love someone again."

"All we can do is pray, Sweetheart. Call me if anything changes."

"I will."

After I hung up, I laid my head on Ryan's arm and cried myself to sleep.

The alarm on the IV monitor woke me. His IV bag was empty. A nurse came and attached another bag. After she left, as I was gently stroking his arm, he squeezed my hand.

"Oh, my God!" I gasped.

"Do you know that you're beautiful when you cry?" he whispered, not moving but quietly looking at me.

"I hardly think so." I sat up and wiped my wet face with a handful of balled-up tissue. "I must be a mess with mascara all over my face."

"Beautiful to me," he said.

"How long have you been awake?"

"Long enough to enjoy watching you sleep," he said weakly.

I reached for the emergency call button. "I'm calling the doctor."

"No, not yet. The doctor can wait."

"How do you feel?"

"Not sure." He rotated is head in a small slow circle. "My head really hurts and my knee's sore, but otherwise I feel fine. Where am I?

"Chicago Hope."

"Are the girls okay?"

"They're scared, but with your parents at my house."

"Mom and Dad are here?"

"They were in your room earlier but left to give the girls dinner."

Ryan glanced around the room. "I don't remember anything after getting into the taxi at the airport. What happened?"

"The taxi slid off the interstate and rolled over. They didn't find you right away because you were buried deep in the snow. It was a miracle you weren't killed."

Ryan closed his eyes for a moment. "So, you were worried about me, huh?"

"Don't get any big ideas or I'll hide your bed pan."

"Aaahh, that's what I like about you—sweet and sensitive." He grinned and repositioned his head on the pillow, then asked, "What about the taxi driver?"

"He's fine. He was knocked unconscious too but lucked out— only minor bruises."

"Thank God." He sighed with relief, then turned his face toward me. "Tearza?"

"What?"

"I'm glad you're here." He squeezed his eyes shut and a bit of moisture leaked onto his cheek. "I don't know how to say this, but I didn't think I was coming back."

"Don't talk like that." I fussed around with his pillow and sheets. "You don't have to explain."

Embarrassed, he looked away. "I'm not afraid anymore."

"What do you mean?"

"We have to talk."

"Not now, you need you rest."

"But—" he started to speak again.

I pressed my index finger to his lips. "Shhhh!"

He nodded and sank back into the pillow. I tingled all over as we continued to hold hands. Suddenly, he winced.

"The nurse can give you something if you need it." I said, gently brushing his cheek with the back of my hand. "Why were you in a taxi?" I pulled the blanket up to his neck. "We thought you were on a plane to New York."

"I was coming home."

"What?" I said, shocked.

He stared at the ceiling for a minute, as if he were still drifting between two worlds. Finally, he spoke. "When I opened my eyes a few minutes ago, you were the first thing I saw. I had no idea where I was. I couldn't tell if I was still dreaming or awake."

Leaning forward, I kissed him on the lips. Ryan gently cupped my face in his hands, and I started to cry all over again.

"I'm sorry, I can't help it." I said.

He wiped away my tears with his thumbs. I remembered how he had done the same thing to Marci when she froze her feet.

"I was coming home because I decided to turn down the transfer."

"Why?" I said.

"It's a long story. But when I woke up and saw you, I knew I'd made the right decision."

"What if they fire you?"

"I don't care. I can always move to another firm. I'm switching to family practice. I'm tired of the stress and conflict in litigation. I want to try help people, and I want control of my life. Don't worry about me. I'll be fine whether I stay or leave the firm."

I laid my head on his chest. The longer I lay there, the rhythm of my breathing began to match his until we became one with the same breath, the same heartbeat. With his heartbeat echoing in my ear, I whispered, "I love you."

He didn't respond, so I raised my head and placed my chin on his chest to confess again.

"I love you more than anything in the world," I said even louder, but still got no response. His eyes were closed, and I realized that he was asleep. *Maybe it's just as well*, I thought, *because this is going to get complicated.*

My phone vibrated in my purse. It was Stella.

"How is he?" she asked.

"You won't believe it. He woke up briefly. He's fine and taking a nap right now."

"Thank God," she said, sobbing.

"Sorry I didn't call earlier, but he was awake for just a short time. Tell the girls that I'll be home in a little while to kiss them goodnight."

I hung up, said a quick prayer, and then gave Ryan a little kiss on the cheek.

"I'll be back in the morning. Sleep tight, my love."

Chapter 3

Ryan

"Where are we?" I asked.

Deep in the woods, Tearza pulled me along an abandoned trail strewn with fallen logs, wet grass, and wildflowers. Suddenly, she stopped and pointed into the underbrush. I didn't notice it at first, but a tiny path broke off to our right.

"Where are you taking me?"

"It's a secret," she said. "You have to promise to never reveal what I'm showing you."

With my finger, I made a big X over my heart. "Cross my heart."

She led me deeper into the woods. The path became steeper as we passed through dark ravines and jagged rock formations. At last, we came to a small clearing under a thick canopy of trees. She stopped again and cocked her head. "Can you hear it?"

She grabbed my hand and put her index finger to her lips, telling me to wait. The rain had stopped a few minutes ago. Eerily, there was almost no sound this deep in the forest after the passing of a storm.

"I don't hear anything," I whispered.

"That's the point." She let go of my hand, bent over, picked up two dandelions next to the path and held them under my chin.

"Stand still," she commanded.

"Why?"

"If you love me, your chin will turn yellow," she said with a mischievous grin.

I stared at the top of her head as she peered at my chin.

"Well…"

"I'm not telling." She giggled as she rubbed the flowers under my chin, then ran down the trail. I chased after her until we emerged from the thick undergrowth onto the edge of a waterfall that spilled over huge granite boulders from a hundred feet above. The water poured like milk from a pitcher, frothing and foaming as it hit the bottom.

Standing next to the water's edge, she said, "We're here. Now hold out your hands, palms up, and close your eyes."

Obediently, I shut my eyes, held out my hands, and waited. When she touched her fingertips to mine, she began vibrating like a tuning fork to some universal wavelength that connected us together. The pulsating energy made my entire body tremble.

"Tearza?" I called out with my eyes still closed. "What's happening?"

No answer.

"Tearza?"

"It's not Tearza," a voice said.

My eyes fluttered open. A ghost held my hands. I squinted at the outline of a woman's face in the pre-dawn light. "Clair?" I rubbed my eyes in disbelief, "is that you?"

She pulled her hands slowly away.

"You talked in your sleep. It sounded like a good dream, so I decided not to wake you."

Confused, I closed my eyes for a second and reopened them.

"What are you doing here?"

"Your mom called me last night."

"What?" I tried to sit up, but my head felt like it was on fire.

"We've stayed in touch, your mom and me, over the last two years."

"I don't understand."

"Don't blame her. She's been a big help to me as I've struggled to stay clean. She only called because the doctor told her that you might not live. I jumped on the red-eye from Los Angeles and came straight to the hospital." She let go of my hands and pulled a chair close to the bed. "Anyway, here I am."

Her once-thick, dark hair was now thin and hung limply around her shoulders. Her lips were dry and cracked and she constantly licked them as if they burned. She was a shadow of the woman I had married.

Suddenly, Clair lost her bravery and stared at the floor, fidgeting with her purse.

"I shouldn't have come. I didn't know until I got here that you'd regained consciousness." She shifted nervously in her chair and then frowned and twisted her hair just like Sara did.

"I feel pretty stupid now, but I didn't know what else to do."

"Don't worry. I'm glad you came."

She leaned toward me. "What's around your neck? It's beautiful."

I reached down, surprised to find a necklace.

"It's a guardian angel," she said. "Somebody's looking out for you."

"I guess."

She paused, lifted a strand of hair away from my eyes and lightly ran her finger down my cheek. "I'm so glad you're safe."

"Thanks." I noticed her hands shaking. "Are you okay?"

Embarrassed, she sat down and hid them in her lap. "It's the medications. The side effects aren't the greatest, although it's better than the alternative."

A nurse poked her head into the room, interrupting us again. "Do you need anything for pain?"

"No, but thanks," I said.

Once the door closed, I asked Clair, "Where are you living?"

"Orange County, south of LA," she said. "I work in a halfway house. It's good for me. They help me when I need it and I make a little money, plus free room and board. I've found I'm good at something. I can help people who struggle with demons like mine."

We sat quietly for a minute, searching for the right thing to say.

"It's been a long time," she said.

I nodded.

"It's not that I don't care about the girls, it's only…" She struggled, unsure how to finish her thought.

"Don't worry. The girls know you love them."

"I think about them all the time, wondering what they look like, what they're doing, if they ever think about me."

"Funny you say that because whenever I look at the girls, I see you. Your eyes, your smile… I remember the way we used to be, before all the bad things started." I paused, then added, "Can you ever forgive me?"

"What? You want me to forgive you?" She looked surprised. "Why?"

"It was my fault."

"You can't blame yourself for what happened to us." She reached for my hand. Her fingers felt cold and clammy. "I know that now. I was so angry with you, with *everything* for so long, until I realized that I couldn't live in the past."

She slowly let go, tucked a magazine into her purse, grabbed her coat and stood up.

"I'm sorry I came. I wanted to be here for you in case…"

"In case, what?"

She hesitated, "In case you needed me."

Clair looked out the frosted window. The sun was almost above the horizon. Her gaze went beyond this room. She rubbed her tired eyes as if debating what to say next. She glanced at a brown paper package on the table next to his bed.

"What's this?" she asked.

I glanced at the table. "I have no idea. I didn't know it was there. Go ahead, open it."

Clair tore the wrapping off the package and pulled out an old, worn-out photo album. "It looks like a scrapbook." Clair turned the first page and gasped.

"What?" I said.

"Look." Clair stepped closer and held the album so I could see a large portrait of a beautiful, young woman. "It's your mother."

Shocked, I asked, "Where did you get this?"

"I don't know. It was on the table when I arrived."

Clair pulled a chair close to my bed. We studied each page for a long time. After all these years, without any information about Mom, it was fun to cry over the photos of my parents at their wedding and Mom showing off her "baby-bump" of me—and so much more.

When we finished, I closed my eyes for a minute. "Why?" I asked Clair. "He destroyed everything that reminded him of Charlotte—everything but me."

"I don't know. Billy's a wounded soul." Clair stood and walked to the window. "It's been a long time since we saw a sunrise together. Remember how we used to play our old records all night until the sun came up?"

"I do."

"And your favorite song?" she asked.

"Desperado."

"Of course. And do you remember the line, 'you better let somebody love you before it's too late.'"

"What do you mean?"

She leaned over and kissed me. To my surprise, she still smelled like lilies of the valley.

"It's too late for us, but not for you."

"I don't understand."

"Life's full of choices." She forced a smile and for a second all I saw was the old Clair—my Clair. She smoothed her jacket, brushed her hair back from her eyes and walked toward the door.

"Clair, wait. Do you want to see the girls?"

Halfway across the room, with her back to me, she stopped. Her body sagged, and then she straightened her shoulders and turned to face me.

"Not yet, not like this."

"Is there anything I can do for you?"

"Let me think about it." The previous dullness in her eyes was gone. "Do you still have our snow globe?"

"Of course."

"Make one last wish for us."

Moving my lips, I tried to speak, but nothing came out. Finally, I gave up and nodded.

"Maybe I'll see you tomorrow."

"Clair, come here for a second. There's something I want to tell you."

She came over to me.

"I've made too many mistakes, but I'm changing. The girls have taught me how to be a better father and a better person. Maybe I'd be a better friend than a husband if I had a second chance."

"What are you saying?"

"If you can stay sober, the girls would love to have you back in their lives."

Clair shoulders shook as she wept. "What about you?"

"I'm not suggesting that we remarry. That part of us is over, but we can be friends. Once you're ready, maybe you could come back. It might be difficult at first, but we could try hard to make it work."

"Are you suggesting that I move back here?"

"The girls love you. You'll always be their mother."

"I don't know."

"Why not?"

She sat down on the edge of my bed. "Because I'm afraid."

"Then we can be afraid together. I don't want to make another mistake any more than you do. We can be a family again, just not the same way as before."

"Thank you." She cleared her throat and blew her nose. "This is not what I expected."

"Me neither." I touched her hand. "Please, think about?"

She nodded. "I will."

After she left, my head pounded and I stared at the ceiling wondering, *Now what?*

Chapter 4

Tearja

The next morning, I walked through the ICU with a happy heart, two coffees, a newspaper, and a bag of glazed doughnuts. At Ryan's room, I saw the outline of him through the glass, but somebody else moved in the room. A woman was standing over him, talking, and waving her arms. She wasn't dressed as a nurse. Then she leaned over and kissed him. My mind raced with possibilities. I'd never met her before, but could that be Clair?

I panicked as the woman opened the door and came out. There wasn't any time to think, so I quickly set the coffee and doughnuts on the counter and opened the newspaper. As she got closer, I glanced up. Our eyes met for an instant and then I looked down at the paper again, pretending to read. *It had to be her,* I thought. She stopped, hesitated for a second, then resumed her pace. Her footsteps down the hall grew fainter before I finally looked up.

Still shaking, I picked up the coffee and doughnuts and carried them into Ryan's room. Not knowing what to expect, I knocked. Ryan waved and struggled to sit up.

"I thought you might want some real coffee," I said.

Ryan leaned around me and looked out the door. "Ah, thanks. I feel much better today."

"Really? Your face is flushed," I said. "Do you have a temperature?"

He shook his head and glanced at the tray next to his bed. "Could you hand me some water?"

"Sure."

He took a huge gulp of water and set the glass down.

"Thirsty?"

"Must be the pain medication," he said. "How are the girls?"

"Fine," I said. "Everyone's so relieved."

"How did you sleep last night?" I asked.

"Good."

"How was your morning so far?" I asked carefully.

"Good." Ryan squirmed in bed, while playing with the bed controls. Then he pointed to his necklace.

"Tearza, where did this come from?"

"Sara."

"Is that the same one you gave to her?"

"Yes, she was scared."

"She's something."

For the next half-hour, we talked about the weather, his parents, the girls, and work—everything but the woman in his room. Now I'm certain it was Clair. Frustrated, I finally said, "I have to leave."

"But you just got here."

"Something came up." I stood up. "I'll talk to you later."

Gripping my jacket in one hand and cell phone in the other, I fled to my car. All the way home, I thought about Clair and Ryan. *What did this mean? Was she back for good?*

◆ ◆ ◆

Ryan left the hospital after three days and seemed to be recovering well. Christmas was fast approaching. I was behind in my Christmas cards and gift buying. There never seemed to be enough hours in the day.

Marci and Ella had their annual school Christmas concert. I always loved watching each class sing Christmas songs, especially the little ones. The joy and wonder that filled their bright faces was contagious.

The girls wanted to ride to the concert with Sara and Gracie, so we picked them up. Ryan got into the car slowly, still not fully healed. When we arrived, the girls raced into the church to put on their costumes. I turned off the car and Ryan and I sat there in awkward silence. The last week had been frantic. Ryan had to work overtime to catch up, so we hadn't connected. He still had never brought up Clair. Our breath fogged the windows as we each waited for the other to speak.

"Well, should we go in?" he finally asked.

"I guess so," was all I could muster.

Inside the church, we found an empty pew. We were early and Ryan fiddled with the video camera for a few minutes then turned to me.

"I know this isn't the time or place, but what's wrong?"

I shrugged. "You tell me."

"I can't read your mind," Ryan said.

"What did Jamison say when you turned down the transfer?"

"He was furious at first."

"Does that mean you'll stay with the firm?"

"We'll see. I don't want to work for Jamison." He turned to face me. "What do you think?"

"You have to make that decision.

"I'm still confused. It's as if we had a fight or something. You've acted funny ever since the hospital."

"How can you say that?" I glanced around and lowered my voice. "What am I supposed to think? I saw your wife in your room. I saw her kiss you."

Ryan's face paled. "You saw Clair?"

"Yes."

"Did you talk to her?"

"No."

A blast of cold air hit us as the rear door opened and families started to arrive.

Ryan leaned toward me. "Let's step outside for a second. I can explain everything."

We went into the corridor. Ryan seemed to struggle with how to begin, but finally settled on: "Have you ever seen your past—reincarnated—appearing like a ghost?"

Nodding, I thought of all the times that Jim had returned to me in my dreams over the last two years.

"Seeing Clair…" He shook his head. "I was stunned."

"Is she coming back?" I asked.

"She might if she can stay sober. To be honest, I don't know what she wants at this point."

"Has she been successful in her outpatient program?"

"She claims to feel much better and said she's working a steady job in a halfway house." Ryan stepped closer. "I have my doubts and fears. However, having her nearby would be good for the girls—she's still their mother."

"Where does that leave us?"

He looked way, then seemed to gather some strength and looked me in the eye. "Clair will always be a part of my past. But you are my present." He smiled. "And my future."

I leaned into him and he lifted my chin so I could look into his eyes.

"I know it might be hard for you to understand," he said, "but Clair deserves a second chance at happiness, don't you think?"

"You're right. I'm acting silly. It's just that…" I stopped because I didn't know how to say this. "You understand how much I love Sara and Gracie."

"I know you do, and they love you too. We have to trust each other."

"I don't want Clair to change things."

"She won't," he said, squeezing my hands. "I'm so sorry. I should've told you about Clair at the hospital. I just didn't know what to say."

"Thanks. I understand now."

"Shall we go back in? The concert will start in a few minutes."

The kids marched in and lined up on stage, and when they sang, I felt as close to God as anytime in my life. Ryan and I sat holding hands as if we'd always been together. As we listened to the girls sing "Away in a Manger," I realized I wanted to take a chance on love again.

After we got home, I pondered what I wanted to say to Ryan, and how I should say it. What if he didn't feel the same way I did? But it was impossible to go back now. Our kiss in the barn at Thanksgiving changed everything. I could accept the consequences for myself, but was that fair to the girls? If Ryan didn't love me, the change between us could affect the girls forever.

Sleep was a stranger, so I went to the kitchen for something to drink. The family room was cold without a fire in the fireplace. I walked into the studio to get a blanket out of an old cedar chest. I pulled out the wool blanket and found beneath it my old paintbrushes. Like abandoned friends, they had waited patiently for the day I returned.

Picking up one of the brushes, I felt a strange surge of energy. I pulled the rest of the brushes out and set them on the floor. Then I opened the closet next to the chest. The small room was filled with stacks of canvas paintings—some finished, others in various stages. Most were not very good, but a few had promise. Flipping through the old frames, my heart stopped when I saw the unfinished painting from the morning Jim had died.

Empty suitcases blocked the doorway, so I moved those aside and dragged the unfinished painting and easel out of the closet. It took a while to organize my materials. Finally, I sat on a stool and stared at the painting I had begun two years ago. The canvas had a preliminary foundation of color, but no form yet. I felt like Michelangelo staring at raw marble. I knew something good was in there waiting for me. I just couldn't figure out how to begin. I closed my eyes and my mother's sweet voice whispered in my ear. "From where you dream…"

Then I saw it. I knew what to do and quickly picked up the brush.

Suddenly it was four o'clock in the morning. The painting was finished. Exhausted, but strangely content, I closed my eyes and drifted off,. To my surprise, for the first time, Ryan instead of Jim appeared in dream. Ryan was standing on the shore of Lake Superior skipping rocks with all four girls.

I woke with a strange sense of urgency. The dream lingered as I prepared a box with six smooth skipping stones that we'd brought home from our camping trip. I wrapped the stones in red and green tissue paper and placed them on top of a small note that said, "Each stone is like the six of us—not perfect, yet the same. You are my Christmas wish. I wish that someday we become a family."

I kissed the box and later went to the post office to mail it.

Chapter 5

Ryan

Since I'd left the hospital, Tearza had been constantly on my mind. I had suppressed my true feelings for months—holding back, afraid. Afraid I'd screw up another relationship. Afraid I'd hurt Tearza or my girls again. But the car accident changed everything. I could never replace Jim—I knew that. I was far from perfect. But maybe, just maybe, I could be good enough.

After I put the girls to bed, I poured myself a glass of wine and sat in front of the fireplace. Our Christmas tree was still only half decorated, and the extra ornaments lay scattered in boxes around the floor. I put my feet on the coffee table and closed my eyes.

Next to me, Gracie had left my favorite book, *A Christmas Memory,* on the couch. The cover was slightly beaten up from countless times of reading it to Sara and Gracie. I thumbed through the pages and found several pressed flowers, the ones picked on a bike ride with Tearza and the girls last spring. It was irrational, but I lifted the dandelion to my chin and decided. I had to know for sure, or I'd regret it for the rest of my life.

I drove to Franco's shop the next morning. When I arrived, he greeted me, "*Buon giorno*, my friend. How's my favorite girl?"

"That's why I'm here. I need a special favor from Sofi."

"Sofi, we have a special visitor!" he called. Sofi didn't answer, so we walked to the rear of the store where Sofi was hunched over dried flowers on a large worktable. Her tiny hands were almost crippled with arthritis, yet she handled the small flowers as if they were as fragile as love. Franco surprised her by kissing her on the back of the neck and she batted him away, chastising him loudly in Italian.

"See," Franco laughed, "she's crazy about me."

"I need a special favor," I said.

"Anything, my boy," Sofi said.

I pulled out the flowers from an envelope. "We pressed these in a book last spring and I'd like you to frame them for me."

Sofi and Franco shared a smile. Then Franco twisted his moustache. "Why not have Tearza frame them for you? She'll be here tomorrow. They have a lot of orders to fill before the holidays."

"It's a present for her."

"I can see that. But what's the occasion?"

I blushed.

"Something special?" he teased.

Sofi said, "Franco, leave the poor boy alone. You never sent me flowers when you were his age?" She rolled her eyes and nodded in his direction. "He was romantic as a plow horse."

They both started to argue loudly in Italian until I put my hands in the air and called for a truce.

"She has memory of an elephant." He pointed to his head. "But I love her anyway."

"When do you need it?"

"As soon as possible."

"Let's see. I could have it done today. Will that work?"

"Great. Then I can mail it tomorrow."

The pressed flowers were perfect. Six of Tearza's favorite flowers pressed together forever—like us. I wrote a short note, wrapped the frame, mailed the box and prayed for the best.

◆ ◆ ◆

Seven days before Christmas, I took the afternoon off to shop for Christmas presents. After walking around the mall for an hour, I came up empty. I grabbed a cup of coffee from a kiosk and strolled over to watch Santa holding children on his lap for pictures. This was Clair's favorite Christmas activity. A woman tapped me on the shoulder. "Are you in line?"

I sighed. "Wish I were."

She picked up her tiny daughter and waved at her husband who scurried across the busy court to join them.

"First time?" I asked.

"Yes, and I'm terrified that she'll scream bloody murder when I set her on Santa's lap."

"She'll be fine. Enjoy, because everything goes too fast..." My voice trailed off as emotion was overtaking me.

"Are you okay?" the woman asked.

"Yes," I lied and moved on.

◆ ◆ ◆

The rest of the week was agony. I anticipated slow mail service after I mailed the frame with my note, yet still had no response from Tearza. Not a good sign. She should've received the package, but if she hadn't called by now—well, it didn't take a genius to figure out what that meant.

Then the doorbell rang. It was the mail carrier holding a small box along with a stack of Christmas cards. I thanked him and looked at the box. The return address was Tearza's. I untied the bow and took a quick look. Inside, wrapped in red and green tissue, were six smooth stones. A small card was placed beneath the stones, but it was sealed. I didn't open it because I was sure it was meant for the girls. I quickly closed the box, retied the bow, and put it aside for the girls to open when they got home.

Chapter 6
Tearza

It had been a long, sleepless week and I still had heard nothing from Ryan. The mail carrier pulled up to our mailbox, so I ran out to give her our Christmas present. "Merry Christmas!" I shouted.

She leaned out the window. "Same to you."

I handed her a bag of Christmas cookies with one of our homemade cards.

"You didn't have to do that," she said.

"It's Christmas Eve and you deserve it."

Although I had a heavy heart, I thumbed through the stack of Christmas cards from our friends. The mail included a small package, but I decided to wait until after I looked at all the cards before opening it. I always enjoyed the Christmas letters and photos.

Finally, I examined the small package and noticed the return address was Ryan's. Sadly, I realized why he hadn't called. I assumed he didn't want to hurt my feelings, so he had sent me a book or something to let me down easy.

I wiped my eyes, steeled myself, and sliced open the flaps of the package. Choking back the tears, I felt awful—this was like Jim dying all over again. I slowly removed the white tissue paper on top, discovering not a book but a picture frame of five hand-pressed daisies and one dandelion. I couldn't stop shaking as I peeled off the small note taped to the glass. I struggled to read his note because my tears kept blurring the letters. When the words finally came into focus, I was shocked. I read and reread it again to make sure I had read it correctly, then dropped to my knees. I realized Ryan had never received my box because he didn't mention it in his note. Our packages must have passed each other in the mail.

I stared at the note in disbelief,. In Ryan's nearly illegible handwriting, it said, "Are you sure my chin wasn't yellow?"

Chapter 7
Ryan

The smell of baking cookies made the whole house warm and cozy. Sara was proud of me because I had only burned two batches. The counters were a mess, covered with mixing bowls, cookie sheets, sticks of butter, pink and green frosting, and empty bottles of vanilla.

The doorbell rang as I finished the last batch. "I'll be right there," I yelled.

I licked frosting off my fingers, wiped my hands on my jeans, opened the door and discovered Tearza standing there. She didn't say anything at first. I was mesmerized for a second, watching large, lazy snowflakes sprinkle her hair and eyelashes with stardust.

"Ryan," she gave me a helpless look as she lifted my framed flowers in the air, "from last spring?"

I nodded and stepped through the doorway.

"Why now?" she asked.

"Because I had to know," I said.

Her tears streamed down her face. Suddenly, I realized the stones in the box were for me, and they were meant to represent the six of us. I'm such an idiot! I should have just read the note.

"I—you—we—us." She struggled to speak and then stopped.

"Does that mean?"

"Yes."

"Are you sure?" I hesitated. "What if you're wrong?"

"I'll take the chance," she said.

"But—"

She put her hand over my mouth. "Lawyers talk too much." She stood on her tiptoes and kissed me. "I love you."

"I never thought I'd hear you say that."

Snowflakes continued to cover us as we rocked back and forth on the stoop. Suddenly, Cooper bounced through the deep snow and tried to wedge himself between us. I gently pushed him away as we continued to kiss. But then a voice stopped us.

"What're you doing?" Marci called out loudly.

Knee deep in the fresh snow, dragging their sleds behind them, all four girls had stopped in their tracks with their mouths wide open.

"What? You mean this?" I leaned down and kissed Tearza.

"No, I think she means this." Tearza stood on her toes, wrapped her arms around my neck and kissed me back—twice.

The girls stood like statues until we burst out laughing, which made Cooper bark and run in a circle around us. Sara turned to Marci and they gave each other a high-five, while yelling, "Yeeess!" at the same time.

"Come on," I said, waving to them all. "Let's go inside. I baked cookies and they're still warm."

◆ ◆ ◆

Later that evening, Tearza picked us up to attend the Christmas Eve candlelight service together. In the foyer, we shook the snow off our coats. Burning candles, pine and cedar scented, infused the church with the fragrance of Christmas. A large Christmas tree decorated the altar and hundreds of candles illuminated the sanctuary with a soft, flickering glow. The organ was playing Christmas carols. Halfway up the aisle, Gracie suddenly poked me in the side and opened her palm to reveal a bright penny.

"What's that?"

"Remember, the homeless man gave it to me last fall?"

"Yes," I said.

"Tearza gave it back to me after you left the hospital." Gracie slipped the penny into my pocket. "It's yours now."

"Why?"

"We got our wish. Now it's yours." She smiled. "Who knows. Someday you may need to make a wish."

I kissed the top of her head. "Love you, honey."

She hugged me around the waist. "Love you too."

We hurried to catch up with the others. Once we settled into our pew, I pulled the penny out of my pocket and rubbed it until it became warm. Slowly, I understood. *Darn that Gracie,* I thought.

Tearza leaned over. "What are you smiling about?"

"Gracie," I said, turning the penny over in my hand.

"You're a good daddy."

"You think so?"

She kissed me on the cheek and whispered, "I know so."

I glanced over her shoulder at Sara and Marci. They were sharing a songbook and Marci smiled back at me. Satisfied, I turned my gaze to the large cross hanging in the front of the church when a flash of golden light caught my eye. On the altar, next to the manger scene, five golden angels were spinning above five tall, white candles. Spellbound, I watched the heat from the candle flames propel the five beautiful angels around and around—my guardian angels—my promises to keep.

Acknowledgements

The seeds for this novel emerged in 2004 during a flight from Australia to Minneapolis that took 88 hours to complete due to an earthquake in Hawaii. During the multiple attempts to cross the Pacific, I reminisced about the wonderful memories Marsha and I created raising three amazing boys. As with my first novel Ukrainian Nights, I'm eternally grateful for the collaboration with Gary Lindberg and Ian Graham Leask. Without their encouragement, mentoring, coaching and editing, this novel would not be possible. It's my pleasure to continue our collaboration on novel three, expected to be published in 2021.

About the Author

Pete Carlson's debut novel has won national recognition. "Ukrainian Nights" won the Finalist Award in the General Fiction category of the highly prestigious Eric Hoffer Awards 2020 program.

Carlson has had a diverse forty-year career in commercial real estate development throughout the country. Carlson moved to Denver from Minnesota in 2017 and recently developed a luxury condominium project called Altus Vail in Vail Village. He has been a frequent speaker on various webinars and a guest in KFAI *Write On Radio*. He serves on the board of the Colorado Authors League and is a member of The Authors Guild and Lighthouse Writers. He is blessed with his wife, Marsha, three sons and their spouses. He currently lives in Denver, Colorado.